BY THE SAME AUTHOR

Hateship, Friendship, Courtship, Loveship, Marriage

The Love of a Good Woman

Selected Stories

Open Secrets

Friend of My Youth

The Progress of Love

The Moons of Jupiter

The Beggar Maid

Something I've Been Meaning to Tell You

Lives of Girls and Women

Dance of the Happy Shades

RUNAWAY

RUNAWAY

Stories

ALICE MUNRO

Chatto & Windus
LONDON

Published by Chatto & Windus 2005

First published in the United States of America in 2004 by Knopf

3 5 7 9 10 8 6 4 2

'Runaway', 'Chance', 'Soon', 'Silence', and 'Passion' previously appeared in
The New Yorker

Grateful acknowledgment is made to Ludlow Music, Inc., for permission to reprint
an excerpt from the song lyric 'Goodnight Irene', words and music by
Huddie Ledbetter and John A. Lomax. TRO-Copyright © 1936 (Renewed), 1950
(Renewed) by Ludlow Music, Inc., New York, NY. Reprinted by permission of
Ludlow Music, Inc.

First published in Great Britain in 2005 by
Chatto & Windus
Random House, 20 Vauxhall Bridge Road,
London SW1V 2SA

Random House Australia (Pty) Limited
20 Alfred Street, Milsons Point, Sydney,
New South Wales 2061, Australia

Random House New Zealand Limited
18 Poland Road, Glenfield,
Auckland 10, New Zealand

Random House (Pty) Limited
Endulini, 5A Jubliee Road, Parktown 2193, South Africa

The Random House Group Limited Reg. No. 954009
www.randomhouse.co.uk

ISBN 0 7011 7750 0

Papers used by Random House are natural,
recyclable products made from wood grown in sustainable forests;
the manufacturing processes conform to the environmental
regulations of the country of origin

Printed and bound in Great Britain by
Mackays of Chatham plc, Chatham, Kent

In memory of my friends,

Mary Carey

Jean Livermore

Melda Buchanan

Contents

RUNAWAY
3

CHANCE
48

SOON
87

SILENCE
126

PASSION
159

TRESPASSES
197

TRICKS
236

POWERS
270

RUNAWAY

RUNAWAY

Carla heard the car coming before it topped the little rise in the road that around here they called a hill. It's her, she thought. Mrs. Jamieson—Sylvia—home from her holiday in Greece. From the barn door—but far enough inside that she could not readily be seen—she watched the road Mrs. Jamieson would have to drive by on, her place being half a mile farther along the road than Clark and Carla's.

If it was somebody getting ready to turn in at their gate it would be slowing down by now. But still Carla hoped. *Let it not be her.*

It was. Mrs. Jamieson turned her head once, quickly—she had all she could do maneuvering her car through the ruts and puddles the rain had made in the gravel—but she didn't lift a hand off the wheel to wave, she didn't spot Carla. Carla got a glimpse of a tanned arm bare to the shoulder, hair bleached a lighter color than it had been before, more white now than silver-blond, and an expression that was determined and exasperated and amused at her own exasperation—just the way Mrs. Jamieson would look negotiating such a road. When she turned her head there was something like a bright flash—of inquiry, of hopefulness—that made Carla shrink back.

So.

Maybe Clark didn't know yet. If he was sitting at the computer he would have his back to the window and the road.

But Mrs. Jamieson might have to make another trip. Driving home from the airport, she might not have stopped for groceries—not until she'd been home and figured out what she needed. Clark might see her then. And after dark, the lights of her house would show. But this was July, and it didn't get dark till late. She might be so tired that she wouldn't bother with the lights, she might go to bed early.

On the other hand, she might telephone. Any time now.

This was the summer of rain and more rain. You heard it first thing in the morning, loud on the roof of the mobile home. The trails were deep in mud, the long grass soaking, leaves overhead sending down random showers even in those moments when there was no actual downpour from the sky and the clouds looked like clearing. Carla wore a high, wide-brimmed old Australian felt hat every time she went outside, and tucked her long thick braid down her shirt.

Nobody showed up for trail rides, even though Clark and Carla had gone around posting signs in all the camping sites, in the cafes, and on the tourist office billboard and anywhere else they could think of. Only a few pupils were coming for lessons and those were regulars, not the batches of schoolchildren on vacation, the busloads from summer camps, that had kept them going through last summer. And even the regulars that they counted on were taking time off for holiday trips, or simply cancelling their lessons because of the weather being so discouraging. If they called too late, Clark charged them for the time anyway. A couple of them had complained, and quit for good.

There was still some income from the three horses that were boarded. Those three, and the four of their own, were out in the field now, poking around in the grass under the trees. They looked as if they couldn't be bothered to notice that the rain was holding off for the moment, the way it often did for a while in the afternoon. Just enough to get your hopes up—the clouds whitening and thinning and letting through a diffuse brightness that never got around to being real sunshine, and was usually gone before supper.

Carla had finished mucking out in the barn. She had taken her time—she liked the rhythm of her regular chores, the high space under the barn roof, the smells. Now she went over to the exercise ring to see how dry the ground was, in case the five o'clock pupil did show up.

Most of the steady showers had not been particularly heavy, or borne on any wind, but last week there had come a sudden stirring and then a blast through the treetops and a nearly horizontal blinding rain. In a quarter of an hour the storm had passed over. But branches lay across the road, hydro lines were down, and a large chunk of the plastic roofing over the ring had been torn loose. There was a puddle like a lake at that end of the track, and Clark had worked until after dark, digging a channel to drain it away.

The roof had not yet been repaired. Clark had strung fence wire across to keep the horses from getting into the mud, and Carla had marked out a shorter track.

On the Web, right now, Clark was hunting for someplace to

buy roofing. Some salvage outlet, with prices that they could afford, or somebody trying to get rid of such material second-hand. He would not go to Hy and Robert Buckley's Building Supply in town, which he called Highway Robbers Buggery Supply, because he owed them too much money and had had a fight with them.

Clark had fights not just with the people he owed money to. His friendliness, compelling at first, could suddenly turn sour. There were places he would not go into, where he always made Carla go, because of some row. The drugstore was one such place. An old woman had pushed in front of him—that is, she had gone to get something she'd forgotten and come back and pushed in front, rather than going to the end of the line, and he had complained, and the cashier had said to him, "She has emphysema," and Clark had said, "Is that so? I have piles, myself," and the manager had been summoned, to say that was uncalled-for. And in the coffee shop out on the highway the advertised breakfast discount had not been allowed, because it was past eleven o'clock in the morning, and Clark had argued and then dropped his takeout cup of coffee on the floor—just missing, so they said, a child in its stroller. He said the child was half a mile away and he dropped the cup because no cuff had been provided. They said he had not asked for a cuff. He said he shouldn't have had to ask.

"You flare up," said Carla.

"That's what men do."

She had not said anything to him about his row with Joy Tucker. Joy Tucker was the librarian from town who boarded her horse with them. The horse was a quick-tempered little chestnut mare named Lizzie—Joy Tucker, when she was in a jokey mood, called her Lizzie Borden. Yesterday she had driven out, not in a jokey mood at all, and complained about the roof's not being fixed yet, and Lizzie looking miserable, as if she might have caught a chill.

There was nothing the matter with Lizzie, actually. Clark had tried—for him—to be placating. But then it was Joy Tucker who flared up and said that their place was a dump, and Lizzie deserved better, and Clark said, "Suit yourself." Joy had not—or not yet—removed Lizzie, as Carla had expected. But Clark, who had formerly made the little mare his pet, had refused to have anything more to do with her. Lizzie's feelings were hurt, in consequence—she was balky when exercised and kicked up a fuss when her hoofs had to be picked out, as they did every day, lest they develop a fungus. Carla had to watch out for nips.

But the worst thing as far as Carla was concerned was the absence of Flora, the little white goat who kept the horses company in the barn and in the fields. There had not been any sign of her for two days. Carla was afraid that wild dogs or coyotes had got her, or even a bear.

She had dreamt of Flora last night and the night before. In the first dream Flora had walked right up to the bed with a red apple in her mouth, but in the second dream—last night—she had run away when she saw Carla coming. Her leg seemed to be hurt but she ran anyway. She led Carla to a barbed-wire barricade of the kind that might belong on some battlefield, and then she—Flora—slipped through it, hurt leg and all, just slithered through like a white eel and disappeared.

The horses had seen Carla go across to the ring and they had all moved up to the fence—looking bedraggled in spite of their New Zealand blankets—so that she would take notice of them on her way back. She talked quietly to them, apologizing for coming empty-handed. She stroked their necks and rubbed their noses and asked whether they knew anything about Flora.

Grace and Juniper snorted and nuzzled up, as if they recognized the name and shared her concern, but then Lizzie butted in between them and knocked Grace's head away from Carla's petting hand. She gave the hand a nip for good measure, and Carla had to spend some time scolding her.

Up until three years ago Carla never really looked at mobile homes. She didn't call them that, either. Like her parents, she would have thought "mobile home" pretentious. Some people lived in trailers, and that was all there was to it. One trailer was no different from another. When Carla moved in here, when she chose this life with Clark, she began to see things in a new way. After that she started saying "mobile home" and she looked to see how people had fixed them up. The kind of curtains they had hung, the way they had painted the trim, the ambitious decks or patios or extra rooms that had been built on. She could hardly wait to get at such improvements herself.

Clark had gone along with her ideas, for a while. He had built new steps, and spent a lot of time looking for an old wrought-iron railing for them. He didn't make any complaint about the money spent on paint for the kitchen and bathroom or the material for curtains. Her paint job was hasty—she didn't know, at that time, that you should take the hinges off the cupboard doors. Or that you should line the curtains, which had since faded.

What Clark balked at was tearing up the carpet, which was the same in every room and the thing that she had most counted on replacing. It was divided into small brown squares, each with a pattern of darker brown and rust and tan squiggles and shapes. For a long time she had thought these were the same squiggles and shapes, arranged in the same way, in each square. Then when she had had more time, a lot of time, to examine them, she decided that there were four patterns joined together to make identical larger squares. Sometimes she could pick out the arrangement easily and sometimes she had to work to see it.

She did this when it was raining outside and Clark's mood weighted down all their inside space, and he did not want to pay attention to anything but the computer screen. But the best thing to do then was to invent or remember some job to do in the barn. The horses would not look at her when she was unhappy, but Flora, who was never tied up, would come and rub against her, and look up with an expression that was not quite sympathy—it was more like comradely mockery—in her shimmering yellow-green eyes.

Flora had been a half-grown kid when Clark brought her home from a farm where he had gone to bargain for some horse tackle. The people there were giving up on the country life, or at least on the raising of animals—they had sold their horses but failed to get rid of their goats. He had heard about how a goat was able to bring a sense of ease and comfort into a horse stable and he wanted to try it. They had meant to breed her someday but there had never been any signs of her coming into heat.

At first she had been Clark's pet entirely, following him everywhere, dancing for his attention. She was quick and graceful and provocative as a kitten, and her resemblance to a guileless girl in love had made them both laugh. But as she grew older she seemed to attach herself to Carla, and in this attachment she was suddenly much wiser, less skittish—she seemed capable, instead, of a subdued and ironic sort of humor. Carla's behavior with the horses was tender and strict and rather maternal, but the comradeship with Flora was quite different, Flora allowing her no sense of superiority.

"Still no sign of Flora?" she said, as she pulled off her barn boots. Clark had posted a Lost Goat notice on the Web.

"Not so far," he said, in a preoccupied but not unfriendly voice. He suggested, not for the first time, that Flora might have just gone off to find herself a billy.

No word about Mrs. Jamieson. Carla put the kettle on. Clark was humming to himself as he often did when he sat in front of the computer.

Sometimes he talked back to it. *Bullshit*, he would say, replying to some challenge. Or he would laugh—but could not remember what the joke was, when she asked him afterwards.

Carla called, "Do you want tea?" and to her surprise he got up and came into the kitchen.

"So," he said. "So, Carla."

"What?"

"So she phoned."

"Who?"

"Her Majesty. Queen Sylvia. She just got back."

"I didn't hear the car."

"I didn't ask you if you did."

"So what did she phone for?"

"She wants you to go and help her straighten up the house. That's what she said. Tomorrow."

"What did you tell her?"

"I told her sure. But you better phone up and confirm."

Carla said, "I don't see why I have to, if you told her." She poured out their mugs of tea. "I cleaned up her house before she left. I don't see what there could be to do so soon."

"Maybe some coons got in and made a mess of it while she was gone. You never know."

"I don't have to phone her right this minute," she said. "I want to drink my tea and I want to have a shower."

"The sooner the better."

Carla took her tea into the bathroom, calling back, "We have to go to the laundromat. Even when the towels dry out they smell moldy."

"We're not changing the subject, Carla."

Even after she'd got in the shower he stood outside the door and called to her.

"I am not going to let you off the hook, Carla."

She thought he might still be standing there when she came out, but he was back at the computer. She dressed as if she was going to town—she hoped that if they could get out of here, go to the laundromat, get a takeout at the cappuccino place, they might be able to talk in a different way, some release might be possible. She went into the living room with a brisk step and put her arms around him from behind. But as soon as she did that a wave of grief swallowed her up—it must have been the heat of the shower, loosening her tears—and she bent over him, all crumbling and crying.

He took his hands off the keyboard but sat still.

"Just don't be mad at me," she said.

"I'm not mad. I hate when you're like this, that's all."

"I'm like this because you're mad."

"Don't tell me what I am. You're choking me. Start supper."

That was what she did. It was obvious by now that the five o'clock person wasn't coming. She got out the potatoes and began to peel them, but her tears would not stop and she could not see what she was doing. She wiped her face with a paper towel and tore off a fresh one to take with her and went out into the rain. She didn't go into the barn because it was too miserable in there without Flora. She walked along the lane back to the woods. The horses were in the other field. They came over to the fence to watch her. All of them except Lizzie, who capered and snorted a bit, had the sense to understand that her attention was elsewhere.

. . .

It had started when they read the obituary, Mr. Jamieson's obituary. That was in the city paper, and his face had been on the evening news. Up until the year before, they had known the Jamiesons only as neighbors who kept to themselves. She taught Botany at the college forty miles away, so she had to spend a good deal of her time on the road. He was a poet.

Everybody knew that much. But he seemed to be occupied with other things. For a poet, and for an old man—perhaps twenty years older than Mrs. Jamieson—he was rugged and active. He improved the drainage system on his place, cleaning out the culvert and lining it with rocks. He dug and planted and fenced a vegetable garden, cut paths through the woods, looked after repairs on the house.

The house itself was an odd-looking triangular affair that he had built years ago, with some friends, on the foundation of an old wrecked farmhouse. Those people were spoken of as hippies—though Mr. Jamieson must have been a bit old for that, even then, before Mrs. Jamieson's time. There was a story that they grew marijuana in the woods, sold it, and stored the money in sealed glass jars, which were buried around the property. Clark had heard this from the people he got to know in town. He said it was bullshit.

"Else somebody would have got in and dug it up, before now. Somebody would have found a way to make him tell where it was."

When they read the obituary Carla and Clark learned for the first time that Leon Jamieson had been the recipient of a large prize, five years before his death. A prize for poetry. Nobody had ever mentioned this. It seemed that people could believe in dope money buried in glass jars, but not in money won for writing poetry.

Shortly after this Clark said, "We could've made him pay."

Carla knew at once what he was talking about, but she took it as a joke.

"Too late now," she said. "You can't pay once you're dead."

"He can't. She could."

"She's gone to Greece."

"She's not going to stay in Greece."

"She didn't know," said Carla more soberly.

"I didn't say she did."

"She doesn't have a clue about it."

"We could fix that."

Carla said, "No. No."

Clark went on as if she had not spoken.

"We could say we're going to sue. People get money for stuff like that all the time."

"How could you do that? You can't sue a dead person."

"Threaten to go to the papers. Big-time poet. The papers would eat it up. All we have to do is threaten and she'd cave in."

"You're just fantasizing," Carla said. "You're joking."

"No," said Clark. "Actually, I'm not."

Carla said she did not want to talk about it anymore and he said okay.

But they talked about it the next day, and the next and the next. He sometimes got notions like this that were not practicable, which might even be illegal. He talked about them with growing excitement and then—she wasn't sure why—he dropped them. If the rain had stopped, if this had turned into something like a normal summer, he might have let this idea go the way of the others. But that had not happened, and during the last month he had harped on the scheme as if it was perfectly feasible and serious. The question was how much money to ask for. Too little, and the woman might not take them seriously, she might be inclined to see if they were bluffing. Too much might get her back up and she might become stubborn.

Carla had stopped saying that it was a joke. Instead she told him that it wouldn't work. She said that for one thing, people expected poets to be that way. So it wouldn't be worth paying out money to cover it up.

He said that it would work if it was done right. Carla was to break down and tell Mrs. Jamieson the whole story. Then Clark would move in, as if it had all been a surprise to him, he had just found out. He would be outraged, he would talk about telling the world. He would let Mrs. Jamieson be the one who first mentioned money.

"You were injured. You were molested and humiliated and I was injured and humiliated because you are my wife. It's a question of respect."

Over and over again he talked to her in this way and she tried to deflect him but he insisted.

"Promise," he said. "Promise."

This was because of what she had told him, things she could not now retract or deny.

Sometimes he gets interested in me?

The old guy?

Sometimes he calls me into the room when she's not there?

Yes.

When she has to go out shopping and the nurse isn't there either.

A lucky inspiration of hers, one that instantly pleased him.

So what do you do then? Do you go in?

She played shy.

Sometimes.

He calls you into his room. So? Carla? So, then?

I go in to see what he wants.

So what does he want?

This was asked and told in whispers, even if there was nobody to hear, even when they were in the neverland of their bed. A bedtime story, in which the details were important and had to be added to every time, and this with convincing reluctance, shyness, giggles, *dirty, dirty*. And it was not only he who was eager and grateful. She was too. Eager to please and excite him, to excite herself. Grateful every time it still worked.

And in one part of her mind it *was* true, she saw the randy old man, the bump he made in the sheet, bedridden indeed, almost beyond speech but proficient in sign language, indicating his desire, trying to nudge and finger her into complicity, into obliging stunts and intimacies. (Her refusal a necessity, but also perhaps strangely, slightly disappointing, to Clark.)

Now and then came an image that she had to hammer down, lest it spoil everything. She would think of the real dim and sheeted body, drugged and shrinking every day in its rented hospital bed, glimpsed only a few times when Mrs. Jamieson or the visiting nurse had neglected to close the door. She herself never actually coming closer to him than that.

In fact she had dreaded going to the Jamiesons', but she needed the money, and she felt sorry for Mrs. Jamieson, who seemed so haunted and bewildered, as if she was walking in her sleep. Once or twice Carla had burst out and done something really silly just to loosen up the atmosphere. The kind of thing she did when clumsy and terrified first-time horseback riders were feeling humiliated. She used to try that too when Clark was stuck in his moods. It didn't work with him anymore. But the story about Mr. Jamieson had worked, decisively.

There was no way to avoid the puddles in the path or the tall soaked grass alongside it, or the wild carrot which had recently come into flower. But the air was warm enough so that she didn't get chilly. Her clothes were soaked through as if by her own sweat or the tears that ran down her face with the drizzle of rain. Her weeping petered out in time. She had nothing to wipe her nose on—the paper towel now soggy—but she leaned over and blew it hard into a puddle.

She lifted her head and managed the long-drawn-out, vibrating whistle that was her signal—Clark's too—for Flora. She waited a couple of minutes and then called Flora's name. Over and over again, whistle and name, whistle and name.

Flora did not respond.

It was almost a relief, though, to feel the single pain of missing Flora, of missing Flora perhaps forever, compared to the mess she had got into concerning Mrs. Jamieson, and her seesaw misery with Clark. At least Flora's leaving was not on account of anything that she—Carla—had done wrong.

At the house, there was nothing for Sylvia to do except to open the windows. And to think—with an eagerness that dismayed without really surprising her—of how soon she could see Carla.

All the paraphernalia of illness had been removed. The room that had been Sylvia and her husband's bedroom and then his death chamber had been cleaned out and tidied up to look as if nothing had ever happened in it. Carla had helped with all that during the few frenzied days between the crematorium and the departure for Greece. Every piece of clothing Leon had ever worn and some things he hadn't, including gifts from his sisters that had never been taken out of their packages, had been piled in the backseat of the car and delivered to the Thrift Shop. His pills, his shaving things, unopened cans of the fortified drink that had sustained him as long as anything could, cartons of the sesame seed snaps that at one time he had eaten by the dozens, the plastic bottles full of the lotion that had eased his back, the sheepskins on which he had lain—all of that was dumped into plastic bags to be hauled away as garbage, and Carla didn't question a thing. She never said, "Maybe somebody could use that," or pointed out that whole cartons of cans were unopened. When Sylvia said, "I wish I hadn't taken the clothes to town. I wish I'd burned them all up in the incinerator," Carla had shown no surprise.

They cleaned the oven, scrubbed out the cupboards, wiped down the walls and the windows. One day Sylvia sat in the living room going through all the condolence letters she had received. (There was no accumulation of papers and notebooks to be attended to, as you might have expected with a writer, no unfinished work or scribbled drafts. He had told her, months before, that he had pitched everything. *And no regrets.*)

The south-sloping wall of the house was made up of big windows. Sylvia looked up, surprised by the watery sunlight that had come out—or possibly surprised by the shadow of Carla, bare-legged, bare-armed, on top of a ladder, her resolute face crowned with a frizz of dandelion hair that was too short for the braid. She was vigorously spraying and scrubbing the glass. When she saw Sylvia looking at her she stopped and flung out her arms as if she was splayed there, making a silly gargoyle-like face. They both began to laugh. Sylvia felt this laughter running all through her like a playful stream. She went back to her letters as Carla resumed the cleaning. She decided that all of these kind words—genuine or perfunctory, the tributes and regrets—could go the way of the sheepskins and the crackers.

When she heard Carla taking the ladder down, heard boots on the deck, she was suddenly shy. She sat where she was with her head bowed as Carla came into the room and passed behind her on her way to the kitchen to put the pail and the cloths back under the sink. Carla hardly halted, she was quick as a bird, but she managed to drop a kiss on Sylvia's bent head. Then she went on whistling something to herself.

That kiss had been in Sylvia's mind ever since. It meant nothing in particular. It meant *Cheer up*. Or *Almost done*. It meant that they were good friends who had got through a lot of depressing work together. Or maybe just that the sun had come out. That Carla was thinking of getting home to her horses. Nevertheless, Sylvia saw it as a bright blossom, its petals spreading inside her with tumultuous heat, like a menopausal flash.

Every so often there had been a special girl student in one of her botany classes—one whose cleverness and dedication and awkward egotism, or even genuine passion for the natural world, reminded her of her young self. Such girls hung around her worshipfully, hoped for some sort of intimacy they could not—in most cases—imagine, and they soon got on her nerves.

Carla was nothing like them. If she resembled anybody in Sylvia's life, it would have to be certain girls she had known in high school—those who were bright but never too bright, easy athletes but not strenuously competitive, buoyant but not rambunctious. Naturally happy.

"Where I was, this little village, this little tiny village with my two old friends, well, it was the sort of place where the very occasional tourist bus would stop, just as if it had got lost, and the tourists would get off and look around and they were absolutely bewildered because they weren't anywhere. There was nothing to buy."

Sylvia was speaking about Greece. Carla was sitting a few feet away from her. The large-limbed, uncomfortable, dazzling girl was sitting there at last, in the room that had been filled with thoughts of her. She was faintly smiling, belatedly nodding.

"And at first," Sylvia said, "at first I was bewildered too. It was so hot. But it's true about the light. It's wonderful. And then I figured out what there was to do, and there were just these few simple things but they could fill the day. You walk half a mile down the road to buy some oil and half a mile in the other direction to buy your bread or your wine, and that's the morning, and you eat some lunch under the trees and after lunch it's too hot to do anything but close the shutters and lie on your bed and maybe read. At first you read. And then it gets so you don't even do that. Why read? Later on you notice the shadows are longer and you get up and go for a swim.

"Oh," she interrupted herself. "Oh, I forgot."

She jumped up and went to get the present she had brought, which in fact she had not forgotten about at all. She had not wanted to hand it to Carla right away, she had wanted the moment to come more naturally, and while she was speaking she had thought ahead to the moment when she could mention the sea, going swimming. And say, as she now said, "Swimming reminded me of this because it's a little replica, you know, it's a little replica of the horse they found under the sea. Cast in bronze. They dredged it up, after all this time. It's supposed to be from the second century B.C."

When Carla had come in and looked around for work to do, Sylvia had said, "Oh, just sit down a minute, I haven't had anybody to talk to since I got back. Please." Carla had sat down on the edge of a chair, legs apart, hands between her knees, looking somehow desolate. As if reaching for some distant politeness she had said, "How was Greece?"

Now she was standing, with the tissue paper crumpled around the horse, which she had not fully unwrapped.

"It's said to represent a racehorse," Sylvia said. "Making that final spurt, the last effort in a race. The rider, too, the boy, you can see he's urging the horse on to the limit of its strength."

She did not mention that the boy had made her think of Carla, and she could not now have said why. He was only about ten or eleven years old. Maybe the strength and grace of the arm that must have held the reins, or the wrinkles in his childish forehead, the absorption and the pure effort there was in some way like Carla cleaning the big windows last spring. Her strong legs in her shorts, her broad shoulders, her big swipes at the glass, and then the way she had splayed herself out as a joke, inviting or even commanding Sylvia to laugh.

"You can see that," Carla said, now conscientiously examining the little bronzy-green statue. "Thank you very much."

"You are welcome. Let's have coffee, shall we? I've just made some. The coffee in Greece was quite strong, a little stronger than I liked, but the bread was heavenly. And the ripe figs, they were astounding. Sit down another moment, please do. You should stop me going on and on this way. What about here? How has life been here?"

"It's been raining most of the time."

"I can see that. I can see it has," Sylvia called from the kitchen end of the big room. Pouring the coffee, she decided that she would keep quiet about the other gift she had brought. It hadn't cost her anything (the horse had cost more than the girl could probably guess), it was only a beautiful small pinkish-white stone she had picked up along the road.

"This is for Carla," she had said to her friend Maggie, who was walking beside her. "I know it's silly. I just want her to have a tiny piece of this land."

She had already mentioned Carla to Maggie, and to Soraya, her other friend there, telling them how the girl's presence had come to mean more and more to her, how an indescribable bond had seemed to grow up between them, and had consoled her in the awful months of last spring.

"It was just to see somebody—somebody so fresh and full of health coming into the house."

Maggie and Soraya had laughed in a kindly but annoying way.

"There's always a girl," Soraya said, with an indolent stretch of her heavy brown arms, and Maggie said, "We all come to it sometime. A crush on a girl."

Sylvia was obscurely angered by that dated word—*crush.*

"Maybe it's because Leon and I never had children," she said. "It's stupid. Displaced maternal love."

Her friends spoke at the same time, saying in slightly different ways something to the effect that it might be stupid but it was, after all, love.

But the girl was not, today, anything like the Carla Sylvia had been remembering, not at all the calm bright spirit, the carefree and generous young creature who had kept her company in Greece.

She had been hardly interested in her gift. Almost sullen as she reached out for her mug of coffee.

"There was one thing I thought you would have liked a lot," said Sylvia energetically. "The goats. They were quite small even when they were full-grown. Some spotty and some white, and they were leaping around up on the rocks just like—like the spirits of the place." She laughed in an artificial way, she couldn't stop herself. "I wouldn't be surprised if they'd had wreaths on their horns. How is your little goat? I forget her name."

Carla said, "Flora."

"Flora."

"She's gone."

"Gone? Did you sell her?"

"She disappeared. We don't know where."

"Oh, I'm sorry. I'm sorry. But isn't there a chance she'll turn up again?"

No answer. Sylvia looked directly at the girl, something that up to now she had not quite been able to do, and saw that her eyes were full of tears, her face blotchy—in fact it looked grubby—and that she seemed bloated with distress.

She didn't do anything to avoid Sylvia's look. She drew her lips tight over her teeth and shut her eyes and rocked back and forth as if in a soundless howl, and then, shockingly, she did howl. She howled and wept and gulped for air and tears ran down her cheeks and snot out of her nostrils and she began to look around wildly for something to wipe with. Sylvia ran and got handfuls of Kleenex.

"Don't worry, here you are, here, you're all right," she said, thinking that maybe the thing to do would be to take the girl in her arms. But she had not the least wish to do that, and it might make things worse. The girl might feel how little Sylvia wanted to do such a thing, how appalled she was in fact by this noisy fit.

Carla said something, said the same thing again.

"Awful," she said. "Awful."

"No it's not. We all have to cry sometimes. It's all right, don't worry."

"It's awful."

And Sylvia could not help feeling how, with every moment of this show of misery, the girl made herself more ordinary, more like one of those soggy students in her—Sylvia's—office. Some of them cried about their marks, but that was often tactical, a brief unconvincing bit of whimpering. The more infrequent, real waterworks would turn out to have something to do with a love affair, or their parents, or a pregnancy.

"It's not about your goat, is it?"

"No. No."

"You better have a glass of water," said Sylvia.

She took time to run it cold, trying to think what else she should do or say, and when she returned with it Carla was already calming down.

"Now. Now," Sylvia said as the water was being swallowed. "Isn't that better?"

"Yes."

"It's not the goat. What is it?"

Carla said, "I can't stand it anymore."

What could she not stand?

It turned out to be the husband.

He was mad at her all the time. He acted as if he hated her. There was nothing she could do right, there was nothing she could say. Living with him was driving her crazy. Sometimes she thought she already was crazy. Sometimes she thought he was.

"Has he hurt you, Carla?"

No. He hadn't hurt her physically. But he hated her. He despised her. He could not stand it when she cried and she could not help crying because he was so mad.

She did not know what to do.

"Perhaps you do know what to do," said Sylvia.

"Get away? I would if I could." Carla began to wail again. "I'd give anything to get away. I can't. I haven't any money. I haven't anywhere in this world to go."

"Well. Think. Is that altogether true?" said Sylvia in her best counselling manner. "Don't you have parents? Didn't you tell me you grew up in Kingston? Don't you have a family there?"

Her parents had moved to British Columbia. They hated Clark. They didn't care if she lived or died.

Brothers or sisters?

One brother nine years older. He was married and in Toronto. He didn't care either. He didn't like Clark. His wife was a snob.

"Have you ever thought of the Women's Shelter?"

"They don't want you there unless you've been beaten up. And everybody would find out and it would be bad for our business."

Sylvia gently smiled.

"Is this a time to think about that?"

Then Carla actually laughed. "I know," she said, "I'm insane."

"Listen," said Sylvia. "Listen to me. If you had the money to go, would you go? Where would you go? What would you do?"

"I would go to Toronto," Carla said readily enough. "But I wouldn't go near my brother. I'd stay in a motel or something and I'd get a job at a riding stable."

"You think you could do that?"

"I was working at a riding stable the summer I met Clark. I'm more experienced now than I was then. A lot more."

"You sound as if you've figured this out," said Sylvia thoughtfully.

Carla said, "I have now."

"So when would you go, if you could go?"

"Now. Today. This minute."

"All that's stopping you is lack of money?"

Carla took a deep breath. "All that's stopping me," she said.

"All right," said Sylvia. "Now listen to what I propose. I don't think you should go to a motel. I think you should take the bus to Toronto and go to stay with a friend of mine. Her name is Ruth Stiles. She has a big house and she lives alone and she won't mind having somebody to stay. You can stay there till you find a job. I'll help you with some money. There must be lots and lots of riding stables around Toronto."

"There are."

"So what do you think? Do you want me to phone and find out what time the bus goes?"

Carla said yes. She was shivering. She ran her hands up and down her thighs and shook her head roughly from side to side.

"I can't believe it," she said. "I'll pay you back. I mean, thank you. I'll pay you back. I don't know what to say."

Sylvia was already at the phone, dialling the bus depot.

"Shh, I'm getting the times," she said. She listened, and hung up. "I know you will. You agree about Ruth's? I'll let her know. There's one problem, though." She looked critically at Carla's shorts and T-shirt. "You can't very well go in those clothes."

"I can't go home to get anything," said Carla in a panic. "I'll be all right."

"The bus will be air-conditioned. You'll freeze. There must be something of mine you could wear. Aren't we about the same height?"

"You're ten times skinnier."

"I didn't use to be."

In the end they decided on a brown linen jacket, hardly worn—Sylvia had considered it to be a mistake for herself, the style too brusque—and a pair of tailored tan pants and a cream-colored silk shirt. Carla's sneakers would have to do with this outfit, because her feet were two sizes larger than Sylvia's.

Carla went to take a shower—something she had not bothered with in her state of mind that morning—and Sylvia phoned Ruth. Ruth was going to be out at a meeting that evening, but she would leave the key with her upstairs tenants and all Carla would have to do was ring their bell.

"She'll have to take a cab from the bus depot, though. I assume she's okay to manage that?" Ruth said.

Sylvia laughed. "She's not a lame duck, don't worry. She is just a person in a bad situation, the way it happens."

"Well good. I mean good she's getting out."

"Not a lame duck at all," said Sylvia, thinking of Carla trying on the tailored pants and linen jacket. How quickly the young recover from a fit of despair and how handsome the girl had looked in the fresh clothes.

The bus would stop in town at twenty past two. Sylvia decided to make omelettes for lunch, to set the table with the dark-blue cloth, and to get down the crystal glasses and open a bottle of wine.

"I hope you're hungry enough to eat something," she said, when Carla came out clean and shining in her borrowed clothes. Her softly freckled skin was flushed from the shower, and her hair was damp and darkened, out of its braid, the sweet frizz now flat against her head. She said she was hungry, but when she tried to get a forkful of the omelette to her mouth her trembling hands made it impossible.

"I don't know why I'm shaking like this," she said. "I must be excited. I never knew it would be this easy."

"It's very sudden," said Sylvia. "Probably it doesn't seem quite real."

"It does, though. Everything now seems really real. Like the time before now, that's when I was in a daze."

"Maybe when you make up your mind to something, when you really make up your mind, that's how it is. Or that's how it should be."

"If you've got a friend," said Carla with a self-conscious smile and a flush spreading over her forehead. "If you've got a true friend. I mean like you." She laid down the knife and fork and raised her wineglass awkwardly with both hands. "Drinking to a true friend," she said, uncomfortably. "I probably shouldn't even take a sip, but I will."

"Me too," said Sylvia with a pretense of gaiety. She drank, but spoiled the moment by saying, "Are you going to phone him? Or what? He'll have to know. At least he'll have to know where you are by the time he'd be expecting you home."

"Not the phone," said Carla, alarmed. "I can't do it. Maybe if you—"

"No," said Sylvia. "No."

"No, that's stupid. I shouldn't have said that. It's just hard to think straight. What I maybe should do, I should put a note in the mailbox. But I don't want him to get it too soon. I don't want us to even drive past there when we're going into town. I want to go the back way. So if I write it—if I write it, could you, could you maybe slip it in the box when you come back?"

Sylvia agreed to this, seeing no good alternative.

She brought pen and paper. She poured a little more wine. Carla sat thinking, then wrote a few words.

I have gone away. I will be all write.

These were the words that Sylvia read when she unfolded the paper, on her way back from the bus depot. She was sure Carla knew *right* from *write*. It was just that she had been talking about *writing* a note, and she was in a state of exalted confusion. More confusion perhaps than Sylvia had realized. The wine had brought out a stream of talk, but it had not seemed to be accompanied by any particular grief or upset. She had talked about the horse barn where she had worked and met Clark when she was eighteen and just out of high school. Her parents wanted her to go to college, and she had agreed as long as she could choose to be a veterinarian. All she really wanted, and had wanted all her life, was to work with animals and live in the country. She had been one of those dorky girls in high school, one of those girls they made rotten jokes about, but she didn't care.

Clark was the best riding teacher they had. Scads of women were after him, they would take up riding just to get him as their teacher. Carla teased him about his women and at first he seemed to like it, then he got annoyed. She apologized and tried to make up for it by getting him talking about his dream—his plan, really—to have a riding school, a horse stable, someplace out in the country. One day she came into the stable and saw him hanging up his saddle and realized she had fallen in love with him.

Now she considered it was sex. It was probably just sex.

When fall came and she was supposed to quit working and leave for college in Guelph, she refused to go, she said she needed a year off.

Clark was very smart but he hadn't waited even to finish high school. He had altogether lost touch with his family. He thought families were like a poison in your blood. He had been an attendant in a mental hospital, a disc jockey on a radio station in Lethbridge, Alberta, a member of a road crew on the highways near Thunder Bay, an apprentice barber, a salesman in an Army Surplus store. And those were only the jobs he told her about.

She had nicknamed him Gypsy Rover, because of the song, an old song her mother used to sing. Now she took to singing it around the house all the time and her mother knew something was up.

> *"Last night she slept in a feather bed*
> *With a silken quilt for cover*
> *Tonight she'll sleep on the cold hard ground—*
> *Beside her gypsy lo-ov-ver."*

Her mother said, "He'll break your heart, that's a sure thing." Her stepfather, who was an engineer, did not even grant Clark that much power. "A loser," he called him. "One of those drifters." As if Clark was a bug he could just whisk off his clothes.

So Carla said, "Does a drifter save up enough money to buy a farm? Which, by the way, he has done?" and he only said, "I'm not about to argue with you." She was not his daughter anyway, he added, as if that was the clincher.

So, naturally, Carla had to run away with Clark. The way her parents behaved, they were practically guaranteeing it.

"Will you get in touch with your parents after you're settled?" Sylvia said. "In Toronto?"

Carla lifted her eyebrows, pulled in her cheeks and made a saucy O of her mouth. She said, "Nope."

Definitely a little drunk.

Back home, having left the note in the mailbox, Sylvia cleaned up the dishes that were still on the table, washed and polished the omelette pan, threw the blue napkins and tablecloth in the laundry basket, and opened the windows. She did this with a confusing sense of regret and irritation. She had put out a fresh cake of apple-scented soap for the girl's shower and the smell of it lingered in the house, as it had in the air of the car.

The rain was holding off. She could not stay still, so she went for a walk along the path that Leon had cleared. The gravel he had dumped in the boggy places had mostly washed away. They used to go walking every spring, to look for wild orchids. She taught him the name of every wildflower—all of which, except for trillium, he forgot. He used to call her his Dorothy Wordsworth.

Last spring she went out once and picked him a small bunch of dog's-tooth violets, but he looked at them—as he sometimes looked at her—with mere exhaustion, disavowal.

She kept seeing Carla, Carla stepping onto the bus. Her

thanks had been sincere but already almost casual, her wave jaunty. She had got used to her salvation.

Back in the house, at around six o'clock, Sylvia put in a call to Toronto, to Ruth, knowing that Carla would not have arrived yet. She got the answering machine.

"Ruth," said Sylvia. "Sylvia. It's about this girl I sent you. I hope she doesn't turn out to be a bother to you. I hope it'll be all right. You may find her a little full of herself. Maybe it's just youth. Let me know. Okay?"

She phoned again before she went to bed but got the machine, so she said, "Sylvia again. Just checking," and hung up. It was between nine and ten o'clock, not even really dark. Ruth must still be out and the girl would not want to pick up the phone in a strange house. She tried to think of the name of Ruth's upstairs tenants. They surely wouldn't have gone to bed yet. But she could not remember. And just as well. Phoning them would have meant making too much of a fuss, being too anxious, going too far.

She got into the bed but it was impossible to stay there, so she took a light quilt and went out to the living room and lay down on the sofa, where she had slept for the last three months of Leon's life. She did not think it likely that she would get to sleep there either—there were no curtains on the bank of windows and she could tell by the look of the sky that the moon had risen, though she could not see it.

The next thing she knew she was on a bus somewhere—in Greece?—with a lot of people she did not know, and the engine of the bus was making an alarming knocking sound. She woke to find the knocking was at her front door.

Carla?

. . .

31

Carla had kept her head down until the bus was clear of town. The windows were tinted, nobody could see in, but she had to guard herself against seeing out. Lest Clark appear. Coming out of a store or waiting to cross the street, all ignorant of her abandoning him, thinking this an ordinary afternoon. No, thinking it the afternoon when their scheme—his scheme—was put in motion, eager to know how far she had got with it.

Once they were out in the country she looked up, breathed deeply, took account of the fields, which were slightly violet-tinted through the glass. Mrs. Jamieson's presence had surrounded her with some kind of remarkable safety and sanity and had made her escape seem the most rational thing you could imagine, in fact the only self-respecting thing that a person in Carla's shoes could do. Carla had felt herself capable of an unaccustomed confidence, even of a mature sense of humor, revealing her life to Mrs. Jamieson in a way that seemed bound to gain sympathy and yet to be ironic and truthful. And adapted to live up to what, as far as she could see, were Mrs. Jamieson's—Sylvia's—expectations. She did have a feeling that it would be possible to disappoint Mrs. Jamieson, who struck her as a most sensitive and rigorous person, but she thought that she was in no danger of doing that.

If she didn't have to be around her for too long.

The sun was shining, as it had been for some time. When they sat at lunch it had made the wineglasses sparkle. No rain had fallen since early morning. There was enough of a wind blowing to lift the roadside grass, the flowering weeds, out of their drenched clumps. Summer clouds, not rain clouds, were scudding across the sky. The whole countryside was changing, shaking itself loose, into the true brightness of a July day. And as they sped along she was able to see not much trace at all of the recent past—no big puddles in the fields, showing where the seed had washed out, no miserable spindly cornstalks or lodged grain.

It occurred to her that she must tell Clark about this—that perhaps they had chosen what was for some freakish reason a very wet and dreary corner of the country, and there were other places where they could have been successful.

Or could be yet?

Then it came to her of course that she would not be telling Clark anything. Never again. She would not be concerned about what happened to him, or to Grace or Mike or Juniper or Blackberry or Lizzie Borden. If by any chance Flora came back, she would not hear of it.

This was her second time to leave everything behind. The first time was just like the old Beatles song—her putting the note on the table and slipping out of the house at five o'clock in the morning, meeting Clark in the church parking lot down the street. She was actually humming that song as they rattled away. *She's leaving home, bye-bye.* She recalled now how the sun was coming up behind them, how she looked at Clark's hands on the wheel, the dark hairs on his competent forearms, and breathed in the smell of the inside of the truck, a smell of oil and metal, tools and horse barns. The cold air of the fall morning blew in through the truck's rusted seams. It was the sort of vehicle that nobody in her family ever rode in, that scarcely ever appeared on the streets where they lived.

Clark's preoccupation on that morning with the traffic (they had reached Highway 401), his concern about the truck's behavior, his curt answers, his narrowed eyes, even his slight irritation at her giddy delight—all of that thrilled her. As did the disorder of his past life, his avowed loneliness, the tender way he could have with a horse, and with her. She saw him as the architect of the life ahead of them, herself as captive, her submission both proper and exquisite.

"You don't know what you're leaving behind," her mother wrote to her, in that one letter that she received, and never answered. But in those shivering moments of early-morning flight she certainly did know what she was leaving behind, even if she had rather a hazy idea of what she was going to. She despised her parents, their house, their backyard, their photo albums, their vacations, their Cuisinart, their *powder room,* their walk-in closets, their underground lawn-sprinkling system. In the brief note she had written she had used the word *authentic.*

I have always felt the need of a more authentic kind of life. I know I cannot expect you to understand this.

The bus had stopped now at the first town on the way. The depot was a gas station. It was the very station she and Clark used to drive to, in their early days, to buy cheap gas. In those days their world had included several towns in the surrounding countryside and they had sometimes behaved like tourists, sampling the specialties in grimy hotel bars. Pigs' feet, sauerkraut, potato pancakes, beer. And they would sing all the way home like crazy hillbillies.

But after a while all outings came to be seen as a waste of time and money. They were what people did before they understood the realities of their lives.

She was crying now, her eyes had filled up without her realizing it. She set herself to thinking about Toronto, the first steps ahead. The taxi, the house she had never seen, the strange bed she would sleep in alone. Looking in the phone book tomorrow for the addresses of riding stables, then getting to wherever they were, asking for a job.

She could not picture it. Herself riding on the subway or streetcar, caring for new horses, talking to new people, living among hordes of people every day who were not Clark.

A life, a place, chosen for that specific reason—that it would not contain Clark.

The strange and terrible thing coming clear to her about that world of the future, as she now pictured it, was that she would not exist there. She would only walk around, and open her mouth and speak, and do this and do that. She would not really be there. And what was strange about it was that she was doing all this, she was riding on this bus in the hope of recovering herself. As Mrs. Jamieson might say—and as she herself might with satisfaction have said—*taking charge of her own life*. With nobody glowering over her, nobody's mood infecting her with misery.

But what would she care about? How would she know that she was alive?

While she was running away from him—now—Clark still kept his place in her life. But when she was finished running away, when she just went on, what would she put in his place? What else—who else—could ever be so vivid a challenge?

She had managed to stop crying, but she had started to shake. She was in a bad way and would have to take hold, get a grip on herself. "Get a grip on yourself," Clark had sometimes told her, passing through a room where she was scrunched up, trying not to weep, and that indeed was what she must do.

They had stopped in another town. This was the third town away from the one where she had got on the bus, which meant that they had passed through the second town without her even noticing. The bus must have stopped, the driver must have called out the name, and she had not heard or seen anything in her fog of fright. Soon enough they would reach the major highway, they would be tearing along towards Toronto.

And she would be lost.

She would be lost. What would be the point of getting into a taxi and giving the new address, of getting up in the morning and brushing her teeth and going into the world? Why should she get a job, put food in her mouth, be carried by public transportation from place to place?

Her feet seemed now to be at some enormous distance from her body. Her knees, in the unfamiliar crisp pants, were weighted with irons. She was sinking to the ground like a stricken horse who will never get up.

Already the bus had loaded on the few passengers and the parcels that had been waiting in this town. A woman and a baby in its stroller were waving somebody good-bye. The building behind them, the cafe that served as a bus stop, was also in motion. A liquefying wave passed through the bricks and windows as if they were about to dissolve. In peril of her life, Carla pulled her huge body, her iron limbs, forward. She stumbled, she cried out, "Let me off."

The driver braked, he called out irritably, "I thought you were going to Toronto?" People gave her casually curious looks, nobody seemed to understand that she was in anguish.

"I have to get off here."

"There's a washroom in the back."

"No. No. I have to get off."

"I'm not waiting. You understand that? You got luggage underneath?"

"No. Yes. No."

"No luggage?"

A voice in the bus said, "Claustrophobia. That's what's the matter with her."

"You sick?" said the driver.

"No. No. I just want off."

"Okay. Okay. Fine by me."

"Come and get me. Please. Come and get me."

"I will."

. . .

Sylvia had forgotten to lock her door. She realized that she should be locking it now, not opening it, but it was too late, she had it open.

And nobody there.

Yet she was sure, sure, the knocking had been real.

She closed the door and this time she locked it.

There was a playful sound, a tinkling tapping sound, coming from the wall of windows. She switched the light on, but saw nothing there, and switched it off again. Some animal—maybe a squirrel? The French doors that opened between windows, leading to the patio, had not been locked either. Not even really closed, having been left open an inch or so from her airing of the house. She started to close them and somebody laughed, nearby, near enough to be in the room with her.

"It's me," a man said. "Did I scare you?"

He was pressed against the glass, he was right beside her.

"It's Clark," he said. "Clark from down the road."

She was not going to ask him in, but she was afraid to shut the door in his face. He could grab it before she could manage that. She didn't want to turn on the light, either. She slept in a long T-shirt. She should have pulled the quilt from the sofa and wrapped it around herself, but it was too late now.

"Did you want to get dressed?" he said. "What I got in here, it could be the very things you need."

He had a shopping bag in his hand. He thrust it at her, but did not try to come with it.

"What?" she said in a choppy voice.

"Look and see. It's not a bomb. There, take it."

She felt inside the bag, not looking. Something soft. And then she recognized the buttons of the jacket, the silk of the shirt, the belt on the pants.

"Just thought you'd better have them back," he said. "They're yours, aren't they?"

She tightened her jaws so that her teeth wouldn't chatter. A fearful dryness had attacked her mouth and throat.

"I understood they were yours," he said softly.

Her tongue moved like a wad of wool. She forced herself to say, "Where's Carla?"

"You mean my wife Carla?"

Now she could see his face more clearly. She could see how he was enjoying himself.

"My wife Carla is home in bed. Asleep in bed. Where she belongs."

He was both a handsome man and a silly-looking man. Tall, lean, well built, but with a slouch that seemed artificial. A contrived, self-conscious air of menace. A lock of dark hair falling over his forehead, a vain little moustache, eyes that appeared both hopeful and mocking, a boyish smile perpetually on the verge of a sulk.

She had always disliked the sight of him—she had mentioned her dislike to Leon, who said that the man was just unsure of himself, just a bit too friendly.

The fact that he was unsure of himself would not make her any safer now.

"Pretty worn out," he said. "After her little adventure. You should've seen your face—you should've seen the look on you when you recognized those clothes. What did you think? Did you think I'd murdered her?"

"I was surprised," said Sylvia.

"I bet you were. After you were such a big help to her running away."

"I helped her—," Sylvia said with considerable effort, "I helped her because she seemed to be in distress."

"Distress," he said, as if examining the word. "I guess she

was. She was in very big distress when she jumped off that bus and got on the phone to me to come and get her. She was crying so hard I could hardly make out what it was she was saying."

"She wanted to come back?"

"Oh yeah. You bet she wanted to come back. She was in real hysterics to come back. She is a girl who is very up and down in her emotions. But I guess you don't know her as well as I do."

"She seemed quite happy to be going."

"Did she really? Well, I have to take your word for it. I didn't come here to argue with you."

Sylvia said nothing.

"I came here to tell you I don't appreciate you interfering in my life with my wife."

"She is a human being," said Sylvia, though she knew it would be better if she could keep quiet. "Besides being your wife."

"My goodness, is that so? My wife is a human being? Really? Thank you for the information. But don't try getting smart with me. *Sylvia*."

"I wasn't trying to get smart."

"Good. I'm glad you weren't. I don't want to get mad. I just have a couple of important things to say to you. One thing, that I don't want you sticking your nose in anywhere, anytime, in my and my wife's life. Another, that I'm not going to want her coming around here anymore. Not that she is going to particularly want to come, I'm pretty sure of that. She doesn't have too good an opinion of you at the moment. And it's time you learned how to clean your own house.

"Now," he said. "Now. Has that sunk in?"

"Quite sufficiently."

"Oh, I really hope it has. I hope so."

Sylvia said, "Yes."

"And you know what else I think?"

"What?"

"I think you owe me something."

"What?"

"I think you owe me—maybe—you owe me an apology."

Sylvia said, "All right. If you think so. I'm sorry."

He shifted, perhaps just to put out his hand, and with the movement of his body she shrieked.

He laughed. He put his hand on the doorframe to make sure she didn't close it.

"What's that?"

"What's what?" he said, as if she was trying out a trick and it would not work. But then he caught sight of something reflected in the window, and he snapped around to look.

Not far from the house was a wide shallow patch of land that often filled up with night fog at this time of year. The fog was there tonight, had been there all this while. But now at one point there was a change. The fog had thickened, taken on a separate shape, transformed itself into something spiky and radiant. First a live dandelion ball, tumbling forward, then condensing itself into an unearthly sort of animal, pure white, hell-bent, something like a giant unicorn, rushing at them.

"Jesus Christ," Clark said softly and devoutly. And grabbed hold of Sylvia's shoulder. This touch did not alarm her at all—she accepted it with the knowledge that he did it either to protect her or to reassure himself.

Then the vision exploded. Out of the fog, and out of the magnifying light—now seen to be that of a car travelling along this back road, probably in search of a place to park—out of this appeared a white goat. A little dancing white goat, hardly bigger than a sheepdog.

Clark let go. He said, "Where the Christ did you come from?"

"It's your goat," said Sylvia. "Isn't it your goat?"

"Flora," he said. "Flora."

The goat had stopped a yard or so away from them, had turned shy and hung her head.

"Flora," Clark said. "Where the hell did you come from? You scared the shit out of us."

Us.

Flora came closer but still did not look up. She butted against Clark's legs.

"Goddamn stupid animal," he said shakily. "Where'd you come from?"

"She was lost," said Sylvia.

"Yeah. She was. Never thought we'd see her again, actually."

Flora looked up. The moonlight caught a glitter in her eyes.

"Scared the shit out of us," Clark said to her. "Were you off looking for a boyfriend? Scared the shit. Didn't you? We thought you were a ghost."

"It was the effect of the fog," Sylvia said. She stepped out of the door now, onto the patio. Quite safe.

"Yeah."

"Then the lights of that car."

"Like an apparition," he said, recovering. And pleased that he had thought of this description.

"Yes."

"The goat from outer space. That's what you are. You are a goddamn goat from outer space," he said, patting Flora. But when Sylvia put out her free hand to do the same—her other hand still held the bag of clothes that Carla had worn—Flora immediately lowered her head as if to prepare for some serious butting.

"Goats are unpredictable," Clark said. "They can seem tame but they're not really. Not after they grow up."

"Is she grown-up? She looks so small."

"She's big as she's ever going to get."

They stood looking down at the goat, as if expecting she would provide them with more conversation. But this was apparently not going to happen. From this moment they could go neither forward nor back. Sylvia believed that she might have seen a shadow of regret cross his face that this was so.

But he acknowledged it. He said, "It's late."

"I guess it is," said Sylvia, just as if this had been an ordinary visit.

"Okay, Flora. Time for us to go home."

"I'll make other arrangements for help if I need it," she said. "I probably won't need it now, anyway." She added almost laughingly, "I'll stay out of your hair."

"Sure," he said. "You better get inside. You'll get cold."

"People used to think night fogs were dangerous."

"That's a new one on me."

"So good night," she said. "Good night, Flora."

The phone rang then.

"Excuse me."

He raised a hand and turned away. "Good night."

It was Ruth on the phone.

"Ah," Sylvia said. "A change in plans."

She did not sleep, thinking of the little goat, whose appearance out of the fog seemed to her more and more magical. She even wondered if, possibly, Leon could have had something to do with it. If she was a poet she would write a poem about something like this. But in her experience the subjects that she thought a poet could write about did not appeal to Leon.

Carla had not heard Clark go out but she woke when he came in. He told her that he had just been out checking around the barn.

"A car went along the road a while ago and I wondered what they were doing here. I couldn't get back to sleep till I went out and checked whether everything was okay."

"So was it?"

"Far as I could see."

"And then while I was up," he said, "I thought I might as well pay a visit up the road. I took the clothes back."

Carla sat up in bed.

"You didn't wake her up?"

"She woke up. It was okay. We had a little talk."

"Oh."

"It was okay."

"You didn't mention any of that stuff, did you?"

"I didn't mention it."

"It really was all made-up. It really was. You have to believe me. It was all a lie."

"Okay."

"You have to believe me."

"Then I believe you."

"I made it all up."

"Okay."

He got into bed.

"Your feet are cold," she said. "Like they got wet."

"Heavy dew.

"Come here," he said. "When I read your note, it was just like I went hollow inside. It's true. If you ever went away, I'd feel like I didn't have anything left in me."

The bright weather had continued. On the streets, in the stores, in the Post Office, people greeted each other by saying that summer had finally arrived. The pasture grass and even the poor beaten crops lifted up their heads. The puddles dried up, the mud turned to dust. A light warm wind blew and everybody felt like doing things again. The phone rang. Inquiries about trail rides, about riding lessons. Summer camps were interested now, having cancelled their trips to museums. Minivans drew up, with their loads of restless children. The horses pranced along the fences, freed from their blankets.

Clark had managed to get hold of a large enough piece of roofing at a good price. He had spent the whole first day after Runaway Day (that was how they referred to Carla's bus trip) fixing the roof of the exercise ring.

For a couple of days, as they went about their chores, he and Carla would wave at each other. If she happened to pass close to him, and there was nobody else around, Carla might kiss his shoulder through the light material of his summer shirt.

"If you ever try to run away on me again I'll tan your hide," he said to her, and she said, "*Would* you?"

"What?"

"Tan my hide?"

"Damn right." He was high-spirited now, irresistible as when she had first known him.

Birds were everywhere. Red-winged blackbirds, robins, a pair of doves that sang at daybreak. Lots of crows, and gulls on reconnoitering missions from the lake, and big turkey buzzards that sat in the branches of a dead oak about half a mile away, at the edge of the woods. At first they just sat there, drying out their voluminous wings, lifting themselves occasionally for a trial flight, flapping around a bit, then composing themselves to let the sun and the warm air do their work. In a day or so they were restored, flying high, circling and dropping to earth, disappearing over the woods, coming back to rest in the familiar bare tree.

Lizzie's owner—Joy Tucker—showed up again, tanned and friendly. She had just got sick of the rain and gone off on her holidays to hike in the Rocky Mountains. Now she was back.

"Perfect timing weatherwise," Clark said. He and Joy Tucker were soon joking as if nothing had happened.

"Lizzie looks to be in good shape," she said. "But where's her little friend? What's her name—Flora?"

"Gone," said Clark. "Maybe she took off to the Rocky Mountains."

"Lots of wild goats out there. With fantastic horns."

"So I hear."

For three or four days they had been just too busy to go down and look in the mailbox. When Carla opened it she found the phone bill, some promise that if they subscribed to a certain magazine they could win a million dollars, and Mrs. Jamieson's letter.

My Dear Carla,

I have been thinking about the (rather dramatic) events of the last few days and I find myself talking to myself but really to you, so often that I thought I must speak to you, even if—the best way I can do now—only in a letter. And don't worry—you do not have to answer me.

Mrs. Jamieson went on to say that she was afraid that she had involved herself too closely in Carla's life and had made the mistake of thinking somehow that Carla's happiness and freedom were the same thing. All she cared for was Carla's happiness and she saw now that she—Carla—must find that in her marriage. All she could hope was that perhaps Carla's flight and turbulent emotions had brought her true feelings to the surface and perhaps a recognition in her husband of his true feelings as well.

She said that she would perfectly understand if Carla had a wish to avoid her in the future and that she would always be grateful for Carla's presence in her life during such a difficult time.

The strangest and most wonderful thing in this whole string of events seems to me the reappearance of Flora. In fact it seems rather like a miracle. Where had she been all the time and why did she choose just that moment for her reappearance? I am sure your husband has described it to you. We were talking at the patio door and I—facing out—was the first to see this white something—descending on us out of the night. Of course it was the effect of the ground fog. But truly terrifying. I think I shrieked out loud. I had never in my life felt such bewitchment, in the true sense. I suppose I should be honest and say fear. There were we were, two adults, frozen, and then out of the fog comes little lost Flora.

There has to be something special about this. I know of course that Flora is an ordinary little animal and that she probably spent her time away in getting herself pregnant. In a sense her return has no connection at all with our human lives. Yet her appearance at that moment did have a profound effect on your husband and me. When two human beings divided by hostility are both, at the same time, mystified—no, frightened—by the same apparition, there is a bond that springs up between them, and they find themselves united in the most unexpected way. United in their humanity—that is the only way I can describe it. We parted almost as friends. So Flora has her place as a good angel in my life and perhaps also in your husband's life and yours.

With all my good wishes, Sylvia Jamieson

As soon as Carla had read this letter she crumpled it up. Then she burned it in the sink. The flames leapt up alarmingly and she turned on the tap, then scooped up the soft disgusting black stuff and put it down the toilet as she should have done in the first place.

She was busy for the rest of that day, and the next, and the next. During that time she had to take two parties out on the trails, she had to give lessons to children, individually and in groups. At night when Clark put his arms around her—busy as he was now, he was never too tired, never cross—she did not find it hard to be cooperative.

It was as if she had a murderous needle somewhere in her lungs, and by breathing carefully, she could avoid feeling it. But every once in a while she had to take a deep breath, and it was still there.

Sylvia had taken an apartment in the college town where she taught. The house was not up for sale—or at least there wasn't a sign out in front of it. Leon Jamieson had got some kind of posthumous award—news of this was in the papers. There was no mention this time of any money.

As the dry golden days of fall came on—an encouraging and profitable season—Carla found that she had got used to the sharp thought that had lodged in her. It wasn't so sharp anymore—in fact, it no longer surprised her. And she was inhabited now by an almost seductive notion, a constant low-lying temptation.

She had only to raise her eyes, she had only to look in one direction, to know where she might go. An evening walk, once her chores for the day were finished. To the edge of the woods, and the bare tree where the buzzards had held their party.

And then the little dirty bones in the grass. The skull with perhaps some shreds of bloodied skin clinging to it. A skull that she could hold like a teacup in one hand. Knowledge in one hand.

Or perhaps not. Nothing there.

Other things could have happened. He could have chased Flora away. Or tied her in the back of the truck and driven some distance and set her loose. Taken her back to the place they'd got her from. Not to have her around, reminding them.

She might be free.

The days passed and Carla didn't go near that place. She held out against the temptation.

CHANCE

Halfway through June, in 1965, the term at Torrance House is over. Juliet has not been offered a permanent job—the teacher she replaced has recovered—and she could now be on her way home. But she is taking what she has described as a little detour. A little detour to see a friend who lives up the coast.

About a month ago, she went with another teacher—Juanita, who was the only person on the staff near her age, and her only friend—to see a revival of a movie called *Hiroshima Mon Amour*. Juanita confessed afterwards that she herself, like the woman in the picture, was in love with a married man—the father of a student. Then Juliet said that she had found herself in somewhat the same situation but had not allowed things to go on because of the tragic plight of his wife. His wife was a total invalid, more or less brain-dead. Juanita said that she wished her lover's wife was brain-dead but she was not—she was vigorous and powerful and could get Juanita fired.

And shortly after that, as if conjured by such unworthy lies or half-lies, came a letter. The envelope looked dingy, as if it had spent some time in a pocket, and it was addressed only to "Juliet (Teacher), Torrance House, 1482 Mark St., Vancouver, B.C." The headmistress gave it to Juliet, saying, "I assume this is for you. It's strange there's no surname but they've got the address right. I suppose they could look that up."

> *Dear Juliet, I forgot which school it was that you're teaching at but the other day I remembered, out of the blue, so it seemed to me a sign that I should write to you. I hope you are still there but the job would have to be pretty awful for you to quit before the term is up and anyway you didn't strike me as a quitter.*
>
> *How do you like our west coast weather? If you think you have got a lot of rain in Vancouver, then imagine twice as much, and that's what we get up here.*
>
> *I often think of you sitting up looking at the ~~stairs~~ stars. You see I wrote stairs, it's late at night and time I was in bed.*
>
> *Ann is about the same. When I got back from my trip I thought she had failed a good deal, but that was mostly because I was able to see all at once how she had gone downhill in the last two or three years. I had not noticed her decline when I saw her every day.*
>
> *I don't think I told you that I was stopping off in Regina to see my son, who is now eleven years old. He lives there with his mother. I noticed a big change in him too.*
>
> *I'm glad I finally remembered the name of the school but I am awfully afraid now that I can't remember your*

last name. I will seal this anyway and hope the name comes to me.

I often think of you.
I often think of you
I often think of you zzzzzz

The bus takes Juliet from downtown Vancouver to Horseshoe Bay and then onto a ferry. Then across a mainland peninsula and onto another ferry and onto the mainland again and so to the town where the man who wrote the letter lives. Whale Bay. And how quickly—even before Horseshoe Bay—you pass from city to wilderness. All this term she has been living amongst the lawns and gardens of Kerrisdale, with the north shore mountains coming into view like a stage curtain whenever the weather cleared. The grounds of the school were sheltered and civilized, enclosed by a stone wall, with something in bloom at every season of the year. And the grounds of the houses around it were the same. Such trim abundance—rhododendrons, holly, laurel, and wisteria. But before you get even so far as Horseshoe Bay, real forest, not park forest, closes in. And from then on—water and rocks, dark trees, hanging moss. Occasionally a trail of smoke from some damp and battered-looking little house, with a yard full of firewood, lumber and tires, cars and parts of cars, broken or usable bikes, toys, all the things that have to sit outside when people are lacking garages or basements.

The towns where the bus stops are not organized towns at all. In some places a few repetitive houses—company houses—are built close together, but most of the houses are like those in the woods, each one in its own wide cluttered yard, as if they have been built within sight of each other only accidentally. No paved streets, except the highway that goes through, no sidewalks. No big solid buildings to house Post Offices or Municipal Offices, no ornamented blocks of stores, built to be noticed. No war monuments, drinking fountains, flowery little parks. Sometimes a hotel; which looks as if it is only a pub. Sometimes a modern school or hospital—decent, but low and plain as a shed.

And at some time—noticeably on the second ferry—she begins to have stomach-turning doubts about the whole business.

I often think of you often

I think of you often

That is only the sort of thing people say to be comforting, or out of a mild desire to keep somebody on the string.

But there will have to be a hotel, or tourist cabins at least, at Whale Bay. She will go there. She has left her big suitcase at the school, to be picked up later. She has only her travelling bag slung over her shoulder, she won't be conspicuous. She will stay one night. Maybe phone him.

And say what?

That she happens to be up this way to visit a friend. Her friend Juanita, from the school, who has a summer place—where? Juanita has a cabin in the woods, she is a fearless outdoor sort of woman (quite different from the real Juanita, who is seldom out of high heels). And the cabin has turned out to be not far south of Whale Bay. The visit to the cabin and Juanita being over, Juliet has thought—she has thought—since she was nearly there already—she has thought she might as well . . .

Rocks, trees, water, snow. These things, constantly rearranged, made up the scene six months ago, outside the train window on a morning between Christmas and New Year's. The rocks were large, sometimes jutting out, sometimes smoothed like boulders, dark gray or quite black. The trees were mostly evergreens, pine or spruce or cedar. The spruce trees—black spruce—had what looked like little extra trees, miniatures of themselves, stuck right on top. The trees that were not evergreens were spindly and bare—they might be poplar or tamarack or alder. Some of them had spotty trunks. Snow sat in thick caps on top of the rocks and was plastered to the windward side of the trees. It lay in a soft smooth cover over the surface of many big or small frozen lakes. Water was free of ice only in an occasional fast-flowing, dark and narrow stream.

Juliet had a book open on her lap, but she was not reading. She did not take her eyes from what was going by. She was alone in a double seat and there was an empty double seat across from her. This was the space in which her bed was made up at night. The porter was busy in this sleeping car at the moment, dismantling the nighttime arrangements. In some places the dark-green, zippered shrouds still hung down to the floor. There was a smell of that cloth, like tent cloth, and maybe a slight smell of nightclothes and toilets. A blast of fresh winter air whenever anyone opened the doors at either end of the car. The last people were going to breakfast, other people coming back.

There were tracks in the snow, small animal tracks. Strings of beads, looping, vanishing.

Juliet was twenty-one years old and already the possessor of a B.A. and an M.A. in Classics. She was working on her Ph.D. thesis, but had taken time out to teach Latin at a girls' private school in Vancouver. She had no training as a teacher, but an unexpected vacancy at half-term had made the school willing to hire her. Probably no one else had answered the ad. The salary was less than any qualified teacher would be likely to accept. But Juliet was happy to be earning any money at all, after her years on mingy scholarships.

She was a tall girl, fair-skinned and fine-boned, with light-brown hair that even when sprayed did not retain a bouffant style. She had the look of an alert schoolgirl. Head held high, a neat rounded chin, wide thin-lipped mouth, snub nose, bright eyes, and a forehead that was often flushed with effort or appreciation. Her professors were delighted with her—they were grateful these days for anybody who took up ancient languages, and particularly for someone so gifted—but they were worried, as well. The problem was that she was a girl. If she got married—which might happen, as she was not bad-looking for a scholarship girl, she was not bad-looking at all—she would waste all her hard work and theirs, and if she did not get married she would probably become bleak and isolated, losing out on promotions to men (who needed them more, as they had to support families). And she would not be able to defend the oddity of her choice of Classics, to accept what people would see as its irrelevance, or dreariness, to slough that off the way a man could. Odd choices were simply easier for men, most of whom would find women glad to marry them. Not so the other way around.

When the teaching offer came they urged her to take it. Good for you. Get out into the world a bit. See some real life.

Juliet was used to this sort of advice, though disappointed to hear it coming from these men who did not look or sound as if they had knocked about in the real world very eagerly themselves. In the town where she grew up her sort of intelligence was often put in the same category as a limp or an extra thumb, and people had been quick to point out the expected accompanying drawbacks—her inability to run a sewing machine or tie up a neat parcel, or notice that her slip was showing. What would become of her, was the question.

That occurred even to her mother and father, who were proud of her. Her mother wanted her to be popular, and to that end had urged her to learn to skate and to play the piano. She did neither willingly, or well. Her father just wanted her to fit in.

You have to fit in, he told her, otherwise people will make your life hell. (This ignored the fact that he, and particularly Juliet's mother, did not fit in so very well themselves, and were not miserable. Perhaps he doubted Juliet could be so lucky.)

I do, said Juliet once she got away to college. In the Classics Department I fit in. I am extremely okay.

But here came the same message, from her teachers, who had seemed to value and rejoice in her. Their joviality did not hide their concern. Get out into the world, they had said. As if where she had been till now was nowhere.

Nevertheless, on the train, she was happy.

Taiga, she thought. She did not know whether that was the right word for what she was looking at. She might have had, at some level, the idea of herself as a young woman in a Russian novel, going out into an unfamiliar, terrifying, and exhilarating landscape where the wolves would howl at night and where she would meet her fate. She did not care that this fate—in a Russian novel—would likely turn out to be dreary, or tragic, or both.

Personal fate was not the point, anyway. What drew her in—enchanted her, actually—was the very indifference, the repetition, the carelessness and contempt for harmony, to be found on the scrambled surface of the Precambrian shield.

A shadow appeared in the corner of her eye. Then a trousered leg, moving in.

"Is this seat taken?"

Of course it wasn't. What could she say?

Tasselled loafers, tan slacks, tan and brown checked jacket with pencil lines of maroon, dark-blue shirt, maroon tie with flecks of blue and gold. All brand-new and all—except for the shoes—looking slightly too large, as if the body inside had shrunk somewhat since the purchase.

He was a man perhaps in his fifties, with strands of bright

golden-brown hair plastered across his scalp. (It couldn't be dyed, could it, who would dye such a scanty crop of hair?) His eyebrows darker, reddish, peaked and bushy. The skin of his face all rather lumpy, thickened like the surface of sour milk.

Was he ugly? Yes, of course. He was ugly, but so in her opinion were many, many men of around his age. She would not have said, afterwards, that he was remarkably ugly.

His eyebrows went up, his light-colored, leaky eyes widened, as if to project conviviality. He settled down opposite her. He said, "Not much to see out there."

"No." She lowered her eyes to her book.

"Ah," he said, as if things were opening up in a comfortable way. "And how far are you going?"

"Vancouver."

"Me too. All the way across the country. May as well see it all while you're at it, isn't that right?"

"Mm."

But he persisted.

"Did you get on at Toronto too?"

"Yes."

"That's my home, Toronto. I lived there all my life. Your home there too?"

"No," said Juliet, looking at her book again and trying hard to prolong the pause. But something—her upbringing, her embarrassment, God knows perhaps her pity, was too strong for her, and she dealt out the name of her hometown, then placed it for him by giving its distance from various larger towns, its position as regarded Lake Huron, Georgian Bay.

"I've got a cousin in Collingwood. That's nice country, up there. I went up to see her and her family, a couple of times. You travelling on your own? Like me?"

He kept flapping his hands one over the other.

"Yes." No more, she thinks. No more.

"This is the first time I went on a major trip anywhere. Quite a trip, all on your own."

Juliet said nothing.

"I just saw you there reading your book all by yourself and I thought, maybe she's all by herself and got a long way to go too, so maybe we could just sort of chum around together?"

At those words, *chum around*, a cold turbulence rose in Juliet. She understood that he was not trying to pick her up. One of the demoralizing things that sometimes happened was that rather awkward and lonely and unattractive men would make a bald bid for her, implying that she had to be in the same boat as they were. But he wasn't doing that. He wanted a friend, not a girlfriend. He wanted a *chum*.

Juliet knew that, to many people, she might seem to be odd and solitary—and so, in a way, she was. But she had also had the experience, for much of her life, of feeling surrounded by people who wanted to drain away her attention and her time and her soul. And usually, she let them.

Be available, be friendly (especially if you are not *popular*)—that was what you learned in a small town and also in a girls' dormitory. Be accommodating to anybody who wants to suck you dry, even if they know nothing about who you are.

She looked straight at this man and did not smile. He saw her resolve, there was a twitch of alarm in his face.

"Good book you got there? What's it about?"

She was not going to say that it was about ancient Greece and the considerable attachment that the Greeks had to the irrational. She would not be teaching Greek, but was supposed to be teaching a course called Greek Thought, so she was reading Dodd again to see what she could pick up. She said, "I do want to read. I think I'll go to the observation car."

And she got up and walked away, thinking that she shouldn't have said where she was going, it was possible that he might get up and follow her, apologizing, working up to another plea. Also, that it would be cold in the observation car, and she would wish that she had brought her sweater. Impossible to go back now to get it.

The wraparound view from the observation car, at the back of the train, seemed less satisfying to her than the view from the sleeping-car window. There was now always the intrusion of the train itself, in front of you.

Perhaps the problem was that she was cold, just as she had thought she would be. And disturbed. But not sorry. One moment more and his clammy hand would have been proffered—she thought that it would have been either clammy or dry and scaly—names would have been exchanged, she would have been locked in. It was the first victory of this sort that she had ever managed, and it was against the most pitiable, the saddest opponent. She could hear him now, chewing on the words *chum around*. Apology and insolence. Apology his habit. And insolence the result of some hope or determination breaking the surface of his loneliness, his hungry state.

It was necessary but it hadn't been easy, it hadn't been easy at all. In fact it was more of a victory, surely, to stand up to someone in such a state. It was more of a victory than if he had been slick and self-assured. But for a while she would be somewhat miserable.

There were only two other people sitting in the observation car. Two older women, each of them sitting alone. When Juliet saw a large wolf crossing the snowy, perfect surface of a small lake, she knew that they must see it too. But neither broke the silence, and that was pleasing to her. The wolf took no notice of the train, he did not hesitate or hurry. His fur was long, silvery shading into white. Did he think it made him invisible?

While she was watching the wolf, another passenger had arrived. A man, who took the seat across the aisle from hers.

He too carried a book. An elderly couple followed—she small and sprightly, he large and clumsy, taking heavy disparaging breaths.

"Cold up here," he said, when they were settled.

"Do you want me to go get your jacket?"

"Don't bother."

"It's no bother."

"I'll be all right."

In a moment the woman said, "You certainly do get a view here." He did not answer, and she tried again. "You can see all round."

"What there is to see."

"Wait till we go through the mountains. That'll be something. Did you enjoy your breakfast?"

"The eggs were runny."

"I know." The woman commiserated. "I was thinking, I should just have barged into the kitchen and done them myself."

"Galley. They call it a galley."

"I thought that was on a boat."

Juliet and the man across the aisle raised their eyes from their books at the same moment, and their glances met, with a calm withholding of any expression. And in this second or two the train slowed, then stopped, and they looked elsewhere.

They had come to a little settlement in the woods. On the one side was the station, painted a dark red, and on the other a few houses painted the same color. Homes or barracks, for the railway workers. There was an announcement that there would be a stop here for ten minutes.

The station platform had been cleared of snow, and Juliet, peering ahead, saw some people getting off the train to walk about. She would have liked to do this herself, but not without a coat.

The man across the aisle got up and went down the steps

without a look around. Doors opened somewhere below, bringing a stealthy stream of cold air. The elderly husband asked what they were doing here, and what was the name of this place anyway. His wife went to the front of the car to try to see the name, but she was not successful.

Juliet was reading about maenadism. The rituals took place at night, in the middle of winter, Dodd said. The women went up to the top of Mount Parnassus, and when they were, at one time, cut off by a snowstorm, a rescue party had to be sent. The would-be maenads were brought down with their clothes stiff as boards, having, in all their frenzy, accepted rescue. This seemed rather like contemporary behavior to Juliet, it somehow cast a modern light on the celebrants' carrying-on. Would the students see it so? Not likely. They would probably be armed against any possible entertainment, any involvement, as students were. And the ones who weren't so armed wouldn't want to show it.

The call to board sounded, the fresh air was cut off, there were reluctant shunting movements. She raised her eyes to watch, and saw, some distance ahead, the engine disappearing around a curve.

And then a lurch or a shudder, a shudder that seemed to pass along the whole train. A sense, up here, of the car rocking. An abrupt stop.

Everybody sat waiting for the train to start again, and nobody spoke. Even the complaining husband was silent. Minutes passed. Doors were opening and closing. Men's voices calling, a spreading feeling of fright and agitation. In the club car, which was just below, a voice of authority—maybe the conductor's. But it was not possible to hear what he was saying.

Juliet got up and went to the front of the car, looking over the tops of all the cars ahead. She saw some figures running in the snow.

One of the lone women came up and stood beside her.

"I felt there was something going to happen," the woman said. "I felt it back there, when we were stopped. I didn't want us to start up again, I thought something was going to happen."

The other lone woman had come to stand behind them.

"It won't be anything," she said. "Maybe a branch across the tracks."

"They have that thing that goes ahead of the train," the first woman told her. "It goes on purpose to catch things like a branch across the tracks."

"Maybe it had just fallen."

Both women spoke with the same north-of-England accent and without the politeness of strangers or acquaintances. Now that Juliet got a good look at them she saw that they were probably sisters, though one had a younger, broader face. So they travelled together but sat separately. Or perhaps they'd had a row.

The conductor was mounting the stairs to the observation car. He turned, halfway up, to speak.

"Nothing serious to worry about, folks, it seems like we hit an obstacle on the track. We're sorry for the delay and we'll get going again as soon as we can, but we could be here a little while. The steward tells me there's going to be free coffee down here in a few minutes."

Juliet followed him down the stairs. She had become aware, as soon as she stood up, that there was a problem of her own which would make it necessary for her to go back to her seat and her travelling case, whether the man she snubbed was still there or not. As she made her way through the cars she met other people on the move. People were pressing against the windows on one side of the train, or they had halted between the cars, as if they expected the doors to open. Juliet had no time to ask questions, but as she slid past she heard that it might have been a bear, or an elk, or a cow. And people wondered what a cow would be doing up here in the bush, or why the bears were not all asleep now, or if some drunk had fallen asleep on the tracks.

In the dining car people were sitting at the tables, whose white cloths had all been removed. They were drinking the free coffee.

Nobody was in Juliet's seat, or in the seat across from it. She picked up her case and hurried along to the Ladies. Monthly bleeding was the bane of her life. It had even, on occasion, interfered with the writing of important three-hour examinations, because you couldn't leave the room for reinforcements.

Flushed, crampy, feeling a little dizzy and sick, she sank down on the toilet bowl, removed her soaked pad and wrapped it in toilet paper and put it in the receptacle provided. When she stood up she attached the fresh pad from her bag. She saw that the water and urine in the bowl was crimson with her blood. She put her hand on the flush button, then noticed in front of her eyes the warning not to flush the toilet while the train was standing still. That meant, of course, when the train was standing near the station, where the discharge would take place, very disagreeably, right where people could see it. Here, she might risk it.

But just as she touched the button again she heard voices close by, not in the train but outside the toilet window of pebbled glass. Maybe train workers walking past.

She could stay till the train moved, but how long would that be? And what if somebody desperately wanted in? She decided that all she could do was to put down the lid and get out.

She went back to her own seat. Across from her, a child four or five years old was slashing a crayon across the pages of a coloring book. His mother spoke to Juliet about the free coffee.

"It may be free but it looks like you have to go and get it yourself," she said. "Would you mind watching him while I go?"

"I don't want to stay with her," the child said, without looking up.

"I'll go," said Juliet. But at that moment a waiter entered the car with the coffee wagon.

"There. I shouldn't't've complained so soon," the mother said. "Did you hear it was a b-o-d-y?"

Juliet shook her head.

"He didn't have a coat on even. Somebody saw him get off and walk on up ahead but they never realized what he was doing. He must've just got round the curve so the engineer couldn't see him till it was too late."

A few seats ahead, on the mother's side of the aisle, a man said, "Here they come back," and some people got up, from Juliet's side, and stooped to see. The child stood up too, pressed his face to the glass. His mother told him to sit down.

"You color. Look at the mess you made, all over the lines."

"I can't look," she said to Juliet. "I can't stand to look at anything like that."

Juliet got up and looked. She saw a small group of men tramping back towards the station. Some had taken off their coats, which were piled on top of the stretcher that a couple of them were carrying.

"You can't see anything," a man behind Juliet said to a woman who had not stood up. "They got him all covered."

Not all of the men who proceeded with their heads lowered were railway employees. Juliet recognized the man who had sat across from her up in the observation car.

After ten or fifteen minutes more, the train began to move. Around the curve there was no blood to be seen, on either side of the car. But there was a trampled area, a shovelled mound of snow. The man behind her was up again. He said, "That's where it happened, I guess," and watched for a little while to see if there was anything else, then turned around and sat down.

The train, instead of speeding to make up for lost time, seemed to be going more slowly than previously. Out of respect, perhaps, or with apprehension about what might lie ahead, around the next curve. The headwaiter went through the car announcing the first seating for lunch, and the mother and child at once got up and followed him. A procession began, and Juliet heard a woman who was passing say, "Really?"

The woman talking to her said softly, "That's what she said. Full of blood. So it must have splashed in when the train went over—"

"Don't say it."

A little later, when the procession had ended and the early lunchers were eating, the man came through—the man from the observation car who had been seen outside walking in the snow.

Juliet got up and quickly pursued him. In the black cold space between the cars, just as he was pushing the heavy door in front of him, she said, "Excuse me. I have to ask you something."

This space was full of sudden noise, the clanking of heavy wheels on the rails.

"What is it?"

"Are you a doctor? Did you see the man who—"

"I'm not a doctor. There's no doctor on the train. But I have some medical experience."

"How old was he?"

The man looked at her with a steady patience and some displeasure.

"Hard to say. Not young."

"Was he wearing a blue shirt? Did he have blondish-brown-colored hair?"

He shook his head, not to answer her question but to refuse it.

"Was this somebody you knew?" he said. "You should tell the conductor if it was."

"I didn't know him."

"Excuse me, then." He pushed open the door and left her.

Of course. He thought she was full of disgusting curiosity, like many other people.

Full of blood. That was disgusting, if you liked.

She could never tell anybody about the mistake that had been made, the horrid joke of it. People would think her exceptionally crude and heartless, were she ever to speak of it. And what was at one end of the misunderstanding—the suicide's smashed body—would seem, in the telling, to be hardly more foul and frightful than her own menstrual blood.

Never tell that to anybody. (Actually she did tell it, a few years later, to a woman named Christa, a woman whose name she did not yet know.)

But she wanted very much to tell somebody something. She got out her notebook and on one of its ruled pages began to write a letter to her parents.

> *We have not yet reached the Manitoba border and most people have been complaining that the scenery is rather monotonous but they cannot say that the trip has been lacking in dramatic incident. This morning we stopped at some godforsaken little settlement in the northern woods, all painted Dreary Railway Red. I was sitting at the back of the train in the Observation Car, and freezing to death because they skimp on the heat up there (the idea must be that the scenic glories will distract you from your discomfort) and I was too lazy to trudge back and get my sweater. We sat around there for ten or fifteen minutes and then started up again, and I could see*

the engine rounding a curve up ahead, and then suddenly there was a sort of Awful Thump . . .

She and her father and her mother had always made it their business to bring entertaining stories into the house. This had required a subtle adjustment not only of the facts but of one's position in the world. Or so Juliet had found, when her world was school. She had made herself into a rather superior, invulnerable observer. And now that she was away from home all the time this stance had become habitual, almost a duty.

But as soon as she had written the words *Awful Thump,* she found herself unable to go on. Unable, in her customary language, to go on.

She tried looking out the window, but the scene, composed of the same elements, had changed. Less than a hundred miles on, it seemed as if there was a warmer climate. The lakes were fringed with ice, not covered. The black water, black rocks, under the wintry clouds, filled the air with darkness. She grew tired watching, and she picked up her Dodd, opening it just anywhere, because, after all, she had read it before. Every few pages she seemed to have had an orgy of underlining. She was drawn to these passages, but when she read them she found that what she had pounced on with such satisfaction at one time now seemed obscure and unsettling.

. . . what to the partial vision of the living appears as the act of a fiend, is perceived by the wider insight of the dead to be an aspect of cosmic justice . . .

The book slipped out of her hands, her eyes closed, and she was now walking with some children (students?) on the surface of a lake. Everywhere each of them stepped there appeared a five-sided crack, all of these beautifully even, so that the ice became like a tiled floor. The children asked her the name of these ice tiles, and she answered with confidence, *iambic pentameter.* But they laughed and with this laughter the cracks widened. She realized her mistake then and knew that only the right word would save the situation, but she could not grasp it.

She woke and saw the same man, the man she had followed and pestered between the cars, sitting across from her.

"You were sleeping." He smiled slightly at what he had said. "Obviously."

She had been sleeping with her head hanging forward, like an old woman, and there was a dribble at the corner of her mouth. Also, she knew she must get to the Ladies Toilet at once, hoping there was nothing on her skirt. She said "Excuse me" (just what he had last said to her) and took up her case and walked away with as little self-conscious haste as she could manage.

When she came back, washed and tidied and reinforced, he was still there.

He spoke at once. He said that he wanted to apologize.

"It occurred to me I was rude to you. When you asked me—"

"Yes," she said.

"You had it right," he said. "The way you described him."

This seemed less an offering, on his part, than a direct and necessary transaction. If she did not care to speak he might just get up and walk away, not particularly disappointed, having done what he'd come to do.

Shamefully, Juliet's eyes overflowed with tears. This was so unexpected that she had no time to look away.

"Okay," he said. "It's okay."

She nodded quickly, several times, sniffled wretchedly, blew her nose on the tissue she eventually found in her bag.

"It's all right," she said, and then she told him, in a straightforward way, just what had happened. How the man bent over and asked her if the seat was taken, how he sat down, how she had been looking out the window and how she couldn't do that any longer so she had tried or had pretended to read her book, how he had asked where she had got on the train, and found out where she lived, and kept trying to make headway with the conversation, till she just picked up and left him.

The only thing she did not reveal to him was the expression *chum around*. She had a notion that if she were to say that she would burst into tears all over again.

"People interrupt women," he said. "Easier than men."

"Yes. They do."

"They think women are bound to be nicer."

"But he just wanted somebody to talk to," she said, shifting sides a little. "He wanted somebody worse than I *didn't* want somebody. I realize that now. And I don't look mean. I don't look cruel. But I was."

A pause, while she once more got her sniffling and her leaky eyes under control.

He said, "Haven't you ever wanted to do that to anybody before?"

"*Yes*. But I've never done it. I never have gone so far. And why I did it this time—it was that he was so humble. And he had all new clothes on he'd probably bought for the trip. He was probably depressed and thought he'd go on a trip and it was a good way to meet people and make friends.

"Maybe if he'd just been going a little way—," she said. "But he said he was going to Vancouver and I would have been saddled with him. For days."

"Yes."

"I really might have been."

"Yes."

"So."

"Rotten luck," he said, smiling a very little. "The first time you get up the nerve to give somebody the gears he throws himself under a train."

"It could have been the last straw," she said, now feeling slightly defensive. "It could have been."

"I guess you'll just have to watch out, in future."

Juliet raised her chin and looked at him steadily.

"You mean I'm exaggerating."

Then something happened that was as sudden and unbidden as her tears. Her mouth began to twitch. Unholy laughter was rising.

"I guess it is a little extreme."

He said, "A little."

"You think I'm dramatizing?"

"That's natural."

"But you think it's a mistake," she said, with the laughter under control. "You think feeling guilty is just an indulgence?"

"What I think is—," he said. "I think that this is minor. Things will happen in your life—things will probably happen in your life—that will make this seem minor. Other things you'll be able to feel guilty about."

"Don't people always say that, though? To somebody who is younger? They say, oh, you won't think like this someday. You wait and see. As if you didn't have a right to any serious feelings. As if you weren't capable."

"Feelings," he said. "I was talking about experience."

"But you are sort of saying that guilt isn't any use. People do say that. Is it true?"

"You tell me."

They went on talking about this for a considerable time, in low voices, but so forcefully that people passing by sometimes looked astonished, or even offended, as people may when they overhear debates that seem unnecessarily abstract. Juliet realized, after a while, that though she was arguing—rather well, she thought—for the necessity of some feelings of guilt both in public and in private life, she had stopped feeling any, for the moment. You might even have said that she was enjoying herself.

He suggested that they go forward to the lounge, where they could drink coffee. Once there Juliet discovered that she was quite hungry, though the lunch hours were long over. Pretzels and peanuts were all that could be procured, and she gobbled them up in such a way that the thoughtful, slightly competitive conversation they were having before was not retrievable. So they talked instead about themselves. His name was Eric Porteous, and he lived in a place called Whale Bay, somewhere north of Vancouver, on the west coast. But he was not going there immediately, he was breaking the trip in Regina, to see some people he had not seen for a long time. He was a fisherman, he caught prawns. She asked about the medical experience he had referred to, and he said, "Oh, it's not very extensive. I did some medical study. When you're out in the bush or on the boat anything can happen. To the people you're working with. Or to yourself."

He was married, his wife's name was Ann.

Eight years ago, he said, Ann had been injured in a car accident. For several weeks she was in a coma. She came out of that, but she was still paralyzed, unable to walk or even to feed herself. She seemed to know who he was, and who the woman who looked after her was—with the help of this woman he was able to keep her at home—but her attempts to talk, and to understand what was going on around her, soon faded away.

They had been to a party. She hadn't particularly wanted to go but he had wanted to go. Then she decided to walk home by herself, not being very happy with things at the party.

It was a gang of drunks from another party who ran off the road and knocked her down. Teenagers.

Luckily, he and Ann had no children. Yes, luckily.

"You tell people about it and they feel they have to say, how terrible. What a tragedy. Et cetera."

"Can you blame them?" said Juliet, who had been about to say something of the sort herself.

No, he said. But it was just that the whole thing was a lot more complicated than that. Did Ann feel that it was a tragedy? Probably not. Did he? It was something you got used to, it was a new kind of life. That was all.

All of Juliet's enjoyable experience of men had been in fantasy. One or two movie stars, the lovely tenor—not the virile heartless hero—on a certain old recording of *Don Giovanni.* Henry V, as she read about him in Shakespeare and as Laurence Olivier had played him in the movie.

This was ridiculous, pathetic, but who ever needed to know? In actual life there had been humiliation and disappointment, which she had tried to push out of her mind as quickly as possible.

There was the experience of being stranded head and shoulders above the gaggle of other unwanted girls at the high school dances, and being bored but making a rash attempt to be lively on college dates with boys she didn't much like, who did not much like her. Going out with the visiting nephew of her thesis adviser last year and being broken into—you couldn't call it rape, she too was determined—late at night on the ground in Willis Park.

On the way home he had explained that she wasn't his type. And she had felt too humiliated to retort—or even to be aware, at that moment—that he was not hers.

She had never had fantasies about a particular, real man—

least of all about any of her teachers. Older men—in real life—seemed to her to be slightly unsavory.

This man was how old? He had been married for at least eight years—and perhaps two years, two or three years, more than that. Which made him probably thirty-five or thirty-six. His hair was dark and curly with some gray at the sides, his forehead wide and weathered, his shoulders strong and a little stooped. He was hardly any taller than she was. His eyes were wide set, dark, and eager but also wary. His chin was rounded, dimpled, pugnacious.

She told him about her job, the name of the school—Torrance House. ("What do you want to bet it's called Torments?") She told him that she was not a real teacher but that they were glad to get anybody who had majored in Greek and Latin at college. Hardly anybody did anymore.

"So why did you?"

"Oh, just to be different, I guess."

Then she told him what she had always known that she should never tell any man or boy, lest he lose interest immediately.

"And because I love it. I love all that stuff. I really do."

They ate dinner together—each drinking a glass of wine—and then went up to the observation car, where they sat in the dark, all by themselves. Juliet had brought her sweater this time.

"People must think there's nothing to see up here at night," he said. "But look at the stars you can see on a clear night."

Indeed the night was clear. There was no moon—at least not yet—and the stars appeared in dense thickets, both faint and bright. And like anyone who had lived and worked on boats, he was familiar with the map of the sky. She was able to locate only the Big Dipper.

"That's your start," he said. "Take the two stars on the side of the Dipper opposite the handle. Got them? Those are the pointers. Follow them up. Follow them, you'll find the pole-star." And so on.

He found for her Orion, which he said was the major constellation in the Northern Hemisphere in winter. And Sirius, the Dog Star, at that time of year the brightest star in the whole northern sky.

Juliet was pleased to be instructed but also pleased when it came her turn to be the instructor. He knew the names but not the history.

She told him that Orion was blinded by Enopion but had got his sight back by looking at the sun.

"He was blinded because he was so beautiful, but Hephaestus came to his rescue. Then he was killed anyway, by Artemis, but he got changed into a constellation. It often happened when somebody really valuable got into bad trouble, they were changed into a constellation. Where is Cassiopeia?"

He directed her to a not very obvious W.

"It's supposed to be a woman sitting down."

"That was on account of beauty too," she said.

"Beauty was dangerous?"

"You bet. She was married to the king of Ethiopia and she was the mother of Andromeda. And she bragged about her beauty and for punishment she was banished to the sky. Isn't there an Andromeda, too?"

"That's a galaxy. You should be able to see it tonight. It's the most distant thing you can see with the naked eye."

Even when guiding her, telling her where to look in the sky, he never touched her. Of course not. He was married.

"Who was Andromeda?" he asked her.

"She was chained to a rock but Perseus rescued her."

. . .

Whale Bay.

A long dock, a number of large boats, a gas station and store that has a sign in the window saying that it is also the bus stop and the Post Office.

A car parked at the side of this store has in its window a homemade taxi sign. She stands just where she stepped down from the bus. The bus pulls away. The taxi toots its horn. The driver gets out and comes towards her.

"All by yourself," he says. "Where are you headed for?"

She asks if there is a place where tourists stay. Obviously there won't be a hotel.

"I don't know if there's anybody renting rooms out this year. I could ask them inside. You don't know anybody around here?"

Nothing to do but to say Eric's name.

"Oh sure," he says with relief. "Hop in, we'll get you there in no time. But it's too bad, you pretty well missed the wake."

At first she thinks that he said *wait*. Or *weight*? She thinks of fishing competitions.

"Sad time," the driver says, now getting in behind the wheel. "Still, she wasn't ever going to get any better."

Wake. The wife. Ann.

"Never mind," he says. "I expect there'll still be some people hanging around. Of course you did miss the funeral. Yesterday. It was a monster. Couldn't get away?"

Juliet says, "No."

"I shouldn't be calling it a wake, should I? Wake is what you have before they're buried, isn't it? I don't know what you call what takes place after. You wouldn't want to call it a party, would you? I can just run you up and show you all the flowers and tributes, okay?"

Inland, off the highway, after a quarter of a mile or so of rough dirt road, is Whale Bay Union Cemetery. And close to the fence is the mound of earth altogether buried in flowers. Faded real flowers, bright artificial flowers, a little wooden cross with the name and date. Tinselly curled ribbons that have blown about all over the cemetery grass. He draws her attention to all the ruts, the mess the wheels of so many cars made yesterday.

"Half of them had never even seen her. But they knew him, so they wanted to come anyway. Everybody knows Eric."

They turn around, drive back, but not all the way back to the highway. She wants to tell the driver that she has changed her mind, she does not want to visit anybody, she wants to wait at the store to catch the bus going the other way. She can say that she really did get the day wrong, and now she is so ashamed of having missed the funeral that she does not want to show up at all.

But she cannot get started. And he will report on her, no matter what.

They are following narrow, winding back roads, past a few houses. Every time they go by a driveway without turning in, there is a feeling of reprieve.

"Well, here's a surprise," the driver says, and now they do turn in. "Where's everybody gone? Half a dozen cars when I drove past an hour ago. Even his truck's gone. Party over. Sorry—I shouldn't've said that."

"If there's nobody here," Juliet says eagerly, "I could just go back down."

"Oh, somebody's here, don't worry about that. Ailo's here. There's her bike. You ever meet Ailo? You know, she's the one took care of things?" He is out and opening her door.

As soon as Juliet steps out, a large yellow dog comes bounding and barking, and a woman calls from the porch of the house.

"Aw go on, Pet," the driver says, pocketing the fare and getting quickly back into the car.

"Shut up. Shut up, Pet. Settle down. She won't hurt you," the woman calls. "She's just a pup."

Pet's being a pup, Juliet thinks, would not make her any less likely to knock you down. And now a small reddish-brown dog arrives to join in the commotion. The woman comes down the steps, yelling, "Pet. Corky. You behave. If they think you are scared of them they will just get after you the worse."

Her *just* sounds something like *chust*.

"I'm not scared," says Juliet, jumping back when the yellow dog's nose roughly rubs her arm.

"Come on in, then. Shut up, the two of you, or I will knock your heads. Did you get the day mixed up for the funeral?"

Juliet shakes her head as if to say that she is sorry. She introduces herself.

"Well, it is too bad. I am Ailo." They shake hands.

Ailo is a tall, broad-shouldered woman with a thick but not flabby body, and yellowish-white hair loose over her shoulders. Her voice is strong and insistent, with some rich production of sounds in the throat. A German, Dutch, Scandinavian accent?

"You better sit down here in the kitchen. Everything is in a mess. I will get you some coffee."

The kitchen is bright, with a skylight in the high, sloping ceiling. Dishes and glasses and pots are piled everywhere. Pet and Corky have followed Ailo meekly into the kitchen, and have started to lap out whatever is in the roasting pan that she has set down on the floor.

Beyond the kitchen, up two broad steps, there is a shaded, cavernous sort of living room, with large cushions flung about on the floor.

Ailo pulls out a chair at the table. "Now sit down. You sit down here and have some coffee and some food."

"I'm fine without," says Juliet.

"No. There is the coffee I have just made, I will drink mine while I work. And there are so much things left over to eat."

She sets before Juliet, with the coffee, a piece of pie—bright green, covered with some shrunken meringue.

"Lime Jell-O," she says, withholding approval. "Maybe it tastes all right, though. Or there is rhubarb?"

Juliet says, "Fine."

"So much mess here. I clean up after the wake, I get it all settled. Then the funeral. Now after the funeral I have to clean up all over again."

Her voice is full of sturdy grievance. Juliet feels obliged to say, "When I finish this I can help you."

"No. I don't think so," Ailo says. "I know everything." She is moving around not swiftly but purposefully and effectively. (Such women never want your help. They can tell what you're like.) She continues drying the glasses and plates and cutlery, putting what she has dried away in cupboards and drawers. Then scraping the pots and pans—including the one she retrieves from the dogs—submerging them in fresh soapy water, scrubbing the surfaces of the table and the counters, wringing the dishcloths as if they were chickens' necks. And speaking to Juliet, with pauses.

"You are a friend of Ann? You know her from before?"

"No."

"No. I think you don't. You are too young. So why do you want to come to her funeral?"

"I didn't," says Juliet. "I didn't know. I just came by to visit." She tries to sound as if this was a whim of hers, as if she had lots of friends and wandered about making casual visits.

With singular fine energy and defiance Ailo polishes a pot, as she chooses not to reply to this. She lets Juliet wait through several more pots before she speaks.

"You come to visit Eric. You found the right house. Eric lives here."

"You don't live here, do you?" says Juliet, as if this might change the subject.

"No. I do not live here. I live down the hill, with my hussband." The word *hussband* carries a weight, of pride and reproach.

Without asking, Ailo fills up Juliet's coffee cup, then her own. She brings a piece of pie for herself. It has a rosy layer on the bottom and a creamy layer on top.

"Rhubarb cusstart. It has to be eaten or it will go bad. I do not need it, but I eat it anyway. Maybe I get you a piece?"

"No. Thank you."

"Now. Eric has gone. He will not be back tonight. I do not think so. He has gone to Christa's place. Do you know Christa?"

Juliet tightly shakes her head.

"Here we all live so that we know the other people's situations. We know well. I do not know what it is like where you live. In Vancouver?" (Juliet nods.) "In a city. It is not the same. For Eric to be so good to look after his wife he must need help, do you see? I am one to help him."

Quite unwisely Juliet says, "But do you not get paid?"

"Certain I am paid. But it is more than a job. Also the other kind of help from a woman, he needs that. Do you understand what I am saying? Not a woman with a hussband, I do not believe in that, it is not nice, that is a way to have fights. First Eric had Sandra, then she has moved away and he has Christa. There was a little while both Christa and Sandra, but they were good friends, it was all right. But Sandra has her kids, she wants to move away to bigger schools. Christa is an artist. She makes things out of wood that you find on the beach. What is it you call that wood?"

"Driftwood," says Juliet unwillingly. She is paralyzed by disappointment, by shame.

"That is it. She takes them to places and they sell them for her. Big things. Animals and birds but not realist. Not realist?"

"Not realistic?"

"Yes. Yes. She has never had any children. I don't think she will want to be moving away. Eric has told you this? Would you like more coffee? There is still some in the pot."

"No. No thanks. No he hasn't."

"So. Now I have told you. If you have finish I will take the cup to wash."

She detours to nudge with her shoe the yellow dog lying on the other side of the refrigerator.

"You got to get up. Lazy girl. Soon we are going home.

"There is a bus goes back to Vancouver, it goes through at ten after eight," she says, busy at the sink with her back to the room. "You can come home with me and when it is time my hussband will drive you. You can eat with us. I ride my bike, I ride slow so you can keep up. It is not far."

The immediate future seems set in place so firmly that Juliet gets up without a thought, looks around for her bag. Then she sits down again, but in another chair. This new view of the kitchen seems to give her resolve.

"I think I'll stay here," she says.

"Here?"

"I don't have anything much to carry. I'll walk to the bus."

"How will you know your way? It is a mile."

"That's not far." Juliet wonders about knowing the way, but thinks that, after all, you just have to head downhill.

"He is not coming back, you know," says Ailo. "Not tonight."

"That doesn't matter."

Ailo gives a massive, perhaps disdainful, shrug.

"Get up, Pet. Up." Over her shoulder she says, "Corky stays here. Do you want her in or out?"

"I guess out."

"I will tie her up, then, so she cannot follow. She may not want to stay with a stranger."

Juliet says nothing.

"The door locks when we go out. You see? So if you go out and want to come back in, you have to press this. But when you leave you don't press. It will be locked. Do you understand?"

"Yes."

"We did not use to bother locking here, but now there are too many strangers."

After they had been looking at the stars, the train had stopped for a while in Winnipeg. They got out and walked in a wind so cold that it was painful for them to breathe, let alone speak. When they boarded the train again they sat in the lounge and he ordered brandy.

"Warm us up and put you to sleep," he said.

He was not going to sleep. He would sit up until he got off at Regina, some time towards morning.

Most of the berths were already made up, the dark-green curtains narrowing the aisles, when he walked her back to her car. All the cars had names, and the name of hers was Miramichi.

"This is it," she whispered, in the space between the cars, his hand already pushing the door for her.

"Say good-bye here, then." He withdrew his hand, and they balanced themselves against the jolting so that he could kiss her thoroughly. When that was finished he did not let go, but held her and stroked her back, and then began to kiss her all over her face.

But she pulled away, she said urgently, "I'm a virgin."

"Yes, yes." He laughed, and kissed her neck, then released her and pushed the door open in front of her. They walked down the aisle till she located her own berth. She flattened herself against the curtain, turning, and rather expecting him to kiss her again or touch her, but he slid by almost as if they had met by accident.

How stupid, how disastrous. Afraid, of course, that his stroking hand would go farther down and reach the knot she had made securing the pad to the belt. If she had been the sort of girl who could rely on tampons this need never have happened.

And why *virgin*? When she had gone to such unpleasant lengths, in Willis Park, to insure that such a condition would not be an impediment? She must have been thinking of what she would tell him—she would never be able to tell him that she was menstruating—in the event that he hoped to carry things further. How could he have had plans like that, anyway? How? Where? In her berth, with so little room and all the other passengers very likely still awake around them? Standing up, swaying back and forth, pressed against a door, which anybody could come along and open, in that precarious space between the cars?

So now he could tell someone how he listened all evening to this fool girl showing off what she knew about Greek mythology, and in the end—when he finally kissed her good night, to get rid of her—she started screaming that she was a virgin.

He had not seemed the sort of man to do that, to talk like that, but she could not help imagining it.

She lay awake far into the night, but had fallen asleep when the train stopped at Regina.

. . .

Left alone, Juliet could explore the house. But she does no such thing. It is twenty minutes, at least, before she can be rid of the presence of Ailo. Not that she is afraid that Ailo might come back to check up on her, or to get something she has forgotten. Ailo is not the sort of person who forgets things, even at the end of a strenuous day. And if she had thought Juliet would steal anything, she would simply have kicked her out.

She is, however, the sort of woman who lays claim to space, particularly to kitchen space. Everything within Juliet's gaze speaks of Ailo's occupation, from the potted plants (herbs?) on the windowsill to the chopping block to the polished linoleum.

And when she has managed to push Ailo back, not out of the room but perhaps back beside the old-fashioned refrigerator, Juliet comes up against Christa. Eric has a woman. Of course he has. Christa. Juliet sees a younger, a more seductive Ailo. Wide hips, strong arms, long hair—all blond with no white—breasts bobbing frankly under a loose shirt. The same aggressive—and in Christa, sexy—lack of chic. The same relishing way of chewing up and then spitting out her words.

Two other women come into her mind. Briseis and Chryseis. Those playmates of Achilles and Agamemnon. Each of them described as being "of the lovely cheeks." When the professor read that word (which she could not now remember), his forehead had gone quite pink and he seemed to be suppressing a giggle. For that moment, Juliet despised him.

So if Christa turns out to be a rougher, more northerly version of Briseis/Chryseis, will Juliet be able to start despising Eric as well?

But how will she ever know, if she walks down to the highway and gets on the bus?

The fact is that she never intended to get on that bus. So it seems. With Ailo out of the way, it is easier to discover her own intentions. She gets up at last and makes more coffee, then pours it into a mug, not one of the cups that Ailo has put out.

She is too keyed up to be hungry, but she examines the bottles on the counter, which people must have brought for the wake. Cherry brandy, peach schnapps, Tia Maria, sweet vermouth. These bottles have been opened but the contents have not proved popular. The serious drinking has been done from the empty bottles ranged by Ailo beside the door. Gin and whisky, beer and wine.

She pours Tia Maria into her coffee, and takes the bottle with her up the steps into the big living room.

This is one of the longest days of the year. But the trees around here, the big bushy evergreens and the red-limbed arbutus, shut out the light from the descending sun. The skylight keeps the kitchen bright, while the windows in the living room are nothing but long slits in the wall, and there the darkness has already begun to accumulate. The floor is not finished—old shabby rugs are laid down on squares of plywood—and the room is oddly and haphazardly furnished. Mostly with cushions, lying about on the floor, a couple of hassocks covered in leather, which has split. A huge leather chair, of the sort that leans back and has a rest for your feet. A couch covered by an authentic but ragged patchwork quilt, an ancient television set, and brick-and-plank bookshelves—on which there are no books, only stacks of old *National Geographic*s, with a few sailing magazines and issues of *Popular Mechanics.*

Ailo obviously has not got around to cleaning up this room. There are smudges of ashes where ashtrays have been upset onto the rugs. And crumbs everywhere. It occurs to Juliet that she might look for the vacuum cleaner, if there is one, but then she thinks that even if she could get it to work it is likely that some mishap would occur—the thin rugs might get scrunched up and caught in the machine, for instance. So she just sits in the leather chair, adding more Tia Maria as the level of her coffee goes down.

Nothing is much to her liking on this coast. The trees are too large and crowded together and do not have any personality of their own—they simply make a forest. The mountains are too grand and implausible and the islands that float upon the waters of the Strait of Georgia are too persistently picturesque. This house, with its big spaces and slanted ceilings and unfinished wood, is stark and self-conscious.

The dog barks from time to time, but not urgently. Maybe she wants to come in and have company. But Juliet has never had a dog—a dog in the house would be a witness, not a companion, and would only make her feel uncomfortable.

Perhaps the dog is barking at exploring deer, or a bear, or a cougar. There has been something in the Vancouver papers about a cougar—she thinks it was on this coast—mauling a child.

Who would want to live where you have to share every part of outdoor space with hostile and marauding animals?

Kallipareos. Of the lovely cheeks. Now she has it. The Homeric word is sparkling on her hook. And beyond that she is suddenly aware of all her Greek vocabulary, of everything which seems to have been put in a closet for nearly six months now. Because she was not teaching Greek, she put it away.

That is what happens. You put it away for a little while, and now and again you look in the closet for something else and you remember, and you think, *soon*. Then it becomes something that is just there, in the closet, and other things get crowded in front of it and on top of it and finally you don't think about it at all.

The thing that was your bright treasure. You don't think about it. A loss you could not contemplate at one time, and now it becomes something you can barely remember.

That is what happens.

And even if it's not put away, even if you make your living from it, every day? Juliet thinks of the older teachers at the school, how little most of them care for whatever it is that they teach. Take Juanita, who chose Spanish because it goes with her Christian name (she is Irish) and who wants to speak it well, to use it in her travels. You cannot say that Spanish is her treasure.

Few people, very few, have a treasure, and if you do you must hang on to it. You must not let yourself be waylaid, and have it taken from you.

The Tia Maria has worked in a certain way with the coffee. It makes her feel careless, but powerful. It enables her to think that Eric, after all, is not so important. He is someone she might dally with. Dally is the word. As Aphrodite did, with Anchises. And then one morning she will slip away.

She gets up and finds the bathroom, then comes back and lies down on the couch with the quilt over her—too sleepy to notice Corky's hairs on it, or Corky's smell.

When she wakes it is full morning, though only twenty past six by the kitchen clock.

She has a headache. There is a bottle of aspirin in the bathroom—she takes two, and washes herself and combs her hair and gets her toothbrush from her bag and brushes her teeth. Then she makes a fresh pot of coffee and eats a slice of home-made bread without bothering to heat or butter it. She sits at the kitchen table. Sunlight, slipping down through the trees, makes coppery splashes on the smooth trunks of the arbutus. Corky begins to bark, and barks for quite a long time before the truck turns into the yard and silences her.

Juliet hears the door of the truck close, she hears him speaking to the dog, and dread comes over her. She wants to hide somewhere (she says later, *I could have crawled under the table*, but of course she does not think of doing anything so ridiculous). It's like the moment at school before the winner of the prize is announced. Only worse, because she has no reasonable hope. And because there will never be another chance so momentous in her life.

When the door opens she cannot look up. On her knees the fingers of both hands are interwoven, clenched together.

"You're here," he says. He is laughing in triumph and admiration, as if at a most spectacular piece of impudence and daring. When he opens his arms it's as if a wind has blown into the room and made her look up.

Six months ago she did not know this man existed. Six months ago, the man who died under the train was still alive, and perhaps picking out the clothes for his trip.

"You're here."

She can tell by his voice that he is claiming her. She stands up, quite numb, and sees that he is older, heavier, more impetuous than she has remembered. He advances on her and she feels herself ransacked from top to bottom, flooded with relief, assaulted by happiness. How astonishing this is. How close to dismay.

It turns out that Eric was not taken so much by surprise as he pretended. Ailo phoned him last night, to warn him about the strange girl, Juliet, and offered to check for him as to whether the girl had got on the bus. He had thought it somehow right to take the chance that she would do so—to test fate, maybe—but when Ailo phoned to say that the girl had not gone he was startled by the joy he felt. Still, he did not come home right away, and he did not tell Christa, though he knew he would have to tell her, very soon.

All this Juliet absorbs bit by bit in the weeks and months that follow. Some information arrives accidentally, and some as the result of her imprudent probing.

Her own revelation (of nonvirginity) is considered minor.

Christa is nothing like Ailo. She does not have wide hips or blond hair. She is a dark-haired, thin woman, witty and sometimes morose, who will become Juliet's great friend and mainstay during the years ahead—though she will never quite forgo a habit of sly teasing, the ironic flicker of a submerged rivalry.

SOON

Two profiles face each other. One the profile of a pure white heifer, with a particularly mild and tender expression, the other that of a green-faced man who is neither young nor old. He seems to be a minor official, maybe a postman—he wears that sort of cap. His lips are pale, the whites of his eyes shining. A hand that is probably his offers up, from the lower margin of the painting, a little tree or an exuberant branch, fruited with jewels.

At the upper margin of the painting are dark clouds, and underneath them some small tottery houses and a toy church with its toy cross, perched on the curved surface of the earth. Within this curve a small man (drawn to a larger scale, however, than the buildings) walks along purposefully with a scythe on his shoulder, and a woman, drawn to the same scale, seems to wait for him. But she is hanging upside down.

There are other things as well. For instance, a girl milking a cow, within the heifer's cheek.

Juliet decided at once to buy this print for her parents' Christmas present.

"Because it reminds me of them," she said to Christa, her friend who had come down with her from Whale Bay to do some shopping. They were in the gift shop of the Vancouver Art Gallery.

Christa laughed. "The green man and the cow? They'll be flattered."

Christa never took anything seriously at first, she had to make some joke about it. Juliet wasn't bothered. Three months pregnant with the baby that would turn out to be Penelope, she was suddenly free of nausea, and for that reason, or some other, she was subject to fits of euphoria. She thought of food all the time, and hadn't even wanted to come into the gift shop, because she had spotted a lunchroom.

She loved everything in the picture, but particularly the little figures and rickety buildings at the top of it. The man with the scythe and the woman hanging upside down.

She looked for the title. *I and the Village.*

It made exquisite sense.

"Chagall. I like Chagall," said Christa. "Picasso was a bastard."

Juliet was so happy with what she had found that she could hardly pay attention.

"You know what he is supposed to have said? *Chagall is for shopgirls,*" Christa told her. "So what's wrong with shopgirls? Chagall should have said, Picasso is for people with funny faces."

"I mean, it makes me think of their life," Juliet said. "I don't know why, but it does."

She had already told Christa some things about her

parents—how they lived in a curious but not unhappy isolation, though her father was a popular schoolteacher. Partly they were cut off by Sara's heart trouble, but also by their subscribing to magazines nobody around them read, listening to programs on the national radio network, which nobody around them listened to. By Sara's making her own clothes—sometimes ineptly—from *Vogue* patterns, instead of Butterick. Even by the way they preserved some impression of youth instead of thickening and slouching like the parents of Juliet's schoolfellows. Juliet had described Sam as looking like her—long neck, a slight bump to the chin, light-brown floppy hair—and Sara as a frail pale blonde, a wispy untidy beauty.

When Penelope was thirteen months old, Juliet flew with her to Toronto, then caught the train. This was in 1969. She got off in a town twenty miles or so away from the town where she had grown up, and where Sam and Sara still lived. Apparently the train did not stop there anymore.

She was disappointed to get off at this unfamiliar station and not to see reappear, at once, the trees and sidewalks and houses she remembered—then, very soon, her own house, Sam and Sara's house, spacious but plain, no doubt with its same blistered and shabby white paint, behind its bountiful soft-maple tree.

Sam and Sara, here in this town where she'd never seen them before, were smiling but anxious, diminished.

Sara gave a curious little cry, as if something had pecked her. A couple of people on the platform turned to look.

Apparently it was only excitement.

"We're long and short, but still we match," she said.

At first Juliet did not understand what was meant. Then she figured it out—Sara was wearing a black linen skirt down to her calves and a matching jacket. The jacket's collar and cuffs were of a shiny lime-green cloth with black polka dots. A turban of the same green material covered her hair. She must have made the outfit herself, or got some dressmaker to make it for her. Its colors were unkind to her skin, which looked as if fine chalk dust had settled over it.

Juliet was wearing a black minidress.

"I was wondering what you'd think of me, black in the summertime, like I'm all in mourning," Sara said. "And here you're dressed to match. You look so smart, I'm all in favor of these short dresses."

"And long hair," said Sam. "An absolute hippy." He bent to look into the baby's face. "Hello, Penelope."

Sara said, "What a dolly."

She reached out for Penelope—though the arms that slid out of her sleeves were sticks too frail to hold any such burden. And they did not have to, because Penelope, who had tensed at the first sound of her grandmother's voice, now yelped and turned away, and hid her face in Juliet's neck.

Sara laughed. "Am I such a scarecrow?" Again her voice was ill controlled, rising to shrill peaks and falling away, drawing stares. This was new—though maybe not entirely. Juliet had an idea that people might always have looked her mother's way when she laughed or talked, but in the old days it would have been a spurt of merriment they noticed, something girlish and attractive (though not everybody would have liked that either, they would have said she was always trying to get attention).

Juliet said, "She's so tired."

Sam introduced the young woman who was standing behind them, keeping her distance as if she was taking care not to be identified as part of their group. And in fact it had not occurred to Juliet that she was.

"Juliet, this is Irene. Irene Avery."

Juliet stuck out her hand as well as she could while holding

Penelope and the diaper bag, and when it became evident that Irene was not going to shake hands—or perhaps did not notice the intention—she smiled. Irene did not smile back. She stood quite still but gave the impression of wanting to bolt.

"Hello," said Juliet.

Irene said, "Pleased to meet you," in a sufficiently audible voice, but without expression.

"Irene is our good fairy," Sara said, and then Irene's face did change. She scowled a little, with sensible embarrassment.

She was not as tall as Juliet—who was tall—but she was broader in the shoulders and hips, with strong arms and a stubborn chin. She had thick, springy black hair, pulled back from her face into a stubby ponytail, thick and rather hostile black eyebrows, and the sort of skin that browns easily. Her eyes were green or blue, a light surprising color against this skin, and hard to look into, being deep set. Also because she held her head slightly lowered and twisted her face to the side. This wariness seemed hardened and deliberate.

"She does one heck of a lot of work for a fairy," Sam said, with his large strategic grin. "I'll tell the world she does."

And now of course Juliet recalled the mention in letters of some woman who had come in to help, because of Sara's strength having gone so drastically downhill. But she had thought of somebody much older. Irene was surely no older than she was herself.

The car was the same Pontiac that Sam had got secondhand maybe ten years ago. The original blue paint showed in streaks here and there but was mostly faded to gray, and the effects of winter road salt could be seen in its petticoat fringe of rust.

"The old gray mare," said Sara, almost out of breath after the short walk from the railway platform.

"She hasn't given up," said Juliet. She spoke admiringly, as seemed to be expected. She had forgotten that this was what they called the car, though it was the name she had thought up herself.

"Oh, she never gives up," said Sara, once she was settled with Irene's help in the backseat. "And we'd never give up on her."

Juliet got into the front seat, juggling Penelope, who was beginning again to whimper. The heat inside the car was shocking, even though it had been parked with the windows down in the scanty shade of the station poplars.

"Actually I'm considering—," said Sam as he backed out, "I'm considering turning her in for a truck."

"He doesn't mean it," shrieked Sara.

"For the business," Sam continued. "It'd be a lot handier. And you'd get a certain amount of advertising every time you drove down the street, just from the name on the door."

"He's teasing," Sara said. "How am I going to ride around in a vehicle that says *Fresh Vegetables*? Am I supposed to be the squash or the cabbage?"

"Better pipe down, Missus," Sam said, "or you won't have any breath left when we reach home."

After nearly thirty years of teaching in the public schools around the county—ten years in the last school—Sam had suddenly quit and decided to get into the business of selling vegetables, full-time. He had always cultivated a big vegetable garden, and raspberry canes, in the extra lot beside their house, and they had sold their surplus produce to a few people around town. But now, apparently, this was to change into his way of making a living, selling to grocery stores and perhaps eventually putting up a market stall at the front gate.

"You're serious about all this?" said Juliet quietly.

"Darn right I am."

"You're not going to miss teaching?"

"Not on your Nelly-O. I was fed up. I was fed up to the eyeballs."

It was true that after all those years, he had never been offered, in any school, the job of principal. She supposed that was what he was fed up with. He was a remarkable teacher, the one whose antics and energy everyone would remember, his Grade Six unlike any other year in his pupils' lives. Yet he had been passed over, time and again, and probably for that very reason. His methods could be seen to undercut authority. So you could imagine Authority saying that he was not the sort of man to be in charge, he'd do less harm where he was.

He liked outdoor work, he was good at talking to people, he would probably do well, selling vegetables.

But Sara would hate it.

Juliet did not like it either. If there was a side to be on, however, she would have to choose his. She was not going to define herself as a snob.

And the truth was that she saw herself—she saw herself and Sam and Sara, but particularly herself and Sam—as superior in their own way to everybody around them. So what should his peddling vegetables matter?

Sam spoke now in a quieter, conspiratorial voice.

"What's her name?"

He meant the baby's.

"Penelope. We're never going to call her Penny. Penelope."

"No, I mean—I mean her last name."

"Oh. Well, it's Henderson-Porteous I guess. Or Porteous-Henderson. But maybe that's too much of a mouthful, when she's already called Penelope? We knew that but we wanted Penelope. We'll have to settle it somehow."

"So. He's given her his name," Sam said. "Well, that's something. I mean, that's good."

Juliet was surprised for a moment, then not.

"Of course he has," she said. Pretending to be mystified and amused. "She's his."

"Oh yes. Yes. But given the circumstances."

"I forget about the circumstances," she said. "If you mean the fact that we're not married, it's hardly anything to take into account. Where we live, the people we know, it is not a thing anybody thinks about."

"Suppose not," said Sam. "Was he married to the first one?"

Juliet had told them about Eric's wife, whom he had cared for during the eight years that she had lived after her car accident.

"Ann? Yes. Well, I don't really know. But yes. I think so. Yes."

Sara called into the front seat, "Wouldn't it be nice to stop for ice cream?"

"We've got ice cream in the fridge at home," Sam called back. And added quietly, shockingly, to Juliet, "Take her into anyplace for a treat, and she'll put on a show."

The windows were still down, the warm wind blew through the car. It was full summer—a season which never arrived, as far as Juliet could see, on the west coast. The hardwood trees were humped over the far edge of the fields, making blue-black caves of shade, and the crops and the meadows in front of them, under the hard sunlight, were gold and green. Vigorous young wheat and barley and corn and beans—fairly blistering your eyes.

Sara said, "What's this conference in aid of? In the front seat? We can't hear back here for the wind."

Sam said, "Nothing interesting. Just asking Juliet if her fellow's still doing the fishing."

Eric made his living prawn fishing, and had done so for a long time. Once he had been a medical student. That had come to an end because he had performed an abortion, on a friend (not a girlfriend). All had gone well, but somehow the story got out. This was something Juliet had thought of revealing to her broad-minded parents. She had wanted, perhaps, to establish him as an educated man, not just a fisherman. But why should that matter, especially now that Sam was a vegetable man? Also, their broad-mindedness was possibly not so reliable as she had thought.

There was more to be sold than fresh vegetables and berries. Jam, bottled juice, relish, were turned out in the kitchen. The first morning of Juliet's visit, raspberry-jam making was in progress. Irene was in charge, her blouse wet with steam or sweat, sticking to her skin between the shoulder blades. Every so often she flashed a look at the television set, which had been wheeled down the back hall to the kitchen doorway, so that you had to squeeze around it to get into the room. On the screen was a children's morning program, showing a Bullwinkle cartoon. Now and then Irene gave a loud laugh at the cartoon antics, and Juliet laughed a little, to be comradely. Of this Irene took no notice.

Counter space had to be cleared so that Juliet could boil and mash an egg for Penelope's breakfast, and make some coffee and toast for herself. "Is that enough room?" Irene asked her, in a voice that was dubious, as if Juliet was an intruder whose demands could not be foreseen.

Close-up, you could see how many fine black hairs grew on Irene's forearms. Some grew on her cheeks, too, just in front of her ears.

In her sidelong way she watched everything Juliet did, watched her fiddle with the knobs on the stove (not remembering at first which burners they controlled), watched her lifting the egg out of the saucepan and peeling off the shell (which stuck, this time, and came away in little bits rather than in large easy pieces), then watched her choosing the saucer to mash it in.

"You don't want her to drop that on the floor." This was a

reference to the china saucer. "Don't you got a plastic dish for her?"

"I'll watch it," Juliet said.

It turned out that Irene was a mother, too. She had a boy three years old and a daughter just under two. Their names were Trevor and Tracy. Their father had been killed last summer in an accident at the chicken barn where he worked. She herself was three years younger than Juliet—twenty-two. The information about the children and the husband came out in answer to Juliet's questions, and the age could be figured from what she said next.

When Juliet said, "Oh, I'm sorry"—speaking about the accident and feeling that she had been rude to pry, and that it was now hypocritical of her to commiserate—Irene said, "Yeah. Right in time for my twenty-first birthday," as if misfortunes were something to accumulate, like charms on a bracelet.

After Penelope had eaten all of the egg that she would accept, Juliet hoisted her onto one hip and carried her upstairs.

Halfway up she realized that she had not washed the saucer.

There was nowhere to leave the baby, who was not yet walking but could crawl very quickly. Certainly she could not be left for even five minutes in the kitchen, with the boiling water in the sterilizer and the hot jam and the chopping knives—it was too much to ask Irene to watch her. And first thing this morning she had again refused to make friends with Sara. So Juliet carried her up the enclosed stairs to the attic—having shut the door behind—and set her there on the steps to play, while she herself looked for the old playpen. Fortunately Penelope was an expert on steps.

The house was a full two stories tall, its rooms high-ceilinged but boxlike—or so they seemed to Juliet now. The roof was steeply pitched, so that you could walk around in the middle of the attic. Juliet used to do that, when she was a child.

She walked around telling herself some story she had read, with certain additions or alterations. Dancing—that too—in front of an imaginary audience. The real audience consisted of broken or simply banished furniture, old trunks, an immensely heavy buffalo coat, the purple martin house (a present from long-ago students of Sam's, which had failed to attract any purple martins), the German helmet supposed to have been brought home by Sam's father from the First World War, and an unintentionally comic amateur painting of the *Empress of Ireland* sinking in the Gulf of St. Lawrence, with matchstick figures flying off in all directions.

And there, leaning against the wall, was *I and the Village*. Face out—no attempt had been made to hide it. And no dust on it to speak of, so it had not been there long.

She found the playpen, after a few moments of searching. It was a handsome heavy piece of furniture, with a wooden floor and spindle sides. And the baby carriage. Her parents had kept everything, had hoped for another child. There had been one miscarriage at least. Laughter in their bed, on Sunday mornings, had made Juliet feel as if the house had been invaded by a stealthy, even shameful, disturbance, not favorable to herself.

The baby carriage was of the kind that folded down to become a stroller. This was something Juliet had forgotten about, or hadn't known. Sweating by now, and covered with dust, she got to work to effect this transformation. This sort of job was never easy for her, she never grasped right away the manner in which things were put together, and she might have dragged the whole thing downstairs and gone out to the garden to get Sam to help her, but for the thought of Irene. Irene's flickering pale eyes, indirect but measuring looks, competent hands. Her vigilance, in which there was something that couldn't quite be called contempt. Juliet didn't know what it could be called. An attitude, indifferent but uncompromising, like a cat's.

She managed at last to get the stroller into shape. It was cumbersome, half again as big as the stroller she was used to. And filthy, of course. As she was herself by now, and Penelope, on the steps, even more so. And right beside the baby's hand was something Juliet hadn't even noticed. A nail. The sort of thing you paid no attention to, till you had a baby at the hand-to-mouth stage, and that you had then to be on the lookout for all the time.

And she hadn't been. Everything here distracted her. The heat, Irene, the things that were familiar and the things that were unfamiliar.

I and the Village.

"Oh," said Sara. "I hoped you wouldn't notice. Don't take it to heart."

The sunroom was now Sara's bedroom. Bamboo shades had been hung on all the windows, filling the small room—once part of the verandah—with a brownish-yellow light and a uniform heat. Sara, however, was wearing woolly pink pajamas. Yesterday, at the station, with her pencilled eyebrows and raspberry lipstick, her turban and suit, she had looked to Juliet like an elderly Frenchwoman (not that Juliet had seen many elderly Frenchwomen), but now, with her white hair flying out in wisps, her bright eyes anxious under nearly nonexistent brows, she looked more like an oddly aged child. She was sitting up against the pillows with the quilts pulled up to her waist. When Juliet had walked her to the bathroom, earlier, it had been revealed that in spite of the heat she was wearing both socks and slippers in bed.

A straight-backed chair had been placed by her bed, its seat being easier for her to reach than a table. On it were pills and medicines, talcum powder, moisturizing lotion, a half-drunk cup of milky tea, a glass filmed with the traces of some dark tonic, probably iron. On top of the bed were magazines—old copies of *Vogue* and the *Ladies' Home Journal*.

"I'm not," said Juliet.

"We did have it hanging up. It was in the back hall by the dining-room door. Then Daddy took it down."

"Why?"

"He didn't say anything about it to me. He didn't say that he was going to. Then came a day when it was just gone."

"Why would he take it down?"

"Oh. It would be some notion he had, you know."

"What sort of a notion?"

"Oh. I think—you know, I think it probably had to do with Irene. That it would disturb Irene."

"There wasn't anybody naked in it. Not like the Botticelli."

For indeed there was a print of *The Birth of Venus* hanging in Sam and Sara's living room. It had been the subject of nervous jokes years ago on the occasion when they had the other teachers to supper.

"No. But it was *modern*. I think it made Daddy uncomfortable. Or maybe looking at it with Irene looking at it—that made him uncomfortable. He might be afraid it would make her feel—oh, sort of contemptuous of us. You know—that we were weird. He wouldn't like for Irene to think we were that kind of people."

Juliet said, "The kind of people who would hang that kind of picture? You mean he'd care so much what she thought of our *pictures*?"

"You know Daddy."

"He's not afraid to disagree with people. Wasn't that the trouble in his job?"

"What?" said Sara. "Oh. Yes. He can disagree. But he's careful sometimes. And Irene. Irene is—he's careful of her. She's very valuable to us, Irene."

"Did he think she'd quit her job because she thought we had a weird picture?"

"I would have left it up, dear. I value anything that comes from you. But Daddy . . ."

Juliet said nothing. From the time when she was nine or ten until she was perhaps fourteen, she and Sara had an understanding about Sam. *You know Daddy.*

That was the time of their being women together. Home permanents were tried on Juliet's stubborn fine hair, dressmaking sessions produced the outfits like nobody else's, suppers were peanut-butter-and-tomato-and-mayonnaise sandwiches on the evenings Sam stayed late for a school meeting. Stories were told and retold about Sara's old boyfriends and girlfriends, the jokes they played and the fun they had, in the days when Sara was a schoolteacher too, before her heart got too bad. Stories from the time before that, when she lay in bed with rheumatic fever and had the imaginary friends Rollo and Maxine who solved mysteries, even murders, like the characters in certain children's books. Glimpses of Sam's besotted courtship, disasters with the borrowed car, the time he showed up at Sara's door disguised as a tramp.

Sara and Juliet, making fudge and threading ribbons through the eyelet trim on their petticoats, the two of them intertwined. And then abruptly, Juliet hadn't wanted any more of it, she had wanted instead to talk to Sam late at night in the kitchen, to ask him about black holes, the Ice Age, God. She hated the way Sara undermined their talk with wide-eyed ingenuous questions, the way Sara always tried somehow to bring the subject back to herself. That was why the talks had to be late at night and there had to be the understanding neither she nor Sam ever spoke about. *Wait till we're rid of Sara.* Just for the time being, of course.

There was a reminder going along with that. *Be nice to Sara. She risked her life to have you, that's worth remembering.*

"Daddy doesn't mind disagreeing with people that are *over* him," Sara said, taking a deep breath. "But you know how he is with people that are *under* him. He'll do anything to make sure they don't feel he's any different from them, he just has to put himself down on their level—"

Juliet did know, of course. She knew the way Sam talked to the boy at the gas pumps, the way he joked in the hardware store. But she said nothing.

"He has to suck up to them," said Sara with a sudden change of tone, a wavering edge of viciousness, a weak chuckle.

Juliet cleaned up the stroller, and Penelope, and herself, and set off on a walk into town. She had the excuse that she needed a certain brand of mild disinfectant soap with which to wash the diapers—if she used ordinary soap the baby would get a rash. But she had other reasons, irresistible though embarrassing.

This was the way she had walked to school for years of her life. Even when she was going to college, and came home on a visit, she was still the same—a girl going to school. Would she never be done going to school? Somebody asked Sam that at a time when she had just won the Intercollegiate Latin Translation Prize, and he had said, " 'Fraid not." He told this story on himself. God forbid that he should mention prizes. Leave Sara to do that—though Sara might have forgotten just what the prize was for.

And here she was, redeemed. Like any other young woman, pushing her baby. Concerned about the diaper soap. And this wasn't just her baby. Her love child. She sometimes spoke of Penelope that way, just to Eric. He took it as a joke, she said it as a joke, because of course they lived together and had done so for some time, and they intended to go on together. The fact that they were not married meant nothing to him, so far as she knew, and she often forgot about it, herself. But occasionally—and now, especially, here at home, it was the fact of her unmarried state that gave her some flush of accomplishment, a silly surge of bliss.

"So—you went upstreet today," Sam said. (Had he always said *upstreet*? Sara and Juliet said *uptown*.) "See anybody you knew?"

"I had to go to the drugstore," Juliet said. "So I was talking to Charlie Little."

This conversation took place in the kitchen, after eleven o'clock at night. Juliet had decided that this was the best time to make up Penelope's bottles for tomorrow.

"Little Charlie?" said Sam—who had always had this other habit she hadn't remembered, the habit of continuing to call people by their school nicknames. "Did he admire the offspring?"

"Of course."

"And well he might."

Sam was sitting at the table, drinking rye and smoking a cigarette. His drinking whisky was new. Because Sara's father had been a drunk—not a down-and-out drunk, he had continued to practice as a veterinarian, but enough of a terror around the house to make his daughter horrified by drinking—Sam had never used to so much as drink a beer, at least to Juliet's knowledge, at home.

Juliet had gone into the drugstore because that was the only place to buy the diaper soap. She hadn't expected to see Charlie, though it was his family's store. The last she had heard of him, he was going to be an engineer. She had mentioned that to him, today, maybe tactlessly, but he had been easy and jovial when he told her that it hadn't worked out. He had put on weight around the middle, and his hair had thinned, had lost some of its wave and glisten. He had greeted Juliet with enthusiasm, with flattery for herself as well as her baby, and this had confused her, so that she had felt her face and neck hot, slightly perspiring, all the time he talked to her. In high school he would have had no time for her—except for a decent greeting, since his manners were always affable, democratic. He took out the most desirable girls in the school, and was now, as he told her, married to one of them. Janey Peel. They had two children, one of them about Penelope's age, one older. That was the reason, he said, with a candor that seemed to owe something to Juliet's own situation—that was the reason he hadn't gone on to become an engineer.

So he knew how to win a smile and a gurgle from Penelope, and he chatted with Juliet as a fellow parent, somebody now on the same level. She felt idiotically flattered and pleased. But there was more to his attention than that—the quick glance at her unadorned left hand, the joke about his own marriage. And something else. He appraised her, covertly, perhaps he saw her now as a woman displaying the fruits of a boldly sexual life. Juliet, of all people. The gawk, the scholar.

"Does she look like you?" he had asked, when he squatted down to peer at Penelope.

"More like her father," said Juliet casually, but with a flood of pride, the sweat now pearling on her upper lip.

"Does she?" said Charlie, and straightened up, speaking confidentially. "I'll tell you one thing, though. I thought it was a shame—"

. . .

Juliet said to Sam, "He told me he thought it was a shame what happened with you."

"He did, did he? What did you say to that?"

"I didn't know what to say. I didn't know what he meant. But I didn't want him to know that."

"No."

She sat down at the table. "I'd like a drink but I don't like whisky."

"So you drink now, too?"

"Wine. We make our own wine. Everybody in the Bay does."

He told her a joke then, the sort of joke that he would never have told her before. It involved a couple going to a motel, and it ended up with the line "So it's like what I always tell the girls at Sunday school—you don't have to drink and smoke to have a good time."

She laughed but felt her face go hot, as with Charlie.

"Why did you quit your job?" she said. "Were you let go because of me?"

"Come on now." Sam laughed. "Don't think you're so important. I wasn't let go. I wasn't fired."

"All right then. You quit."

"I quit."

"Did it have anything at all to do with me?"

"I quit because I got goddamn sick of my neck always in that noose. I was on the point of quitting for years."

"It had nothing to do with me?"

"All right," Sam said. "I got into an argument. There were things said."

"What things?"

"You don't need to know.

"And don't worry," he said after a moment. "They didn't fire me. They couldn't have fired me. There are rules. It's like I told you—I was ready to go anyway."

"But you don't realize," said Juliet. "You don't *realize*. You don't realize just how *stupid* this is and what a disgusting place this is to live in, where people say that kind of thing, and how if I told people I know this, they wouldn't believe it. It would seem like a joke."

"Well. Unfortunately your mother and I don't live where you live. Here is where we live. Does that fellow of yours think it's a joke too? I don't want to talk any more about this tonight, I'm going to bed. I'm going to look in on Mother and then I'm going to bed."

"The passenger train—," said Juliet with continued energy, even scorn. "It does still stop here. Doesn't it? You didn't want me getting off here. *Did you?*"

On his way out of the room, her father did not answer.

Light from the last streetlight in town now fell across Juliet's bed. The big soft maple tree had been cut down, replaced by a patch of Sam's rhubarb. Last night she had left the curtains closed to shade the bed, but tonight she felt that she needed the outside air. So she had to switch the pillow down to the foot of the bed, along with Penelope, who had slept like an angel with the full light in her face.

She wished she had drunk a little of the whisky. She lay stiff with frustration and anger, composing in her head a letter to Eric. *I don't know what I'm doing here, I should never have come here, I can't wait to go home.*

Home.

. . .

When it was barely light in the morning, she woke to the noise of a vacuum cleaner. Then a voice—Sam's—interrupted this noise, and she must have fallen asleep again. When she woke up later, she thought it must have been a dream. Otherwise Penelope would have woken up, and she hadn't.

The kitchen was cooler this morning, no longer full of the smell of simmering fruit. Irene was fixing little caps of gingham cloth, and labels, onto all the jars.

"I thought I heard you vacuuming," said Juliet, dredging up cheerfulness. "I must have dreamed it. It was only about five o'clock in the morning."

Irene did not answer for a moment. She was writing on a label. She wrote with great concentration, her lips caught between her teeth.

"That was her," she said when she had finished. "She woke your dad up and he had to go and make her quit."

This seemed unlikely. Yesterday Sara had left her bed only to go to the bathroom.

"He told me," said Irene. "She wakes up in the middle of the night and thinks she's going to do something and then he has to get up and make her quit."

"She must have a spurt of energy then," said Juliet.

"Yeah." Irene was getting to work on another label. When that was done, she faced Juliet.

"Wants to wake your dad up and get attention, that's it. Him dead tired and he's got to get out of bed and tend to her."

Juliet turned away. Not wanting to set Penelope down—as if the child wasn't safe here—she juggled her on one hip while she fished the egg out with a spoon, tapped and shelled and mashed it with one hand.

While she fed Penelope she was afraid to speak, lest the tone of her voice alarm the baby and set her wailing. Something communicated itself to Irene, however. She said in a more subdued voice—but with an undertone of defiance—"That's just the way they get. When they're sick like that, they can't help it. They can't think about nobody but themselves."

Sara's eyes were closed, but she opened them immediately. "Oh, my dear ones," she said, as if laughing at herself. "My Juliet. My Penelope."

Penelope seemed to be getting used to her. At least she did not cry, this morning, or turn her face away.

"Here," said Sara, reaching for one of her magazines. "Set her down and let her work at this."

Penelope looked dubious for a moment, then grabbed a page and tore it vigorously.

"There you go," said Sara. "All babies love to tear up magazines. I remember."

On the bedside chair there was a bowl of Cream of Wheat, barely touched.

"You didn't eat your breakfast?" Juliet said. "Is that not what you wanted?"

Sara looked at the bowl as if serious consideration was called for, but couldn't be managed.

"I don't remember. No, I guess I didn't want it." She had a little fit of giggling and gasping. "Who knows? Crossed my mind—she could be poisoning me.

"I'm just kidding," she said when she recovered. "But she's very fierce. Irene. We mustn't underestimate—Irene. Did you see the hairs on her arms?"

"Like cats' hairs," said Juliet.

"Like skunks'."

"We must hope none of them get into the jam."

"Don't make me—laugh any more—"

Penelope became so absorbed in tearing up magazines that in

a while Juliet was able to leave her in Sara's room and carry the Cream of Wheat out to the kitchen. Without saying anything, she began to make an eggnog. Irene was in and out, carrying boxes of jam jars to the car. On the back steps, Sam was hosing off the earth that clung to the newly dug potatoes. He had begun to sing—too softly at first for his words to be heard. Then, as Irene came up the steps, more loudly.

"Irene, good ni-i-ight,
Irene, good night,
Good night, Irene, good night, Irene,
I'll see you in my dreams."

Irene, in the kitchen, swung around and yelled, "Don't sing that song about me."

"What song about you?" said Sam, with feigned amazement. "Who's singing a song about you?"

"You were. You just were."

"Oh—that song. That song about Irene? The girl in the song? By golly—I forgot that was your name too."

He started up again, but humming, stealthily. Irene stood listening, flushed, with her chest going up and down, waiting to pounce if she should hear a word.

"Don't you sing about me. If it's got my name in it, it's about me."

Suddenly Sam burst out in full force.

"Last Saturday night I got married,
Me and my wife settled down—"

"Stop it. You stop it," cried Irene, wide-eyed, inflamed. "If you don't stop I'll go out there and squirt the hose on you."

. . .

Sam was delivering jam, that afternoon, to various grocery stores and a few gift shops which had placed orders. He invited Juliet to come along. He had gone to the hardware store and bought a brand-new baby's car seat for Penelope.

"That's one thing we don't have in the attic," he said. "When you were little, I don't know if they had them. Anyway, it wouldn't have mattered. We didn't have a car."

"It's very spiffy," said Juliet. "I hope it didn't cost a fortune."

"A mere bagatelle," said Sam, bowing her into the car.

Irene was in the field picking more raspberries. These would be for pies. Sam tooted the horn twice and waved as they set off, and Irene decided to respond, raising one arm as if batting away a fly.

"That's a dandy girl," Sam said. "I don't know how we would have survived without her. But I imagine she seems pretty rough to you."

"I hardly know her."

"No. She's scared stiff of you."

"Surely not." And trying to think of something appreciative or at least neutral to say about Irene, Juliet asked how her husband had been killed at the chicken barn.

"I don't know if he was a criminal type or just immature. Anyway, he got in with some goons who were planning a sideline in stolen chickens and of course they managed to set off the alarm and the farmer came out with a gun and whether he meant to shoot him or not he did—"

"My God."

"So Irene and her in-laws went to court but the fellow got off. Well, he would. It must have been pretty hard on her, though. Even if it doesn't seem that the husband was much of a prize."

Juliet said that of course it must have been, and asked him if Irene was somebody he had taught at school.

"No no no. She hardly got to school, as far as I can make out."

He said that her family had lived up north, somewhere near Huntsville. Yes. Somewhere near there. One day they all went into town. Father, mother, kids. And the father told them he had things to do and he would meet them in a while. He told them where. When. And they walked around with no money to spend, until it was time. And he just never showed up.

"Never intended to show up. Ditched them. So they had to go on welfare. Lived in some shack out in the country, where it was cheap. Irene's older sister, the one who was the mainstay, more than the mother, I gather—she died of a burst appendix. No way of getting her into town, snowstorm on and they didn't have a phone. Irene didn't want to go back to school then, because her sister had sort of protected her from the way the other kids would act towards them. She may seem thick-skinned now but I guess she wasn't always. Maybe even now it's more of a masquerade."

And now, he said, now Irene's mother was looking after the little boy and the little girl, but guess what, after all these years the father had shown up and was trying to get the mother to go back to him, and if that should happen Irene didn't know what she'd do, since she didn't want her kids near him.

"They're cute kids, too. The little girl has some problem with a cleft palate and she's already had one operation but she'll need another later on. She'll be all right. But that's just one more thing."

One more thing.

What was the matter with Juliet? She felt no real sympathy. She felt herself rebelling, deep down, against this wretched litany. It was too much. When the cleft palate appeared in the story what she had really wanted to do was complain. *Too much.*

She knew she was wrong, but the feeling would not budge. She was afraid to say anything more, lest out of her mouth she betray her hard heart. She was afraid she would say to Sam, "Just what is so wonderful about all this misery, does it make her a saint?" Or she might say, most unforgivably, "I hope you don't mean to get us mixed up with people like that."

"I'm telling you," Sam said, "at the time she came to help us out I was at wits' end. Last fall, your mother was a downright catastrophe. And not exactly that she was letting everything go. No. Better if she had let everything go. Better if she'd done nothing. What she did, she'd start one job up and then she could not get on with it. Over and over. Not that this was anything absolutely new. I mean, I always had to pick up after her and look after her and help her do the housework. Me and you both—remember? She'd always been this sweet pretty girl with a bad heart and she was used to being waited on. Once in a while over the years it did occur to me she could have tried harder.

"But it got so bad," he said. "It got so I'd come home to the washing machine in the middle of the kitchen floor and wet clothes slopping all over the place. And some baking mess she'd started on and given up on, stuff charred to a crisp in the oven. I was scared she'd set herself on fire. Set the house on fire. I'd tell her and tell her, stay in bed. But she wouldn't and then she'd be all in this mess, crying. I tried a couple of girls coming in and they just couldn't handle her. So then—Irene.

"Irene," he said with a robust sigh. "I bless the day. I tell you. Bless the day."

But like all good things, he said, this must come to an end. Irene was getting married. To a forty- or fifty-year-old widower. Farmer. He was supposed to have money and for her sake Sam guessed he hoped it was true. Because the man did not have much else to recommend him.

"By Jesus he doesn't. As far as I can see he's only got one tooth in his head. Bad sign, in my opinion. Too proud or stingy to get choppers. Think of it—a grand-looking girl like her."

"When is the event?"

"In the fall sometime. In the fall."

Penelope had been sleeping all this time—she had gone to sleep in her car seat almost as soon as they started to move. The front windows were down and Juliet could smell the hay, which was freshly cut and baled—nobody made hay coils anymore. Some elm trees were still standing, marvels now, in their isolation.

They stopped in a village built all along one street in a narrow valley. Bedrock stuck out of the valley walls—the only place for many miles around where such massive rocks were to be seen. Juliet remembered coming here when there was a special park which you paid to enter. In the park there was a fountain, a teahouse where they served strawberry shortcake and ice cream—and surely other things which she could not remember. Caves in the rock were named after each of the Seven Dwarfs. Sam and Sara had sat on the ground by the fountain eating ice cream while she had rushed ahead to explore the caves. (Which were nothing much, really—quite shallow.) She had wanted them to come with her but Sam had said, "You know your mother can't climb."

"You run," Sara had said. "Come back and tell us all about it." She was dressed up. A black taffeta skirt that spread in a circle around her on the grass. Those were called ballerina skirts.

It must have been a special day.

Juliet asked Sam about this when he came out of the store. At first he could not remember. Then he did. A gyp joint, he said. He didn't know when it had disappeared.

Juliet could see no trace anywhere along the street of a fountain or a teahouse.

"A bringer of peace and order," Sam said, and it took a moment for her to recognize that he was still talking about Irene. "She'll turn her hand to anything. Cut the grass and hoe the garden. Whatever she's doing she gives it her best and she behaves as if it's a privilege to do it. That's what never ceases to amaze me."

What could the carefree occasion have been? A birthday, a wedding anniversary?

Sam spoke insistently, even solemnly, over the noise of the car's struggle up the hill.

"She restored my faith in women."

Sam charged into every store after telling Juliet that he wouldn't be a minute, and came back to the car quite a while later explaining that he had not been able to get away. People wanted to talk, people had been saving up jokes to tell him. A few followed him out to see his daughter and her baby.

"So that's the girl who talks Latin," one woman said.

"Getting a bit rusty nowadays," Sam said. "Nowadays she has her hands full."

"I bet," the woman said, craning to get a look at Penelope. "But aren't they a blessing? Oh, the wee ones."

Juliet had thought she might talk to Sam about the thesis she was planning to return to—though at present that was just a dream. Such subjects used to come up naturally between them. Not with Sara. Sara would say, "Now, you must tell me what you're doing in your studies," and Juliet would sum things up, and Sara might ask her how she kept all those Greek names straight. But Sam had known what she was talking about. At college she had mentioned how her father had explained to her what *thaumaturgy* meant, when she ran across the word at the age of twelve or thirteen. She was asked if her father was a scholar.

"Sure," she said. "He teaches Grade Six."

Now she had a feeling that he would subtly try to undermine her. Or maybe not so subtly. He might use the word *airy-fairy*. Or claim to have forgotten things she could not believe he had forgotten.

But maybe he had. Rooms in his mind closed up, the windows blackened—what was in there judged by him to be too useless, too discreditable, to meet the light of day.

Juliet spoke out more harshly than she intended.

"Does she want to get married? Irene?"

This question startled Sam, coming as it did in that tone and after a considerable silence.

"I don't know," he said.

And after a moment, "I don't see how she could."

"Ask her," Juliet said. "You must want to, the way you feel about her."

They drove for a mile or two before he spoke. It was clear she had given offense.

"I don't know what you're talking about," he said.

"Happy, Grumpy, Dopey, Sleepy, Sneezy," Sara said.

"Doc," said Juliet.

"Doc. *Doc*. Happy, Sneezy, *Doc,* Grumpy, *Bashful*, Sneezy—No. Sneezy, Bashful, Doc, Grumpy—*Sleepy,* Happy, Doc, Bashful—"

Having counted on her fingers, Sara said, "Wasn't that eight?

"We went there more than once," she said. "We used to call it the Shrine of Strawberry Shortcake—oh, how I'd like to go again."

"Well, there's nothing there," Juliet said. "I couldn't even see where it was."

"I'm sure I could have. Why didn't I go with you? A summer drive. What strength does it take to ride in a car? Daddy's always saying I haven't the strength."

"You came to meet me."

"Yes I did," said Sara. "But he didn't want me to. I had to throw a fit."

She reached around to pull up the pillows behind her head, but she could not manage it, so Juliet did it for her.

"Drat," said Sara. "What a useless piece of goods I am. I think I could handle a bath, though. What if company comes?"

Juliet asked if she was expecting anybody.

"No. But what if?"

So Juliet took her into the bathroom and Penelope crawled after them. Then when the water was ready and her grandmother hoisted in, Penelope decided that the bath must be for her as well. Juliet undressed her, and the baby and the old woman were bathed together. Though Sara, naked, did not look like an old woman as much as an old girl—a girl, say, who had suffered some exotic, wasting, desiccating disease.

Penelope accepted her presence without alarm, but kept a firm hold on her own duck-shaped yellow soap.

It was in the bath that Sara finally brought herself to ask, circumspectly, about Eric.

"I'm sure he is a nice man," she said.

"Sometimes," said Juliet casually.

"He was so good to his first wife."

"Only wife," Juliet corrected her. "So far."

"But I'm sure now you have this baby—you're happy, I mean. I'm sure you're happy."

"As happy as is consistent with living in sin," Juliet said, surprising her mother by wringing out a dripping washcloth over her soaped head.

"That's what I mean," said Sara after ducking and covering her face, with a joyful shriek. Then, "Juliet?"

"Yes?"

"You know I don't mean it if I ever say mean things about Daddy. I know he loves me. He's just unhappy."

Juliet dreamed she was a child again and in this house, though the arrangement of the rooms was somewhat different. She looked out the window of one of the unfamiliar rooms, and saw an arc of water sparkling in the air. This water came from the hose. Her father, with his back to her, was watering the garden. A figure moved in and out among the raspberry canes and was revealed, after a while, to be Irene—though a more childish Irene, supple and merry. She was dodging the water sprinkled from the hose. Hiding, reappearing, mostly successful but always caught again for an instant before she ran away. The game was supposed to be lighthearted, but Juliet, behind the window, watched it with disgust. Her father always kept his back to her, yet she believed—she somehow *saw*—that he held the hose low, in front of his body, and that it was only the nozzle of it that he turned back and forth.

The dream was suffused with a sticky horror. Not the kind of horror that jostles its shapes outside your skin, but the kind that curls through the narrowest passages of your blood.

When she woke that feeling was still with her. She found the dream shameful. Obvious, banal. A dirty indulgence of her own.

. . .

There was a knock on the front door in the middle of the afternoon. Nobody used the front door—Juliet found it a bit stiff to open.

The man who stood there wore a well-pressed yellow shirt with short sleeves, and tan pants. He was perhaps a few years older than she was, tall but rather frail-looking, slightly hollow-chested, but vigorous in his greeting, relentless in his smiling.

"I've come to see the lady of the house," he said.

Juliet left him standing there and went into the sunroom.

"There's a man at the door," she said. "He might be selling something. Should I get rid of him?"

Sara was pushing herself up. "No, no," she said breathlessly. "Tidy me a bit, can you? I heard his voice. It's Don. It's my friend Don."

Don had already entered the house and was heard outside the sunroom door.

"No fuss, Sara. It's only me. Are you decent?"

Sara, with a wild and happy look, reached for the hairbrush she could not manage, then gave up and ran her fingers through her hair. Her voice rang out gaily. "I'm as decent as I'll ever be, I'm afraid. Come in here."

The man appeared, hurried up to her, and she lifted her arms to him. "You smell of summer," she said. "What is it?" She fingered his shirt. "Ironing. Ironed cotton. My, that's nice."

"I did it myself," he said. "Sally's over at the church messing about with the flowers. Not a bad job, eh?"

"Lovely," said Sara. "But you almost didn't get in. Juliet thought you were a salesman. Juliet's my daughter. My dear daughter. I told you, didn't I? I told you she was coming. Don is my minister, Juliet. My friend and minister."

Don straightened up, grasped Juliet's hand.

"Good you're here—I'm very glad to meet you. And you weren't so far wrong, actually. I am a sort of salesman."

Juliet smiled politely at the ministerial joke.

"What church are you the minister of?"

The question made Sara laugh. "Oh dear—that gives the show away, doesn't it?"

"I'm from Trinity," said Don, with his unfazed smile. "And as for giving the show away—it's no news to me that Sara and Sam were not involved with any of the churches in the community. I just started dropping in anyway, because your mother is such a charming lady."

Juliet could not remember whether it was the Anglican or United Church that was called Trinity.

"Would you get Don a reasonable sort of chair, dear?" said Sara. "Here he is bending over me like a stork. And some sort of refreshment, Don? Would you like an eggnog? Juliet makes me the most delicious eggnogs. No. No, that's probably too heavy. You've just come in from the heat of the day. Tea? That's hot too. Ginger ale? Some kind of juice? What juice do we have, Juliet?"

Don said, "I don't need anything but a glass of water. That would be welcome."

"No tea? Really?" Sara was quite out of breath. "But I think I'd like some. You could drink half a cup, surely. Juliet?"

In the kitchen, by herself—Irene could be seen in the garden, today she was hoeing around the beans—Juliet wondered if the tea was a ruse to get her out of the room for a few private words. A few private words, perhaps even a few words of prayer? The notion sickened her.

Sam and Sara had never belonged to any church, though Sam had told someone, early in their life here, that they were Druids. Word had gone around that they belonged to a church not represented in town, and that information had moved them up a notch from having no religion at all. Juliet herself had gone to Sunday school for a while at the Anglican Church, though that was mostly because she had an Anglican friend. Sam, at school, had never rebelled at having to read the Bible and say the Lord's Prayer every morning, any more than he objected to "God Save the Queen."

"There's times for sticking your neck out and times not to," he had said. "You satisfy them this way, maybe you can get away with telling the kids a few facts about evolution."

Sara had at one time been interested in the Baha'i faith, but Juliet believed that this interest had waned.

She made enough tea for the three of them and found some digestive biscuits in the cupboard—also the brass tray which Sara had usually taken out for fancy occasions.

Don accepted a cup, and gulped down the ice water which she had remembered to bring him, but shook his head at the cookies.

"Not for me, thanks."

He seemed to say this with special emphasis. As if godliness forbade him.

He asked Juliet where she lived, what was the nature of the weather on the west coast, what work her husband did.

"He's a prawn fisherman, but he's actually not my husband," said Juliet pleasantly.

Don nodded. Ah, yes.

"Rough seas out there?"

"Sometimes."

"Whale Bay. I've never heard of it but now I'll remember it. What church do you go to in Whale Bay?"

"We don't go. We don't go to church."

"Is there not a church of your sort handy?"

Smiling, Juliet shook her head.

"There *is* no church of our sort. We don't believe in God."

Don's cup made a little clatter as he set it down in its saucer. He said he was sorry to hear that.

"Truly sorry to hear that. How long have you been of this opinion?"

"I don't know. Ever since I gave it any serious thought."

"And your mother's told me you have a child. You have a little girl, don't you?"

Juliet said yes, she had.

"And she has never been christened? You intend to bring her up a heathen?"

Juliet said that she expected Penelope would make up her own mind about that, someday.

"But we intend to bring her up without religion. Yes."

"That is sad," said Don quietly. "For yourselves, it's sad. You and your—whatever you call him—you've decided to reject God's grace. Well. You are adults. But to reject it for your child—it's like denying her nourishment."

Juliet felt her composure cracking. "But we don't *believe*," she said. "We don't believe in God's grace. It's not like denying her nourishment, it's refusing to bring her up on lies."

"Lies. What millions of people all over the world believe in, you call lies. Don't you think that's a little presumptuous of you, calling God a lie?"

"Millions of people don't believe it, they just go to church," said Juliet, her voice heating. "They just don't think. If there is a God, then God gave me a mind, and didn't he intend me to use it?

"Also," she said, trying to hold herself steady. "Also, millions of people believe something different. They believe in Buddha, for instance. So how does millions of people believing in anything make it true?"

"Christ is alive," said Don readily. "Buddha isn't."

"That's just something to say. What does it mean? I don't see any proof of either one being alive, as far as that goes."

"*You* don't. But others do. Do you know that Henry Ford—Henry Ford the second, who has everything anybody in life could desire—nevertheless he gets down on his knees and prays to God every night of his life?"

"Henry Ford?" cried Juliet. "Henry Ford? What does anything *Henry Ford* does matter to me?"

The argument was taking the course that arguments of this sort are bound to take. The minister's voice, which had started out more sorrowful than angry—though always indicating ironclad conviction—was taking on a shrill and scolding tone, while Juliet, who had begun, as she thought, in reasonable resistance—calm, shrewd, rather maddeningly polite—was now in a cold and biting rage. Both of them cast around for arguments and refutations that would be more insulting than useful.

Meanwhile Sara nibbled on a digestive biscuit, not looking up at them. Now and then she shivered, as if their words struck her, but they were beyond noticing.

What did bring their display to an end was the loud wailing of Penelope, who had wakened wet and had complained softly for a while, then complained more vigorously, and finally given way to fury. Sara heard her first, and tried to attract their attention.

"Penelope," she said faintly, then, with more effort, "Juliet. Penelope." Juliet and the minister both looked at her distractedly, and then the minister said, with a sudden drop in his voice, "Your baby."

Juliet hurried from the room. She was shaking when she picked Penelope up, she came close to stabbing her when she was pinning on the dry diaper. Penelope stopped crying, not because she was comforted but because she was alarmed by this rough attention. Her wide wet eyes, her astonished stare, broke into Juliet's preoccupation, and she tried to settle herself down, talking as gently as she could and then picking her child up, walking with her up and down the upstairs hall. Penelope was not immediately reassured, but after a few minutes the tension began to leave her body.

Juliet felt the same thing happening to her, and when she thought that a certain amount of control and quiet had returned to both of them, she carried Penelope downstairs.

The minister had come out of Sara's room and was waiting for her. In a voice that might have been contrite, but seemed in fact frightened, he said, "That's a nice baby."

Juliet said, "Thank you."

She thought that now they might properly say good-bye, but something was holding him. He continued to look at her, he did not move away. He put his hand out as if to catch hold of her shoulder, then dropped it.

"Do you know if you have—," he said, then shook his head slightly. The *have* had come out sounding like *hab*.

"Jooze," he said, and slapped his hand against his throat. He waved in the direction of the kitchen.

Juliet's first thought was that he must be drunk. His head was wagging slightly back and forth, his eyes seemed to be filmed over. Had he come here drunk, had he brought something in his pocket? Then she remembered. A girl, a pupil at the school where she had once taught for half a year. This girl, a diabetic, would suffer a kind of seizure, become thick-tongued, distraught, staggering, if she had gone too long without food.

Shifting Penelope to her hip, she took hold of his arm and steadied him along towards the kitchen. Juice. That was what they had given the girl, that was what he was talking about.

"Just a minute, just a minute, you'll be all right," she said. He held himself upright, hands pressed down on the counter, head lowered.

There was no orange juice—she remembered giving Penelope the last of it that morning, thinking she must get more. But there was a bottle of grape soda, which Sam and Irene liked to drink when they came in from work in the garden.

"Here," she said. Managing with one hand, as she was used to doing, she poured out a glassful. "Here." And as he drank she said, "I'm sorry there's no juice. But it's the sugar, isn't it? You have to get some sugar?"

He drank it down, he said, "Yeah. Sugar. Thanks." Already his voice was clearing. She remembered this too, about the girl at the school—how quick and apparently miraculous the recovery. But before he was quite recovered, or quite himself, while he was still holding his head at a slant, he met her eyes. Not on purpose, it seemed, just by chance. The look in his eyes was not grateful, or forgiving—it was not really personal, it was just the raw look of an astounded animal, hanging on to whatever it could find.

And within a few seconds the eyes, the face, became the face of the man, the minister, who set down his glass and without another word fled out of the house.

Sara was either asleep or pretending to be, when Juliet went to pick up the tea tray. Her sleeping state, her dozing state, and her waking state had now such delicate and shifting boundaries that it was hard to identify them. At any rate, she spoke, she said in little more than a whisper, "Juliet?"

Juliet paused in the doorway.

"You must think Don is—rather a simpleton," Sara said. "But he isn't well. He's a diabetic. It's serious."

Juliet said, "Yes."

"He needs his faith."

"Foxhole argument," said Juliet, but quietly, and perhaps Sara did not hear, for she went on talking.

"My faith isn't so simple," said Sara, her voice all shaky (and seeming to Juliet, at this moment, strategically pathetic). "I can't describe it. But it's—all I can say—it's *something*. It's a—wonderful—*something*. When it gets really bad for me—when it gets so bad I—you know what I think then? I think, all right. I think— Soon. *Soon I'll see Juliet.*"

Dreaded (Dearest) Eric,

Where to begin? I am fine and Penelope is fine. Considering. She walks confidently now around Sara's bed but is still leery of striking out with no support. The summer heat is amazing, compared with the west coast. Even when it rains. It's a good thing it does rain because Sam is going full-tilt at the market garden business. The other day I rode around with him in the ancient vehicle delivering fresh raspberries and raspberry jam (made by a sort of junior Ilse Koch person who inhabits our kitchen) and newly dug first potatoes of the season. He is quite gung-ho. Sara stays in bed and dozes or looks at outdated fashion magazines. A minister came to visit her and he and I got into a big stupid row about the existence of God or some such hot topic. The visit is going okay though . . .

This was a letter that Juliet found years later. Eric must have saved it by accident—it had no particular importance in their lives.

. . .

She had gone back to the house of her childhood once more, for Sara's funeral, some months after that letter was written. Irene was no longer around, and Juliet had no memory of asking or being told where she was. Most probably she had married. As Sam did again, in a couple of years. He married a fellow teacher, a good-natured, handsome, competent woman. They lived in her house—Sam tore down the house where he and Sara had lived, and extended the garden. When his wife retired, they bought a trailer and began to go on long winter trips. They visited Juliet twice at Whale Bay. Eric took them out in his boat. He and Sam got along well. As Sam said, like a house afire.

When she read the letter, Juliet winced, as anybody does on discovering the preserved and disconcerting voice of some past fabricated self. She wondered at the sprightly cover-up, contrasting with the pain of her memories. Then she thought that some shift must have taken place, at that time, which she had not remembered. Some shift concerning where home was. Not at Whale Bay with Eric but back where it had been before, all her life before.

Because it's what happens at home that you try to protect, as best you can, for as long as you can.

But she had not protected Sara. When Sara had said, *soon I'll see Juliet,* Juliet had found no reply. Could it not have been managed? Why should it have been so difficult? Just to say *Yes.* To Sara it would have meant so much—to herself, surely, so little. But she had turned away, she had carried the tray to the kitchen, and there she washed and dried the cups and also the glass that had held grape soda. She had put everything away.

SILENCE

On the short ferry ride from Buckley Bay to Denman Island, Juliet got out of her car and stood at the front of the boat, in the summer breeze. A woman standing there recognized her, and they began to talk. It is not unusual for people to take a second look at Juliet and wonder where they've seen her before, and, sometimes, to remember. She appears regularly on the Provincial Television channel, interviewing people who are leading singular or notable lives, and deftly directing panel discussions, on a program called *Issues of the Day*. Her hair is cut short now, as short as possible, and has taken on a very dark auburn color, matching the frames of her glasses. She often wears black pants—as she does today—and an ivory silk shirt, and sometimes a black jacket. She is what her mother would have called a striking-looking woman.

"Forgive me. People must be always bothering you."

"It's okay," Juliet says. "Except when I've just been to the dentist or something."

The woman is about Juliet's age. Long black hair streaked with gray, no makeup, long denim skirt. She lives on Denman, so Juliet asks her what she knows about the Spiritual Balance Centre.

"Because my daughter is there," Juliet says. "She's been on a retreat there or taking a course, I don't know what they call it. For six months. This is the first time I've got to see her, in six months."

"There are a couple of places like that," the woman says. "They sort of come and go. I don't mean there's anything suspect about them. Just that they're generally off in the woods, you know, and don't have much to do with the community. Well, what would be the point of a retreat if they did?"

She says that Juliet must be looking forward to seeing her daughter again, and Juliet says yes, very much.

"I'm spoiled," she says. "She's twenty years old, my daughter—she'll be twenty-one this month, actually—and we haven't been apart much."

The woman says that she has a son of twenty and a daughter of eighteen and another of fifteen, and there are days when she'd *pay* them to go on a retreat, singly or all together.

Juliet laughs. "Well. I've only the one. Of course, I won't guarantee that I won't be all for shipping her back, given a few weeks."

This is the kind of fond but exasperated mother-talk she finds it easy to slip into (Juliet is an expert at reassuring responses), but the truth is that Penelope has scarcely ever given her cause for complaint, and if she wanted to be totally honest, at this point she would say that one day without some contact with her daughter is hard to bear, let alone six months. Penelope has worked at Banff, as a summer chambermaid, and she has gone on bus trips to Mexico, a hitchhiking trip to Newfoundland. But she has always lived with Juliet, and there has never been a six-month break.

She gives me delight, Juliet could have said. *Not that she is one of those song-and-dance purveyors of sunshine and cheer and looking-on-the-bright-side. I hope I've brought her up better than that. She has grace and compassion and she is as wise as if she'd been on this earth for eighty years. Her nature is reflective, not all over the map like mine. Somewhat reticent, like her father's. She is also angelically pretty, she's like my mother, blond like my mother but not so frail. Strong and noble. Molded, I should say, like a caryatid. And contrary to popular notions I am not even faintly jealous. All this time without her—and with no word from her, because Spiritual Balance does not allow letters or phone calls—all this time I've been in a sort of desert, and when her message came I was like an old patch of cracked earth getting a full drink of rain.*

Hope to see you Sunday afternoon. It's time.

Time to go home, was what Juliet hoped this meant, but of course she would leave that up to Penelope.

Penelope had drawn a rudimentary map, and Juliet shortly found herself parked in front of an old church—that is, a church building seventy-five or eighty years old, covered with stucco, not as old or anything like as impressive as churches usually were in the part of Canada where Juliet had grown up. Behind it was a more recent building, with a slanting roof and windows all across its front, also a simple stage and some seating benches and what looked like a volleyball court with a sagging net. Everything was shabby, and the once-cleared patch of land was being reclaimed by juniper and poplars.

A couple of people—she could not tell whether men or women—were doing some carpentry work on the stage, and others sat on the benches in separate small groups. All wore ordinary clothes, not yellow robes or anything of that sort. For a few minutes no notice was taken of Juliet's car. Then one of the people on the benches rose and walked unhurriedly towards her. A short, middle-aged man wearing glasses.

She got out of the car and greeted him and asked for Penelope. He did not speak—perhaps there was a rule of silence—but nodded and turned away and went into the church. From which there shortly appeared, not Penelope, but a heavy, slow-moving woman with white hair, wearing jeans and a baggy sweater.

"What an honor to meet you," she said. "Do come inside. I've asked Donny to make us some tea."

She had a broad fresh face, a smile both roguish and tender, and what Juliet supposed must be called twinkling eyes. "My name is Joan," she said. Juliet had been expecting an assumed name like Serenity, or something with an Eastern flavor, nothing so plain and familiar as Joan. Later, of course, she thought of Pope Joan.

"I've got the right place, have I? I'm a stranger on Denman," she said disarmingly. "You know I've come to see Penelope?"

"Of course. Penelope." Joan prolonged the name, with a certain tone of celebration.

The inside of the church was darkened with purple cloth hung over the high windows. The pews and other church furnishings had been removed, and plain white curtains had been strung up to form private cubicles, as in a hospital ward. The cubicle into which Juliet was directed had, however, no bed, just a small table and a couple of plastic chairs, and some open shelves piled untidily with loose papers.

"I'm afraid we're still in the process of getting things fixed up in here," Joan said. "Juliet. May I call you Juliet?"

"Yes, of course."

"I'm not used to talking to a celebrity." Joan held her hands together in a prayer pose beneath her chin. "I don't know whether to be informal or not."

"I'm not much of a celebrity."

"Oh, you are. Now don't say things like that. And I'll just get it off my chest right away, how I admire you for the work you do. It's a beam in the darkness. The only television worth watching."

"Thank you," said Juliet. "I had a note from Penelope—"

"I know. But I'm sorry to have to tell you, Juliet, I'm very sorry and I don't want you to be too disappointed—Penelope is not here."

The woman says those words—*Penelope is not here*—as lightly as possible. You would think that Penelope's absence could be turned into a matter for amused contemplation, even for their mutual delight.

Juliet has to take a deep breath. For a moment she cannot speak. Dread pours through her. Foreknowledge. Then she pulls herself back to reasonable consideration of this fact. She fishes around in her bag.

"She said she hoped—"

"I know. I know," says Joan. "She did intend to be here, but the fact was, she could not—"

"Where is she? Where did she go?"

"I cannot tell you that."

"You mean you can't or you won't?"

"I can't. I don't know. But I can tell you one thing that may put your mind at rest. Wherever she has gone, whatever she has decided, it will be the right thing for her. It will be the *right* thing for her spirituality and her growth."

Juliet decides to let this pass. She gags on the word *spirituality*, which seems to take in—as she often says—everything from prayer wheels to High Mass. She never expected that Penelope, with her intelligence, would be mixed up in anything like this.

"I just thought I should know," she says, "in case she wanted me to send on any of her things."

"Her possessions?" Joan seems unable to suppress a wide smile, though she modifies it at once with an expression of tenderness. "Penelope is not very concerned right now about her *possessions.*"

Sometimes Juliet has felt, in the middle of an interview, that the person she faces has reserves of hostility that were not apparent before the cameras started rolling. A person whom Juliet has underestimated, whom she has thought rather stupid, may have strength of that sort. Playful but deadly hostility. The thing then is never to show that you are taken aback, never to display any hint of hostility in return.

"What I mean by growth is our inward growth, of course," Joan says.

"I understand," says Juliet, looking her in the eye.

"Penelope has had such a wonderful opportunity in her life to meet interesting people—goodness, she hasn't needed to meet interesting people, she's *grown up* with an interesting person, you're her *mother*—but you know, sometimes there's a dimension that is missing, grown-up children feel that they've *missed out* on something—"

"Oh yes," says Juliet. "I know that grown-up children can have all sorts of complaints."

Joan has decided to come down hard.

"The spiritual dimension—I have to say this—was it not altogether lacking in Penelope's life? I take it she did not grow up in a faith-based home."

"Religion was not a banned subject. We could talk about it."

"But perhaps it was the way you talked about it. Your intellectual way? If you know what I mean. You are so clever," she adds, kindly.

"So you say."

Juliet is aware that any control of the interview, and of herself, is faltering, and may be lost.

"Not so *I* say, Juliet. So *Penelope* says. Penelope is a dear fine girl, but she has come to us here in great hunger. Hunger for the things that were not available to her in her home. There you were, with your wonderful busy successful life—but Juliet, I must tell you that your daughter has known loneliness. She has known unhappiness."

"Don't most people feel that, one time or another? Loneliness and unhappiness?"

"It's not for me to say. Oh, Juliet. You are a woman of marvellous insights. I've often watched you on television and I've thought, how does she get right to the heart of things like that, and all the time being so nice and polite to people? I never thought I'd be sitting talking to you face-to-face. And what's more, that I'd be in a position to *help* you—"

"I think that maybe you're mistaken about that."

"You feel hurt. It's natural that you should feel hurt."

"It's also my own business."

"Ah well. Perhaps she'll get in touch with you. After all."

Penelope did get in touch with Juliet, a couple of weeks later. A birthday card arrived on her own—Penelope's—birthday, the 19th of June. Her twenty-first birthday. It was the sort of card you send to an acquaintance whose tastes you cannot guess. Not a crude jokey card or a truly witty card or a sentimental card. On the front of it was a small bouquet of pansies tied by a thin purple ribbon whose tail spelled out the words *Happy Birthday.* These words were repeated inside, with the words *Wishing you a very* added in gold letters above them.

And there was no signature. Juliet thought at first that someone had sent this card to Penelope, and forgotten to sign it, and that she, Juliet, had opened it by mistake. Someone who had Penelope's name and the date of her birth on file. Her dentist, maybe, or her driving teacher. But when she checked the writing on the envelope she saw that there had been no mistake—there was her own name, indeed, written in Penelope's own handwriting.

Postmarks gave you no clue anymore. They all said *Canada Post.* Juliet had some idea that there were ways of telling at least which province a letter came from, but for that you would have to consult the Post Office, go there with the letter and very likely be called upon to prove your case, your right to the information. And somebody would be sure to recognize her.

She went to see her old friend Christa, who had lived in Whale Bay when she herself lived there, even before Penelope was born. Christa was in Kitsilano, in an assisted-living facility. She had multiple sclerosis. Her room was on the ground floor, with a small private patio, and Juliet sat with her there, looking out at a sunny bit of lawn, and the wisteria all in bloom along the fence that concealed the garbage bins.

Juliet told Christa the whole story of the trip to Denman Island. She had told nobody else, and had hoped perhaps not to have to tell anybody. Every day when she was on her way home from work she had wondered if perhaps Penelope would be waiting in the apartment. Or at least that there would be a letter. And then there had been—that unkind card—and she had torn it open with her hands shaking.

"It means something," Christa said. "It lets you know she's okay. Something will follow. It will. Be patient."

Juliet talked bitterly for a while about Mother Shipton. That was what she finally decided to call her, having toyed with and become dissatisfied with Pope Joan. What bloody chicanery, she said. What creepiness, nastiness, behind the second-rate, sweetly religious facade. It was impossible to imagine Penelope's having been taken in by her.

Christa suggested that perhaps Penelope had visited the place because she had considered writing something about it. Some sort of investigative journalism. Fieldwork. The personal angle—the long-winded personal stuff that was so popular nowadays.

Investigating for six months? said Juliet. Penelope could have figured out Mother Shipton in ten minutes.

"It's weird," admitted Christa.

"You don't know more than you're letting on, do you?" said Juliet. "I hate to even ask that. I feel so at sea. I feel stupid. That woman intended me to feel stupid, of course. Like the character who blurts out something in a play and everybody turns away because they all know something she doesn't know—"

"They don't do that kind of play anymore," Christa said. "Now nobody knows anything. No—Penelope didn't take me into her confidence any more than she did you. Why should she? She'd know I'd end up telling you."

Juliet was quiet for a moment, then she muttered sulkily, "There have been things you didn't tell me."

"Oh, for God's sake," said Christa, but without any animosity. "Not that again."

"Not that again," Juliet agreed. "I'm in a lousy mood, that's all."

"Just hold on. One of the trials of parenthood. She hasn't

given you many, after all. In a year this will all be ancient history."

Juliet didn't tell her that in the end she had not been able to walk away with dignity. She had turned and cried out beseechingly, furiously.

"What did she tell you?"

And Mother Shipton was standing there watching her, as if she had expected this. A fat pitying smile had stretched her closed lips as she shook her head.

During the next year Juliet would get phone calls, now and then, from people who had been friendly with Penelope. Her reply to their inquiries was always the same. Penelope had decided to take a year off. She was travelling. Her travelling agenda was by no means fixed, and Juliet had no way of contacting her, nor any address she could supply.

She did not hear from anybody who had been a close friend. This might mean that people who had been close to Penelope knew quite well where she was. Or it might be that they too were off on trips to foreign countries, had found jobs in other provinces, were embarked on new lives, too crowded or chancy at present to allow them to wonder about old friends.

(Old friends, at that stage in life, meaning somebody you had not seen for half a year.)

Whenever she came in, the first thing Juliet did was to look for the light flashing on her answering machine—the very thing she used to avoid, thinking there would be someone pestering her about her public utterances. She tried various silly tricks, to do with how many steps she took to the phone, how she picked it up, how she breathed. *Let it be her.*

Nothing worked. After a while the world seemed emptied

of the people Penelope had known, the boyfriends she had dropped and the ones who had dropped her, the girls she had gossiped with and probably confided in. She had gone to a private girls' boarding school—Torrance House—rather than to a public high school, and this meant that most of her longtime friends—even those who were still her friends at college—had come from places out of town. Some from Alaska or Prince George or Peru.

There was no message at Christmas. But in June, another card, very much in the style of the first, not a word written inside. Juliet had a drink of wine before she opened it, then threw it away at once. She had spurts of weeping, once in a while of uncontrollable shaking, but she came out of these in quick fits of fury, walking around the house and slapping one fist into her palm. The fury was directed at Mother Shipton, but the image of that woman had faded, and finally Juliet had to recognize that she was really only a convenience.

All pictures of Penelope were banished to her bedroom, with sheaves of drawings and crayonings she had done before they left Whale Bay, her books, and the European one-cup coffeemaker with the plunger that she had bought as a present for Juliet with the first money she had made in her summer job at McDonald's. Also such whimsical gifts for the apartment as a tiny plastic fan to stick on the refrigerator, a wind-up toy tractor, a curtain of glass beads to hang in the bathroom window. The door of that bedroom was shut and in time could be passed without disturbance.

Juliet gave a great deal of thought to getting out of this apartment, giving herself the benefit of new surroundings. But she said to Christa that she could not do that, because that was the address Penelope had, and mail could be forwarded for only three months, so there would be no place then where her daughter could find her.

"She could always get to you at work," said Christa.

"Who knows how long I'll be there?" Juliet said. "She's probably in some commune where they're not allowed to communicate. With some guru who sleeps with all the women and sends them out to beg on the streets. If I'd sent her to Sunday school and taught her to say her prayers this probably wouldn't have happened. I should have. I should have. It would have been like an inoculation. I neglected her *spirituality.* Mother Shipton said so."

When Penelope was barely thirteen years old, she had gone away on a camping trip to the Kootenay Mountains of British Columbia, with a friend from Torrance House, and the friend's family. Juliet was in favor of this. Penelope had been at Torrance House for only one year (accepted on favorable financial terms because of her mother's once having taught there), and it pleased Juliet that she had already made so firm a friend and been accepted readily by the friend's family. Also that she was going camping—something that regular children did and that Juliet, as a child, had never had the chance to do. Not that she would have wanted to, being already buried in books—but she welcomed signs that Penelope was turning out to be a more normal sort of girl than she herself had been.

Eric was apprehensive about the whole idea. He thought Penelope was too young. He didn't like her going on a holiday with people he knew so little about. And now that she went to boarding school they saw too little of her as it was—so why should that time be shortened?

Juliet had another reason—she simply wanted Penelope out of the way for the first couple of weeks of the summer holidays, because the air was not clear between herself and Eric. She wanted things resolved, and they were not resolved. She did not want to have to pretend that all was well, for the sake of the child.

Eric, on the other hand, would have liked nothing better than to see their trouble smoothed over, hidden out of the way. To Eric's way of thinking, civility would restore good feeling, the semblance of love would be enough to get by on until love itself might be rediscovered. And if there was never anything more than a semblance—well, that would have to do. Eric could manage with that.

Indeed he could, thought Juliet, despondently.

Having Penelope at home, a reason for them to behave well—for Juliet to behave well, since she was the one, in his opinion, who stirred up all the rancor—that would suit Eric very well.

So Juliet told him, and created a new source of bitterness and blame, because he missed Penelope badly.

The reason for their quarrel was an old and ordinary one. In the spring, through some trivial disclosure—and the frankness or possibly the malice of their longtime neighbor Ailo, who had a certain loyalty to Eric's dead wife and some reservations about Juliet—Juliet had discovered that Eric had slept with Christa. Christa had been for a long time her close friend, but she had been, before that, Eric's girlfriend, his *mistress* (though nobody said that anymore). He had given her up when he asked Juliet to live with him. She had known all about Christa then and she could not reasonably object to what had happened in the time before she and Eric were together. She did not. What she did object to—what she claimed had broken her heart—had happened after that. (But still a long time ago, said Eric.) It had happened when Penelope was a year old, and Juliet had taken her back to Ontario. When Juliet had gone home to visit her parents. To visit—as she always pointed out now—to visit her dying mother. When she was away, and loving and missing Eric with every shred of her being (she now believed this), Eric had simply returned to his old habits.

At first he confessed to once (drunk), but with further prodding, and some drinking in the here-and-now, he said that possibly it had been more often.

Possibly? He could not remember? So many times he could not remember?

He could remember.

Christa came to see Juliet, to assure her that it had been nothing serious. (This was Eric's refrain, as well.) Juliet told her to go away and never come back. Christa decided that now would be a good time to go to see her brother in California.

Juliet's outrage at Christa was actually something of a formality. She did understand that a few rolls in the hay with an old girlfriend (Eric's disastrous description, his ill-judged attempt to minimize things) were nowhere near as threatening as a hot embrace with some woman newly met. Also, her outrage at Eric was so fierce and irrepressible as to leave little room for blame of anybody else.

Her contentions were that he did not love her, had never loved her, had mocked her, with Christa, behind her back. He had made her a laughingstock in front of people like Ailo (who had always hated her). That he had treated her with contempt, he regarded the love she felt (or had felt) for him with contempt, he had lived a lie with her. Sex meant nothing to him, or at any rate it did not mean what it meant (had meant) to her, he would have it off with whoever was handy.

Only the last of these contentions had the least germ of truth in it, and in her quieter states she knew that. But even that little truth was enough to pull everything down around her. It shouldn't do that, but it did. And Eric was not able—in all honesty he was not able—to see why that should be so. He was not surprised that she should object, make a fuss, even weep (though a woman like Christa would never have done that), but that she should really be damaged, that she should consider herself bereft of all that had sustained her—and for something that had happened *twelve years ago*—this he could not understand.

Sometimes he believed that she was shamming, making the most of it, and at other times he was full of real grief, that he had made her suffer. Their grief aroused them, and they made love magnificently. And each time he thought that would be the end of it, their miseries were over. Each time he was mistaken.

In bed, Juliet laughed and told him about Pepys and Mrs. Pepys, inflamed with passion under similar circumstances. (Since more or less giving up on her classical studies, she was reading widely, and nowadays everything she read seemed to have to do with adultery.) Never so often and never so hot, Pepys had said, though he recorded as well that his wife had also thought of murdering him in his sleep. Juliet laughed about this, but half an hour later, when he came to say good-bye before going out in the boat to check his prawn traps, she showed a stony face and gave him a kiss of resignation, as if he'd been going to meet a woman out in the middle of the bay and under a rainy sky.

There was more than rain. The water was hardly choppy when Eric went out, but later in the afternoon a wind came up suddenly, from the southeast, and tore up the waters of Desolation Sound and Malaspina Strait. It continued almost till dark—which did not really close down until around eleven o'clock in this last week of June. By then a sailboat from Campbell River was missing, with three adults and two children aboard. Also two fish boats—one with two men aboard and the other with only one man—Eric.

The next morning was calm and sunny—the mountains, the waters, the shores, all sleek and sparkling.

It was possible, of course, that none of these people were lost, that they had found shelter and spent the night in any of the multitude of little bays. That was more likely to be true of the fishermen than of the family in the sailboat, who were not local people but vacationers from Seattle. Boats went out at once, that morning, to search the mainland and island shores and the water.

The drowned children were found first, in their life jackets, and by the end of the day the bodies of their parents were located as well. A grandfather who had accompanied them was not found until the day after. The bodies of the men who had been fishing together never showed up, though the remnants of their boat washed up near Refuge Cove.

Eric's body was recovered on the third day. Juliet was not allowed to see it. Something had got at him, it was said (meaning some animal), after the body was washed ashore.

It was perhaps because of this—because there was no question of viewing the body and no need for an undertaker—that the idea caught hold amongst Eric's old friends and fellow fishermen of burning Eric on the beach. Juliet did not object to this. A death certificate had to be made out, so the doctor who came to Whale Bay once a week was telephoned at his office in Powell River, and he gave Ailo, who was his weekly assistant and a registered nurse, the authority to do this.

There was plenty of driftwood around, plenty of the sea-salted bark which makes a superior fire. In a couple of hours all was ready. News had spread—somehow, even at such short notice, women began arriving with food. It was Ailo who took charge—her Scandinavian blood, her upright carriage and flowing white hair, seeming to fit her naturally for the role of Widow of the Sea. Children ran about on the logs, and were shooed away from the growing pyre, the shrouded, surprisingly meager bundle that was Eric. A coffee urn was supplied to this half-pagan ceremony by the women from one of the churches, and cartons of beer, bottles of drink of all sorts, were left discreetly, for the time being, in the trunks of cars and cabs of trucks.

The question arose of who would speak, and who would light the pyre. They asked Juliet, would she do it? And Juliet—brittle and busy, handing out mugs of coffee—said that they had it wrong, as the widow she was supposed to throw herself into the flames. She actually laughed as she said this, and those who had asked her backed off, afraid that she was getting hysterical. The man who had partnered Eric most often in the boat agreed to do the lighting, but said he was no speaker. It occurred to some that he would not have been a good choice anyway, since his wife was an Evangelical Anglican, and he might have felt obliged to say things which would have distressed Eric if he had been able to hear them. Then Ailo's husband offered—he was a little man disfigured by a fire on a boat, years ago, a grumbling socialist and atheist, and in his talk he rather lost track of Eric, except to claim him as a Brother in the Battle. He went on at surprising length, and this was ascribed, afterwards, to the suppressed life he led under the rule of Ailo. There might have been some restlessness in the crowd before his recital of grievances got stopped, some feeling that the event was turning out to be not so splendid, or solemn, or heartrending, as might have been expected. But when the fire began to burn this feeling vanished, and there was great concentration, even, or especially, among the children, until the moment when one of the men cried, "Get the kids out of here." This was when the flames had reached the body, bringing the realization, coming rather late, that consumption of fat, of heart and kidneys and liver, might produce explosive or sizzling noises disconcerting to hear. So a good many of the children were hauled away by their mothers—some willingly, some to their own dismay. So the final act of the fire became a mostly male ceremony, and slightly scandalous, even if not, in this case, illegal.

Juliet stayed, wide-eyed, rocking on her haunches, face pressed against the heat. She was not quite there. She thought of whoever it was—Trelawny?—snatching Shelley's heart out of the flames. The heart, with its long history of significance. Strange to think how even at that time, not so long ago, one fleshly organ should be thought so precious, the site of courage and love. It was just flesh, burning. Nothing connected with Eric.

Penelope knew nothing of what was going on. There was a short item in the Vancouver paper—not about the burning on the beach, of course, just about the drowning—but no newspapers or radio reports reached her, deep in the Kootenay Mountains. When she got back to Vancouver she phoned home, from her friend Heather's house. Christa answered—she had got back too late for the ceremony, but was staying with Juliet, and helping as she could. Christa said that Juliet was not there—it was a lie—and asked to speak to Heather's mother. She explained what had happened, and said that she was driving Juliet to Vancouver, they would leave at once, and Juliet would tell Penelope herself when they got there.

Christa dropped Juliet at the house where Penelope was, and Juliet went inside alone. Heather's mother left her in the sunroom, where Penelope was waiting. Penelope received the news with an expression of fright, then—when Juliet rather formally put her arms around her—of something like embarrassment. Perhaps in Heather's house, in the white and green and orange sunroom, with Heather's brothers shooting baskets in the backyard, news so dire could hardly penetrate. The burning was not mentioned—in this house and neighborhood it would surely have seemed uncivilized, grotesque. In this house, also, Juliet's manner was sprightly beyond anything intended—her behavior close to that of *a good sport*.

Heather's mother entered after a tiny knock—with glasses of iced tea. Penelope gulped hers down and went to join Heather, who had been lurking in the hall.

Heather's mother then had a talk with Juliet. She apologized for intruding with practical matters but said that time was short. She and Heather's father were driving east in a few days' time to see relatives. They would be gone for a month, and had planned to take Heather with them. (The boys were going to camp.) But now Heather had decided she did not want to go, she had begged to stay here in the house, with Penelope. A fourteen-year-old and a thirteen-year-old could not really be left alone, and it had occurred to her that Juliet might like some time away, a respite, after what she had been through. After her loss and tragedy.

So Juliet shortly found herself living in a different world, in a large spotless house brightly and thoughtfully decorated, with what are called conveniences—but to her were luxuries—on every hand. This on a curving street lined with similar houses, behind trimmed bushes and showy flower beds. Even the weather, for that month, was flawless—warm, breezy, bright. Heather and Penelope went swimming, played badminton in the backyard, went to the movies, baked cookies, gorged, dieted, worked on their tans, filled the house with music whose lyrics seemed to Juliet sappy and irritating, sometimes invited girlfriends over, did not exactly invite boys but held long, taunting, aimless conversations with some who passed the house or had collected next door. By chance, Juliet heard Penelope say to one of the visiting girls, "Well, I hardly knew him, really."

She was speaking about her father.

How strange.

She had never been afraid to go out in the boat, as Juliet was, when there was a chop on the water. She had pestered him to be taken and was often successful. When following after Eric, in her businesslike orange life jacket, carrying what gear she could manage, she always wore an expression of particular seriousness and dedication. She took note of the setting of the traps and became skilful, quick, and ruthless at the deheading and bagging of the catch. At a certain stage of her childhood—say from eight to eleven—she had always said that she was going to go out fishing when she grew up, and Eric had told her there were girls doing that nowadays. Juliet had thought it was possible, since Penelope was bright but not bookish, and exuberantly physical, and brave. But Eric, out of Penelope's hearing, said that he hoped the idea would wear off, he wouldn't wish the life on anybody. He always spoke this way, about the hardship and uncertainty of the work he had chosen, but took pride, so Juliet thought, in those very things.

And now he was dismissed. By Penelope, who had recently painted her toenails purple and was sporting a false tattoo on her midriff. He who had filled her life. She dismissed him.

But Juliet felt as if she was doing the same. Of course, she was busy looking for a job and a place to live. She had already put the house in Whale Bay up for sale—she could not imagine remaining there. She had sold the truck and given away Eric's tools, and such traps as had been recovered, and the dinghy. Eric's grown son from Saskatchewan had come and taken the dog.

She had applied for a job in the reference department of the college library, and a job in the public library, and she had a feeling she would get one or the other. She looked at apartments in the Kitsilano or Dunbar or Point Grey areas. The cleanness, tidiness, and manageability of city life kept surprising her. This was how people lived where the man's work did not take place out of doors, and where various operations connected with it did not end up indoors. And where the weather might be a factor in your mood but never in your life, where such dire matters as the changing habits and availability of prawns and salmon were merely interesting, or not remarked upon at all. The life she had been leading at Whale Bay, such a short time ago, seemed haphazard, cluttered, exhausting, by comparison. And she herself was cleansed of the moods of the last months—she was brisk and competent, and better-looking.

Eric should see her now.

She thought about Eric in this way all the time. It was not that she failed to realize that Eric was dead—that did not happen for a moment. But nevertheless she kept constantly referring to him, in her mind, as if he was still the person to whom her existence mattered more than it could to anyone else. As if he was still the person in whose eyes she hoped to shine. Also the person to whom she presented arguments, information, surprises. This was such a habit with her, and took place so automatically, that the fact of his death did not seem to interfere with it.

Nor was their last quarrel entirely resolved. She held him to account, still, for his betrayal. When she flaunted herself a little now, it was against that.

The storm, the recovery of the body, the burning on the beach—that was all like a pageant she had been compelled to watch and compelled to believe in, which still had nothing to do with Eric and herself.

. . .

She got the job in the reference library, she found a two-bedroom apartment that she could just afford, Penelope went back to Torrance House as a day student. Their affairs at Whale Bay were wound up, their life there finished. Even Christa was moving out, coming to Vancouver in the spring.

On a day before that, a day in February, Juliet stood in the shelter at the campus bus stop when her afternoon's work was over. The day's rain had stopped, there was a band of clear sky in the west, red where the sun had gone down, out over the Strait of Georgia. This sign of the lengthening days, the promise of the change of season, had an effect on her that was unexpected and crushing.

She realized that Eric was dead.

As if all this time, while she was in Vancouver, he had been waiting somewhere, waiting to see if she would resume her life with him. As if being with him was an option that had stayed open. Her life since she came here had still been lived against a backdrop of Eric, without her ever quite understanding that Eric did not exist. Nothing of him existed. The memory of him in the daily and ordinary world was in retreat.

So this is grief. She feels as if a sack of cement has been poured into her and quickly hardened. She can barely move. Getting onto the bus, getting off the bus, walking half a block to her building (why is she living here?), is like climbing a cliff. And now she must hide this from Penelope.

At the supper table she began to shake, but could not loosen her fingers to drop the knife and fork. Penelope came around the table and pried her hands open. She said, "It's Dad, isn't it?"

Juliet afterwards told a few people—such as Christa—that these seemed the most utterly absolving, the most tender words, that anybody had ever said to her.

Penelope ran her cool hands up and down the insides of Juliet's arms. She phoned the library the next day to say that her mother was sick, and she took care of her for a couple of days, staying home from school until Juliet recovered. Or until, at least, the worst was over.

During those days Juliet told Penelope everything. Christa, the fight, the burning on the beach (which she had so far managed, almost miraculously, to conceal from her). Everything.

"I shouldn't burden you with all this."

Penelope said, "Yeah, well, maybe not." But added staunchly, "I forgive you. I guess I'm not a baby."

Juliet went back into the world. The sort of fit she had had in the bus stop recurred, but never so powerfully.

Through her research work in the library, she met some people from the Provincial Television channel, and took a job they offered. She had worked there for about a year when she began to do interviews. All the indiscriminate reading she'd done for years (and that Ailo had so disapproved of, in the days at Whale Bay), all the bits and pieces of information she'd picked up, her random appetite and quick assimilation, were now to come in handy. And she cultivated a self-deprecating, faintly teasing manner that usually seemed to go over well. On camera, few things fazed her. Though in fact she would go home and march back and forth, letting out whimpers or curses as she recalled some perceived glitch or fluster or, worse still, a mispronunciation.

After five years the birthday cards stopped coming.

"It doesn't mean anything," Christa said. "All they were for was to tell you she's alive somewhere. Now she figures you've got the message. She trusts you not to send some tracker after her. That's all."

"Did I put too much on her?"

"Oh, Jul."

"I don't mean just with Eric dying. Other men, later. I let her see too much misery. My stupid misery."

For Juliet had had two affairs during the years that Penelope was between fourteen and twenty-one, and during both of these she had managed to fall hectically in love, though she was ashamed afterwards. One of the men was much older than she, and solidly married. The other was a good deal younger, and was alarmed by her ready emotions. Later she wondered at these herself. She really had cared nothing for him, she said.

"I wouldn't think you did," said Christa, who was tired. "I don't know."

"Oh Christ. I was such a fool. I don't get like that about men anymore. Do I?"

Christa did not mention that this might be because of a lack of candidates.

"No, Jul. No."

"Actually I didn't do anything so terrible," Juliet said then, brightening up. "Why do I keep lamenting that it's my fault? She's a conundrum, that's all. I need to face that.

"A conundrum and a cold fish," she said, in a parody of resolution.

"No," said Christa.

"No," said Juliet. "No—that's not true."

After the second June had passed without any word, Juliet decided to move. For the first five years, she told Christa, she had waited for June, wondering what might come. The way things were now, she had to wonder every day. And be disappointed every day.

She moved to a high-rise building in the West End. She meant to throw away the contents of Penelope's room, but in the end she stuffed it all into garbage bags and carried it with her. She had only one bedroom now but there was storage space in the basement.

She took up jogging in Stanley Park. Now she seldom mentioned Penelope, even to Christa. She had a boyfriend—that was what you called them now—who had never heard anything about her daughter.

Christa grew thinner and moodier. Quite suddenly, one January, she died.

You don't go on forever, appearing on television. However agreeable the viewers have found your face, there comes a time when they'd prefer somebody different. Juliet was offered other jobs—researching, writing voice-over for nature shows—but she refused them cheerfully, describing herself as in need of a total change. She went back to Classical Studies—an even smaller department than it used to be—she meant to resume writing her thesis for her Ph.D. She moved out of the high-rise apartment and into a bachelor flat, to save money.

Her boyfriend had got a teaching job in China.

Her flat was in the basement of a house, but the sliding doors at the back opened out at ground level. And there she had a little brick-paved patio, a trellis with sweet peas and clematis, herbs and flowers in pots. For the first time in her life, and in a very small way, she was a gardener, as her father had been.

Sometimes people said to her—in stores, or on the campus bus—"Excuse me, but your face is so familiar," or, "Aren't you the lady that used to be on television?" But after a year or so this passed. She spent a lot of time sitting and reading, drinking coffee at sidewalk tables, and nobody noticed her. She let her hair grow out. During the years that it had been dyed red it had lost the vigor of its natural brown—it was a silvery brown now, fine and wavy. She was reminded of her mother, Sara. Sara's soft, fair, flyaway hair, going gray and then white.

She did not have room to have people to dinner anymore, and

she had lost interest in recipes. She ate meals that were nourishing enough, but monotonous. Without exactly meaning to, she lost contact with most of her friends.

It was no wonder. She lived now a life as different as possible from the life of the public, vivacious, concerned, endlessly well-informed woman that she had been. She lived amongst books, reading through most of her waking hours and being compelled to deepen, to alter, whatever premise she had started with. She often missed the world news for a week at a time.

She had given up on her thesis and become interested in some writers referred to as the Greek novelists, whose work came rather late in the history of Greek literature (starting in the first century B.C.E., as she had now learned to call it, and continuing into the early Middle Ages). Aristeides, Longus, Heliodorus, Achilles Tatius. Much of their work is lost or fragmentary and is also reported to be indecent. But there is a romance written by Heliodorus, and called the *Aethiopica* (originally in a private library, retrieved at the siege of Buda), that has been known in Europe since it was printed at Basle in 1534.

In this story the queen of Ethiopia gives birth to a white baby, and is afraid she will be accused of adultery. So she gives the child—a daughter—into the care of the gymnosophists—that is, the naked philosophers, who are hermits and mystics. The girl, who is called Charicleia, is finally taken to Delphi, where she becomes one of the priestesses of Artemis. There she meets a noble Thessalian named Theagenes, who falls in love with her and, with the help of a clever Egyptian, carries her off. The Ethiopian queen, as it turns out, has never ceased to long for her daughter and has hired this very Egyptian to search for her. Mischance and adventures continue until all the main characters meet at Meroe, and Charicleia is rescued—again—just as she is about to be sacrificed by her own father.

Interesting themes were thick as flies here, and the tale had a natural continuing fascination for Juliet. Particularly the part about the gymnosophists. She tried to find out as much as she could about these people, who were usually referred to as Hindu philosophers. Was India, in this case, presumed to be adjacent to Ethiopia? No—Heliodorus came late enough to know his geography better than that. The gymnosophists would be wanderers, far spread, attracting and repelling those they lived amongst with their ironclad devotion to purity of life and thought, their contempt for possessions, even for clothing and food. A beautiful maiden reared amongst them might well be left with some perverse hankering for a bare, ecstatic life.

Juliet had made a new friend named Larry. He taught Greek, and he had let Juliet store the garbage bags in the basement of his house. He liked to imagine how they might make the *Aethiopica* into a musical. Juliet collaborated in this fantasy, even to making up the marvellously silly songs and the preposterous stage effects. But she was secretly drawn to devising a different ending, one that would involve renunciation, and a backward search, in which the girl would be sure to meet fakes and charlatans, impostors, shabby imitations of what she was really looking for. Which was reconciliation, at last, with the erring, repentant, essentially great-hearted queen of Ethiopia.

Juliet was almost certain that she had seen Mother Shipton here in Vancouver. She had taken some clothes that she would never wear again (her wardrobe had grown increasingly utilitarian) to a Salvation Army Thrift Store, and as she set the bag down in the receiving room she saw a fat old woman in a muumuu fixing tags onto trousers. The woman was chatting with the other workers. She had the air of a supervisor, a cheerful but vigilant overseer—or perhaps the air of a woman who would assume that role whether she had any official superiority or not.

If she was in fact Mother Shipton, she had come down in the world. But not by very much. For if she was Mother Shipton, would she not have reserves of buoyancy and self-approbation, such as to make real downfall impossible?

Reserves of advice, pernicious advice, as well.

She has come to us here in great hunger.

Juliet had told Larry about Penelope. She had to have one person who knew. "Should I have talked to her about a noble life?" she said. "Sacrifice? Opening your life to the needs of strangers? I never thought of it. I must have acted as if it would have been good enough if she turned out like me. Would that sicken her?"

Larry was not a man who wanted anything from Juliet but her friendship and good humor. He was what used to be called an old-fashioned bachelor, asexual as far as she could tell (but probably she could not tell far enough), squeamish about any personal revelations, endlessly entertaining.

Two other men had appeared who wanted her as a partner. One of them she had met when he sat down at her sidewalk table. He was a recent widower. She liked him, but his loneliness was so raw and his pursuit of her so desperate that she became alarmed.

The other man was Christa's brother, whom she had met several times during Christa's life. His company suited her—in many ways he was like Christa. His marriage had ended long ago, he was not desperate—she knew, from Christa, that there had been women ready to marry him whom he had avoided. But he was too rational, his choice of her verged on being cold-blooded, there was something humiliating about it.

But why humiliating? It was not as if she loved him.

It was while she was still seeing Christa's brother—his name was Gary Lamb—that she ran into Heather, on a downtown street in Vancouver. Juliet and Gary had just come out of a theater where they had seen an early-evening movie, and they were talking about where to go for dinner. It was a warm night in summer, the light still not gone from the sky.

A woman detached herself from a group on the sidewalk. She came straight at Juliet. A thin woman, perhaps in her late thirties. Fashionable, with taffy streaks in her dark hair.

"Mrs. Porteous. Mrs. Porteous."

Juliet knew the voice, though she would never have known the face. Heather.

"This is incredible," Heather said. "I'm here for three days and I'm leaving tomorrow. My husband's at a conference. I was thinking that I don't know anybody here anymore and then I turn around and see you."

Juliet asked her where she was living now and she said Connecticut.

"And just about three weeks ago I was visiting Josh—you remember my brother Josh?—I was visiting my brother Josh and his family in Edmonton and I ran into Penelope. Just like this, on the street. No—actually it was in the mall, that humongous mall they have. She had a couple of her kids with her, she'd brought them down to get uniforms for that school they go to. The boys. We were both flabbergasted. I didn't know her right away but she recognized me. She'd flown down, of course. From that place way up north. But she says it's quite civilized, really. And she said you were still living here. But I'm with these people—they're my husband's friends—and I really haven't had time to ring you up—"

Juliet made some gesture to say that of course there would not be time and she had not expected to be rung up.

She asked how many children Heather had.

"Three. They're all monsters. I hope they grow up in a hurry. But my life's a picnic compared with Penelope's. *Five.*"

"Yes."

"I have to run now, we're going to see a movie. I don't even know anything about it, I don't even like French movies. But it was altogether great meeting you like this. My mother and dad moved to White Rock. They used to see you all the time on TV. They used to brag to their friends that you'd lived in our house. They say you're not on anymore, did you get sick of it?"

"Something like that."

"I'm coming, I'm coming." She hugged and kissed Juliet, the way everybody did now, and ran to join her companions.

So. Penelope did not live in Edmonton—she had *come down* to Edmonton. Flown down. That meant she must live in Whitehorse or in Yellowknife. Where else was there that she could describe as *quite civilized*? Maybe she was being ironical, mocking Heather a bit, when she said that.

She had five children and two at least were boys. They were being outfitted with school uniforms. That meant a private school. That meant money.

Heather had not known her at first. Did that mean she had aged? That she was out of shape after five pregnancies, that she had not *taken care of herself*? As Heather had. As Juliet had, to a certain extent. That she was one of those women to whom the whole idea of such a struggle seemed ridiculous, a confession of insecurity? Or just something she had no time for—far outside of her consideration.

Juliet had thought of Penelope being involved with transcendentalists, of her having become a mystic, spending her life in contemplation. Or else—rather the opposite but still radically simple and spartan—earning her living in a rough and risky way, fishing, perhaps with a husband, perhaps also with some husky little children, in the cold waters of the Inside Passage off the British Columbia coast.

Not at all. She was living the life of a prosperous, practical matron. Married to a doctor, maybe, or to one of those civil servants managing the northern parts of the country during the time when their control is being gradually, cautiously, but with some fanfare, relinquished to the native people. If she ever met Penelope again they might laugh about how wrong Juliet had been. When they told about their separate meetings with Heather, how weird that was, they would laugh.

No. No. The fact was surely that she had already laughed too much around Penelope. Too many things had been jokes. Just as too many things—personal things, loves that were maybe just gratification—had been tragedies. She had been lacking in motherly inhibitions and propriety and self-control.

Penelope had said that she, Juliet, was still living in Vancouver. She had not told Heather anything about the breach. Surely not. If she had been told, Heather would not have spoken so easily.

How did Penelope know that she was still here, unless she checked in the phone directory? And if she did, what did that mean?

Nothing. Don't make it mean anything.

She walked to the curb to join Gary, who had tactfully moved away from the scene of the reunion.

Whitehorse, Yellowknife. It was painful indeed to know the names of those places—places she could fly to. Places where she could loiter in the streets, devise plans for catching glimpses.

But she was not so mad. She must not be so mad.

At dinner, she thought that the news she had just absorbed put her into a better situation for marrying Gary, or living with him—whatever it was he wanted. There was nothing to worry about, or hold herself in wait for, concerning Penelope. Penelope was not a phantom, she was safe, as far as anybody is safe, and she was probably as happy as anybody is happy. She had detached herself from Juliet and very likely from the memory of Juliet, and Juliet could not do better than to detach herself in turn.

But she had told Heather that Juliet was living in Vancouver. Did she say *Juliet*? Or *Mother. My mother.*

Juliet told Gary that Heather was the child of old friends. She had never spoken to him about Penelope, and he had never given any sign of knowing about Penelope's existence. It was possible that Christa had told him, and he had remained silent out of a consideration that it was none of his business. Or that Christa had told him, and he had forgotten. Or that Christa had never mentioned anything about Penelope, not even her name.

If Juliet lived with him the fact of Penelope would never surface, Penelope would not exist.

Nor did Penelope exist. The Penelope Juliet sought was gone. The woman Heather had spotted in Edmonton, the mother who had brought her sons to Edmonton to get their school uniforms, who had changed in face and body so that Heather did not recognize her, was nobody Juliet knew.

Does Juliet believe this?

If Gary saw that she was agitated he pretended not to notice. But it was probably on this evening that they both understood they would never be together. If it had been possible for them to be together she might have said to him, *My daughter went away without telling me good-bye and in fact she probably did not know then that she was going. She did not know it was for good. Then gradually, I believe, it dawned on her how much she wanted to stay away. It is just a way that she has found to manage her life.*

"It's maybe the explaining to me that she can't face. Or has not

time for, really. You know, we always have the idea that there is this reason or that reason and we keep trying to find out reasons. And I could tell you plenty about what I've done wrong. But I think the reason may be something not so easily dug out. Something like purity in her nature. Yes. Some fineness and strictness and purity, some rock-hard honesty in her. My father used to say of someone he disliked, that he had no use for that person. Couldn't those words mean simply what they say? Penelope does not have a use for me.

Maybe she can't stand me. It's possible.

Juliet has friends. Not so many now—but friends. Larry continues to visit, and to make jokes. She keeps on with her studies. The word *studies* does not seem to describe very well what she does—*investigations* would be better.

And being short of money, she works some hours a week at the coffee place where she used to spend so much time at the sidewalk tables. She finds this work a good balance for her involvement with the old Greeks—so much so that she believes she wouldn't quit even if she could afford to.

She keeps on hoping for a word from Penelope, but not in any strenuous way. She hopes as people who know better hope for undeserved blessings, spontaneous remissions, things of that sort.

PASSION

Not too long ago, Grace went looking for the Traverses' summer house in the Ottawa Valley. She had not been in that part of the country for many years, and of course there had been changes. Highway 7 now avoided towns that it used to go right through, and it went straight in places where, as she remembered, there used to be curves. And this part of the Canadian Shield has many small lakes, which the usual sort of map has no room to identify. Even when she had located Little Sabot Lake, or thought she had, there seemed to be too many roads leading into it from the county road, and then, when she had chosen one of those roads, too many paved roads crossing it, all with names that she did not recall. In fact there had not been any street names when she had been here over forty years ago. And there was no pavement. There was just the one dirt road running towards the lake, then the one dirt road running rather haphazardly along the lake's edge.

Now there was a village. Or a suburb, perhaps you could call it, because she did not see any Post Office or even the most unpromising convenience store. The settlement lay four or five streets deep along the lake, with small houses strung close together on small lots. Some of them were undoubtedly summer places—the windows already boarded up, as was always done for the winter season. But many others showed all the signs of year-round habitation—habitation, in many cases, by people who filled the yards with plastic gym sets and outdoor grills and training bikes and motorcycles and picnic tables, where some of them sat having lunch or beer on this September day which was still warm. And by other people, not so visible—they were students maybe, or old hippies living alone—who put up flags or sheets of tinfoil for curtains. Small, mostly decent, cheap houses, some fixed to withstand the winter, and some not.

Grace would have decided to turn back if she had not seen the octagonal house, with the fretwork along the roof, and the doors in every other wall. The Woodses' house. She had always remembered it as having eight doors, but it seemed there were only four. She had never been inside to see how, or if, the space was divided into rooms. She didn't think any of the Travers family had ever been inside, either. The house was surrounded by great hedges, in the old days, and by the sparkling poplar trees that were always rustled by a wind along the shore. Mr. and Mrs. Woods were old—as Grace was now—and had not seemed to be visited by any friends or children. Their quaint original house had now a forlorn, a mistaken, look. Neighbors with their ghetto blasters and their sometimes dismembered vehicles, their toys and washing, were bunched up against either side of it.

It was the same with the Travers house when she found it, a

quarter of a mile or so along this road. The road went past it now, instead of ending there, and the houses on either side were only a few feet away from the wraparound deep verandah.

It had been the first house that Grace had ever seen built in this way—one story high, the main roof continuing without a break out over that verandah, on all sides. Later she had seen many like it, in Australia. A style that made you think of hot summers.

You used to be able to run from the verandah across the dusty end of the driveway, across a sandy trampled patch of weeds and wild strawberries, also the Traverses' property, and then jump—no, actually, wade—into the lake. Now you would hardly be able to see the lake, because of the substantial house—one of the few regular suburban houses here, with a two-car garage—that had been built across that very route.

What was Grace really looking for when she had undertaken this expedition? Maybe the worst thing would have been to get just what she might have thought she was after. Sheltering roof, screened windows, the lake in front, the stand of maple and cedar and balm of Gilead trees behind. Perfect preservation, the past intact, when nothing of the kind could be said of herself. To find something so diminished, still existing but made irrelevant—as the Travers house now seemed to be, with its added dormer windows, its startling blue paint—might be less hurtful in the long run.

And what if you find it gone altogether? You make a fuss. If anybody has come along to listen to you, you bewail the loss. But mightn't a feeling of relief pass over you, of old confusions or obligations wiped away?

Mr. Travers had built the house—that is, he had it built, as a surprise wedding present for Mrs. Travers. When Grace first saw it, it would have been perhaps thirty years old. Mrs. Travers' children were widely spaced—Gretchen around twenty-eight or twenty-nine, already married and a mother herself, and Maury twenty-one, going into his last year at college. And then there was Neil, in his midthirties. But Neil was not a Travers. He was Neil Borrow. Mrs. Travers had been married before, to a man who had died. She had earned her living, and supported her child, as a teacher of Business English at a secretarial school. Mr. Travers, when he referred to this time in her life before he met her, spoke of it as a time of hardship almost like penal servitude, something hardly to be made up for by a whole lifetime of comfort, which he would happily provide.

Mrs. Travers herself didn't speak of it this way at all. She had lived with Neil in a big old house broken up into apartments, not far from the railway tracks in the town of Pembroke, and many of the stories she told at the dinner table were about events there, about her fellow tenants, and the French-Canadian landlord, whose harsh French and tangled English she imitated. The stories might have had titles, like the stories of Thurber's that Grace had read in *The Anthology of American Humor,* found unaccountably on the library shelf at the back of her Grade Ten classroom. (Also on that shelf was *The Last of the Barons,* and *Two Years Before the Mast.*)

"The Night Old Mrs. Cromarty Got Out on the Roof." "How the Postman Courted Miss Flowers." "The Dog Who Ate Sardines."

Mr. Travers never told stories and had little to say at dinner, but if he came upon you looking, say, at the fieldstone fireplace, he might say, "Are you interested in rocks?" and tell you where each of them had come from, and how he had searched and searched for the particular pink granite, because Mrs. Travers had once exclaimed over a rock like that, glimpsed in a road cut. Or he might show you such not really unusual features as he himself had added to the house design—the corner cupboard shelves swinging outwards in the kitchen, the storage space under the window seats. He was a tall stooped man with a soft voice and thin hair slicked over his scalp. He wore bathing shoes when he went into the water, and though he did not look fat in his usual clothes, he displayed then a pancake fold of white flesh slopping over the top of his bathing trunks.

Grace worked that summer at the hotel at Bailey's Falls, north of Little Sabot Lake. Early in the season the Travers family had come to dinner there. She had not noticed them—they were not at one of her tables and it was a busy night. She was setting up a table for a new party when she realized that someone was waiting to speak to her.

It was Maury. He said, "I was wondering if you would like to go out with me sometime?"

Grace barely looked up from shooting out the silverware. She said, "Is this a dare?" Because his voice was high and nervous and he stood there stiffly, as if forcing himself. And it was known that sometimes a party of young men from the cottages would dare one another to ask a waitress out. It wasn't entirely a joke—they really would show up, if accepted, though sometimes they only meant to park, without taking you to a movie or even for coffee. So it was considered rather shameful, rather hard up, for a girl to agree.

"What?" he said painfully, and then Grace did stop and look at him. It seemed to her that she saw the whole of him in that moment, the true Maury. Scared, fierce, innocent, determined.

"Okay," she said quickly. She might have meant, okay, calm down, I know it's not a dare, I know you wouldn't do that. Or, okay, I'll go out with you. She herself hardly knew which. But he took it as agreement, and at once arranged—without lowering his voice, or noticing the looks he was getting from diners around them—that he would pick her up after work on the following night.

He did take her to the movies. They saw *Father of the Bride*. Grace hated it. She hated girls like Elizabeth Taylor in that movie, she hated spoiled rich girls of whom nothing was ever asked but that they wheedle and demand. Maury said that it was only supposed to be a comedy, but she said that was not the point. She could not make clear what the point was. Anybody would think that it was because she worked as a waitress and was too poor to go to college, and that if she wanted anything like that kind of wedding she would have to spend years saving up to pay for it herself. (Maury did think this, and was stricken with respect for her, almost with reverence.)

She could not explain or quite understand that it wasn't altogether jealousy she felt, it was rage. And not because she couldn't shop like that or dress like that. It was because that was what girls were supposed to be like. That was what men—people, everybody—thought they should be like. Beautiful, treasured, spoiled, selfish, pea-brained. That was what a girl should be, to be fallen in love with. Then she would become a mother and she'd be all mushily devoted to her babies. Not selfish anymore, but just as pea-brained. Forever.

She was fuming about this while sitting beside a boy who had fallen in love with her because he had believed—instantly—in the integrity and uniqueness of her mind and soul, and had seen her poverty as a romantic gloss on that. (He would have known she was poor not just because of the job she was working at but because of her strong Ottawa Valley accent, of which she was as yet unaware.)

He honored her feelings about the movie. Indeed, now that he had listened to her angry struggles to explain, he struggled to tell her something in turn. He said that he saw now that it was not anything so simple, so *feminine*, as jealousy. He saw that. It was that she would not stand for frivolity, was not content to be like most girls. She was special.

Grace always remembered what she was wearing on that night. A dark-blue ballerina skirt, a white blouse, through whose eyelet frills you could see the tops of her breasts, a wide rose-colored elasticized belt. There was a discrepancy, no doubt, between the way she presented herself and the way she wanted to be judged. But nothing about her was dainty or pert or polished in the style of the time. A bit ragged round the edges, in fact, giving herself gypsy airs, with the very cheapest silver-painted bangles, and the long, wild-looking curly dark hair that she had to put into a snood when she waited on tables.

Special.

He had told his mother about her and his mother had said, "You must bring this Grace of yours to dinner."

It was all new to her, all immediately delightful. In fact she fell in love with Mrs. Travers, rather as Maury had fallen in love with her. It was not in her nature, of course, to be so openly dumbfounded, so worshipful, as he was.

Grace had been brought up by her aunt and uncle, really her great-aunt and great-uncle. Her mother had died when she was three years old, and her father had moved to Saskatchewan, where he had another family. Her stand-in parents were kind, even proud of her, though bewildered, but they were not given to conversation. The uncle made his living caning chairs, and he had taught Grace how to cane, so that she could help him, and eventually take over as his eyesight failed. But then she had got the job at Bailey's Falls for the summer, and though it was hard for him—for her aunt as well—to let her go, they believed she needed a taste of life before she settled down.

She was twenty years old, and had just finished high school. She should have finished a year ago, but she had made an odd choice. In the very small town where she lived—it was not far from Mrs. Travers' Pembroke—there was nevertheless a high school, which offered five grades, to prepare you for the government exams and what was then called senior matriculation. It was never necessary to study all the subjects offered, and at the end of her first year—what should have been her final year, Grade Thirteen—Grace tried examinations in History and Botany and Zoology and English and Latin and French, receiving unnecessarily high marks. But there she was in September, back again, proposing to study Physics and Chemistry, Trigonometry, Geometry, and Algebra, though these subjects were considered particularly hard for girls. When she had finished that year, she would have covered all Grade Thirteen subjects except Greek and Italian and Spanish and German, which were not taught by any teacher in her school. She did creditably well in all three branches of mathematics and in the sciences, though her results were nothing like so spectacular as the year before. She had even thought, then, of teaching herself Greek and Spanish and Italian and German so that she could try those exams the next year. But the principal of the school had a talk with her, telling her this was getting her nowhere since she was not going to be able to go to college, and anyway no college course required such a full plate. Why was she doing it? Did she have any plans?

No, said Grace, she just wanted to learn everything you could learn for free. Before she started her career of caning.

It was the principal who knew the manager of the inn, and said he would put in a word for her if she wanted to try for a summer waitressing job. He too mentioned getting a taste of life.

So even the man in charge of all learning in that place did not believe that learning had to do with life. And anybody Grace told about what she had done—she told it to explain why she was late leaving high school—had said something like *you must have been crazy.*

Except for Mrs. Travers, who had been sent to business college instead of a real college because she was told she had to be useful, and who now wished like anything—she said—that she had crammed her mind instead, or first, with what was useless.

"Though you do have to earn a living," she said. "Caning chairs seems like a useful sort of thing to do anyway. We'll have to see."

See what? Grace didn't want to think ahead at all. She wanted life to continue just as it was now. By trading shifts with another girl, she had managed to get Sundays off, from breakfast on. This meant that she always worked late on Saturdays. In effect, it meant that she had traded time with Maury for time with Maury's family. She and Maury could never see a movie now, never have a real date. But he would pick her up when her work was finished, around eleven o'clock, and they would go for a drive, stop for ice cream or a hamburger—Maury was scrupulous about not taking her into a bar, because she was not yet twenty-one—then end up parking somewhere.

Grace's memories of these parking sessions—which might last till one or two in the morning—proved to be much hazier than her memories of sitting at the Traverses' round dining table or—when everybody finally got up and moved, with coffee or fresh drinks—sitting on the tawny leather sofa, the rockers, the cushioned wicker chairs, at the other end of the room. (There was no fuss about doing the dishes and cleaning up the kitchen—a woman Mrs. Travers called "my friend the able Mrs. Abel" would come in the morning.)

Maury always dragged cushions onto the rug and sat there. Gretchen, who never dressed for dinner in anything but jeans or army pants, usually sat cross-legged in a wide chair. Both she and Maury were big and broad-shouldered, with something of their mother's good looks—her wavy caramel-colored hair, and warm hazel eyes. Even, in Maury's case, a dimple. *Cute,* the other waitresses called Maury. They whistled softly. *Hubba hubba.* Mrs. Travers, however, was barely five feet tall, and under her bright muumuus she seemed not fat but sturdily plump, like a child who hasn't stretched up yet. And the shine, the intentness, of her eyes, the gaiety always ready to break out, had not or could not be imitated or inherited. No more than the rough red, almost a rash, on her cheeks. That was probably the result of going out in any weather without taking thought of her complexion, and like her figure, like her muumuus, it showed her independence.

There were sometimes guests, besides family, on these Sunday evenings. A couple, maybe a single person as well, usually close to Mr. and Mrs. Travers' age, and usually resembling them in the way the women would be eager and witty and the men quieter, slower, tolerant. People told amusing stories, in which the joke was often on themselves. (Grace has been an engaging talker for so long now that she sometimes gets sick of herself, and it's hard for her to remember how novel these dinner conversations once seemed to her. Where she came from, most of the lively conversation took the form of dirty jokes, which of course her aunt and uncle did not go in for. On the rare occasions when they had company, there was praise of and apology for the food, discussion of the weather, and a fervent wish for the meal to be finished as soon as possible.)

After dinner at the Traverses', if the evening was cool

enough, Mr. Travers lit a fire. They played what Mrs. Travers called "idiotic word games," at which, in fact, people had to be fairly clever, even if they thought up silly definitions. And here was where somebody who had been rather quiet at dinner might begin to shine. Mock arguments could be built up around claims of great absurdity. Gretchen's husband Wat did this, and so after a bit did Grace, to Mrs. Travers' and Maury's delight (Maury calling out, to everyone's amusement but Grace's own, "See? I told you. She's smart"). And it was Mrs. Travers herself who led the way in this making up of words with outrageous defenses, insuring that the play should not become too serious or any player too anxious.

The only time there was a problem of anyone's being unhappy with a game was when Mavis, who was married to Mrs. Travers' son Neil, came to dinner. Mavis and her two children were staying not far away, at her parents' place down the lake. That night there was only family, and Grace, as Mavis and Neil had been expected to bring their small children. But Mavis came by herself—Neil was a doctor, and it turned out that he was busy in Ottawa that weekend. Mrs. Travers was disappointed but she rallied, calling out in cheerful dismay, "But the children aren't in Ottawa, surely?"

"Unfortunately not," said Mavis. "But they're not being particularly charming. I'm sure they'd shriek all through dinner. The baby's got prickly heat and God knows what's the matter with Mikey."

She was a slim suntanned woman in a purple dress, with a matching wide purple band holding back her dark hair. Handsome, but with little pouches of boredom or disapproval hiding the corners of her mouth. She left most of her dinner untouched on her plate, explaining that she had an allergy to curry.

"Oh, Mavis. What a shame," said Mrs. Travers. "Is this new?"

"Oh no. I've had it for ages but I used to be polite about it. Then I got sick of throwing up half the night."

"If you'd only told me— What can we get you?"

"Don't worry about it, I'm fine. I don't have any appetite anyway, what with the heat and the joys of motherhood."

She lit a cigarette.

Afterwards, in the game, she got into an argument with Wat over a definition he used, and when the dictionary proved it acceptable she said, "Oh, I'm sorry. I guess I'm just outclassed by you people." And when it came time for everybody to hand in their own word on a slip of paper for the next round, she smiled and shook her head.

"I don't have one."

"Oh, Mavis," said Mrs. Travers. And Mr. Travers said, "Come on, Mavis. Any old word will do."

"But I don't have any old word. I'm so sorry. I just feel stupid tonight. The rest of you just play around me."

Which they did, everybody pretending nothing was wrong, while Mavis smoked and continued to smile her determined sweetly hurt unhappy smile. In a little while she got up and said she was awfully tired, and she couldn't leave her children on their grandparents' hands any longer, she'd had a lovely and instructive visit, and she must now go home.

"I have to give you an Oxford dictionary next Christmas," she said to nobody in particular as she went out with a bitter tinkle of a laugh.

The Traverses' dictionary that Wat had used was an American one.

When she was gone none of them looked at each other. Mrs. Travers said, "Gretchen, do you have the strength to make us all a pot of coffee?" And Gretchen went off to the kitchen, muttering, "What fun. Jesus wept."

"Well. Her life is trying," said Mrs. Travers. "With the two little ones."

During the week Grace got a break, for one day, between clearing breakfast and setting up dinner, and when Mrs. Travers found out about this she started driving up to Bailey's Falls to bring her down to the lake for those free hours. Maury would be at work then—he was working for the summer with the road gang repairing Highway 7—and Wat would be in his office in Ottawa and Gretchen would be swimming with the children or rowing with them on the lake. Usually Mrs. Travers herself would announce that she had shopping to do, or preparations to make for supper, or letters to write, and she would leave Grace on her own in the big, cool, shaded living-dining room, with its permanently dented leather sofa and crowded bookshelves.

"Read anything that takes your fancy," Mrs. Travers said. "Or curl up and go to sleep if that's what you'd like. It's a hard job, you must be tired. I'll make sure you're back on time."

Grace never slept. She read. She barely moved, and below her shorts her bare legs became sweaty and stuck to the leather. Perhaps it was because of the intense pleasure of reading. Quite often she saw nothing of Mrs. Travers until it was time for her to be driven back to work.

Mrs. Travers would not start any sort of conversation until enough time had passed for Grace's thoughts to have got loose from whatever book she had been in. Then she might mention having read it herself, and say what she had thought of it—but always in a way that was both thoughtful and lighthearted. For instance she said, about *Anna Karenina,* "I don't know how many times I've read it, but I know that first I identified with Kitty, and then it was Anna—oh, it was awful, with Anna, and now, you know, the last time I found myself sympathizing all the time with Dolly. Dolly when she goes to the country, you know, with all those children, and she has to figure out how to do the washing, there's the problem about the washtubs—I suppose that's just how your sympathies change as you get older. Passion gets pushed behind the washtubs. Don't pay any attention to me, anyway. You don't, do you?"

"I don't know if I pay much attention to anybody." Grace was surprised at herself and wondered if she sounded conceited or juvenile. "But I like listening to you talk."

Mrs. Travers laughed. "I like listening to myself."

Somehow, around this time, Maury had begun to talk about their being married. This would not happen for quite a while—not until after he was qualified and working as an engineer—but he spoke of it as of something that she as well as he must be taking for granted. *When we are married*, he would say, and instead of questioning or contradicting him, Grace would listen curiously.

When they were married they would have a place on Little Sabot Lake. Not too close to his parents, not too far away. It would be just a summer place, of course. The rest of the time they would live wherever his work as an engineer should take them. That might be anywhere—Peru, Iraq, the Northwest Territories. Grace was delighted by the idea of such travels—rather more than she was delighted by the idea of what he spoke of, with a severe pride, as *our own home*. None of this seemed at all real to her, but then, the idea of helping her uncle, of taking on the life of a chair caner, in the town and the very house where she had grown up, had never seemed real either.

Maury kept asking her what she had told her aunt and uncle about him, when she was going to take him home to meet them.

Even his easy use of that word—*home*—seemed slightly off kilter to her, though surely it was one she herself had used. It seemed more fitting to say *my aunt and uncle's house.*

In fact she had said nothing in her brief weekly letters, except to mention that she was "going out with a boy who works around here for the summer." She might have given the impression that he worked at the hotel.

It wasn't as if she had never thought of getting married. That possibility—half a certainty—had been in her thoughts, along with the life of caning chairs. In spite of the fact that nobody had ever courted her, she had thought that it would happen, someday, and in exactly this way, with the man making up his mind immediately. He would see her—perhaps he would have brought a chair to be fixed—and seeing her, he would fall in love. He would be handsome, like Maury. Passionate, like Maury. Pleasurable physical intimacies would follow.

This was the thing that had not happened. In Maury's car, or out on the grass under the stars, she was willing. And Maury was ready, but not willing. He felt it his responsibility to protect her. And the ease with which she offered herself threw him off balance. He sensed, perhaps, that it was cold. A deliberate offering which he could not understand and which did not fit in at all with his notions of her. She herself did not understand how cold she was—she believed that her show of eagerness must be leading to the pleasures she knew about, in solitude and imagining, and she felt it was up to Maury to take over. Which he would not do.

These sieges left them both disturbed and slightly angry or ashamed, so that they could not stop kissing, clinging, using fond words, to make it up to each other as they said good night. It was a relief to Grace to be alone, to get into bed in the dormitory and blot the last couple of hours out of her mind. And she thought it must be a relief to Maury to be driving down the highway by himself, rearranging his impressions of his Grace so that he could stay wholeheartedly in love with her.

Most of the waitresses left after Labour Day to go back to school or college. But the hotel was staying open till Thanksgiving with a reduced staff—Grace among them. There was talk, this year, about opening again in early December for a winter season, or at least a Christmas season, but nobody amongst the kitchen or dining-room staff seemed to know if this would really happen. Grace wrote to her aunt and uncle as if the Christmas season was a certainty. In fact she did not mention any closing at all, unless possibly after New Year's. So they should not expect her.

Why did she do this? It was not as if she had any other plans. She had told Maury that she thought she should spend this one year helping her uncle, maybe trying to find somebody else to learn caning, while he, Maury, was taking his final year at college. She had even promised to have him visit at Christmas so that he could meet her family. And he had said that Christmas would be a good time to make their engagement formal. He was saving from his summer wages to buy her a diamond ring.

She too had been saving her wages. So she would be able to take the bus to Kingston, to visit him during his school term.

She spoke of this, promised it, so easily. But did she believe, or even wish, that it would happen?

"Maury is a sterling character," said Mrs. Travers. "Well, you can see that for yourself. He will be a dear uncomplicated man, like his father. Not like his brother. His brother Neil is very bright. I don't mean that Maury isn't, you certainly don't get to be an engineer without a brain or two in your head, but Neil is—he's deep." She laughed at herself. "*Deep unfathomable caves of ocean bear*—what am I talking about? A long time Neil and I didn't have anybody but each other. So I think he's special. I don't mean he can't be fun. But sometimes people who are the most fun can be melancholy, can't they? You wonder about them. But what's the use of worrying about your grown-up children? With Neil I worry a bit, with Maury only a tiny little bit. And Gretchen I don't worry about at all. Because women always have got something, haven't they, to keep them going? That men haven't got."

The house on the lake was never closed up till Thanksgiving. Gretchen and the children had to go back to Ottawa, of course, because of school. And Maury, whose job was finished, had to go to Kingston. Mr. Travers would come out only on weekends. But usually, Mrs. Travers had told Grace, she stayed on, sometimes with guests, sometimes by herself.

Then her plans were changed. She went back to Ottawa with Mr. Travers in September. This happened unexpectedly—the weekend dinner was cancelled.

Maury said that she got into trouble, now and then, with her nerves. "She has to have a rest," he said. "She has to go into the hospital for a couple of weeks or so and they get her stabilized. She always comes out fine."

Grace said that his mother was the last person she would have expected to have such troubles.

"What brings it on?"

"I don't think they know," Maury said.

But after a moment he said, "Well. It could be her husband. I mean, her first husband. Neil's father. What happened with him, et cetera."

What had happened was that Neil's father had killed himself.

"He was unstable, I guess.

"But it maybe isn't that," he continued. "It could be other

stuff. Problems women have around her age. It's okay though—they can get her straightened around easy now, with drugs. They've got terrific drugs. Not to worry about it."

By Thanksgiving, as Maury had predicted, Mrs. Travers was out of the hospital and feeling well. Thanksgiving dinner was taking place at the lake as usual. And it was being held on Sunday—that was also as usual, to allow for packing up and closing the house on Monday. And it was fortunate for Grace, because Sunday had remained her day off.

The whole family would be there. No guests—unless you counted Grace. Neil and Mavis and their children would be staying at Mavis' parents' place, and having dinner there on Monday, but they would be spending Sunday at the Traverses'.

By the time Maury brought Grace down to the lake on Sunday morning, the turkey was already in the oven. Because of the children, dinner would be early, around five o'clock. The pies were on the kitchen counter—pumpkin, apple, wild blueberry. Gretchen was in charge of the kitchen—as coordinated a cook as she was an athlete. Mrs. Travers sat at the kitchen table, drinking coffee and working at a jigsaw puzzle with Gretchen's younger daughter, Dana.

"Ah, Grace," she said, jumping up for an embrace—the first time she had ever done this—and with a clumsy motion of her hand scattering the jigsaw pieces.

Dana wailed, *"Grandma,"* and her older sister, Janey, who had been watching critically, scooped up the pieces.

"We can put them back together," she said. "Grandma didn't mean to."

"Where do you keep the cranberry sauce?" said Gretchen.

"In the cupboard," said Mrs. Travers, still squeezing Grace's arms and ignoring the destroyed puzzle.

"*Where* in the cupboard?"

"Oh. Cranberry sauce," Mrs. Travers said. "Well—I make it. First I put the cranberries in a little water. Then I keep it on low heat—no, I think I soak them first—"

"Well, I haven't got time for all that," Gretchen said. "You mean you don't have any canned?"

"I guess not. I must not have, because I make it."

"I'll have to send somebody to get some."

"Maybe you could ask Mrs. Woods?"

"No. I've hardly even spoken to her. I haven't got the nerve. Somebody'll have to go to the store."

"Dear—it's Thanksgiving," said Mrs. Travers gently. "Nowhere will be open."

"That place down the highway, it's always open." Gretchen raised her voice. "Where's Wat?"

"He's out in the rowboat," called Mavis from the back bedroom. She made it sound like a warning, because she was trying to get her baby to sleep. "He took Mikey out in the boat."

Mavis had driven over in her own car with Mikey and the baby. Neil was coming later—he had some phone calls to make. And Mr. Travers had gone golfing.

"It's just that I need somebody to go to the store," Gretchen said. She waited, but no offer came from the bedroom. She raised her eyebrows at Grace.

"You can't drive, can you?"

Grace said no.

Mrs. Travers looked around to see where her chair was, and sat down, with a grateful sigh.

"Well," said Gretchen. "Maury can drive. Where's Maury?"

Maury was in the front bedroom looking for his swimming trunks, though everybody had told him that the water would be too cold for swimming. He said the store would not be open.

"It will be," said Gretchen. "They sell gas. And if it isn't there's that one just coming into Perth, you know, with the ice-cream cones—"

Maury wanted Grace to come with him, but the two little girls, Janey and Dana, were pulling her to come with them to see the swing their grandfather had put up under the Norway maple at the side of the house.

Going down the steps, she felt the strap of one of her sandals break. She took both shoes off and walked without difficulty on the sandy soil, the flat-pressed plantain, and the many curled leaves that had already fallen.

First she pushed the children in the swing, then they pushed her. It was when she jumped off, barefoot, that one leg crumpled and she let out a yelp of pain, not knowing what had happened.

It was her foot, not her leg. The pain had shot up from the sole of her left foot, which had been cut by the sharp edge of a clamshell.

"Dana brought those shells," Janey said. "She was going to make a house for her snail."

"He got away," said Dana.

Gretchen and Mrs. Travers and even Mavis had come hurrying out of the house, thinking the cry came from one of the children.

"She's got a bloody foot," said Dana. "There's blood all over the ground."

Janey said, "She cut it on a shell. Dana left those shells here, she was going to build a house for Ivan. Ivan her snail."

Then there was a basin brought out, water to wash the cut, a towel, and everyone was asking how much it hurt.

"Not too bad," said Grace, limping to the steps, with both little girls competing to hold her up and generally getting in her way.

"Oh, that's nasty," Gretchen said. "But why weren't you wearing your shoes?"

"Broke her strap," said Dana and Janey together, as a wine-colored convertible, making very little sound, swerved neatly round in the parking space.

"Now, that is what I call opportune," said Mrs. Travers. "Here's the very man we need. The doctor."

This was Neil, the first time Grace had ever seen him. He was tall, spare, quick-moving.

"Your bag," cried Mrs. Travers gaily. "We've already got a case for you."

"Nice piece of junk you've got there," said Gretchen. "New?"

Neil said, "Piece of folly."

"Now the baby's wakened." Mavis gave a sigh of unspecific accusation and she went back into the house.

Janey said severely, "You can't do anything without that baby waking up."

"*You* better be quiet," said Gretchen.

"Don't tell me you haven't got it with you," said Mrs. Travers. But Neil swung a doctor's bag out of the backseat, and she said, "Oh, yes you have, that's good, you never know."

"You the patient?" Neil said to Dana. "What's the matter? Swallow a toad?"

"It's her," said Dana with dignity. "It's *Grace*."

"I see. She swallowed the toad."

"She *cut her foot*. It's bleeding and bleeding."

"On a clamshell," said Janey.

Now Neil said "Move over" to his nieces, and sat on the step below Grace, and carefully lifted the foot and said, "Give me that cloth or whatever," then carefully blotted away the blood to get a look at the cut. Now that he was so close to her, Grace noticed a smell she had learned to identify this summer working at the inn—the smell of liquor edged with mint.

"It sure is," he said. "It's bleeding and bleeding. That's a good thing, clean it out. Hurts?"

Grace said, "Some."

He looked searchingly, though briefly, into her face. Perhaps wondering if she had caught the smell, and what she thought about it.

"I bet. See that flap? We have to get under there and make sure it's clean, then I'll put a stitch or two in it. I've got some stuff I can rub on so that won't hurt as bad as you might think." He looked up at Gretchen. "Hey. Let's get the audience out of the way here."

He had not spoken a word, as yet, to his mother, who now repeated that it was such a good thing that he had come along just when he did.

"Boy Scout," he said. "Always at the ready."

His hands didn't feel drunk, and his eyes didn't look it. Neither did he look like the jolly uncle he had impersonated when he talked to the children, or the purveyor of reassuring patter he had chosen to be with Grace. He had a high pale forehead, a crest of tight curly gray-black hair, bright gray eyes, a wide thin-lipped mouth that seemed to curl in on some vigorous impatience, or appetite, or pain.

When the cut had been bandaged, out on the steps—Gretchen having gone back to the kitchen and made the children come with her, but Mrs. Travers remaining, watching intently, with her lips pressed together as if promising that she would not make any interruptions—Neil said that he thought it would be a good idea to run Grace into town, to the hospital.

"For an anti-tetanus shot."

"It doesn't feel too bad," said Grace.

Neil said, "That's not the point."

“I agree,” said Mrs. Travers. “Tetanus—that’s terrible.”

“We shouldn’t be long,” he said. “Here. Grace? Grace, I’ll get you to the car.” He held her under one arm. She had strapped on the one sandal, and managed to get her toes into the other so that she could drag it along. The bandage was very neat and tight.

“I’ll just run in,” he said, when she was sitting in the car. “Make my apologies.”

To Gretchen? To Mavis.

Mrs. Travers came down from the verandah, wearing the look of hazy enthusiasm that seemed natural to her, and indeed irrepressible, on this day. She put her hand on the car door.

“This is good,” she said. “This is very good. Grace, you are a godsend. You’ll try to keep him away from drinking today, won’t you? You’ll know how to do it.”

Grace heard these words, but gave them hardly any thought. She was too dismayed by the change in Mrs. Travers, by what looked like an increase in bulk, a stiffness in all her movements, a random and rather frantic air of benevolence, a weepy gladness leaking out of her eyes. And a faint crust showing at the corners of her mouth, like sugar.

The hospital was in Carleton Place, three miles away. There was a highway overpass above the railway tracks, and they took this at such speed that Grace had the impression that at its crest the car had lifted off the pavement, they were flying. There was hardly any traffic about, she was not frightened, and anyway there was nothing she could do.

Neil knew the nurse who was on duty in Emergency, and after he had filled out a form and let her take a passing look at Grace’s foot ("Nice job," she said without interest), he was able to go ahead and give the tetanus shot himself. ("It won't hurt now, but it could later.") Just as he finished, the nurse came back into the cubicle and said, "There's a guy in the waiting room to take her home."

She said to Grace, "He says he's your fiancé."

"Tell him she's not ready yet," Neil said. "No. Tell him we've already gone."

"I said you were in here."

"But when you came back," said Neil, "we were gone."

"He said you were his brother. Won't he see your car in the lot?"

"I parked out back. I parked in the doctors' lot."

"Pret-ty tric-ky," said the nurse, over her shoulder.

And Neil said to Grace, "You didn't want to go home yet, did you?"

"No," said Grace, as if she'd seen the word written in front of her, on the wall. As if she was having her eyes tested.

Once more she was helped to the car, sandal flopping from the toe strap, and settled on the creamy upholstery. They took a back street out of the lot, an unfamiliar way out of the town. She knew they wouldn't see Maury. She did not have to think of him. Still less of Mavis.

Describing this passage, this change in her life, later on, Grace might say—she did say—that it was as if a gate had clanged shut behind her. But at the time there was no clang—acquiescence simply rippled through her, the rights of those left behind were smoothly cancelled.

Her memory of this day remained clear and detailed, though there was a variation in the parts of it she dwelt on.

And even in some of those details she must have been wrong.

. . .

First they drove west on Highway 7. In Grace's recollection, there is not another car on the highway, and their speed approaches the flight on the highway overpass. This cannot have been true—there must have been people on the road, people on their way home that Sunday morning, on their way to spend Thanksgiving with their families. On their way to church or coming home from church. Neil must have slowed down when driving through villages or the edges of towns, and for the many curves on the old highway. She was not used to driving in a convertible with the top down, wind in her eyes, wind taking charge of her hair. That gave her the illusion of constant speed, perfect flight—not frantic but miraculous, serene.

And though Maury and Mavis and the rest of the family were wiped from her mind, some scrap of Mrs. Travers did remain, hovering, delivering in a whisper and with a strange, shamed giggle, her last message.

You'll know how to do it.

Grace and Neil did not talk, of course. As she remembers it, you would have had to scream to be heard. And what she remembers is, to tell the truth, hardly distinguishable from her idea, her fantasies at that time, of what sex should be like. The fortuitous meeting, the muted but powerful signals, the nearly silent flight in which she herself would figure more or less as a captive. An airy surrender, flesh nothing now but a stream of desire.

They stopped, finally, at Kaladar, and went into the hotel—the old hotel which is still there. Taking her hand, kneading his fingers between hers, slowing his pace to match her uneven steps. Neil led her into the bar. She recognized it as a bar, though she had never been in one before. (Bailey's Falls Inn did not yet have a license—drinking was done in people's rooms, or in a rather ramshackle so-called nightclub across the road.) This was just as she would have expected—an airless darkened big room, with the chairs and tables put back in a careless way after a hasty cleanup, a smell of Lysol not erasing the smell of beer, whisky, cigars, pipes, men.

There was nobody there—perhaps it wasn't open till afternoon. But might it not now be afternoon? Her idea of time seemed faulty.

Now a man came in from another room, and spoke to Neil. He said, "Hello there, Doc," and went behind the bar.

Grace believed that it would be like this—everywhere they went, there would be somebody Neil knew already.

"You know it's Sunday," the man said in a raised, stern, almost shouting voice, as if he wanted to be heard out in the parking lot. "I can't sell you anything in here on a Sunday. And I can't sell anything to her, ever. She shouldn't even be in here. You understand that?"

"Oh yes, sir. Yes indeed, sir," said Neil. "I heartily agree, sir."

While both men were talking, the man behind the bar had taken a bottle of whisky from a hidden shelf and poured some into a glass and shoved it to Neil across the counter.

"You thirsty?" he said to Grace. He was already opening a Coke. He gave it to her without a glass.

Neil put a bill on the counter and the man shoved it away.

"I told you," he said. "Can't sell."

"What about the Coke?" said Neil.

"Can't sell."

The man put the bottle away, Neil drank what was in the glass very quickly. "You're a good man," he said. "Spirit of the law."

"Take the Coke along with you. Sooner she's out of here the happier I'll be."

"You bet," Neil said. "She's a good girl. My sister-in-law. Future sister-in-law. So I understand."

"Is that the truth?"

They didn't go back to Highway 7. Instead they took the road north, which was not paved, but wide enough and decently graded. The drink seemed to have had the opposite effect to what drinks were supposed to have on Neil's driving. He had slowed down to the seemly, even cautious, rate this road required.

"You don't mind?" he said.

Grace said, "Mind what?"

"Being dragged into any old place."

"No."

"I need your company. How's your foot?"

"It's fine."

"It must hurt some."

"Not really. It's okay."

He picked up the hand that was not holding the Coke bottle, pressed the palm of it to his mouth, gave it a lick, and let it drop.

"Did you think I was abducting you for fell purposes?"

"No," lied Grace, thinking how like his mother that word was. *Fell.*

"There was a time when you would have been right," he said, just as if she had answered yes. "But not today. I don't think so. You're safe as a church today."

The changed tone of his voice, which had become intimate, frank, and quiet, and the memory of his lips pressed to, then his tongue flicked across, her skin, affected Grace to such an extent that she was hearing the words, but not the sense, of what he was telling her. She could feel a hundred, hundreds of flicks of his tongue, a dance of supplication, all over her skin. But she thought to say, "Churches aren't always safe."

"True. True."

"And I'm not your sister-in-law."

"Future. Didn't I say future?"

"I'm not that either."

"Oh. Well. I guess I'm not surprised. No. Not surprised."

Then his voice changed again, became businesslike.

"I'm looking for a turnoff up here, to the right. There's a road I ought to recognize. Do you know this country at all?"

"Not around here, no."

"Don't know Flower Station? Oompah, Poland? Snow Road?"

She had not heard of them.

"There's somebody I want to see."

A turn was made, to the right, with some dubious mutterings on his part. There were no signs. This road was narrower and rougher, with a one-lane plank-floored bridge. The trees of the hardwood forest laced their branches overhead. The leaves were late to turn this year because of the strangely warm weather, so these branches were still green, except for the odd one here and there that flashed out like a banner. There was a feeling of sanctuary. For miles Neil and Grace were quiet, and there was still no break in the trees, no end to the forest. But then Neil broke the peace.

He said, "Can you drive?" and when Grace said no, he said, "I think you should learn."

He meant, right then. He stopped the car, got out and came around to her side, and she had to move behind the wheel.

"No better place than this."

"What if something comes?"

"Nothing will. We can manage if it does. That's why I picked a straight stretch. And don't worry, you do all the work with your right foot."

They were at the beginning of a long tunnel under the trees, the ground splashed with sunlight. He did not bother explaining anything about how cars ran—he simply showed her where to put her foot, and made her practice shifting the gears, then said, "Now go, and do what I tell you."

The first leap of the car terrified her. She ground the gears, and she thought he would put an end to the lesson immediately, but he laughed. He said, "Whoa, easy. Easy. Keep going," and she did. He did not comment on her steering, or the way the steering made her forget about the accelerator, except to say, "Keep going, keep going, keep on the road, don't let the engine die."

"When can I stop?" she said.

"Not till I tell you how."

He made her keep driving until they came out of the tunnel, and then instructed her about the brake. As soon as she had stopped she opened the door so that they could trade sides, but he said, "No. This is just a breather. Soon you'll be getting to like it." And when they started again she began to see that he might be right. Her momentary surge of confidence almost took them into the ditch. Still, he laughed when he had to grab the wheel, and the lesson continued.

He did not let her stop until they had driven for what seemed miles, and even gone—slowly—around several curves. Then he said they had better switch, because he could not get a feeling of direction unless he was driving.

He asked how she felt now, and though she was shaking all over, she said, "Okay."

He rubbed her arm from shoulder to elbow and said, "What a liar." But he did not touch her, beyond that, did not let any part of her feel his mouth again.

He must have got the feeling of direction back some miles on when they came to a crossroads, for he turned left, and the trees thinned out and they climbed a rough road up a long hill, and after a few miles they came to a village, or at least a roadside collection of buildings. A church and a store, neither of them open to serve their original purposes, but probably lived in, to judge by vehicles around them and the sorry-looking curtains in the windows. A couple of houses in the same state and behind one of them a barn that had fallen in on itself, with old dark hay bulging out between its cracked beams like swollen innards.

Neil exclaimed in celebration at the sight of this place, but did not stop there.

"What a relief," he said. "What—a—relief. Now I know. Thank you."

"Me?"

"For letting me teach you to drive. It calmed me down."

"Calmed you down?" said Grace. "Really?"

"True as I live." Neil was smiling, but did not look at her. He was busy looking from side to side across the fields that lay along the road after it had passed through the village. He was talking as if to himself.

"This is it. Got to be it. Now we know."

And so on, till he turned onto a lane that didn't go straight but wound around through a field, avoiding rocks and patches of juniper. At the end of the lane was a house in no better shape than the houses in the village.

"Now, this place," he said, "this place I am not going to take you in. I won't be five minutes."

He was longer than that.

She sat in the car, in the house's shade. The door to the house was open, just the screen door closed. The screen had mended patches in it, newer wire woven in with the old. Nobody came to look at her, not even a dog. And now that the car had stopped, the day filled up with an unnatural silence. Unnatural because you would expect such a hot afternoon to be full of the buzzing and humming and chirping of insects in the grass, in the juniper bushes. Even if you couldn't see them anywhere, their noise would seem to rise out of everything growing on the earth, as far as the horizon. But it was too late in the year, maybe too late even to hear geese honking as they flew south. At any rate, she didn't hear any.

It seemed they were up on top of the world here, or on one of the tops. The field fell away on all sides, the trees around being only partly visible because they grew on lower ground.

Who did he know here, who lived in this house? A woman? It didn't seem possible that the sort of woman he would want could live in a place like this, but there was no end to the strangeness Grace could encounter today. No end to it.

Once this had been a brick house, but someone had begun to take the brick walls down. Plain wooden walls had been bared, underneath, and the bricks that had covered them were roughly piled in the yard, maybe waiting to be sold. The bricks left on this wall of the house formed a diagonal line, stairsteps, and Grace, with nothing to do, leaned back, pushed her seat back, in order to count them. She did this both foolishly and seriously, the way you could pull petals off a flower, but not with any words so blatant as *He loves me, he loves me not.*

Lucky. Not. Lucky. Not. That was all she dared.

She found that it was hard to keep track of bricks arranged in this zigzag fashion, especially since the line flattened out above the door.

She knew. What else could this be? A bootlegger's place. She thought of the bootlegger at home—a raddled, skinny old man, morose and suspicious. He sat on his front step with a shotgun on Halloween night. And he painted numbers on the sticks of firewood stacked by his door so he'd know if any were stolen. She thought of him—or this one—dozing in the heat in his dirty but tidy room (she knew it would be that way by the mended patches in the screen). Getting up from his creaky cot or couch, with the stained quilt on it that some woman relative of his, some woman now dead, had made long ago.

Not that she had ever been inside a bootlegger's house, but the partitions were thin, at home, between some threadbare ways of living that were respectable, and some that were not. She knew how things were.

How strange that she'd thought of marrying Maury. A kind of treachery it would be. A treachery to herself. But not a treachery to be riding with Neil, because he knew some of the same things she did. And she knew more and more, all the time, about him.

And now in the doorway it seemed that she could see her uncle, stooped and baffled, looking out at her, as if she had been away for years and years. As if she had promised to go home and then she had forgotten about it, and in all this time he should have died but he hadn't.

She struggled to speak to him, but he was lost. She was waking up, moving. She was in the car with Neil, on the road again. She had been asleep with her mouth open and she was thirsty. He turned to her for a moment, and she noticed, even with the wind that they made blowing round them, a fresh smell of whisky.

It was true.

"You awake? You were fast asleep when I came out of there," he said. "Sorry—I had to be sociable for a while. How's your bladder?"

That was a problem she had been thinking about, in fact, when they were stopped at the house. She had seen a toilet back there, beyond the house, but had felt shy about getting out and walking to it.

He said, "This looks like a possible place," and stopped the car. She got out and walked in amongst some blooming goldenrod and Queen Anne's lace and wild aster, to squat down. He stood in such flowers on the other side of the road, with his back to her. When she got back into the car she saw the bottle on the floor beside her feet. More than a third of its contents seemed already to be gone.

He saw her looking.

"Oh, don't worry," he said. "I just poured some in here." He held up a flask. "Easier when I'm driving."

On the floor there was also another Coca-Cola. He told her to look in the glove compartment and find the bottle opener.

"It's cold," she said in surprise.

"Icebox. They cut ice off the lakes in the winter and store it in sawdust. He keeps it under the house."

"I thought I saw my uncle in the doorway of that house," she said. "But I was dreaming."

"You could tell me about your uncle. Tell me about where you live. Your job. Anything. I just like to hear you talk."

There was a new strength in his voice, and a change in his face, but it wasn't any manic glow of drunkenness. It was just as if he'd been sick—not terribly sick, just down, under the weather—and was now wanting to assure you he was better. He capped the flask and laid it down and reached for her hand. He held it lightly, a comrade's clasp.

"He's quite old," said Grace. "He's really my great-uncle. He's a caner—that means he canes chairs. I can't explain that to you, but I could show you if we had a chair to cane—"

"I don't see one."

She laughed, and said, "It's boring, really."

"Tell me about what interests you, then. What interests you?"

She said, "You do."

"Oh. What interests you about me?" His hand slid away.

"What you're doing now," said Grace determinedly. "Why."

"You mean drinking? Why I'm drinking?" The cap came off the flask again. "Why don't you ask me?"

"Because I know what you'd say."

"What's that? What would I say?"

"You'd say, what else is there to do? Or something like that."

"That's true," he said. "That's about what I'd say. Well, then you'd try to tell me why I was wrong."

"No," said Grace. "No. I wouldn't."

When she'd said that, she felt cold. She had thought she was serious, but now she saw that she'd been trying to impress him with these answers, trying to show herself as worldly as he was, and in the middle of that she had come on this rock-bottom truth. This lack of hope—genuine, reasonable, and everlasting.

Neil said, "You wouldn't? No. You wouldn't. That's a relief. You are a relief, Grace."

In a while, he said, "You know—I'm sleepy. Soon as we find a good spot I'm going to pull over and go to sleep. Just for a little while. You don't mind that?"

"No. I think you should."

"You'll watch over me?"

"Yes."

"Good."

The spot he found was in a little town called Fortune. There was a park on the outskirts, beside a river, and a gravelled space for cars. He settled the seat back, and at once fell asleep. Evening had come on as it did now, around suppertime, proving that this wasn't a summer day after all. A short while ago people had been having a Thanksgiving picnic here—there was still some smoke rising from the outdoor fireplace, and a smell of hamburgers in the air. The smell did not make Grace hungry, exactly—it made her remember being hungry in other circumstances.

He went to sleep immediately, and she got out. Some dust had settled on her with all the stopping and starting of her driving lesson. She washed her arms and hands and her face as well as she could at an outdoor tap. Then, favoring her cut foot, she walked slowly to the edge of the river, saw how shallow it was, with reeds breaking the surface. A sign there warned that profanity, obscenity, or vulgar language was forbidden in this place and would be punished.

She tried the swings, which faced west. Pumping herself high, she looked into the clear sky—faint green, fading gold, a fierce pink rim at the horizon. Already the air was getting cold.

She'd thought it was touch. Mouths, tongues, skin, bodies, banging bone on bone. Inflammation. Passion. But that wasn't what had been meant for them at all. That was child's play, compared to how she knew him, how far she'd seen into him, now.

What she had seen was final. As if she was at the edge of a flat dark body of water that stretched on and on. Cold, level water. Looking out at such dark, cold, level water, and knowing it was all there was.

It wasn't the drinking that was responsible. The same thing was waiting, no matter what, and all the time. Drinking, needing to drink—that was just some sort of distraction, like everything else.

She went back to the car and tried to wake him up. He stirred but wouldn't waken. So she walked around again to keep warm, and to practice the easiest way with her foot—she understood now that she would be working again, serving breakfast, in the morning.

She tried once more, talking to him urgently. He answered with various promises and mutters, and once more he fell asleep. By the time it was really dark she had given up. Now with the cold of night settled in some other facts became clear to her. That they could not remain here, that they were still in the world after all. That she had to get back to Bailey's Falls.

With some difficulty she got him over into the passenger seat. If that did not wake him, it was clear nothing could. She took a while to figure out how the headlights went on, and then she began to move the car, jerkily, slowly, back onto the road.

She had no idea of directions, and there was not a soul on the street to ask. She just kept driving to the other side of the town, and there, most blessedly, there was a sign pointing the way to Bailey's Falls, among other places. Only nine miles.

She drove along the two-lane highway at never more than thirty miles an hour. There was little traffic. Once or twice a car passed her, honking, and the few she met honked also. In one case it was probably because she was going so slowly, and in the other, because she did not know how to dim the lights. Never mind. She couldn't stop to get her courage up again in the middle of the road. She could just keep going, as he had said. Keep going.

At first she did not recognize Bailey's Falls, coming upon it in this unfamiliar way. When she did, she became more frightened than she had been in all the nine miles. It was one thing to drive in unknown territory, another to turn in at the inn gates.

He was awake when she got stopped in the parking lot. He didn't show any surprise at where they were, or at what she had done. In fact, he told her, the honking had wakened him, miles back, but he had pretended to be still asleep, because the important thing was not to startle her. He hadn't been worried, though. He knew she would make it.

She asked if he was awake enough to drive now.

"Wide-awake. Bright as a dollar."

He told her to slip her foot out of its sandal, and he felt and pressed it here and there before saying, "Nice. No heat. No swelling. Your arm hurt? Maybe it won't." He walked her to the door, and thanked her for her company. She was still amazed to be safely back. She hardly realized it was time to say good-bye.

As a matter of fact she does not know to this day if those words were spoken, or if he only caught her, wound his arms around her, held her so tightly, with such continual, changing pressures that it seemed more than two arms were needed, that she was surrounded by him, his body strong and light, demanding and renouncing all at once, as if he was telling her she was wrong to give up on him, everything was possible, but then again that she was not wrong, he meant to stamp himself on her and go.

Early in the morning, the manager knocked on the dormitory door, calling for Grace.

"Somebody on the phone," he said. "Don't bother, they just wanted to know if you were here. I said I'd go and check. Okay now."

It would be Maury, she thought. One of them, anyway. But probably Maury. Now she'd have to deal with Maury.

When she went down to serve breakfast—wearing her canvas shoes—she heard about the accident. A car had gone into a bridge abutment halfway down the road to Little Sabot Lake. It had been rammed right in, it was totally smashed and burned up. There were no other cars involved, and apparently no passengers. The driver would have to be identified by dental records. Or probably had been, by this time.

"One hell of a way," the manager said. "Better to go and cut your throat."

"It could've been an accident," said the cook, who had an optimistic nature. "Could've just fell asleep."

"Yeah. Sure."

Her arm hurt now as if it had taken a wicked blow. She couldn't balance her tray but had to carry it in front of her, using both hands.

. . .

She did not have to deal with Maury face-to-face. He wrote her a letter.

Just say he made you do it. Just say you didn't want to go.

She wrote back five words. *I did want to go.* She was going to add *I'm sorry*, but stopped herself.

Mr. Travers came to the inn to see her. He was polite and businesslike, firm, cool, not unkind. She saw him now in circumstances that let him come into his own. A man who could take charge, who could tidy things up. He said that it was very sad, they were all very sad, but that alcoholism was a terrible thing. When Mrs. Travers was a little better he was going to take her on a trip, a vacation, somewhere warm.

Then he said that he had to be going, many things to do. As he shook her hand good-bye he put an envelope into it.

"We both hope you'll make good use of this," he said.

The cheque was for one thousand dollars. Immediately she thought of sending it back or tearing it up, and sometimes even now she thinks that would have been a grand thing to do. But in the end, of course, she was not able to do it. In those days, it was enough money to insure her a start in life.

TRESPASSES

They drove out of town around midnight—Harry and Delphine in the front seat and Eileen and Lauren in the back. The sky was clear and the snow had slid off the trees but had not melted underneath them or on the rocks that jutted out beside the road. Harry stopped the car by a bridge.

"This'll do."

"Somebody might see us stopped here," Eileen said. "They might stop to check out what we're up to."

He started to drive again. They turned onto the first little country road, where they all got out of the car and walked carefully down the bank, just a short way, among black lacy cedars. There was a slight crackle to the snow, though the ground underneath was soft and mucky. Lauren was still wearing her pajamas under her coat, but Eileen had made her put on her boots.

"Okay here?" Eileen said.

Harry said, "It's not very far off the road."

"It's far enough."

This was the year after Harry had quit his job on a newsmagazine because he was burned out. He had bought the weekly newspaper in this small town which he remembered from his childhood. His family used to have a summer place on one of the little lakes around here, and he remembered drinking his first beer in the hotel on the main street. He and Eileen and Lauren went there for dinner on their first Sunday night in town.

But the bar was closed. Harry and Eileen had to drink water.

"How come?" said Eileen.

Harry raised his eyebrows at the hotel owner, who was also their waiter.

"Sunday?" he said.

"No license." The owner had a thick—and, it seemed, disdainful—accent. He wore a shirt and tie, a cardigan, and trousers that looked as if they had grown together—all soft, rumpled, fuzzy, like an outer skin that was flaky and graying as his real skin must be underneath.

"Change from the old days," said Harry, and when the man did not reply he went on to order roast beef all round.

"Friendly," Eileen said.

"European," said Harry. "It's cultural. They don't feel obliged to smile all the time." He pointed out things in the dining room that were just the same—the high ceiling, the slowly rotating fan, even a murky oil painting showing a hunting dog with a rusty-feathered bird in its mouth.

In came some other diners. A family party. Little girls in patent shoes and scratchy frills, a toddling baby, a teenaged boy in a suit, half-dead with embarrassment, various parents and parents of parents—a skinny and distracted old man and an old woman flopped sideways in a wheelchair and wearing a corsage. Any one of the women in their flowery dresses would have made about four of Eileen.

"Wedding anniversary," Harry whispered.

On the way out he stopped to introduce himself and his family, to tell them that he was the new fellow at the paper, and to offer his congratulations. He hoped they wouldn't mind if he took down their names. Harry was a broad-faced, boyish-looking man with a tanned skin and shining light-brown hair. His glow of well-being and general appreciation spread around the table—though not perhaps to the teenaged boy or the old couple. He asked how long those two had been married and was told sixty-five years.

"Sixty-five years," cried Harry, reeling at the thought. He asked if he might kiss the bride and did, touching his lips to the long flap of her ear as she moved her head aside.

"Now you have to kiss the groom," he said to Eileen, who smiled tightly and pecked the old man on the top of his head.

Harry asked the recipe for a happy marriage.

"Momma can't talk," said one of the big women. "But let me ask Daddy." She shouted in her father's ear, "Your advice for a happy marriage?"

He wrinkled up his face roguishly.

"All-eeze keep a foot on er neck."

All the grown-ups laughed, and Harry said, "Okay. I'll just put in the paper that you always made sure to get your wife's agreement."

Outside, Eileen said, "How do they manage to get that fat? I don't understand it. You'd have to eat day and night to get that fat."

"Strange," said Harry.

"Those were canned green beans," she said. "In August. Isn't that when green beans are ripe? And out here in the middle of the country, where they are supposed to grow things?"

"Stranger than strange," he said happily.

Almost immediately changes came to the hotel. In the former dining room there was a false ceiling put in—paperboard squares supported by strips of metal. The big round tables were replaced by small square tables, and the heavy wooden chairs by light metal chairs with maroon plastic-covered seats. Because of the lowered ceiling, the windows had to be reduced to squat rectangles. A neon sign in one of them said WELCOME COFFEE SHOP.

The owner, whose name was Mr. Palagian, never smiled or said a word more than he could help to anybody, in spite of the sign.

Just the same, the coffee shop filled up with customers at noon, or in the later hours of the afternoon. The customers were high school students, mostly from Grade Nine to Grade Eleven. Also some of the older students from the grade school. The great attraction of the place was that anybody could smoke there. Not that you could buy cigarettes if you looked to be under sixteen. Mr. Palagian was strict about that. *Not you,* he would say, in his thick, dreary voice. *Not you.*

By this time he had hired a woman to work for him, and if somebody who was too young tried buying cigarettes from her she would laugh.

"Who are you kidding, baby face."

But someone who was sixteen or over could collect the money from those who were younger and buy a dozen packs.

Letter of the law, Harry said.

Harry stopped eating his lunch there—it was too noisy—but

he still came in for breakfast. He was hoping that one day Mr. Palagian would thaw out and tell the story of his life. Harry kept a file full of ideas for books and was always on the lookout for life stories. Someone like Mr. Palagian—or even that fat tough-talking waitress, he said—could be harboring a contemporary tragedy or adventure which would make a best seller.

The thing about life, Harry had told Lauren, was to live in the world with interest. To keep your eyes open and see the possibilities—see the humanity—in everybody you met. To be aware. If he had anything at all to teach her it was that. *Be aware.*

Lauren made her own breakfast, usually cereal with maple syrup instead of milk. Eileen took her coffee back to bed and drank it slowly. She didn't want to talk. She had to get herself in gear to face the day, working in the newspaper office. When she got herself sufficiently in gear—sometime after Lauren went off to school—she got out of bed and had a shower and got dressed in one of her casually provocative outfits. As the fall wore on this was usually a bulky sweater and a short leather skirt and brightly colored tights. Like Mr. Palagian, Eileen managed easily to look different from anybody else in that town, but unlike him she was beautiful, with her cropped black hair and her thin gold earrings like exclamation points, and her faintly mauve eyelids. Her manner in the newspaper office was crisp and her expression remote, but this was broken by strategic, vivid smiles.

They had rented a house at the edge of town. Just beyond their backyard began a vacationland wilderness of rocky knobs and granite slopes, cedar bogs, small lakes, and a transitional forest of poplars, soft maples, tamarack, and spruce. Harry loved it. He said that they might wake up one morning and look out at a moose in the backyard. Lauren came home after school when the sun was already getting low in the sky and the middling warmth of the autumn day was turning out to be a fraud. The house was chilly and smelled of last night's dinner, of stale coffee grounds and the garbage which it was her job to take out. Harry was making a compost heap—next year he meant to have a vegetable garden. Lauren carried the pail of peelings, apple cores, coffee grounds, leftovers, out to the edge of the woods, from which a moose or a bear might appear. The poplar leaves had turned yellow, the tamaracks held furry orange spikes up against the dark evergreens. She dumped the garbage, and shovelled dirt and grass cuttings over it, the way that Harry had shown her.

Her life was a lot different now from the way it had been just a few weeks ago, when she and Harry and Eileen were driving to one of the lakes to swim in the hot afternoons. Then later in the evenings, she and Harry had gone on adventure walks around the town, while Eileen sanded and painted and wallpapered the house, claiming she could do that faster and better on her own. All that she had wanted Harry to do then was to get all his boxes of papers and his filing cabinet and desk into a ratty little room in the basement, out of her way. Lauren had helped him.

One cardboard box she picked up was oddly light and it seemed to hold something soft, not like paper, more like cloth or yarn. Just as she said, "What's this?" Harry saw her holding it and he said, "Hey." Then he said, "Oh God."

He took the box out of her hands and put it into a drawer of the filing cabinet, which he banged shut. "Oh God," he said again.

He had hardly ever spoken to her in such a rough and exasperated way. He looked around as if there might have been somebody watching them and clapped his hands on his trousers.

"Sorry," he said. "I wasn't expecting you to pick that up." He put his elbows on the top of the filing cabinet and leaned his forehead on his hands.

"Now," he said. "Now, Lauren. I could make up some kind of a lie to tell you, but I am going to tell you the truth. Because I believe that children should be told the truth. At least by the time they're your age, they should be. But in this case it has got to be a secret. Okay?"

Lauren said, "Okay." Something made her wish, already, that he wouldn't do this.

"There's ashes in there," Harry said. His voice dropped in a peculiar way when he said *ashes*. "Not ordinary ashes. Cremated ashes of a baby. This baby died before you were born. Okay? Sit down."

She sat on a pile of hardcover notebooks that contained Harry's writing. He raised his head and looked at her.

"See—what I'm telling you is very upsetting to Eileen and that's why it has got to be a secret. That's why you never were told about it, because Eileen cannot stand to be reminded. So now you understand?"

She said what she had to say. Yes.

"Okay now—what happened was, we had this baby before we had you. A baby girl, and when the baby was just very tiny Eileen got pregnant. And this was a terrible shock to her because she was just finding out what a terrible lot of work a new baby is and here she was, not getting any sleep and throwing up because she had morning sickness. It wasn't just morning, it was morning noon and *night* sickness, and she just did not know how she could face it. Being pregnant. So one night when she was just beside herself she somehow got the idea that she had to get out. And she got in the car and the baby in with her in its cot and it was after dark, raining, and she was driving too fast and she missed a curve. So. The baby wasn't fixed in properly and it bounced out of the cot. And Eileen had broken ribs and concussion and it looked for a while as if we were going to lose both babies."

He took a deep breath.

"I mean, we had lost the one already. When it bounced out of its cot it was killed. But we didn't lose the one Eileen was carrying. Because. That was you. You understand? You."

Lauren nodded, minimally.

"So the reason we didn't tell you this—besides the state of Eileen's emotions—is that it might not make you feel very welcome. Not in the first circumstances. But you just have to believe me you were. Oh, Lauren. You were. You are."

He removed his arm from the filing cabinet and came and hugged her. He smelled of sweat and the wine he and Eileen had drunk at dinner and Lauren felt very uncomfortable and embarrassed. The story didn't upset her, although the ashes were a little ghoulish. But she took his word for it that it did upset Eileen.

"Is that what you have the fights about?" she said, in an offhand way, and he let her go.

"The fights," he said sadly. "I suppose there could be something about that underlying. Underlying her hysteria. You know I feel bad about all that stuff. I really do."

When they went out on their walks he occasionally asked her if she was worried, or sad, about what he had told her. She said, "No," in a firm, rather impatient, voice, and he said, "Good."

Every street had a curiosity—the Victorian mansion (now a nursing home), the brick tower that was all that was left of a broom factory, the graveyard going back to 1842. And for a couple of days there was a fall fair. They watched trucks ploughing one by one through the dirt, pulling a platform loaded with cement blocks which slipped forward, causing the trucks to fishtail, and halt and have their distance measured. Harry and Lauren each picked a truck to cheer for.

Now it seemed to Lauren that all of that time had a false glow to it, a reckless silly sort of enthusiasm, that did not take any account of the weight of dailiness, or reality, that she had to carry around once school began and the paper started coming out and the weather changed. A bear or a moose was a real wild animal brooding over its own necessities—it was not some kind of thrill. And she would not now jump up and down and scream as she had done at the fairgrounds, cheering for her truck. Somebody from school might see her and think she was a freak.

Which was close to what they thought anyway.

Her isolation at school was based on knowledge and experience, which, as she half knew, could look like innocence and priggishness. The things that were wicked mysteries to others were not so to her and she did not know how to pretend about them. And that was what separated her, just as much as knowing how to pronounce L'Anse aux Meadows and having read *The Lord of the Rings*. She had drunk half a bottle of beer when she was five and puffed on a joint when she was six, though she had not liked either one. She sometimes had a little wine at dinner, and she liked that all right. She knew about oral sex and all methods of birth control and what homosexuals did. She had regularly seen Harry and Eileen naked, also a party of their friends naked around a campfire in the woods. On that same holiday she had sneaked out with other children to watch fathers slipping by sly agreement into the tents of mothers who were not their wives. One of the boys had suggested sex to her and she had agreed, but he could not make any progress and they became cross with each other and later she hated the sight of him.

This was all a burden to her here—it gave her a sense of embarrassment and peculiar sadness, even of deprivation. And there wasn't much she could do except remember, at school, to call Harry and Eileen Dad and Mom. That seemed to make them larger, but not so sharp. Their tense outlines were slightly blurred when they were spoken of in this way, their personalities slightly glossed over. Face-to-face with them, she had no technique for making this happen. She couldn't even acknowledge that it might be a comfort.

Some girls in Lauren's class, finding the vicinity of the coffee shop irresistible but not being brave enough to go in, would enter the hotel lobby and make their way to the Ladies Room. There they would spend a quarter or a half hour fixing their own and each other's hair in different styles, putting on lipstick that they might have stolen from Stedmans, sniffing each other's necks and wrists, which they had sprayed with all the free trial perfumes in the drugstore.

When they asked Lauren to go with them she suspected some sort of trick, but agreed anyway, partly because she so disliked going home alone in the ever-shortening afternoons to the house on the edge of the forest.

As soon as they were inside the lobby a couple of these girls took hold of her and pushed her up to the desk, where the woman from the restaurant was seated on a high stool, working out some figures on a calculator.

This woman's name—Lauren already knew it from Harry—was Delphine. She had long fine hair that might be whitish blond or might be really white, because she was not young. She must often have to shake that hair back out of her face, as she did now. Her eyes, behind dark-rimmed glasses, were hooded by purple lids. Her face was broad, like her body, pale and smooth. But there was nothing indolent about her. Her eyes, now lifted, were a light flat blue, and she looked from one girl to another as if no contemptible behavior of theirs would surprise her.

"This is her," the girls said.

The woman—Delphine—now looked at Lauren. She said, "Lauren? You sure?"

Lauren, bewildered, said yes.

"Well, I asked them was there anybody at their school called Lauren," Delphine said—referring to the other girls as if they were already at a distance, shut out of her conversation with Lauren. "I asked them because of something that was found in here. Somebody must've dropped it in the coffee shop."

She opened a drawer and lifted out a gold chain. Dangling from the chain were the letters that spelled LAUREN.

Lauren shook her head.

"Not yours?" said Delphine. "Too bad. I already asked the kids in high school. So I guess I'll just have to keep it around. Somebody might come back looking for it."

Lauren said, "You could put an ad in my dad's paper." She did not realize that she should have said just "the paper" until the next day, when she passed a couple of girls in the school hallway and heard a mincing voice say *my dad's paper*.

"I could," said Delphine. "But then I might get all kinds of people coming in and saying it's theirs. Lying about what their name was, even. It's gold."

"But they couldn't wear it," Lauren pointed out, "if it wasn't their real name."

"Maybe not. But I wouldn't put it past them to claim it anyway."

The other girls had started for the Ladies.

"Hey you," Delphine called after them. "That's out of bounds."

They turned around, surprised.

"How come?"

"Because it's out of bounds, that's how come. You can go and fool around someplace else."

"You never stopped us going in there before."

"Before was before and now is now."

"It's supposed to be public."

"It is not," said Delphine. "The one in the town hall is public. So get lost."

"I wasn't referring to you," she said to Lauren, who was about to follow the others. "I'm sorry the chain wasn't yours. You check back in a day or two. If nobody shows up to ask about it, I'll figure, hey, it's got your name on it, after all."

Lauren came back the next day. She did not care about the chain at all, really—she could not imagine going around with your name hanging on your neck. She just wanted to have an errand to do, someplace to go. She could have gone to the newspaper office, but after hearing the way they said *my dad's paper*, she didn't want to do that.

She had decided not to go in if Mr. Palagian and not Delphine was behind the desk. But Delphine was right there, watering an ugly plant in the front window.

"Oh good," Delphine said. "Nobody's come and asked about it. Give it till the end of the week, I have a feeling it's going to be yours yet. You can always come in, this time of day. I don't work the coffee shop in the afternoons. If I'm not in the lobby you just ring the bell, I'll be around somewhere."

Lauren said, "Okay," and turned to go.

"You feel like sitting down a minute? I was thinking I'd get a cup of tea. Do you ever drink tea? Are you allowed to? Would you rather have a soft drink?"

"Lemon-lime," said Lauren. "Please."

"In a glass? Would you like a glass? Ice?"

"It's okay just the way it is," said Lauren. "Thank you."

Delphine brought a glass anyway, with ice. "It didn't seem quite cooled off enough to me," she said. She asked Lauren where she would rather sit—in one of the worn-down old leather chairs by the window or on a high stool behind the desk. Lauren picked the stool, and Delphine sat on the other stool.

"Now, you want to tell me what you learned in school today?"

Lauren said, "Well—"

Delphine's wide face broke into a smile.

"I just asked you that for a joke. I used to hate it, people asking me that. For one thing, I could never remember anything I learned that day. And for another thing, I could do without talking about school when I wasn't at it. So we skip that."

Lauren was not surprised by this woman's evident wish to be friends. She had been brought up to believe that children and adults could be on equal terms with each other, though she had noticed that many adults did not understand this and it was as well not to press the point. She saw that Delphine was a little nervous. That was why she kept talking without a break, and laughing at odd moments, and why she resorted to the maneuver of reaching into the drawer and pulling out a chocolate bar.

"Just a little treat with your drink. Got to make it worthwhile to come and see me again, eh?"

Lauren was embarrassed on the woman's behalf, though glad to accept the chocolate bar. She never got candy at home.

"You don't have to bribe me to come and see you," she said. "I'd like to."

"Oh-ho. So I don't, don't I? You're quite the kid. Okay, then give me that back."

She grabbed for the chocolate bar, and Lauren ducked to protect it. Now she laughed too.

"I meant next time. Next time you don't have to bribe me."

"One bribe is okay, though. That it?"

"I like to have something to do," Lauren said. "Not just go on home."

"Don't you go visit your friends?"

"I don't really have any. I only started this school in September."

"Well. If that bunch that was coming in here is any sample of what you've got to pick from, I'd say you're better off. How do you like this town?"

"It's small. Some things are nice."

"It's a dump. They're all dumps. I have experienced so many dumps in my time you'd think the rats would have ate off my nose by now." She tapped her fingers up and down her nose. Her nails matched her eyelids. "Still there," she said doubtfully.

It's a dump. Delphine said things like that. She spoke vehemently—she did not discuss but stated, and her judgments were severe and capricious. She spoke about herself—her tastes, her physical workings—as about a monumental mystery, something unique and final.

She had an allergy to beets. If even a drop of beet juice made its way down her throat, her tissues would swell up and she would have to go to the hospital, she would need an emergency operation so that she could breathe.

"How's it with you? You got any allergies? No? Good."

She believed a woman should keep her hands nice, no matter what kind of work she had to do. She liked to wear inky-blue or plum fingernail polish. And she liked to wear earrings, big and clattery ones, even at her work. She had no use for the little button kind.

She was not afraid of snakes, but she had a weird feeling about cats. She thought that a cat must have come and lain on top of her when she was a baby, being attracted to the smell of milk.

"So what about you?" she said to Lauren. "What are you scared of? What's your favorite color? Did you ever walk in your sleep? Do you get a tan or a sunburn? Does your hair grow fast or slow?"

It was not as if Lauren was unused to somebody being interested in her. Harry and Eileen were interested—particularly Harry—in her thoughts and opinions and what she felt about things. Sometimes this interest got on her nerves. But she had never realized that there could be all these other things, arbitrary facts, that could seem delightfully important. And she never got the feeling—as she did at home—that there was any other question behind Delphine's questions, never the feeling that if she didn't watch out she would be pried open.

Delphine taught her jokes. She said she knew hundreds of jokes, but she would only tell Lauren the ones that were fit. Harry would not have agreed that the jokes about people from Newfoundland (Newfies) were fit, but Lauren laughed obligingly.

She told Harry and Eileen that she was going to a friend's place, after school. That was not really a lie. They seemed pleased. But because of them she did not take the gold chain with her name when Delphine said she could. She pretended to be concerned that somebody it belonged to might still come looking for it.

Delphine knew Harry, she brought him his breakfast in the coffee shop, and she could have mentioned Lauren's visits to him, but apparently she didn't.

She sometimes put up a sign—*Ring Bell for Service*—and took Lauren with her into other parts of the hotel. Guests did stay there once in a while, and their beds had to be made up, their toilets and sinks scrubbed, their floors vacuumed. Lauren was not allowed to help. "Just sit there and talk to me," Delphine said. "It's lonesome kind of work."

But she was the one who talked. She talked about her life without getting it in any kind of order. Characters appeared and disappeared and Lauren was supposed to know who they were without asking. People called Mr. and Mrs. were good bosses. Other bosses were Old Sowbelly, Old Horse's Arse *(Don't repeat my language)*, and they were terrible. Delphine had worked in hospitals *(As a nurse? Are you kidding?)* and in tobacco fields and in okay restaurants and in dives and in a lumber camp where she cooked and in a bus depot where she cleaned and saw things too gross to talk about and in an all-night convenience store where she was held up and quit.

Sometimes she was palling around with Lorraine and sometimes Phyl. Phyl had a way of borrowing your things without asking—she borrowed Delphine's blouse and wore it to a dance and sweated so much she rotted out the underarms. Lorraine had graduated from high school but she made a big mistake when she married the lamebrain she did and now she was surely sorry.

Delphine could have got married. Some men she had gone out with had done well, some had turned into bums, some she had no idea what had happened to them. She was fond of a boy named Tommy Kilbride but he was a Catholic.

"You probably don't know what that means for a woman."

"It means you can't use birth control," Lauren said. "Eileen was a Catholic, but she quit because she didn't agree. Eileen my mom."

"Your mom wouldn't have to worry anyway, the way it turned out."

Lauren did not understand. Then she thought Delphine must

be talking about her—Lauren—being an only child. She must think that Harry and Eileen would have liked to have more children after they had her but that Eileen had not been able to have them. As far as Lauren knew, that wasn't the case.

She said, "They could've had more if they'd wanted. After they had me."

"That what you think, eh?" Delphine said jokingly. "Maybe they couldn't have any. Could have adopted you."

"No. They didn't. I know they didn't." Lauren was on the verge of telling about what happened when Eileen was pregnant, but she held back because Harry had made so much of its being a secret. She was superstitious about breaking a promise, though she had noticed that adults often didn't mind breaking theirs.

"Don't look so serious," Delphine said. She took Lauren's face in her hands and tapped her blackberry fingernails on her cheeks. "I'm only kidding."

The dryer in the hotel laundry was on the blink, Delphine had to hang up the wet sheets and towels, and because it was raining the best place to do that was in the old livery stable. Lauren helped carry the baskets piled with white linen across the little gravelled yard behind the hotel and into the empty stone barn. A cement floor had been put in there, but still a smell seeped through from the earth beneath, or maybe out of the stone-and-rubble walls. Damp dirt, horse hide, rich hints of piss and leather. The space was empty except for the clotheslines and a few broken chairs and bureaus. Their steps echoed.

"Try calling your name," said Delphine.

Lauren called, "Del-phee-een."

"*Your* name. What are you up to?"

"It's better for the echo," said Lauren, and called again, "Del-phee-een."

"I don't like my name," said Delphine. "Nobody likes their own name."

"I don't *not* like mine."

"Lauren's nice. It's a nice name. They picked a nice name for you."

Delphine had disappeared behind the sheet she was pinning to the clothesline. Lauren wandered around whistling.

"It's singing that really sounds good in here," Delphine said. "Sing your favorite song."

Lauren could not think of a song that was her favorite. That seemed to amaze Delphine, just as she had been amazed when she found out that Lauren did not know any jokes.

"I have loads," she said. And she began to sing.

"Moon River, wider than a mile—"

That was a song Harry sang sometimes, always making fun of the song, or himself. Delphine's way of singing it was quite different. Lauren felt the calm sorrow of Delphine's voice pulling her towards the wavering white sheets. The sheets themselves seemed as if they would dissolve around her—no, around her and Delphine—creating a feeling of acute sweetness. Delphine's singing was like an embrace, wide-open, that you could rush into. At the same time, its loose emotion gave Lauren a shiver in her stomach, a distant threat of being sick.

"Waiting round the bend
My huckleberry friend—"

Lauren interrupted by catching up a chair with the seat out and scraping its leg along the floor.

. . .

"Something I've been meaning to ask you," Lauren said resolutely to Harry and Eileen, at the dinner table. "Is there any sort of chance I could be adopted?"

"Where did you get that idea?" said Eileen.

Harry stopped eating, raised his eyebrows warningly at Lauren, then began to joke. "If we were going to adopt a kid," he said, "do you think we'd get one that asked so many nosey questions?"

Eileen stood up, fiddling with her skirt zipper. The skirt fell down, and then she rolled down her tights and underpants.

"Look here," she said. "That ought to tell you."

Her stomach, which looked flat when she was dressed, now showed a slight fullness and sag. Its surface, still lightly tanned down to the bikini mark, was streaked with some dead-white tracks that glistened in the kitchen light. Lauren had seen these before but had thought nothing of them—they had just seemed to be a part of Eileen's particular body, like the twin moles on her collarbone.

"That is from the skin stretching," Eileen said. "I carried you way out in front." She held her hand an impossible distance in front of her body. "So now are you convinced?"

Harry put his head against Eileen, nuzzled her bare stomach. Then he pulled back and spoke to Lauren.

"In case you're wondering why we didn't have any more, the answer is that you are the only kid we need. You're smart and good-looking and you have a sense of humor. How could we be sure we'd get another that good? Plus, we are not your average family. We like to move around. Try things, be flexible. We have got one kid who is perfect and adaptable. No need to push our luck."

His face, which Eileen could not see, was directing at Lauren a look far more serious than his words. A continued warning, mixed with disappointment and surprise.

If Eileen had not been there, Lauren would have questioned him. What if they had lost both babies, instead of just the one? What if she herself had never been inside Eileen and was not responsible for those tracks on her stomach? How could she be sure that they had not got her as a replacement? If there was one big thing she hadn't known about, why could there not be another?

This notion was unsettling, but it had a distant charm.

The next time Lauren came into the hotel lobby after school, she was coughing.

"Come on upstairs," Delphine said. "I got some good stuff for that."

Just as she was putting out the *Ring Bell for Service* sign Mr. Palagian entered the lobby from the coffee shop. On one foot he wore a shoe and on the other a slipper, slit open to accommodate a bandaged foot. Just about where his big toe must be there was a dried blood spot.

Lauren thought that Delphine would take the sign down when she saw Mr. Palagian, but she didn't. All she said to him was, "You better change that bandage when you get a chance."

Mr. Palagian nodded but did not look at her.

"I'll be down in a bit," she told him.

Her room was up on the third floor, under the eaves. Climbing and coughing, Lauren said, "What happened to his foot?"

"What foot?" said Delphine. "Could be somebody stepped on it, I guess. Maybe with the heel of their shoe, eh?"

The ceiling of her room sloped steeply on either side of a dormer window. There was a single bed, a sink, a chair, a bureau. On the chair a hot plate with a kettle on it. On the bureau a crowded array of makeup, combs and pills, a tin of tea bags and a tin of hot chocolate powder. The bedspread was of thin tan-and-white striped seersucker, like the ones on the guest beds.

"Not very fixed up, is it?" Delphine said. "I don't spend a lot of time here." She filled the kettle at the sink and plugged in the hot plate, then yanked off the bedspread to remove a blanket. "Get out of that jacket," she said. "Wrap yourself up warm in this." She touched the radiator. "It takes all day for any heat to get up here."

Lauren did as she was told. Two cups and two spoons were taken out of the top drawer, hot chocolate was measured from the tin. Delphine said, "I only make it with hot water. I guess you're used to milk. I don't take milk in tea or anything. I bring it up here, it just goes sour. I don't have any refrigerator."

"It's fine with water," said Lauren, though she had never drunk hot chocolate that way. She had a sudden wish to be at home, wrapped up on the sofa and watching TV.

"Well, don't just stand there," said Delphine, in a slightly irritated or nervous voice. "Sit down and get comfortable. The kettle won't take long."

Lauren sat on the edge of the bed. Suddenly Delphine turned around, grabbed her under the arms—causing her to start coughing again—and hauled her up so that she was sitting with her back against the wall and her feet sticking out over the floor. Her boots were pulled off, and Delphine quickly squeezed her feet, to see if her socks were wet.

No.

"Hey. I was going to get you something to fix that cough. Where's my cough syrup?"

From the same top drawer came a bottle half-full of amber liquid. Delphine poured out a spoonful. "Open up," she said. "Doesn't taste so dreadful."

Lauren, when she'd swallowed, said, "Is there whisky in it?"

Delphine peered at the bottle, which had no label.

"I don't see where it says so. Can you see? Are your mommy and daddy going to have a fit if I give you a spoon of whisky for your cough?"

"Sometimes my dad makes me a toddy."

"He does, does he?"

Now the kettle was boiling and the water was poured into the cups. Delphine stirred hurriedly, mashing the lumps, talking to them.

"Come on, you buggers. Come on, you." Pretending to be jolly.

There was something wrong with Delphine today. She seemed too flustered and excited, maybe angry underneath. Also, she was way too big, too flouncy and glossy, for this room.

"You look around this place," she said, "and I know what you're thinking. You're thinking, wow, she must be poor. Why doesn't she have more stuff? But I don't accumulate stuff. For the very good reason that I've had too many experiences of having to pick up and move on. Just get settled, you find something happens and you have to move on. I save, though. People would be surprised what I've got in the bank."

She gave Lauren her cup, and settled herself carefully at the head of the bed, the pillow at her back, her stockinged feet on the exposed sheet. Lauren had a particular feeling of disgust about feet in nylon stockings. Not about bare feet, or feet in socks, or feet in shoes, or feet in nylons covered up in shoes, just about feet in nylons out in the open, particularly touching any other cloth. This was just a private queer feeling—like the feeling she had about mushrooms, or cereal slopping around in milk.

"Just when you came in this afternoon I was feeling sad," Delphine said. "I was thinking about a girl I used to know and thinking I should write her a letter if I knew where she was.

Joyce was her name. I was thinking about what happened to her in her life."

The weight of Delphine's body made the mattress sag so that Lauren had trouble not sliding towards her. The effort that she was making not to bump against that body embarrassed her, and made her try to be particularly polite.

"When did you know her?" she said. "When you were young?"

Delphine laughed. "Yeah. When I was young. She was young too and she had to get out of her house and she was hanging around with this guy and she got caught. You know what I mean by that?"

Lauren said, "Pregnant."

"Right. So she was just drifting along, she thought it might go 'way, maybe. Ha-ha. Like the flu. The guy she was with already had two kids with another woman he wasn't married to but that was more or less his wife, and he was always thinking about going back to her. But before he got around to that he got busted. And also she did—Joyce did—because she was carrying stuff around for him. She had it packed into Tampax tubes, you know what they look like? You know what stuff I mean?"

"Yes," said Lauren to both questions. "Sure. Dope."

Delphine made a gurgling sound, swallowing her drink. "This is all top secret, you understand that?"

Not all the lumps of hot chocolate powder had got mashed up and dissolved, and Lauren did not want to mash them with the spoon that would still have the taste of the so-called cough syrup on it.

"She got off with a suspended sentence, so it wasn't all a bad thing she was pregnant, that was what got her off. And what happened next, she got in with these Christians and they knew a doctor and wife that looked after girls when they had their babies and got the babies adopted right away. It was not quite on the up-and-up, they were getting money for these babies, but anyway it kept her clear of the social workers. So, she had her baby and never even saw it. All she knew was that it was a girl."

Lauren looked around for a clock. There didn't seem to be one. Delphine's watch was up under the sleeve of her black sweater.

"So she got out of there and one thing and another happened to her and she didn't give the baby a thought. She thought she'd get married and have some more kids. So, well, that didn't happen. Not that she minded so much, given some of the people it didn't happen with. She even had a couple of operations so it wouldn't. You know what kind of operations?"

"Abortions," Lauren said. "What time is it?"

"You are a kid that is not short of information," Delphine said. "Yeah, that's right. Abortions." She pulled up her sleeve to look at her watch. "It isn't five yet. I was just going to say that she started thinking about that little girl and wondering what became of her so she started investigating to find out. So it happened she got lucky and found those same people. The Christian people. She had to get a bit nasty with them but she got some information. She found out the names of the couple that took her."

Lauren wriggled her way off the bed. Half tripping on the blanket, she set her cup on the bureau.

"I have to go now," she said. She looked out the little window. "It's snowing."

"Is it? So what else is new? Don't you want to know the rest?"

Lauren was putting on her boots, trying to do it in an absent-minded way so that Delphine wouldn't take much notice.

"The man was supposed to be working for this magazine, so

she went there and they said he wasn't there but they told her where he had went to. She didn't know what name they gave her baby but that was another thing she was able to find out. You never know what you'll find out till you try. You trying to run away on me?"

"I have to go. My stomach feels sick. I've got a cold."

Lauren yanked at the jacket that Delphine had hung on the high hook on the back of the door. When she couldn't get it down immediately, her eyes filled with tears.

"I don't even know this person Joyce," she said miserably.

Delphine shifted her feet to the floor, got up slowly from the bed, set her cup on the bureau.

"If your stomach feels sick you should lie down. You probably drank that too fast."

"I just want my jacket."

Delphine lifted the jacket down but held it too high. When Lauren grabbed at it she would not let go.

"What's the matter?" she said. "You're not crying, are you? I wouldn't've took you for a crybaby. Okay. Okay. Here it is. I was just teasing you."

Lauren got her sleeves in but knew she couldn't manage the zipper. She stuck her hands in the pockets.

"Okay?" said Delphine. "You okay now? You still my friend?"

"Thank you for the hot chocolate."

"Don't walk too fast, you want your stomach to settle down."

Delphine bent over. Lauren backed off, scared that the white hair, the silky flopping curtains of hair, were going to get in her mouth.

If you were old enough for your hair to be white, then it shouldn't be long.

"I know you can keep a secret, I know you keep our visits and talks and everything a secret. You'll understand later. You're a wonderful little girl. There."

She kissed Lauren's head.

"You just don't worry about anything," she said.

Large flakes of snow were falling straight down, leaving on the sidewalks a fluffy coating that melted into black tracks where people walked, and then filled up again. The cars moved along cautiously, showing blurred yellow lights. Lauren looked around now and then to see if anybody was following her. She could not see very well because of the thickening snow and the failing light, but she did not think anybody was.

The feeling in her stomach was of both a swelling and a hollow. It seemed as if she might get rid of that just by eating the right sort of food, so when she got into the house she went straight to the kitchen cupboard and poured herself a bowl of the familiar breakfast cereal. There was no maple syrup left, but she found some corn syrup. She stood in the cold kitchen, eating without even having taken her boots and her outdoor clothing off, and looking out at the freshly whitened backyard. Snow made things visible, even with the kitchen light on. She saw herself reflected against the background of snowy yard and dark rocks capped with white, and evergreen branches drooping already under their white load.

She had hardly got the last spoonful into her mouth when she had to run to the bathroom and throw it all up—cornflakes as yet hardly altered, slime of syrup, slick strings of pale chocolate.

When her parents got home she was lying on the sofa, still in her boots and jacket, watching television.

Eileen pulled her outdoor things off and brought her a blanket and took her temperature—it was normal—then felt her stomach to see if it was hard, and made her bend her right knee up to her chest to see if that gave her a pain in her right side. Eileen always worried about appendicitis because she had once been at a party—the sort of party that went on for days—where a girl had died of a burst appendix, with everybody too stoned to realize that she was in any serious trouble. When she decided that Lauren's appendix was not involved she went to get dinner, and Harry kept Lauren company.

"I think you've got schoolitis," he said. "I used to get it myself. Only when I was a kid the cure for it hadn't been invented. You know what the cure is? Lying on the couch and watching TV."

Next morning Lauren said that she was still feeling sick, though it was not true. She refused breakfast, but as soon as Harry and Eileen were out of the house she got a large cinnamon bun, which she ate without warming it up while she watched television. She wiped her sticky fingers on the blanket that covered her, and tried to think about her future. She wanted to spend it right here, inside the house, on the sofa, but unless she could manufacture some genuine sickness she did not see how that would be possible.

The television news was over and one of the daily soap operas had come on. Here was a world she had been familiar with when she had bronchitis last spring, and had since forgotten all about. In spite of her desertion not much seemed to have changed. Most of the same characters appeared—in new circumstances, of course—and they had their same ways of behaving (noble, ruthless, sexy, sad) and their same looks into the distance and same unfinished sentences referring to accidents and secrets. She enjoyed watching them for a while, but then something that came into her mind began to worry her. Children and grown people too in these stories had often turned out to belong to quite different families from those they had always accepted as their own. Strangers who were sometimes crazy and dangerous had appeared out of the blue with their catastrophic claims and emotions, lives were turned upside down.

This might once have seemed to her an attractive possibility, but it didn't any longer.

Harry and Eileen never locked the doors. Imagine that, Harry would say—we live in a place where you can just walk out and never lock your doors. Lauren got up now and locked them, back and front. Then she closed the curtains on all of the windows. It wasn't snowing today, but there was no melting. The new snow already had a gray tinge to it, as if it had got old overnight.

There was no way that she could cover the little windows in the front door. There were three of them, shaped like teardrops, in a diagonal line. Eileen hated them. She had ripped off the wallpaper and painted the walls of this cheap house with unexpected colors—robin's-egg blue, blackberry-rose, lemon yellow—she had taken up ugly carpets and sanded the floors, but there was nothing she could do about those dinky little windows.

Harry said that they weren't so bad, that there was one for each of them, and just at the right height too, for each of them to look out. He named them Papa Bear, Mama Bear, Baby Bear.

When the soap opera ended and a man and woman began talking about indoor plants, Lauren fell into a light sleep which she hardly knew was a sleep. She knew that it must have been when she woke up from a dream of an animal, a wintry sort of gray weasel or skinny fox—she wasn't sure what—watching the house in broad daylight from the backyard. In the dream somebody had told her that this animal was rabid, because it was not scared of humans or the houses where they lived.

The phone was ringing. She pulled the blanket over her head so she would not hear it. She was sure it was Delphine. Delphine wanting to know how she was, why she was hiding, what did she think about the story she had told her, when was she coming to the hotel?

It was really Eileen, checking on how Lauren was feeling and the state of her appendix. Eileen let the phone ring ten or fifteen times, then she ran from the newspaper office without putting on her coat and drove home. When she found the door locked she banged on it with her fist and rattled the knob. She pressed her face to the Mama Bear window and shouted Lauren's name. She could hear the television. She ran around to the back door and banged and shouted again.

Lauren heard all this, of course, with her head under the blanket, but it took a while for her to realize that it was Eileen and not Delphine. When she did realize that, she came creeping into the kitchen with the blanket trailing behind her, still half thinking the voice might be a trick.

"Jesus, what is the matter with you?" Eileen said, throwing her arms around her. "Why was the door locked, why didn't you answer the phone, what kind of game are you up to?"

Lauren held out for about fifteen minutes, with Eileen alternately hugging her and shouting at her. Then she collapsed and told everything. It was a great relief and yet even as she shivered and cried she felt that something private and complex was being traded away for safety and comfort. It wasn't possible to tell the whole truth because she couldn't get it straight herself. She couldn't explain what she had wanted, right up to the point of not wanting it at all.

Eileen phoned Harry and told him that he had to come home. He would have to walk, she could not go to get him, she could not leave Lauren.

She went to unlock the front door and found an envelope, put through the mail slot but unstamped, with nothing written on it but LAUREN.

"Did you hear this come through the slot?" she said. "Did you hear anybody on the porch, how in the fuck did this happen?"

She tore the envelope open and pulled out the gold chain with Lauren's name on it.

"I forgot to tell you that part," said Lauren.

"There's a note."

"Don't read it," Lauren cried. "Don't *read* it. *I don't want to hear it.*"

"Don't be silly. It can't bite. She just says she phoned up the school and you weren't there so she wondered if you were sick and here is a present to cheer you up. She says she bought it for you anyway, nobody lost it. What does that mean? It was going to be a birthday present when you turned eleven in March but she wants you to have it now. Where did she get the idea your birthday was in March? Your birthday is in June."

"I know that," said Lauren, in the exhausted, childish, sulky voice she had now fallen back on.

"You see?" said Eileen. "She's got everything wrong. She's crazy."

"She knew your name, though. She knew where you were. How did she know that if you didn't adopt me?"

"I don't know how the hell she knew, but she is wrong. She has got it all wrong. Look. We'll get out your birth certificate. You were born in Wellesley Hospital in Toronto. We'll take you there, I could show you the exact room—" Eileen looked at the note again and crumpled it in her fist.

"That bitch. Phoning the school," she said. "Coming to our house. Crazy bitch."

"Hide that thing," said Lauren, meaning the chain. "Hide it. Put it away. *Now.*"

Harry was not so angry as Eileen.

"She seemed a perfectly okay person anytime I talked to her," he said. "She never said anything like this to me."

"Well, she wouldn't," said Eileen. "She wanted to get at Lauren. You have got to go and have a talk with her. Or I will. I mean it. Today."

Harry said he would. "I'll straighten her out," he said. "Absolutely. There won't be any more trouble. What a shame."

Eileen made an early lunch. She made hamburgers with mayonnaise and mustard on them, the way Harry and Lauren both liked them. Lauren had finished hers before she realized that it had probably been a mistake to show such an appetite.

"Feeling better?" said Harry. "Back to school this afternoon?"

"I still have got a cold."

Eileen said, "No. Not back to school. And I am staying home with her."

"I don't absolutely see that that's necessary," said Harry.

"And give her this," said Eileen, pushing the envelope into his pocket. "Never mind, don't bother looking at it, it's just her stupid present. And tell her no more of that kind of thing ever or she'll be in trouble. No more ever. No more."

Lauren never had to go back to school, not in that town.

During the afternoon Eileen phoned Harry's sister—whom Harry wasn't speaking to, because of criticisms the sister's husband had made about his, Harry's, way of living his life—and they talked about the school that the sister had gone to, a girls' private school in Toronto. More phone calls followed, an appointment was made.

"It's not a matter of money," Eileen said. "Harry has enough money. Or he can get it.

"It's not just this happening, either," she said. "You don't deserve to have to grow up in this crappy town. You don't deserve to end up sounding like a hick. I've been thinking of this all along. I was only putting it off till you got a bit older."

Harry said, when he came home, that surely it depended on what Lauren wanted.

"You want to leave home, Lauren? I thought you liked it here. I thought you had friends."

"Friends?" said Eileen. "She had that woman. Del-*phine*. Did you really get through to her? Did she get the message?"

"I did," said Harry. "She did."

"Did you give her back the bribe?"

"If you like to call it that. Yes."

"No more trouble? She understands, no more trouble?"

Harry turned on the radio and they listened to the news through dinner. Eileen opened a bottle of wine.

"What's this?" Harry said in a slightly menacing voice. "A celebration?"

Lauren had learned the signs, and she thought she saw what there was to be gone through now, what price there was to be paid for the miraculous rescue—the never having to go back to school or go near the hotel, perhaps never to have to walk in the streets at all, never to go out of the house in the two weeks left before the Christmas holidays.

Wine could be one of the signs. Sometimes. Sometimes not. But when Harry got out the bottle of gin and poured half a tumbler for himself, adding nothing to it but ice—and soon he wouldn't even be adding ice—the course was set. Everything might still be cheerful but the cheerfulness was hard as knives. Harry would talk to Lauren, and Eileen would talk to Lauren, more than either of them usually talked to her. Now and then they would speak to each other, in almost a normal way. But there would be a recklessness in the room that had not yet been expressed in words. Lauren would hope, or try to hope—more accurately, she used to try to hope—that somehow they would stop the fight from breaking out. And she had always believed—she did yet—that she was not the only one to hope this. They did, too. Partly they did. But partly they were eager for what would come. They never overcame this eagerness. There had never been one time when this feeling was in the room, the change in the air, the shocking brightness that made all shapes, all the furniture and utensils, sharper, yet denser—never one time that the worst did not follow.

Lauren used to be unable to stay in her room, she had to be where they were, flinging herself at them, protesting and weeping, till one or the other would pick her up and carry her back to bed, saying, "All right, all right, don't bug us, just don't bug us, it's our life, we have to be able to talk." "To talk" meant to pace around the house delivering precise harangues of condemnation, shrieks of contradiction, until they had to start flinging ashtrays, bottles, dishes, at each other. One time Eileen ran outside and threw herself down on the lawn, tearing up chunks of dirt and grass, while Harry hissed from the doorway, "Oh, that's the style, give them a show." Once Harry bolted himself in the bathroom, calling, "There's only one way to get out of this torment." Both of them threatened the use of pills and razors.

"Oh God, let's not do this," Eileen had said once. "Please, please, let's stop doing this." And Harry had answered in a high whining voice that cruelly imitated hers, "You're the one doing it—*you* stop."

Lauren had got over trying to figure out what the fights were about. Always about a new thing (tonight she lay in the dark and thought it was probably about her going away, about Eileen's making that decision on her own) and always about the same thing—the thing that belonged to them, that they could never give up.

She had also got over her idea that there was a tender spot in both of them—that Harry made jokes all the time because he was sad, and Eileen was brisk and dismissive because of something about Harry that seemed to shut her out—and that if she, Lauren, could only explain each of them to the other one, things would get better.

Next day they would be muted, broken, shamed, and queerly exhilarated. "People have to do this, it's bad to repress your feelings," Eileen had once told Lauren. "There's even a theory that repressing anger gives you cancer."

Harry referred to the fights as rows. "Sorry about the row," he would say. "Eileen is a very volatile woman. All I can say, sweetie—oh God, all I can say is—these things happen."

On this night Lauren actually fell asleep before they had really begun to do their damage. Before she was even sure they would do it. The gin bottle hadn't yet made an appearance when she went away to bed.

Harry woke her up.

"Sorry," he said. "I'm sorry, honey. Could you just get up and come downstairs?"

"Is it morning?"

"No. It's still late at night. Eileen and I want to talk to you. We've got something to talk to you about. It's sort of about what you already know. Come on, now. You want your slippers?"

"I hate slippers," Lauren reminded him. She went ahead of him down the stairs. He was still dressed and Eileen was still dressed too, waiting in the hall. She said to Lauren, "There's somebody else here that you know."

It was Delphine. Delphine was sitting on the sofa, wearing a ski jacket over her usual black pants and sweater. Lauren had never seen her in outdoor clothes before. Her face sagged, her skin looked pouchy, her body immensely defeated.

"Can't we go in the kitchen?" Lauren said. She didn't know why, but the kitchen seemed safer. Somewhere less special, and with the table to hold on to if they all sat around it.

"Lauren wants to go in the kitchen, we'll go in the kitchen," Harry said.

When they were sitting there, he said, "Lauren. I've explained that I told you about the baby. About the baby we had before you and what happened to that baby."

He waited until Lauren said, "Yes."

"May I say something now?" said Eileen. "May I say something to Lauren?"

Harry said, "Well certainly."

"Harry could not stand the idea of another baby," said Eileen, looking down at her hands in her lap under the tabletop. "He couldn't stand the idea of all the domestic chaos. He had his writing to do. He wanted to achieve things, so he couldn't have chaos. He wanted me to have an abortion and I said I would and then I said I wouldn't and then I said I would, but I couldn't do it and we had a fight and I got the baby and got in the car, I was going to go to some friends' place. I wasn't speeding and I certainly was not drunk. It was just the bad light on the road and the bad weather."

"Also the way the carry-cot was not fastened in," said Harry.

"But let that go," he said. "I was not insisting on an abortion. I might have mentioned getting an abortion, but there was no way I would have made you. I didn't talk about that to Lauren because it would be upsetting for her to hear. It's bound to be upsetting."

"Yes, but it's true," Eileen said. "Lauren can take it, she knows it wasn't like it was *her.*"

Lauren spoke up, surprising herself.

"It was me," she said. "Who was it if it wasn't me?"

"Yes, but I wasn't the one wanted to do it," Eileen said.

"You didn't altogether *not* want to do it," said Harry.

Lauren said, "Stop."

"This is just what we promised we would not do," said Harry. "Isn't this what we promised we would not do? And we should apologize to Delphine."

Delphine had not looked up at anybody while this talk was going on. She had not pulled her chair up to the table. She didn't seem to notice when Harry said her name. It wasn't just defeat that kept her still. It was a weight of obstinacy, even disgust, that Harry and Eileen couldn't notice.

"I talked to Delphine this afternoon, Lauren. I told her about the baby. It was her baby. I never told you the baby was adopted because it made everything seem worse—that we adopted that baby, and then the way we screwed up. Five years trying, we never thought we'd get pregnant, so we adopted. But Delphine was its mother in the first place. We called it Lauren and then we called you Lauren—I guess because it was our favorite name and also it gave us a feeling we were starting over. And Delphine wanted to know about her baby and she found out we had taken it and naturally she made the mistake of thinking it was you. She came here to find you. It's all very sad. When I told her the truth she very understandably wanted proof, so I told her to come here tonight and I showed her the documents. She never wanted to steal you away or anything like that, just to make friends with you. She was just lonely and confused."

Delphine yanked down the zipper of her jacket as if she wanted to get more air.

"And I told her we still had—that we never got around to or it never seemed the right time to—" He waved at the cardboard box that was sitting right out on the counter. "So I showed her that too.

"So tonight as a family," he said, "tonight while everything is all wide-open, we are going to go out and do this. And get rid of all this—misery and blame. Delphine and Eileen and me, and we want you to come with us—is that all right with you? Are you all right?"

Lauren said, "I was asleep. I've got a cold."

"You might as well do as Harry says," said Eileen.

Still Delphine never looked up. Harry got the box from the counter and gave it to her. "Maybe you should be the one to carry it," he said. "Are you all right?"

"Everybody is all right," Eileen said. "Let's just go."

Delphine stood there in the snow, holding the box, so Eileen said, "Should I?" and took it respectfully from her. She opened it up and was going to offer it to Harry, then changed her mind and held it out to Delphine. Delphine lifted out a small handful of ashes, but didn't take the box to pass it on. Eileen took a handful and gave the box to Harry. When he had got some ashes he was going to hand the box on to Lauren, but Eileen said, "No. She doesn't have to."

Lauren had already put her hands in her pockets.

There wasn't any wind, so the ashes just fell where Harry and Eileen and Delphine let them drop, into the snow.

Eileen spoke as if her throat was sore. "Our Father which art in Heaven—"

Harry said clearly, "This is Lauren, who was our child and

whom we all loved—let's all say it together." He looked at Delphine, then Eileen, and they all said, "This is Lauren," with Delphine's voice very quiet, mumbling, and Eileen's full of strained sincerity and Harry's sonorous, presiding, deeply serious.

"And we say good-bye to her and commit her to the snow—"

At the end Eileen said hurriedly, "Forgive us our sins. Our trespasses. Forgive us our trespasses."

Delphine got into the backseat with Lauren for the ride into town. Harry had held the door open for her to get into the front seat beside him, but she stumbled past him into the back. Relinquishing the more important seat, now that she was not the bearer of the box. She reached into the pocket of her ski jacket to get a Kleenex and in doing so dragged out something that fell on the floor of the car. She gave an involuntary grunt, reaching down to locate it, but Lauren had been quicker. Lauren picked up one of the earrings she had often seen Delphine wear—shoulder-length earrings of rainbow beads that sparkled through her hair. Earrings she must have been wearing this evening, but had thought better to stuff away in her pocket. And just the feel of this earring, the feeling of the cold bright beads slithering through her fingers, made Lauren long suddenly for any number of things to vanish, for Delphine to turn back into the person she had been at the beginning, sitting behind the hotel desk, bold and frisky.

Delphine did not say a word. She took the earring without their fingers touching. But for the first time that evening she and Lauren looked each other in the face. Delphine's eyes widened and for an instant there was a familiar expression in them, of mockery and conspiracy. She shrugged her shoulders and put the earring in her pocket. That was all—from then on she just looked at the back of Harry's head.

When Harry slowed to let her out at the hotel, he said, "It

would be nice if you could come and have supper with us, some night when you're not working."

"I'm pretty much always working," Delphine said. She got out of the car and said, "Good-bye," to none of them in particular, and stumped along the mushy sidewalk into the hotel.

On the way home Eileen said, "I knew she wouldn't."

Harry said, "Well. Maybe she appreciated that we asked."

"She doesn't care about us. She only cared about Lauren, when she thought Lauren was hers. Now she doesn't care about her either."

"Well, we care," said Harry, his voice rising. "She's ours."

"We love you, Lauren," he said. "I just want to tell you one more time."

Hers. Ours.

Something was prickling Lauren's bare ankles. She reached down and found that burrs, whole clusters of burrs, were clinging to her pajama legs.

"I got burrs from under the snow. I've got *hundreds* of burrs."

"I'll get them off you when we get home," Eileen said. "I can't do anything about them now."

Lauren was furiously pulling the burrs off her pajamas. And as soon as she got those loose she found that they were hanging on to her fingers. She tried to loosen them with the other hand and in no time they were clinging to all the other fingers. She was so sick of these burrs that she wanted to beat her hands and yell out loud, but she knew that the only thing she could do was just sit and wait.

TRICKS

I

I'll die," said Robin, on an evening years ago. "I'll die if they don't have that dress ready."

They were in the screen porch of the dark-green clapboard house on Isaac Street. Willard Greig, who lived next door, was playing rummy at the card table with Robin's sister, Joanne. Robin was sitting on the couch, frowning at a magazine. The smell of nicotiana fought with a smell of ketchup simmering in some kitchen along the street.

Willard watched Joanne barely smile, before she inquired in a neutral voice, "What did you say?"

"I said, I'll die." Robin was defiant. "I'll die if they don't have that dress ready by tomorrow. The cleaners."

"That's what I thought you said. You'd die?"

You could never catch Joanne on any remark of that sort.

Her tone was so mild, her scorn so immensely quiet, her smile—now vanished—was just the tiny lifting of a corner of her mouth.

"Well, I will," said Robin defiantly. "I need it."

"She *needs* it, she'll *die,* she's going to the *play,*" said Joanne to Willard, in a confidential tone.

Willard said, "Now, Joanne." His parents, and he himself, had been friends of the girls' parents—he still thought of these two as *the girls*—and now that all of the parents were dead he felt it was his duty to keep the daughters, as much as possible, out of each other's hair.

Joanne was now thirty years old, Robin twenty-six. Joanne had a childish body, a narrow chest, a long sallow face, and straight, fine, brown hair. She never tried to pretend she was anything but an unlucky person, stunted halfway between childhood and female maturity. Stunted, crippled in a way, by severe and persisting asthma from childhood on. You didn't expect a person who looked like that, a person who couldn't step outside in winter or be left alone at night, to have such a devastating way of catching on to other, more fortunate people's foolishness. Or to have such a fund of contempt. All their lives, it seemed to Willard, he'd been watching Robin's eyes fill up with tears of wrath, and hearing Joanne say, "What's the matter with you *now*?"

Tonight Robin had felt only a slight sting. Tomorrow was her day to go to Stratford, and she felt herself already living outside Joanne's reach.

"What's the play, Robin?" Willard asked, to smooth things as much as he could. "Is it by Shakespeare?"

"Yes. *As You Like It.*"

"And can you follow him all right? Shakespeare?"

Robin said she could.

"You're a wonder."

. . .

For five years Robin had been doing this. One play every summer. It had started when she was living in Stratford, training to be a nurse. She went with a fellow student who had a couple of free tickets from her aunt, who worked on costumes. The girl who had the tickets was bored sick—it was *King Lear*—so Robin had kept quiet about how she felt. She could not have expressed it anyway—she would rather have gone away from the theater alone, and not had to talk to anybody for at least twenty-four hours. Her mind was made up then to come back. And to come by herself.

It wouldn't be difficult. The town where she had grown up, and where, later, she had to find her work because of Joanne, was only thirty miles away. People there knew that the Shakespeare plays were being put on in Stratford, but Robin had never heard of anybody going to see one. People like Willard were afraid of being looked down on by the people in the audience, as well as having the problem of not following the language. And people like Joanne were sure that nobody, ever, could really like Shakespeare, and so if anybody from here went, it was because they wanted to mix with the higher-ups, who were not enjoying it themselves but only letting on they were. Those few people in town who made a habit of seeing stage productions preferred to go to Toronto, to the Royal Alex, when a Broadway musical was on tour.

Robin liked to have a good seat, so she could only afford a Saturday matinee. She picked a play that was being done on one of her weekends off from the hospital. She never read it beforehand, and she didn't care whether it was a tragedy or a comedy. She had yet to see a single person there that she knew, in the theater or out on the streets, and that suited her very well. One of the nurses she worked with had said to her, "I'd never have the nerve to do that all on my own," and that had made Robin realize how different she herself must be from most people. She never felt more at ease than at these times, surrounded by strangers. After the play she would walk downtown, along the river, and find some inexpensive place to eat—usually a sandwich, as she sat on a stool at the counter. And at twenty to eight she would catch the train home. That was all. Yet those few hours filled her with an assurance that the life she was going back to, which seemed so makeshift and unsatisfactory, was only temporary and could easily be put up with. And there was a radiance behind it, behind that life, behind everything, expressed by the sunlight seen through the train windows. The sunlight and long shadows on the summer fields, like the remains of the play in her head.

Last year, she saw *Antony and Cleopatra*. When it was over she walked along the river, and noticed that there was a black swan—the first she had ever seen—a subtle intruder gliding and feeding at a short distance from the white ones. Perhaps it was the glisten of the white swans' wings that made her think of eating at a real restaurant this time, not at a counter. White tablecloth, a few fresh flowers, a glass of wine, and something unusual to eat, like mussels, or Cornish hen. She made a move to check in her purse, to see how much money she had.

And her purse was not there. The seldom-used little paisley-cloth bag on its silver chain was not slung over her shoulder as usual, it was gone. She had walked alone nearly all the way downtown from the theater without noticing that it was gone. And of course her dress had no pockets. She had no return ticket, no lipstick, no comb, and no money. Not a dime.

She remembered that throughout the play she had held the purse on her lap, under her program. She did not have the program now, either. Perhaps both had slipped to the floor? But no—she remembered having the bag in the toilet cubicle of the

Ladies Room. She had hung it by the chain on the hook that was on the back of the door. But she had not left it there. No. She had looked at herself in the mirror over the washbasin, she had got the comb out to fiddle with her hair. Her hair was dark, and fine, and though she visualized it puffed up like Jackie Kennedy's, and did it up in rollers at night, it had a tendency to go flat. Otherwise she had been pleased with what she saw. She had greenish-gray eyes and black eyebrows and a skin that tanned whether she tried or not, and all this was set off well by her tight-waisted, full-skirted dress of avocado-green polished cotton, with the rows of little tucks around the hips.

That was where she had left it. On the counter by the washbasin. Admiring herself, turning and looking over her shoulder to catch sight of the V of the dress at the back—she believed she had a pretty back—and checking that there was no bra strap showing anywhere.

And on a tide of vanity, of silly gratification, she had sallied out of the Ladies Room, leaving the purse behind.

She climbed the bank to the street and started back to the theater by the straightest route. She walked as fast as she could. There was no shade along the street, and there was busy traffic, in the heat of the late afternoon. She was almost running. That caused the sweat to leak out from under the shields in her dress. She trekked across the baking parking lot—now empty—and up the hill. No more shade up there, and nobody in sight around the theater building.

But it was not locked. In the empty lobby she stood a moment to get her sight back after the outdoor glare. She could feel her heart thumping, and the drops of moisture popping out on her upper lip. The ticket booths were closed, and so was the refreshment counter. The inner theater doors were locked. She took the stairway down to the washroom, her shoes clattering on the marble steps.

Let it be open, let it be open, let it be there.

No. There was nothing on the smooth veined counter, nothing in the wastebaskets, nothing on any hook on the back of any door.

A man was mopping the floor of the lobby when she came upstairs. He told her that it might have been turned in to the Lost and Found, but the Lost and Found was locked. With some reluctance he left his mopping and led her down another stairs to a cubbyhole containing several umbrellas, parcels, and even jackets and hats and a disgusting-looking brownish fox scarf. But no paisley-cloth shoulder purse.

"No luck," he said.

"Could it be under my seat?" she begged, though she was sure it could not be.

"Already been swept in there."

There was nothing for her to do then but climb the stairs, walk through the lobby, and go out onto the street.

She walked in the other direction from the parking lot, seeking shade. She could imagine Joanne saying that the cleaning man had already stashed her purse away to take home to his wife or his daughter, that is what they were like in a place like this. She looked for a bench or a low wall to sit down on while she figured things out. She didn't see such a thing anywhere.

A large dog came up behind her and knocked against her as it passed. It was a dark-brown dog, with long legs and an arrogant, stubborn expression.

"Juno. Juno," a man called. "Watch where you're going.

"She is just young and rude," he said to Robin. "She thinks she owns the sidewalk. She's not vicious. Were you afraid?"

Robin said, "No." The loss of her purse had preoccupied her and she had not thought of an attack from a dog being piled on top of that.

"When people see a Doberman they are often frightened.

Dobermans have a reputation to be fierce, and she is trained to be fierce when she's a watchdog, but not when she's walking."

Robin hardly knew one breed of dog from another. Because of Joanne's asthma, they never had dogs or cats around the house.

"It's all right," she said.

Instead of going ahead to where the dog Juno was waiting, her owner called her back. He fixed the leash he was carrying onto her collar.

"I let her loose down on the grass. Down below the theater. She likes that. But she ought to be on the leash up here. I was lazy. Are you ill?"

Robin did not even feel surprised at this change in the conversation's direction. She said, "I lost my purse. It was my own fault. I left it by the washbasin in the Ladies Room at the theater and I went back to look but it was gone. I just walked away and left it there after the play."

"What play was it today?"

"Antony and Cleopatra," she said. "My money was in it and my train ticket home."

"You came on the train? To see *Antony and Cleopatra*?"

"Yes."

She remembered the advice their mother had given to her and to Joanne about travelling on the train, or travelling anywhere. Always have a couple of bills folded and pinned to your underwear. Also, don't get into a conversation with a strange man.

"What are you smiling at?" he said.

"I don't know."

"Well, you can go on smiling," he said, "because I will be happy to lend you some money for the train. What time does it go?"

She told him, and he said, "All right. But before that you should have some food. Or you will be hungry and not enjoy the train ride. I haven't anything with me, because when I go to take Juno on her walk I do not bring any money. But it isn't far to my shop. Come with me and I'll get it out of the till."

She had been too preoccupied, until now, to notice that he spoke with an accent. What was it? It was not French or Dutch—the two accents that she thought she could recognize, French from school and Dutch from the immigrants who were sometimes patients in the hospital. And the other thing she took note of was that he spoke of her enjoying the train ride. Nobody she knew would speak of a grown person doing that. But he spoke of it as being quite natural and necessary.

At the corner of Downie Street, he said, "We turn this way. My house is just along here."

He said *house,* when he had said *shop* before. But it could be that his shop was in his house.

She was not worried. Afterwards she wondered about that. Without a moment's hesitation she had accepted his offer of help, allowed him to rescue her, found it entirely natural that he should not carry money with him on his walks but could get it from the till in his shop.

A reason for this might have been his accent. Some of the nurses mocked the accents of the Dutch farmers and their wives—behind their backs, of course. So Robin had got into the habit of treating such people with special consideration, as if they had speech impediments, or even some mental slowness, though she knew that this was nonsense. An accent, therefore, roused in her a certain benevolence and politeness.

And she had not looked at him at all closely. At first she was too upset, and then it was not easy, because they were walking side by side. He was tall, long-legged, and walked quickly. One thing she had noticed was the sunlight glinting on his hair, which was cut short as stubble, and it seemed to her that it was bright silver. That is, gray. His forehead, being broad and high, also shone in the sun, and she had somehow got the impression that he was a generation beyond her—a courteous, yet slightly impatient, schoolteacherly, high-handed sort of person, who demanded respect, never intimacy. Later, indoors, she was able to see that the gray hair was mixed with a rusty red—though his skin had an olive tint unusual for a redhead—and that his indoor movements were sometimes awkward, as if he wasn't used to having company in his living space. He was probably not more than ten years older than she was.

She had trusted him for faulty reasons. But she had not been mistaken to do so.

The shop really was in a house. A narrow brick house left over from earlier days, on a street otherwise lined with buildings built to be shops. There was the sort of front door and step and window that a regular house would have, and in the window was an elaborate clock. He unlocked the door, but did not turn around the sign that said *Closed*. Juno crowded in ahead of them both, and again he apologized for her.

"She thinks it's her job to check that there's nobody in here who shouldn't be, and not anything different from when she went out."

The place was full of clocks. Dark wood and light wood, painted figures and gilded domes. They sat on shelves and on the floor and even on the counter across which business could be transacted. Beyond that, some sat on benches with their insides exposed. Juno slipped between them neatly, and could be heard thumping up a stairs.

"Are you interested in clocks?"

Robin said "No," before she thought of being polite.

"All right, then I do not have to go into my spiel," he said, and led her along the path Juno had taken, past the door of what was probably a toilet, and up the steep stairway. Then they were in a kitchen where all was clean and bright and tidy, and Juno was waiting beside a red dish on the floor, flopping her tail.

"You just wait," he said. "Yes. Wait. Don't you see we have a guest?"

He stood aside for Robin to enter the big front room, which had no rug on the wide painted floorboards and no curtains, only shades, on the windows. There was a hi-fi system taking up a good deal of space along one wall, and a sofa along the wall opposite, of the sort that would pull out to make a bed. A couple of canvas chairs, and a bookcase with books on one shelf and magazines on the others, tidily stacked. No pictures or cushions or ornaments in sight. A bachelor's room, with everything deliberate and necessary and proclaiming a certain austere satisfaction. Very different from the only other bachelor premises Robin was familiar with—Willard Greig's, which seemed more like a forlorn encampment established casually in the middle of his dead parents' furniture.

"Where would you like to sit?" he said. "The sofa? It is more comfortable than the chairs. I will make you a cup of coffee and you sit here and drink it while I make some supper. What do you do other times, between when the play is over and the train is going home?"

Foreigners talked differently, leaving a bit of space around the words, the way actors do.

"Walk," Robin said. "And I get something to eat."

"The same today, then. Are you bored when you eat alone?"

"No. I think about the play."

The coffee was very strong, but she got used to it. She did not feel that she should offer to help him in the kitchen, as she would have done with a woman. She got up and crossed the room almost on tiptoe and helped herself to a magazine. And even as she picked it up she knew this would be useless—the magazines were all printed on cheap brown paper in a language she could neither read nor identify.

In fact she realized, once she had it open on her lap, that she could not even identify all the letters.

He came in with more coffee.

"Ah," he said. "So do you read my language?"

That sounded sarcastic, but his eyes avoided her. It was almost as if, inside his own place, he had turned shy.

"I don't even know what language it is," she answered.

"It is Serbian. Some people say Serbo-Croatian."

"Is that where you come from?"

"I am from Montenegro."

Now she was stumped. She did not know where Montenegro was. Beside Greece? No—that was Macedonia.

"Montenegro is in Yugoslavia," he said. "Or that is what they tell us. But we don't think so."

"I didn't think you could get out of those countries," she said. "Those Communist countries. I didn't think you could just leave like ordinary people and get out into the West."

"Oh, you can." He spoke as if this did not interest him very much, or as if he had forgotten about it. "You can get out if you really want to. I left nearly five years ago. And now it is easier. Very soon I am going back there and then I expect I will be leaving again. Now I must cook your dinner. Or you will go away hungry."

"Just one thing," said Robin. "Why can't I read these letters? I mean, what letters are they? Is this the alphabet where you come from?"

"The Cyrillic alphabet. Like Greek. Now I'm cooking."

She sat with the strangely printed pages open in her lap and thought that she had entered a foreign world. A small piece of a foreign world on Downie Street in Stratford. Montenegro. Cyrillic alphabet. It was rude, she supposed, to keep asking him things. To make him feel like a specimen. She would have to control herself, though now she could come up with a host of questions.

All the clocks below—or most of them—began to chime the hour. It was already seven o'clock.

"Is there any later train?" he called from the kitchen.

"Yes. At five to ten."

"Will that be all right? Will anybody worry about you?"

She said no. Joanne would be displeased, but you could not exactly call that being worried.

Supper was a stew or thick soup, served in a bowl, with bread and red wine.

"Stroganoff," he said. "I hope you like it."

"It's delicious," she said truthfully. She was not so sure about the wine—she would have liked it sweeter. "Is this what you eat in Montenegro?"

"Not exactly. Montenegrin food is not very good. We are not famous for our food."

So then it was surely all right to say, "What are you famous for?"

"What are you?"

"Canadian."

"No. What are you famous for?"

That vexed her, she felt stupid. Yet she laughed.

"I don't know. I guess nothing."

"What Montenegrins are famous for is yelling and screaming and fighting. They're like Juno. They need discipline."

He got up to put on some music. He did not ask what she wanted to hear, and that was a relief. She did not want to be asked which composers she preferred, when the only two she could think of were Mozart and Beethoven and she was not sure she could tell their work apart. She really liked folk music, but she thought he might find that preference tiresome and condescending, linking it up to some idea she had of Montenegro.

He put on a kind of jazz.

Robin had never had a lover, or even a boyfriend. How had this happened, or not happened? She did not know. There was Joanne, of course, but there were other girls, similarly burdened, who had managed. A reason might have been that she had not given the matter enough attention, soon enough. In the town she lived in, most girls were seriously attached to somebody before they finished high school, and some didn't finish high school, but dropped out to get married. The girls of the better class, of course—the few girls whose parents could afford to send them to college—were expected to detach themselves from any high school boyfriend before going off to look for better prospects. The discarded boys were soon snapped up, and the girls who had not moved quickly enough then found themselves with slim pickings. Beyond a certain age, any new man who arrived was apt to come equipped with a wife.

But Robin had had her opportunity. She had gone away to train to be a nurse, which should have given her a fresh start. Girls who trained to be nurses got a chance at doctors. There too, she had failed. She didn't realize it at the time. She was too serious, maybe that was the problem. Too serious about something like *King Lear* and not about making use of dances and tennis games. A certain kind of seriousness in a girl could cancel out looks. But it was hard to think of a single case in which she envied any other girl the man she had got. In fact she couldn't yet think of anybody she wished she had married.

Not that she was against marriage altogether. She was just

waiting, as if she was a girl of fifteen, and it was only now and then that she was brought up against her true situation. Occasionally one of the women she worked with would arrange for her to meet somebody, and then she would be shocked at the prospect that had been considered suitable. And recently even Willard had frightened her, by making a joke about how he should move in someday, and help her look after Joanne.

Some people were already excusing her, even praising her, taking it for granted that she had planned from the beginning to devote her life to Joanne.

When they had finished eating he asked her if she would like to take a walk along the river before she caught her train. She agreed, and he said that they could not do that unless he knew her name.

"I might want to introduce you," he said.

She told him.

"Robin like the bird?"

"Like Robin Redbreast," she said, as she had often said before, without thinking about it. Now she was so embarrassed that all she could do was go on speaking recklessly.

"It's your turn now to tell me yours."

His name was Daniel. "Danilo. But Daniel here."

"So here is here," she said, still in this saucy tone which was the result of embarrassment at Robin Redbreast. "But where is there? In Montenegro—do you live in a town or the country?"

"I lived in the mountains."

While they were sitting in the room above his shop there had been a distance, and she had never feared—and never hoped—that the distance would be altered by any brusque or clumsy or sly movement of his. On the few occasions when this had happened with other men she had felt embarrassed for them. Now of necessity she and this man walked fairly close to each other and if they met someone their arms might brush together. Or he would move slightly behind her to get out of the way and his arm or chest knocked for a second against her back. These possibilities, and the knowledge that the people they met must see them as a couple, set up something like a hum, a tension, across her shoulders and down that one arm.

He asked her about *Antony and Cleopatra*, had she liked it (yes) and what part she had liked best. What came into her mind then were various bold and convincing embraces, but she could not say so.

"The part at the end," she said, "where she is going to put the asp on her body"—she had been going to say *breast*, then changed it, but *body* did not sound much better—"and the old man comes in with the basket of figs that the asp is in and they joke around, sort of. I think I liked it because you didn't expect that then. I mean, I liked other things too, I liked it all, but that was different."

"Yes," he said. "I like that too."

"Did you see it?"

"No. I'm saving my money now. But I read a lot of Shakespeare once, students read it when they were learning English. In the daytime I learned about clocks, in the nighttime I learned English. What did you learn?"

"Not so much," she said. "Not in school. After that I learned what you have to, to be a nurse."

"That's a lot to learn, to be a nurse. I think so."

After that they spoke about the coolness of the evening, how welcome it was, and how the nights had lengthened noticeably, though there was still all August to get through. And about Juno, how she had wanted to come with them but had settled down immediately when he reminded her that she had to stay and guard the shop. This talk felt more and more like an agreed-upon subterfuge, like a conventional screen for what was becoming more inevitable all the time, more necessary, between them.

But in the light of the railway depot, whatever was promising, or mysterious, was immediately removed. There were people lined up at the window, and he stood behind them, waiting his turn, and bought her ticket. They walked out onto the platform, where passengers were waiting.

"If you will write your full name and address on a piece of paper," she said, "I'll send you the money right away."

Now it will happen, she thought. And *it* was nothing. Now nothing will happen. Good-bye. Thank you. I'll send the money. No hurry. Thank you. It was no trouble. Thank you just the same. Good-bye.

"Let's walk along here," he said, and they walked along the platform away from the light.

"Better not to worry about the money. It is so little and it might not get here anyway, because I am going away so soon. Sometimes the mail is slow."

"Oh, but I must pay you back."

"I'll tell you how to pay me back, then. Are you listening?"

"Yes."

"I will be here next summer in the same place. The same shop. I will be there by June at the latest. Next summer. So you will choose your play and come here on the train and come to the shop."

"I will pay you back then?"

"Oh yes. And I will make dinner and we'll drink wine and I will tell you all about what has happened in the year and you will tell me. And I want one other thing."

"What?"

"You will wear the same dress. Your green dress. And your hair the same."

She laughed. "So you'll know me."

"Yes."

They were at the end of the platform, and he said, "Watch here," then, "All right?" as they stepped down on the gravel.

"All right," said Robin with a lurch in her voice, either because of the uncertain surface of the gravel or because by now he had taken hold of her at the shoulders, then was moving his hands down her bare arms.

"It is important that we have met," he said. "I think so. Do you think so?"

She said, "Yes."

"Yes. Yes."

He slid his hands under her arms to hold her closer, around the waist, and they kissed again and again.

The conversation of kisses. Subtle, engrossing, fearless, transforming. When they stopped they were both trembling, and it was with an effort that he got his voice under control, tried to speak matter-of-factly.

"We will not write letters, letters are not a good idea. We will just remember each other and next summer we will meet. You don't have to let me know, just come. If you still feel the same, you will just come."

They could hear the train. He helped her up to the platform, then did not touch her anymore, but walked briskly beside her, feeling for something in his pocket.

Just before he left her, he handed her a folded piece of paper. "I wrote on it before we left the shop," he said.

On the train she read his name. *Danilo Adzic*. And the words *Bjelojevici. My village.*

She walked from the station, under the dark full trees. Joanne had not gone to bed. She was playing solitaire.

"I'm sorry I missed the early train," Robin said. "I've had my supper. I had Stroganoff."

"So that's what I'm smelling."

"And I had a glass of wine."

"I can smell that too."

"I think I'll go right up to bed."

"I think you'd better."

Trailing clouds of glory, thought Robin on her way upstairs. From God, who is our home.

How silly that was, and even sacrilegious, if you could believe in sacrilege. Being kissed on a railway platform and told to report in a year's time. If Joanne knew about it, what would she say? A foreigner. Foreigners pick up girls that nobody else will have.

For a couple of weeks the two sisters hardly spoke. Then, seeing that there were no phone calls or letters, and that Robin went out in the evenings only to go to the library, Joanne relaxed. She knew that something had changed, but she didn't think it was serious. She began to make jokes to Willard.

In front of Robin she said, "You know that our girl here has started having mysterious adventures in Stratford? Oh yes. I tell you. Came home smelling of drink and goulash. You know what that smells like? Vomit."

What she probably thought was that Robin had gone to some weird restaurant, with some European dishes on the menu, and ordered a glass of wine with her meal, thinking herself to be sophisticated.

Robin was going to the library to read about Montenegro.

"For more than two centuries," she read, "the Montenegrins maintained the struggle against the Turks and the Albanians, which for them was almost the whole duty of man. (Hence the Montenegrins' reputation for dignity, bellicosity, and aversion to work, which last is a standing Yugoslav joke.)"

Which two centuries these were, she could not discover. She read about kings, bishops, wars, assassinations, and the greatest of all Serbian poems, called "The Mountain Garland," written by a Montenegrin king. She hardly retained a word of what she read. Except the name, the real name of Montenegro, which she did not know how to pronounce. *Crna Gora*.

She looked at maps, where it was hard enough to find the country itself, but possible finally, with a magnifying glass, to become familiar with the names of various towns (none of them Bjelojevici) and with the rivers Moraca and Tara, and the shaded mountain ranges, which seemed to be everywhere but in the Zeta Valley.

Her need to follow this investigation was hard to explain, and she did not try to explain it (though of course her presence in the library was noted, and her absorption). What she must have been trying to do—and what she at least half succeeded in doing—was to settle Danilo into some real place and a real past, to think that these names she was learning must have been known to him, this history must have been what he learned in school, some of these places must have been visited by him as a child or as a young man. And were being visited, perhaps, by him now. When she touched a printed name with her finger, she might have touched the very place he was in.

She tried also to learn from books, from diagrams, about clock making, but there she was not successful.

He remained with her. The thought of him was there when she woke up, and in lulls at work. The Christmas celebrations brought her thoughts round to ceremonies in the Orthodox Church, which she had read about, bearded priests in gold vestments, candles and incense and deep mournful chanting in a foreign tongue. The cold weather and the ice far out into the lake made her think of winter in the mountains. She felt as if she had been chosen to be connected to that strange part of the world, chosen for a different sort of fate. Those were words she used to herself. *Fate. Lover.* Not *boyfriend. Lover.* Sometimes she thought of the casual, reluctant way he had spoken about getting in and out of that country, and she was afraid for him, imagining him involved in dark schemes, cinematic plots and dangers. It was probably a good thing that he had decided there should be no letters. Her life would have been drained entirely into composing them and waiting for them. Writing and waiting, waiting and writing. And of course worrying, if they didn't arrive.

She had something now to carry around with her all the time. She was aware of a shine on herself, on her body, on her voice and all her doings. It made her walk differently and smile for no reason and treat the patients with uncommon tenderness. It was her pleasure to dwell on one thing at a time and she could do that while she went about her duties, while she ate supper with Joanne. The bare wall of the room, with the rectangles of streaked light reflected on it through the slatted blinds. The rough paper of the magazines, with their old-fashioned sketched illustrations, instead of photographs. The thick crockery bowl, with a yellow band around it, in which he served the Stroganoff. The chocolate color of Juno's muzzle, and her lean strong legs. Then the cooling air in the streets, and the fragrance from the municipal flower beds and the streetlamps by the river, around which a whole civilization of tiny bugs darted and circled.

The sinking in her chest, then the closing down, when he came back with her ticket. But after that the walk, the measured steps, the descent from the platform to the gravel. Through the thin soles of her shoes she had felt pain from the sharp pebbles.

Nothing faded for her, however repetitive this program might be. Her memories, and the embroidery on her memories, just kept wearing a deeper groove.

It is important that we have met.
Yes. Yes.

Yet when June came, she delayed. She had not yet decided on which play, or sent away for her ticket. Finally she thought it best to choose the anniversary day, the same day as last year. The play on that day was *As You Like It*. It struck her that she could just go on to Downie Street, and not bother with the play, because she would be too preoccupied or excited to notice much of it. She was superstitious, however, about altering the day's pattern. She got her ticket. And she took her green dress to the cleaners. She had not worn it since that day, but she wanted it to be perfectly fresh, crisp as new.

The woman who did the pressing, at the cleaners, had missed some days that week. Her child was sick. But it was promised that she would be back, the dress would be ready on Saturday morning.

"I'll die," said Robin. "I'll die if they don't have that dress ready for tomorrow."

She looked at Joanne and Willard, playing rummy at the table. She had seen them in this pose so often, and now it was possible she might never see them again. How far they were from the tension and defiance, the risk of her life.

The dress was not ready. The child was still sick. Robin considered taking the dress home and ironing it herself, but she thought she would be too nervous to make a good job of it. Especially with Joanne looking on. She went immediately downtown, to the only possible dress shop, and was lucky enough, she thought, to find another green dress, just as good a fit but made along straight lines, and sleeveless. The color was not avocado, but lime, green. The woman in the store said that was the color this year, and that full skirts and pinched waists had gone out.

Through the train window she saw rain starting. She did not even have an umbrella. And in the seat across from her was a passenger she knew, a woman who had had her gallbladder out just a few months ago, at the hospital. This woman had a married daughter in Stratford. She was a person who thought that two people known to each other, meeting on the train and headed for the same place, should keep up a conversation.

"My daughter's meeting me," she said. "We can take you where you're going. Especially when it's raining."

It was not raining when they got to Stratford, the sun was out and it was very hot. Nevertheless Robin saw nothing for it but to accept the ride. She sat in the backseat with two children who were eating Popsicles. It seemed a miracle that she did not get some orange or strawberry liquid dripped onto her dress.

She was not able to wait for the play to be over. She was shivering in the air-conditioned theater because this dress was made of such light material and had no sleeves. Or it might have been from nervousness. She made her apologetic way to the end of the row, and climbed up the aisle with its irregular steps and went out into the daylight of the lobby. Raining again, very hard. Alone in the Ladies Room, the same one where she had lost her purse, she worked at her hair. The damp was destroying her pouf, the hair she had rolled to be smooth was falling into wispy curly black strands around her face. She should have brought hairspray. She did as good a job as she could, backcombing.

The rain had stopped when she came out, and again the sun was shining, glaring on the wet pavement. Now she set out. Her legs felt weak, as on those occasions when she had to go to the blackboard, at school, to demonstrate a math problem, or had to stand in front of the class to recite memory work. Too soon, she was at the corner of Downie Street. Within a few minutes now, her life would be changed. She was not ready, but she could not stand any delay.

In the second block she could see ahead of her that odd little house, held in place by the conventional shop buildings on either side.

Closer she came, closer. The door stood open, as was the case with most shops along the street—not many of them had put in air-conditioning. There was just a screen door in place to keep out the flies.

Up the two steps, then she stood outside the door. But did not push it open for a moment, so that she could get her eyes used to the half-dark interior, and not stumble when she went in.

He was there, in the work space beyond the counter, busy under a single bulb. He was bent forward, seen in profile, engrossed in the work he was doing on a clock. She had feared a change. She had feared in fact that she was not remembering him accurately. Or that Montenegro might have altered something—given him a new haircut, a beard. But no—he was the same. The work light shining on his head showed the same bristle of hair, glinting as before, silver with its red-brown tarnish. A thick shoulder, slightly hunched, sleeve rolled up to bare the muscled forearm. An expression on his face of concentration, keenness, perfect appreciation of whatever he was doing, of the mechanism he was working with. The same look that had been in her mind, though she had never seen him working on his clocks before. She had been imagining that look bent on herself.

No. She didn't want to walk in. She wanted him to get up, come towards her, open the door. So she called to him.

Daniel. Being shy at the last moment of calling him Danilo, for fear she might pronounce the foreign syllables in a clumsy way.

He had not heard—or probably, because of what he was doing, he delayed looking up. Then he did look up, but not at her—he appeared to be searching for something he needed at the moment. But in raising his eyes he caught sight of her. He carefully moved something out of his way, pushed back from the worktable, stood up, came reluctantly towards her.

He shook his head at her slightly.

Her hand was ready to push the door open, but she did not do it. She waited for him to speak, but he did not. He shook his head again. He was perturbed. He stood still. He looked away from her, looked around the shop—looked at the array of clocks, as if they might give him some information or some support. When he looked again at her face, he shivered, and involuntarily—but perhaps not—he bared his front teeth. As if the sight of her gave him a positive fright, an apprehension of danger.

And she stood there, frozen, as if there was a possibility still that this might be a joke, a game.

Now he came towards her again, as if he had made up his mind what to do. Not looking at her anymore, but acting with determination and—so it seemed to her—revulsion, he put a hand against the wooden door, the shop door which stood open, and pushed it shut in her face.

This was a shortcut. With horror she understood what he was doing. He was putting on this act because it was an easier way to get rid of her than making an explanation, dealing with her astonishment and female carrying-on, her wounded feelings and possible collapse and tears.

. . .

Shame, terrible shame, was what she felt. A more confident, a more experienced, woman would have felt anger and walked away in a fine fury. *Piss on him.* Robin had heard a woman at work talk about a man who had abandoned her. *You can't trust anything in trousers.* That woman had acted as if she was not surprised. And deep down, Robin now was not surprised, either, but the blame was for herself. She should have understood those words of last summer, the promise and farewell at the station, as a piece of folly, unnecessary kindness to a lonely female who had lost her purse and came to plays by herself. He would have regretted that before he got home, and prayed that she wouldn't take him seriously.

It was quite possible that he had brought back a wife from Montenegro, a wife upstairs—that would explain the alarm in his face, the shudder of dismay. If he had thought of Robin it would be in fear of her doing just what she had been doing—dreaming her dreary virginal dreams, fabricating her silly plans. Women had probably made fools of themselves over him before now, and he would have found ways to get rid of them. This was a way. Better cruel than kind. No apologies, no explanations, no hope. Pretend you don't recognize her, and if that doesn't work, slam a door in her face. The sooner you can get her to hate you, the better.

Though with some of them it's uphill work.

Exactly. And here she was, weeping. She had managed to hold it back along the street, but on the path by the river, she was weeping. The same black swan swimming alone, the same families of ducklings and their quacking parents, the sun on the water. It was better not to try to escape, better not to ignore this blow. If you did that for a moment, you had to put up with its hitting you again, a great crippling whack in the chest.

. . .

"Better timing this year," Joanne said. "How was your play?"

"I didn't see all of it. Just when I was going into the theater some bug flew into my eye. I blinked and blinked but I couldn't get rid of it and I had to get up and go to the Ladies and try to wash it out. And then I must've got part of it on the towel and rubbed it into the other eye too."

"You look as if you'd been bawling your eyes out. When you came in I thought that must've been a whale of a sad play. You better wash your face in salt water."

"I was going to."

There were other things she was going to do, or not do. Never go to Stratford, never walk on those streets, never see another play. Never wear the green dresses, neither the lime nor the avocado. Avoid hearing any news of Montenegro, which should not be too difficult.

II

Now the real winter has set in and the lake is frozen over almost all the way to the breakwater. The ice is rough, in some places it looks as if big waves had been frozen in place. Workmen are out taking down the Christmas lights. Flu is reported. People's eyes water from walking against the wind. Most women are into their winter uniform of sweatpants and ski jackets.

But not Robin. When she steps off the elevator to visit the third and top floor of the hospital, she is wearing a long black coat, gray wool skirt, and a lilac-gray silk blouse. Her thick, straight, charcoal-gray hair is cut shoulder-length, and she has tiny diamonds in her ears. (It is still noted, just as it used to be, that some of the best-looking, best-turned-out women in town are those who did not marry.) She does not have to dress like a nurse now, because she works part-time and only on this floor.

You can take the elevator up to the third floor in the usual way, but it's more difficult to get down. The nurse behind the desk has to push a hidden button to release you. This is the Psychiatric Ward, though it is seldom called that. It looks west over the lake, like Robin's apartment, and so it is often called Sunset Hotel. And some older people refer to it as the Royal York. The patients there are short-term, though with some of them the short terms keep recurring. Those whose delusions or withdrawals or miseries become permanent are housed elsewhere, in the County Home, properly called the Long Term Care Facility, just outside of town.

In forty years the town has not grown a great deal, but it has changed. There are two shopping malls, though the stores on the square struggle on. There are new houses—an adult community—out on the bluffs, and two of the big old houses overlooking the lake have been converted to apartments. Robin has been lucky enough to get one of these. The house on Isaac Street where she and Joanne used to live has been smartened up with vinyl and turned into a real estate office. Willard's house is still the same, more or less. He had a stroke a few years ago but made a good recovery, though he has to walk with two canes. When he was in the hospital Robin saw quite a lot of him. He talked about what good neighbors she and Joanne had been, and what fun they had playing cards.

Joanne has been dead for eighteen years, and after selling the house Robin has moved away from old associations. She doesn't go to church anymore, and except for those who become patients in the hospital, she hardly ever sees the people she knew when she was young, the people she went to school with.

The prospects of marriage have opened up again, in a limited way, at her time of life. There are widowers looking around, men left on their own. Usually they want a woman experienced at marriage—though a good job doesn't come amiss either. But Robin has made it clear that she isn't interested. The people she has known since she was young say she never has been interested, that's just the way she is. Some of the people she knows now think she must be a lesbian, but that she has been brought up in an environment so primitive and crippling that she can't acknowledge it.

There are different sorts of people in town now, and these are the people she has made friends with. Some of them live together without being married. Some of them were born in India and Egypt and the Philippines and Korea. The old patterns of life, the rules of earlier days, persist to some extent, but a lot of people go their own way without even knowing about such things. You can buy almost any kind of food you want, and on a fine Sunday morning you can sit at a sidewalk table drinking fancy coffee and enjoying the sound of church bells, without any thought of worship. The beach is no longer surrounded by railway sheds and warehouses—you can walk on a boardwalk for a mile along the lake. There is a Choral Society and a Players Society. Robin is still very active in the Players Society, though not onstage so much as she once was. Several years ago she played Hedda Gabler. The general response was that it was an unpleasant play but that she played Hedda splendidly. An especially good job as the character—so people said—was so much the opposite of herself in real life.

Quite a number of people from here go to Stratford these days. She goes instead to see plays at Niagara-on-the-Lake.

Robin notes the three cots lined up against the opposite wall.

"What's up?" she says to Coral, the nurse at the desk.

"Temporary," says Coral, in a dubious tone. "It's the redistribution."

Robin goes to hang her coat and bag up in the closet behind the desk, and Coral tells her that these cases are from Perth

County. It's some kind of switch on account of overcrowding there, she says. Only somebody got their wires crossed and the county facility here isn't ready for them yet, so it's been decided to park them here for the time being.

"Should I go over and say hello?"

"Up to you. Last I looked they were all out of it."

The three cots have their sides up, the patients lying flat. And Coral was right, they all seem to be sleeping. Two old women and one old man. Robin turns away, and then turns back. She stands looking down at the old man. His mouth is open and his false teeth, if he has any, have been removed. He has his hair yet, white and cropped short. Flesh fallen away, cheeks sunken, but still a face broad at the temples, retaining some look of authority and—as when she last saw it—of perturbation. Patches of shrivelled, pale, almost silvery skin, probably where cancerous spots have been cut away. His body worn down, legs almost disappearing under the covers, but still some breadth in the chest and shoulders, very much as she remembers.

She reads the card attached to the foot of his bed.

Alexander Adzic.

Danilo. Daniel.

Perhaps that is his second name. Alexander. Or else he has lied, taken the precaution of telling a lie or half a lie, right from the start and nearly to the end.

She goes back to the desk and speaks to Coral.

"Any info on that man?"

"Why? Do you know him?"

"I think I might."

"I'll see what there is. I can call it up."

"No hurry," Robin says. "Just when you have time. It's only curiosity. I better go now and see my people."

It is Robin's job to talk to these patients twice a week, to write reports on them, as to how their delusions or depressions are clearing up, whether the pills are working, and how their moods are affected by the visits they have had from their relatives or their partners. She has worked on this floor for years, ever since the practice of keeping psychiatric patients close to home was introduced back in the seventies, and she knows many of the people who keep coming back. She took some extra courses to qualify herself for treating psychiatric cases, but it's something she had a feeling for anyway. Sometime after she came back from Stratford, not having seen *As You Like It*, she had begun to be drawn to this work. Something—though not what she was expecting—*had* changed her life.

She saves Mr. Wray till the last, because he generally wants the most time. She isn't always able to give him as much as he would like—it depends on the problems of the others. Today the rest of them are generally on the mend, thanks to their pills, and all they do is apologize about the fuss they have caused. But Mr. Wray, who believes that his contributions to the discovery of DNA have never been rewarded or acknowledged, is on the rampage about a letter to James Watson. Jim, he calls him.

"That letter I sent Jim," he says. "I know enough not to send a letter like that and not keep a copy. But yesterday I went looking through my files and guess what? You tell me what."

"You better tell me," says Robin.

"Not there. Not there. Stolen."

"It could be misplaced. I'll have a look around."

"I'm not surprised. I should have given up long ago. I'm fighting the Big Boys and who ever wins when you fight Them? Tell me the truth. Tell me. Should I give up?"

"You have to decide. Only you."

He begins to recite to her, once more, the particulars of his misfortune. He has not been a scientist, he has worked as a surveyor, but he must have followed scientific progress all his life.

The information he has given her, and even the drawings he has managed with a dull pencil, are no doubt correct. Only the story of his being cheated is clumsy and predictable, and probably owes a lot to the movies or television.

But she always loves the part of the story where he describes how the spiral unzips and the two strands float apart. He shows her how, with such grace, such appreciative hands. Each strand setting out on its appointed journey to double itself according to its own instructions.

He loves that too, he marvels at it, with tears in his eyes. She always thanks him for his explanation, and wishes that he could stop there, but of course he can't.

Nevertheless, she believes he's getting better. When he begins to root around in the byways of the injustice, to concentrate on something like the stolen letter, it means he's probably getting better.

With a little encouragement, a little shift in his attention, he could perhaps fall in love with her. This has happened with a couple of patients, before now. Both were married. But that did not keep her from sleeping with them, after they were discharged. By that time, however, feelings were altered. The men felt gratitude, she felt goodwill, both of them felt some sort of misplaced nostalgia.

Not that she regrets it. There's very little now that she regrets. Certainly not her sexual life, which has been sporadic and secret but, on the whole, comforting. The effort she put into keeping it secret was perhaps hardly necessary, seeing how people had made up their minds about her—the people she knew now had done that just as thoroughly and mistakenly as the people she knew long ago.

. . .

Coral hands her a printout.

"Not much," she says.

Robin thanks her and folds it and takes it to the closet, to put it into her purse. She wants to be alone when she reads it. But she can't wait till she gets home. She goes down to the Quiet Room, which used to be the Prayer Room. Nobody was in there being quiet at the moment.

> Adzic, Alexander. Born July 3, 1924, Bjelojevici, Yugoslavia. Emigrated Canada, May 29, 1962, care of brother Danilo Adzic, born Bjelojevici, July 3, 1924, Canadian citizen.
>
> Alexander Adzic lived with his brother Danilo until the latter's death Sept 7, 1995. He was admitted to Perth County Long Term Care Facility Sept 25, 1995, and has been a patient there since that date.
>
> Alexander Adzic apparently has been deaf-mute since birth or from illness shortly after. No Special Education Facilities available as a child. I.Q. never determined but he was trained to work at clock repairs. No training in sign language. Dependent on brother and to all appearances emotionally inaccessible otherwise. Apathy, no appetite, occasional hostility, general regression since admission.

Outrageous.

Brothers.

Twins.

Robin wants to set this piece of paper in front of someone, some authority.

This is ridiculous. This I do not accept.

Nevertheless.

Shakespeare should have prepared her. Twins are often the reason for mix-ups and disasters in Shakespeare. A means to an end, those tricks are supposed to be. And in the end the mysteries are solved, the pranks are forgiven, true love or something like it is rekindled, and those who were fooled have the good grace not to complain.

He must have gone out on an errand. A brief errand. He would not leave that brother in charge for very long. Perhaps the screen door was hooked—she had never tried to push it open. Perhaps he had told his brother to hook it and not open it while he himself was giving Juno a walk around the block. She had wondered why Juno wasn't there.

If she had come a little later. A little earlier. If she had stayed till the play was over or skipped the play altogether. If she had not bothered with her hair.

And then? How could they have managed, he with Alexander and she with Joanne? By the way Alexander behaved on that day, it did not look as if he would have put up with any intrusion, any changes. And Joanne would certainly have suffered. Less perhaps from having the deaf-mute Alexander in the house than from Robin's marriage to a foreigner.

Hard now to credit, the way things were then.

It was all spoiled in one day, in a couple of minutes, not by fits and starts, struggles, hopes and losses, in the long-drawn-out way that such things are more often spoiled. And if it's true that things are usually spoiled, isn't the quick way the easier way to bear?

But you don't really take that view, not for yourself. Robin doesn't. Even now she can yearn for her chance. She is not going to spare a moment's gratitude for the trick that has been played. But she'll come round to being grateful for the discovery of it. That, at least—the discovery which leaves everything whole, right up to the moment of frivolous intervention. Leaves you outraged, but warmed from a distance, clear of shame.

That was another world they had been in, surely. As much as any world concocted on the stage. Their flimsy arrangement, their ceremony of kisses, the foolhardy faith enveloping them that everything would sail ahead as planned. Move an inch this way or that, in such a case, and you're lost.

Robin has had patients who believe that combs and toothbrushes must lie in the right order, shoes must face in the right direction, steps must be counted, or some sort of punishment will follow.

If she has failed in that department, it would be in the matter of the green dress. Because of the woman at the cleaners, the sick child, she wore the wrong green dress.

She wished she could tell somebody. Him.

POWERS

GIVE DANTE A REST

March 13, 1927. Now we get the winter, just when we are supposed to be in sight of spring. Big storms closing off the roads, schools shut down. And some old fellow they say went for a walk out the tracks and is likely frozen. Today I went in my snowshoes right down the middle of the street and there was not a mark but mine on the snow. And by the time I got back from the store my tracks were entirely filled in. This is because of the lake not being frozen as usual and the wind out of the west picking up loads of moisture and dumping down on us as snow. I went to get coffee and one or two other necessities. Who should I see in the store but Tessa Netterby whom I hadn't seen for maybe a year. I felt badly I'd never got out to see her, because I used to try to keep up a sort of friendship after she dropped out of school. I think I was the only one that did. She was all wrapped up in a big shawl and she looked like something out of a storybook. Top-heavy, actually, because she has that broad face with its black curly mop and her broad shoulders, though she can't be much over five feet tall. She just smiled, the same old Tessa. And I asked how she was—you always do that when you see her, seriously, because of her long siege of whatever it was that took her out of school when she was around fourteen. But also you ask that because there isn't much else to think of to say, she is not in the world that the rest of us are in. She is not in any clubs and can't take part in any sports and she does not have any normal social life. She does have a sort of life involving people and there is nothing wrong with it, but I wouldn't know how to talk about it and maybe neither would she.

Mr. McWilliams was there helping Mrs. McWilliams out in the store because the clerks had not been able to get in. He is a dreadful tease and he started teasing Tessa, asking her if she didn't get word of this storm coming and why she couldn't have let the rest of us know about it, etc. and Mrs. McWilliams told him to stop it. Tessa just looked as if she never heard and asked for a can of sardines. It made me feel suddenly awful, to think of her sitting down for supper to a can of sardines. Which is hardly likely, I don't know any reason she can't cook a meal like anybody else.

The big news I heard at the store was that the roof of the Knights of Pythias Hall has caved in. There goes our stage for The Gondoliers, which was supposed to go on at the end of March. The Town Hall stage is not big enough and the old Opera House is now being used to store coffins from Hay's Furniture. So tonight we are supposed to have a rehearsal but I don't know who will get there or what will be the outcome.

Mar. 16. Decision to shelve The Gondoliers for this year, only six of us out to rehearsal in the Sunday School Hall so we gave up and went over to Wilf's house for coffee. Wilf also announced that he had meant this to be his last performance because his practice was getting too busy, and we would have to find another tenor. That will be a blow because he is the best.

I still feel funny calling a doctor by his first name even if he is only around thirty. His house used to be Dr. Coggan's and a lot of people still call it that. It was built specially to be a doctor's house with the office wing out to one side. But Wilf has had it all done over, some partitions knocked down altogether so that it is very roomy and bright and Sid Ralston was kidding him about getting it all ready for a wife. That was rather a touchy subject with Ginny right there but probably Sid did not know. (Ginny has had three proposals. First one from Wilf Rubstone, then Tommy Shuttles, then Euan McKay. A doctor, then an optometrist, then a minister. She is eight months older than I am but I don't suppose I have a hope of catching up. I think she does lead them on a bit, though she always says she can't understand it and that every time they asked her to marry them it came like a bolt out of the blue. What I think is that there are ways you can turn everything into a joke and let them know you wouldn't welcome a proposal, before you let them go and make a fool of themselves.)

If ever I am seriously ill I hope I am able to destroy this diary or go through and stroke out any mean things in it, in case I die.

We all got talking in a rather serious way, I don't know why, and the conversation got on to the things we learned at school and how much we had already forgotten. Somebody mentioned the Debating Club that used to be in town and how that all got scrapped after the War when everybody got cars to run around in and the movies to go to and started playing golf. What serious subjects they used to talk about. "Is Science or Literature more important in forming Human Character?" Can anybody imagine getting people out nowadays to listen to that? We'd feel silly even sitting around in an unorganized way and talking about it. Then Ginny said we should at least form a Reading Club and that got us on to the important books we always meant to read but never got down to it. The Harvard Classics that just sit there on the shelf behind glass doors in the living room year after year. Why not War and Peace, I said, but Ginny claimed she had already read it. So it came down to a vote between Paradise Lost and The Divine Comedy and the Divine Comedy won out. All we know about it is that it is not much of a comedy and written in Italian, though we will naturally be reading it in English. Sid thought it was in Latin and said he had read enough of that in Miss Hurt's class to last him all his life and we all roared at him, then he pretended he knew all along. Anyway now that The Gondoliers is on hold we should be able to find some time and will meet every couple of weeks to encourage each other.

Wilf showed us all over the house. The dining room is on one side of the hall and living room on the other and the kitchen has built-in cabinets and a double sink and the latest electric stove. There is a new washroom off the back hall and a streamlined bathroom and the closets are big enough to walk into and fixed up with full-length mirrors in the door. Golden oak floors everywhere. When I got home this place looked so poky and the wainscoting so dark and old-fashioned. I got on to Father at breakfast about how we could build a sunroom off the dining room to at least have one room bright and modern. (I forgot to mention that Wilf has a sunroom built out from the opposite side of the house to his office and it makes a good balance.) Father said what do we need that for when we have two verandahs to get the sun in the morning and the evening? So I see it's not likely I'm going to get anywhere with my home improvement scheme.

. . .

Apr. 1. First thing when I waked up I fooled Father. I ran out into the hall screaming that a bat had come down the chimney into my room and he came tearing out of the bathroom with his braces down and lather all over his face and told me to stop hollering and being hysterical and go and get the broom. So I got it, and then I hid on the back stairs pretending I was terrified while he went thumping around without his glasses on trying to find the bat. Eventually I took pity on him and yelled out, "April Fool!"

So the next thing was Ginny phoned up and said, "Nancy, what am I going to do? My hair is falling out, it's all over the pillow, big clumps of my beautiful hair all over the pillow and now I'm half bald, I can never leave this house again, will you run over here and see if we can make a wig out of it?"

So I said quite coolly, "Just mix up some flour and water and paste it back on. And isn't it funny it happened the morning of April Fool's?"

Now comes the part I am not so anxious to record.

I walked over to Wilf's house without even waiting for my breakfast because I know he goes to the Hospital early. He opened the front door himself in his vest and shirtsleeves. I hadn't bothered with the office figuring it would still be shut. That old woman he has keeping house—I don't even know her name—was banging around in the kitchen. I suppose she should have opened the door, but he was right there in the hall just getting ready to go. "Why Nancy," he said.

I never said a word, just made a suffering face and clutched at my throat.

"What's the matter with you, Nancy?"

More clutching and a miserable croaking and shaking my head to indicate I couldn't tell him. Oh, pitiful.

"In here," says Wilf, and leads me through the side hall

through the house door to the office. I saw that old woman having a peek but I didn't let on I saw her, just kept up my charade.

"Now then," he says, pushing me down on the patient's chair and turning on the lights. The blinds were still down on the windows and the place stank of antiseptic or something. He got out one of the sticks that flattens your tongue and the instrument he has for looking down and lighting up your throat.

"Now, open as wide as you can."

So I do, but just as he is about to press the stick down on my tongue I shout, "April Fool!"

There was not a flicker of a smile on his face. He whipped the stick out of the way and snapped off the light on the instrument and never said a word till he yanked open the outside door of the office. Then he said, "I happen to have sick people to see to, Nancy. Why don't you learn to act your age?"

So I just scurried out of there with my tail between my legs. I didn't have the nerve to ask him why couldn't he take a joke. No doubt that nosey female in his kitchen will spread it all over town how mad he was and how I had to slink off humiliated. I have felt terrible all day. And the worst stupid coincidence is that I have even felt sick, feverish and with a slightly sore throat, so I just sat in the front room with a blanket over my legs reading old Dante. Tomorrow night is the meeting of the Reading Club so I should be way ahead of all the rest of them. The trouble is none of it stuck in my head, because all the time I was reading I was also thinking, what a silly stupid thing I did, and I could hear him telling me in such a cutting voice to act my age. But then I would find myself arguing in my head with him that it is not such an awful thing to have a little fun in your life. I believe his father was a minister, does that account for him? Ministers' families move so much that he would never have time to get in with a gang that grows up together to understand and fool around with each other.

I can see him right now holding the door open in his vest and his starchy shirt. Tall and thin as a knife. His neat parted hair and strict moustache. What a disaster.

I wonder about writing him a note to explain that a joke is not a major offense in my opinion? Or should I just write a dignified sort of apology?

I can't consult with Ginny because he proposed to her and that means he thinks of her as a worthier person than I am. And I am in such a mood that I would wonder if she was secretly holding that over me. (Even if she turned him down.)

Apr. 4. Wilf did not show up at the Reading Club because some old fellow had a stroke. So I wrote him a note. Tried to make it apologetic but not too humble. This nags at me like anything. Not the note but what I did.

Apr. 12. I got the surprise of my stupid young life answering the door at noon today. Father had just got home and had sat down to dinner and there was Wilf. He never answered the note I wrote him and I had resigned myself that he intended to be disgusted with me forever and all I could do in future was snoot him because I had no choice.

He asked if he had interrupted my dinner.

He could not have done that because I have decided to give up eating dinner until I lose five pounds. While Father and Mrs. Box eat theirs I just shut myself up and have a go at Dante.

I said, no.

He said, well then, how about coming for a drive with him? We could see the ice go out on the river, he said. He went on and explained that he had been up most of the night and had to open the office at one o'clock, which didn't give him time for a snooze, and the fresh air would revive him better. He didn't say why he had been up during the night so I figured it was a baby being born and he thought that might embarrass me if he told me.

I said I was just getting started on my day's stint of reading.

"Give Dante a rest for a while," he said.

So I got my coat and told Father and we went out and got in his car. We drove out to the North Bridge where several people, mostly men and boys on their lunch hour, had collected to look at the ice. Not such big chunks of it this year with the winter being so late getting started. Still it was knocking up against the bridge supports and grinding away and making a racket the way it usually does with the little streams of water running in between. There was nothing to do but stand and look at this as if you were mesmerized, and my feet got cold. The ice may be breaking but the winter does not seem to have given up yet and spring seems pretty far away. I wondered how on earth some people could stand there and find this entertaining enough to watch for hours.

It didn't take Wilf long to get tired of it either. We got back in the car and were stumped for conversation, till I took the bull by the horns and asked, did he get my note?

He said yes he had.

I said I really felt like a fool for what I had done (that was true but perhaps more contrite-sounding than I had meant).

He said, "Oh, never mind that."

He backed the car and we headed into town and he said, "I was hoping to ask you to marry me. Only I wasn't going to do it like this. I was going to lead up to it more. In a more suitable sort of situation."

I said, "Do you mean you were hoping to but now you're not? Or do you mean that you actually are?"

I swear that when I said that I was not egging him on. I really just wanted it clarified.

"I mean I am," he said.

"Yes" was out of my mouth before I even got over my shock. I don't know how to explain it. I said yes in a nice polite way but not too eagerly. More like yes, I'd like a cup of tea. I didn't even act surprised. It seemed as if I had to get us quickly through this moment and then we could just be relaxed and normal. Though the fact was that I had never been exactly relaxed and normal with Wilf. At one time I was rather mystified by him and thought he was both intimidating and comical, and then since my unlucky April Fool's I have been just stricken with embarrassment. I hope I am not saying that I said yes I'd marry him to get over the embarrassment. I do remember thinking I should take yes back and say I needed time to think it over, but I could hardly do that without landing us both in a worse muddle of embarrassment than ever. And I don't know what there is for me to think over.

I am engaged to Wilf. I can't believe it. Is this the way it happens to everybody?

Apr. 14. Wilf came and talked to Father and I went over and talked to Ginny. I came right out and confessed that I felt awkward telling her, then said I hoped she would not feel awkward being my maid of honour. She said of course she wouldn't and we both got rather emotional and put our arms around each other and had a bit of a sniffle.

"What are fellows compared to friends?" she said.

And I got in one of my devil-may-care moods and told her it was all her fault anyway.

I said I couldn't stand for the poor man to have had two girls turn him down.

May 30. I have not written in here for so long because I am in a whirlwind of things that have to be done. The wedding is scheduled for July 10. I am getting my dress made by Miss Cornish who drives me crazy standing in my underclothes all stuck together with pins and her barking at me to stay still. It is white marquisette and I am not having a train because I am afraid I would somehow find a way to trip over it. Then a trousseau with half a dozen summer nightgowns and a watered-silk lily-patterned Japanese kimono and three pairs of winter pyjamas, all bought at Simpson's in Toronto. Apparently pyjamas are not the ideal for your trousseau but nightgowns are no good to keep you warm and I hate them anyway, because they always end up getting tangled around your middle. A bunch of silk slips and other stuff, all peach or "nude." Ginny says I should stock up while I have the chance, because if there is a War coming in China a lot of silk things will get scarce. She is as usual all up on the news. Her maid of honour's dress is powder blue.

Yesterday Mrs. Box made the cake. It is supposed to have six weeks to ripen so we are just getting in under the wire. I had to stir it for good luck and the dough was so heavy with fruit I thought my arm would drop off. Ollie was here so he took over and stirred a bit for me when Mrs. B. wasn't looking. What kind of luck that will bring I do not know.

Ollie is Wilf's cousin and is visiting here for a couple of months. As Wilf has no brother he—Ollie, that is—is going to be best man. He is seven months older than I am, so it seems as if he and I are still kids in a way Wilf isn't (I can't imagine he ever was). He—Ollie—has been in a T. B. Sanatorium for three years but is now better. They collapsed one of his lungs when he was in there. I had heard about this and believed you had to function then with one lung but apparently not. They just collapse it so it can be out of use while they treat it with medication and encyst (not insist) the infection so that it is dormant. (See how I am getting to be quite the medical authority now, being engaged to marry a doctor!) While Wilf explained this Ollie put his hands over his ears. He says he prefers not to think about what was done and pretends to himself he is hollow like a celluloid doll. He is a very opposite person to Wilf but they seem to get along just fine.

We are going to have the cake professionally iced at the bakery, thank God. I don't think Mrs. Box could stand the strain otherwise.

June 11. Less than a month to go. I should not even be writing here, I should get going on the wedding present lists. I can't believe all this stuff is going to be mine. Wilf is after me to pick out the wallpaper. I thought the rooms were all plastered and painted white because that was the way he liked them, but it seems he just left them so his wife could pick out the paper. I am afraid I just looked dumbfounded at the job but then I pulled myself together and told him I thought that was very considerate of him but I really could not imagine what I wanted until I was living there. (He must have hoped for it to be all done when we got back from the honeymoon.) So that way I got it put off.

I am still going to the Mill my two days a week. I sort of expected that would continue even after I was married but Father says of course not. He went on as if it wouldn't be quite legal hiring a married woman unless she was a widow or in bad straits, but I pointed out it was not hiring since he didn't pay me anyway. Then he said what he had been embarrassed to say at first, that when I was married there would be interruptions.

"Times when you won't be going out in public," he said.

"Oh, I don't know about that," I said, and blushed like an idiot.

So he has got it into his head (Father has) that it would be nice if Ollie would take over what I am doing and he really hopes (Father) that Ollie could work himself into the business and eventually be able to take it all over. Maybe he wished I would marry somebody who could do that—though he thinks Wilf is *just dandy.* And Ollie being at loose ends and smart and educated (I don't know exactly where or how much education but obviously knowing more than practically anybody around here), he might seem like an A-one choice. And for this reason I had to take him to the office yesterday and show him the books etc., and Father took him and introduced him to the men and anybody who happened to be around and it looked as if all went well. Ollie was very attentive and put on a serious business air in the office and then he was cheerful and jokey (but not too jokey) with the men, he even changed his way of talking just the right amount, and Father was so pleased and buoyed up. When I said good night to him he said, "I take it as a real stroke of luck that young fellow showing up here. He's a fellow who is looking for a future and a place to make himself at home."

And I didn't contradict but I believe that there is as much chance of Ollie settling down here and running a chopping-mill as there is of me getting into the Ziegfeld Follies.

He just can't help putting on a nice act.

I was thinking at one time that Ginny would take him off my hands. She is well-read and smokes and though she goes to church her opinions are the kind some people might take for atheistic. And she told me she didn't think Ollie was bad-looking though he is on the short side (I would say five-eight or nine). He has the blue eyes she likes and the butterscotch-coloured hair with a wave drooping over his forehead, which seems so intentionally charming. He was very nice to her of course when they met and led her on to talk a lot, and after she had gone home he said, "Your little friend is quite the intellectual, isn't she?"

"Little." Ginny is at least as tall as he is and I certainly felt like telling him that. But it is pretty mean to point out something concerning height to a man who is a bit lacking in that respect so I kept my mouth shut. I didn't know what to say about the "intellectual" part of it. In my opinion Ginny is an intellectual (for instance has Ollie read *War and Peace*?), but I couldn't tell from his tone whether he meant she was or she wasn't. All I could tell was that if she was, it wasn't something he cared for, and if she wasn't, then she was acting as if she was and he did not care for that either. I should have said something cool and disagreeable, such as, "You're too deep for me," but of course did not think of anything till later. And the worst thing was that as soon as he had said that, I had secretly, in my heart, got an inkling of something about Ginny, and while I was defending her (in my thoughts) I was also in some sly way agreeing with him. I don't know if she will ever seem as smart to me in the future.

Wilf was right there and must have heard the whole exchange but said nothing. I could have asked him if he didn't feel like sticking up for the girl he had once proposed to, but I have never fully let on to him what I know about that. He often just listens to Ollie and me talk, with his head bent forward (the way he has to do with most people, he is so tall) and a little smile on his face. I'm not even sure it's a smile or just the way his mouth is. In the evenings they both come over and it often ends up with Father and Wilf playing cribbage and Ollie and me just fooling around talking. Or Wilf and Ollie and me playing three-handed Bridge. (Father has never taken to Bridge because he somehow thinks it's too High-Hat.) Sometimes Wilf gets a call from the Hospital or Elsie Bainton (his housekeeper whose name I can't remember—I just had to yell and ask Mrs. Box) and he has to go out. Or sometimes when the crib game is finished he goes and sits at the piano and plays by ear. In the dark, maybe. Father wanders out onto the verandah and sits with Ollie and me and we all rock and listen. It seems then that Wilf is just playing the piano for himself and he isn't doing a performance for us. It doesn't bother him if we listen or not or if we start to chat. And sometimes we do that, because it can get to be a bit too classical for Father whose favourite piece is "My Old Kentucky Home." You can see him getting restless, that kind of music makes him feel that the world is going woozy on him, and for his sake we will start up some conversation. Then he—Father—is the one who will make a point of telling Wilf how we all enjoyed his playing and Wilf says thank-you in a polite absent-minded way. Ollie and I know not to say anything because we know that in this case he does not care about our opinions one way or the other.

One time I caught Ollie singing along very faintly with Wilf's playing.

"Morning is dawning and Peer Gynt is yawning—"

I whispered, "What?"

"Nothing," Ollie said. "That's what he's playing."

I made him spell it. P-e-e-r G-y-n-t.

I should learn more about music, it would be something for Wilf and me to have in common.

The weather has suddenly got hot. The peonies are full out as big as babies' bottoms and the flowers on the spirea bushes are dropping like snow. Mrs. Box goes around saying that if this lasts everything will be dried up by the time of the wedding.

While writing this I have had three cups of coffee and have not even fixed my hair. Mrs. Box says, "You're going to have to change your ways pretty soon."

She meant because Elsie Thingamabob has told Wilf she's going to retire so I can be in charge of the house.

So now I am changing my ways and Good-bye Diary at least for the present. I used to have a feeling something really unusual would occur in my life, and it would be important to have recorded everything. Was that just a feeling?

GIRL IN A MIDDY

"Don't think you can loll around here," said Nancy. "I've got a surprise for you."

Ollie said, "You're full of surprises."

This was on a Sunday, and Ollie had rather hoped he could loll around. A thing he didn't always appreciate, in Nancy, was her energy.

He supposed she'd be needing it soon, for the household that Wilf—in his stolid, ordinary way—was counting on.

After church Wilf had gone straight to the Hospital and Ollie had come back to eat dinner with Nancy and her father. They ate a cold meal on Sundays—Mrs. Box went to her own church on that day and spent the afternoon having a long rest in her own little house. Ollie had helped Nancy tidy up the kitchen. There were some thoroughgoing snores from the dining room.

"Your father," Ollie said, after glancing in. "He's asleep in his rocker with the *Saturday Evening Post* on his knee."

"He never admits he's going to sleep Sunday afternoons," Nancy said, "he always thinks he's going to read."

Nancy was wearing an apron that tied around her waist—not the sort of apron worn for serious kitchen work. She took it off and hung it over the doorknob and fluffed up her hair in front of a small mirror by the kitchen door.

"I'm a mess," she said, in a plaintive, not displeased voice.

"It's true. I can't figure out what Wilf sees in you."

"Look out or I'll bat you one."

She led him out the door and around the currant bushes and under the maple tree where—she had already told him two or three times—she used to have her swing. Then along the back lane to the end of the block. Nobody was cutting the grass, this being Sunday. In fact there was nobody out in the backyards at all and the houses had a closed-up, proud, and sheltering look, as if inside every one of them there were dignified people like Nancy's father, temporarily dead to the world as they took their Well Earned Rest.

This did not mean that the town was entirely quiet. Sunday afternoon was the time that the country people and people from the country villages descended on the beach, which was about a quarter of a mile away at the bottom of a bluff. There was a mixture of shrieks from the water slide and the cries of children ducking and splashing, and car horns and toots of the ice-cream truck and the hollers of young men in a frenzy of showing off and the mothers in a frenzy of anxiety. All of this thrown together in one addled shout.

At the end of the lane, across a poorer, unpaved street, was an empty building that Nancy said was the old icehouse, and beyond that was a vacant lot and a plank bridge over a dry ditch, and then they were on a road just wide enough for one car—or preferably for one horse and buggy. On either side of this road was a wall of thorny bushes with bright little green leaves and a scattering of dry pink flowers. They didn't let any breeze in and they didn't provide any shade, and the branches tried to catch his shirtsleeves.

"Wild *roses*," Nancy said, when he asked what in tarnation these were.

"I suppose that's the surprise?"

"You'll see."

He was sweltering in this tunnel, and he wished that she would slow down. He was often surprised at the time he spent hanging around this girl, who was not outstanding in any way, except perhaps in being spoiled, saucy, and egotistical. Maybe he liked to disturb her. She was just enough smarter than the general run of girls so that he could do that.

What he could see, at a distance, was the roof of a house, with some proper trees shading it, and since there was no hope of getting any more information out of Nancy he contented himself with hoping they could sit down when they got there, in some place cool.

"Company," said Nancy. "Might have known."

A dingy Model T was sitting in the turnaround space at the end of the road.

"Anyway it's only one," she said. "And let's hope they're nearly through."

But when they reached the car nobody had come out from the decent one-and-a-half-story house—built of brick that was called "white" in this part of the country and "yellow" where Ollie came from. (It was actually a grimy sort of tan.) There was no hedge—just a dragging wire fence around the yard in which the grass had not been cut. And there was no cement walk leading from the gate up to the door, only a dirt path. Not that this was unusual outside of a town—not many farmers put in a sidewalk, or owned a lawnmower.

Perhaps there had once been flower beds—at least there were white and gold flowers standing up here and there in the long grass. These were daisies, he was pretty sure, but he could not be bothered asking Nancy and possibly listening to her derisive corrections.

Nancy led him through to a genuine relic of more genteel or leisurely days—an unpainted but complete wooden swing, with two facing benches. The grass wasn't trodden down anywhere near it—apparently it was not much used. It stood in the shade of a couple of the heavy-leaved trees. As soon as Nancy had sat down she sprang up again, and bracing herself between the two benches she began to move this creaky contraption to and fro.

"This'll let her know we're here," she said.

"Let who?"

"Tessa."

"Is she a friend of yours?"

"Of course."

"An old-lady friend?" said Ollie, without enthusiasm. He had had plenty of chances to see how prodigal Nancy was with what might have been called—in some girls' book she might have read and taken to heart, it probably *was* called—the sunshine of her personality. Her innocent teasing of the old fellows at the mill came to mind.

"We went to school together, Tessa and me. Tessa and I."

That brought up another thought—the way she had tried to set him up with Ginny.

"And what's so interesting about her?"

"You'll see. Oh!"

She jumped off in midswing and ran to a hand pump close to the house. A lot of vigorous pumping started. She had to pump long and hard before any water came. And even then she didn't seem tired, she kept on pumping for a while before she filled the tin mug that had been waiting on its hook, and carried it, spilling over, to the swing. He thought from the eager look she had that she would offer it at once to him, but in fact she raised it to her own lips and gulped happily.

"It's not town water," she said, handing it to him. "It's well water. It's delicious."

She was a girl who would drink untreated water from any old tin mug hanging over a well. (The calamities that had taken place in his own body had made him more aware of such risks than another young man might have been.) She was something of a show-off, of course. But she was truly, naturally reckless and full of some pure conviction that she led a charmed life.

He wouldn't have said that of himself. Yet he had an idea—he couldn't have mentioned this without making a joke of it—that he was meant for something unusual, that his life would have some meaning to it. Maybe that was what drew them together. But the difference was that he would go on, he would not settle for less. As she would have to do—as she had already done—being a girl. The thought of choices wider than anything girls ever knew put him suddenly at ease, made him feel compassionate towards her, and playful. There were times when he did not need to ask why he was with her, when teasing her, being teased by her, made the time flow by with sparkling ease.

The water *was* delicious, and marvellously cold.

"People come to see Tessa," she said, sitting down across from him. "You never know when there'll be somebody here."

"Do they?" he said. The wild idea occurred to him that she might be perverse enough, independent enough, to be friends with a girl who was a semi-pro, a casual rural prostitute. To have remained friends, anyway, with a girl who had turned bad.

She read his thoughts—she was sometimes smart.

"Oh, *no*," she said. "I didn't mean anything like that. Oh, that is absolutely the worst idea I ever heard. Tessa is the last girl in the world— That's disgusting. You ought to be ashamed of yourself. She is the last girl— Oh, you'll see." Her face had gone quite red.

The door opened, and without any of the usual prolonged good-byes—or any audible good-byes at all—a man and woman, middle-aged, worn but not worn-out, like their car, came along the path, looked towards the swing and saw Nancy and Ollie but didn't say anything. Oddly enough Nancy didn't say anything either, didn't call out any lively greeting. The couple went to opposite sides of the vehicle and got in and drove away.

Then a figure moved out of the doorway's shadow and Nancy did call out.

"Hey. Tessa."

The woman was built like a sturdy child. A large head covered with dark curly hair, broad shoulders, stumpy legs. Her legs were bare and she was wearing an odd costume—a middy blouse and skirt. At least it was odd for a hot day, and considering the fact that she was no longer a schoolgirl. Very likely it was an outfit she had once worn at school, and being the saving type she was wearing it out around home. Such clothes never wear out, and in Ollie's opinion they never flattered a girl's figure either. She looked clumsy in it, no more and no less than most schoolgirls.

Nancy brought him up and introduced him, and he said to Tessa—in the insinuating way that was usually acceptable to girls—that he had been hearing lots about her.

"He has not," said Nancy. "Don't believe a word he says. I just brought him along out here because I didn't know what to do with him, frankly."

Tessa's eyes were heavy-lidded, and not very large, but their color was a surprising deep, soft blue. When she lifted them to look at Ollie they shone out at him without any particular friendliness or animosity, or even curiosity. They were just very deep and sure and they made it impossible for him to go on saying any silly polite things.

"You better come in," she said, and led the way. "I hope you don't mind if I finish my churning. I was churning when my last company came and I did stop it, but if I don't get at it again the butter might go bad on me."

"Churning on Sunday, what a naughty girl," said Nancy. "See, Ollie. This is how you make butter. I bet you just thought it came out of a cow ready-made and wrapped up to go in the store. You go ahead," she said to Tessa. "If you get tired you can let me try it for a while. I just came out to ask you to my wedding, actually."

"I heard something about that," Tessa said.

"I'd send you an invitation, but I don't know if you'd pay any attention to it. I thought I'd better come out here and wring your neck till you said you'd come."

They had gone straight into the kitchen. The window blinds were down to the sills, a fan stirring the air high overhead. The room smelled of cooking, of saucers of fly poison, of coal oil, of dishcloths. All these smells might have been in the walls and floorboards for decades. But somebody—no doubt the heavy-breathing, almost grunting girl at the churn—had gone to the trouble of painting the cupboards and doors robin's-egg blue.

Newspapers were spread around the churn to save the floor, which was worn into hollows on the regular traffic routes around the table and stove. Ollie would have been gallant enough with most farm girls to ask if he could have a go at the churning, but in this case he didn't feel quite sure of himself. She didn't seem a sullen girl, this Tessa, just old for her years, dishearteningly straightforward and self-contained. Even Nancy quieted down, after a while, in her presence.

The butter came. Nancy jumped up to take a look at it, and called on him to do the same. He was surprised at the pale color of it, hardly yellow at all, but he didn't say anything, supposing Nancy would chide him for ignorance. Then the two girls set the sticky pale lump on a cloth on the table and beat it down with wooden paddles and wrapped the cloth all around it. Tessa lifted a door in the floor and the two of them carried it down some cellar steps he wouldn't have known were there. Nancy gave a shriek as she almost lost her footing. He had an idea that Tessa could have managed better by herself but that she did not mind giving Nancy some privileges, such as you would give to a pesky, charming child. She let Nancy tidy up the papers on the floor while she herself opened the bottles of lemonade she brought up from the cellar. She got a chunk of ice from a corner icebox, washed some sawdust off it and bashed it up with a hammer, in the sink, so that she could drop some into their glasses. There again he didn't try to help.

"Now Tessa," said Nancy, after a gulp of lemonade. "Now it's time. Do me a favor. Please do."

Tessa drank her lemonade.

"Tell Ollie," Nancy said. "Tell him what he's got in his pockets. Start with the right one."

Tessa said, without looking up, "Well, I expect he's got his wallet."

"Oh, go on," said Nancy.

"Well, she's right," said Ollie. "I've got my wallet. Now does she have to guess what's in it? Because there isn't much."

"Never mind that," said Nancy. "Tell him what else, Tessa. In his right pocket."

"What is this, anyway?" said Ollie.

"Tessa," said Nancy sweetly. "Come on, Tessa, you know me. Remember we're old friends, we're friends since the first room of school. Just do it for me."

"Is this some game?" said Ollie. "Is this some game you thought up between the two of you?"

Nancy laughed at him.

"What's the matter," she said. "What have you got that you're ashamed of? Have you a smelly old sock?"

"A pencil," said Tessa, very quietly. "Some money. Coins. I can't tell what value. A piece of paper with some writing on it? Some printing?"

"Clean it out, Ollie," cried Nancy. "Clean it out."

"Oh, and a stick of gum," said Tessa. "I think a stick of gum. That's all."

The gum was unwrapped and covered with lint.

"I'd forgotten that was there," said Ollie, though he hadn't. Out came the stub of a pencil, some nickels and coppers, a folded-up, worn clipping from a newspaper.

"Somebody gave me that," he said, as Nancy snatched it up and unfolded it.

"We are in the market for original manuscripts of superior quality, both poetry and prose," she read aloud. *"Serious consideration will be given—"*

Ollie had grabbed it out of her hand.

"Somebody *gave* me that. They wanted my opinion, whether I thought it was a valid outfit."

"Oh, Ollie."

"I didn't even know it was still there. Same with the gum."

"Aren't you surprised?"

"Of course I am. I'd forgotten."

"Aren't you surprised at Tessa? What she *knew*?"

Ollie managed a smile for Tessa, though he was hotly disturbed. It was not her fault.

"It's what a lot of fellows would have in their pockets," he said. "Coins? Naturally. Pencil—"

"Gum?" said Nancy.

"Possible."

"And the paper with the printing. She said *printing*."

"She said a piece of paper. She didn't know what was on it. You didn't, did you?" he said to Tessa.

She shook her head. She looked towards the door, listening.

"I think there's a car in the lane."

She was right. They all heard it now. Nancy went to peek through the curtain and at that moment Tessa gave Ollie an unexpected smile. It was not a smile of complicity or apology or the usual coquetry. It might have been a smile of welcome, but without any explicit invitation. It was just the offering of some warmth, some easy spirit in her. And at the same time there was a movement of her wide shoulders, a peaceable settling there, as if the smile was spreading through her whole self.

"Oh, shoot," said Nancy. But she had to get control of her excitement and Ollie of his off-kilter attraction and surprise.

Tessa opened the door just as a man was getting out of the car. He waited by the gate for Nancy and Ollie to come down the path. He was probably in his sixties, thick-shouldered, serious-faced, wearing a pale summer suit and a Christie hat. His car was a new-model coupe. He nodded to Nancy and Ollie with the brief respect and deliberate lack of curiosity he might have shown if he was holding the door for them as they came out of a doctor's office.

Tessa's door was not long shut behind him when another car appeared at the far end of the lane.

"Lineup," Nancy said. "Sunday afternoon is busy. In summer, anyway. People come from miles away to see her."

"So she can tell them what they've got in their pockets?"

Nancy let that pass.

"Mostly asking her about things that are lost. Valuable things. Anyway, to them valuable."

"Does she charge?"

"I don't think so."

"She must."

"Why must she?"

"Isn't she poor?"

"She's not starving."

"Maybe she doesn't very often get it right."

"Well, I think she must, or people wouldn't keep coming to see her, would they?"

The tone of their conversation changed as they walked along between the rosebushes in the bright airless tunnel. They wiped sweat from their faces, and lost the energy to snipe at each other.

Ollie said, "I don't understand it."

Nancy said, "I don't know if anybody does. It isn't just things that people lose, either. She has located bodies."

"*Bodies?*"

"There was a man who they thought walked out the railway track and was caught in a snowstorm and froze to death and they couldn't find him, and she told them, look down by the lake at the bottom of the cliff. And sure enough. Not the railway track at all. And once a cow that had gone missing, she told them it was drowned."

"So?" said Ollie. "If that's true, why hasn't anybody investigated? I mean, scientifically?"

"It's perfectly true."

"I don't mean I don't trust her. But I want to know how she does it. Didn't you ever ask her?"

Nancy surprised him. "Wouldn't that be rude?" she said.

Now she was the one who seemed to have had enough of the conversation.

"So," he insisted, "was she seeing things when she was a kid at school?"

"No. I don't know. Not that she ever let on."

"Was she just like everybody else?"

"She wasn't exactly like everybody else. But who is? I mean, I never thought *I* was. Or Ginny didn't think *she* was. With Tessa it was just that she lived out where she did and she had to milk the cow before she came to school in the morning, which none of the rest of us did. I always tried to be friends with her."

"I'm sure," said Ollie mildly.

She went on as if she hadn't heard.

"I think it started, though—I think it must have started when she was sick. Our second year in high school she got sick, she had seizures. She quit school and she never came back, and that's when she sort of fell out of things."

"Seizures," said Ollie. "Epileptic fits?"

"I never heard that. Oh"—she turned away from him—"I've been really disgusting."

Ollie stopped walking. He said, "Why?"

Nancy stopped too.

"I took you out there on purpose to show you we had something special here. Her. Tessa. I mean, to show you Tessa."

"Yes. Well?"

"Because you don't think we have anything here worth noticing. You think we're only worth making fun of. All of us around here. So I was going to show her to you. Like a freak."

"*Freak* is not a word I would use about her."

"That was my intention, though. I should have my head kicked in."

"Not quite."

"I should go and beg her pardon."

"I wouldn't do that."

"Wouldn't you?"

"No."

That evening Ollie helped Nancy set out a cold supper. Mrs. Box had left a cooked chicken and jellied salads in the fridge, and Nancy had made an angel food cake on Saturday, to be served with strawberries. They set everything out on the verandah that got the afternoon shade. Between the main course and the dessert Ollie carried the plates and salad dishes back to the kitchen.

Out of the blue he said, "I wonder if any of them think to bring her some treat or other? Like chicken or strawberries?"

Nancy was dipping the best-looking berries in fruit sugar. After a moment she said, "Sorry?"

"That girl. Tessa."

"Oh," said Nancy. "She's got chickens, she could kill one if she wanted to. I wouldn't be surprised if she's got a berry patch too. They mostly do, in the country."

Her burst of contrition on the way back had done her good, and now it was over.

"It's not just that she isn't a freak," said Ollie. "It's that she doesn't think of herself as a freak."

"Well of course not."

"She's content to be whatever she is. She has remarkable eyes."

Nancy called to Wilf to ask if he wanted to play the piano while she was fussing around getting the dessert out.

"I have to whip the cream, and in this weather it will take forever."

Wilf said they could wait, he was tired.

He did play, though, later when the dishes were done and it was getting dark. Nancy's father did not go to the evening church service—he thought it was too much to ask—but he did not allow any sort of card game or board game on Sunday. He looked through the *Post* again, while Wilf played. Nancy sat on the verandah steps, out of his sight, and smoked a cigarette which she hoped her father would not smell.

"When I'm married—," she said to Ollie, who was leaning against the railing, "when I am married I'll smoke whenever I like."

Ollie, of course, was not smoking, because of his lungs.

He laughed. He said, "Now now. Is that a good enough reason?"

Wilf was playing, by ear, "Eine Kleine Nachtmusik."

"He's good," said Ollie. "He's got good hands. But the girls used to say they were cold."

He was not thinking, however, of Wilf or Nancy or their sort of marriage. He was thinking of Tessa, of her oddity and composure. Wondering what she was doing on this long hot evening at the end of her wild-rose lane. Did she still have callers, was she still busy solving the problems of people's lives? Or did she go out and sit on the swing, and creak back and forth, with no company but the rising moon?

He was to discover, in a little while, that she spent the evenings carrying pails of water from the pump to her tomato plants, and hilling up the beans and potatoes, and that if he wanted to get any chance of talking to her, this would have to be his occupation as well.

During that time Nancy would get more and more wrapped up in the wedding preparations, without a thought to spare for Tessa, and hardly any for him, except to remark once or twice that he never seemed to be around now, when she needed him.

April 29. Dear Ollie,

I have been thinking we would hear from you ever since we got back from Quebec City, and was surprised that we didn't (not even at Christmas!), but then I guess I could say I found out why—I have started several times to write but had to delay till I got my feelings in order. I could say I suppose that the article or story or whatever you call it in Saturday Night was well-written and it is a feather in your cap I am sure to get into a magazine. Father does not like the reference to a "little" lake port and would like to remind you that this is the best and busiest harbour on this side of Lake Huron and I am not sure I like the word "prosaic." I don't know if this is any more a prosaic place than anywhere else and what do you expect it to be—poetic?

The main problem however is Tessa and what this will do to her life. I don't imagine you thought of that. I have not been able to get her on the phone and I cannot get behind the wheel of a car too comfortably (reasons I will leave to your imagination) to go out and see her. Anyway from what I hear she is swamped with people coming and it is the worst possible time for cars to get in where she lives and the wreckers have been hauling people out of the ditch (for which they don't get any thanks, just a lecture on our backward conditions). The road is an awful mess, getting chewed up past repair. The wild roses will certainly be a thing of the past. Already the township council is in an uproar as to how much this will end up costing and a lot of people are very mad because they think Tessa was behind all the publicity and is raking in the money. They don't believe she is doing it all for nothing and if anybody made money out of this it is you. I am quoting Father when I say that—I know you are not a mercenary-minded person. For you it is all the glory of getting into print. Forgive me if that strikes you as sarcastic. It is fine to be ambitious but what about other people?

Well maybe you were expecting a letter of congratulations but I hope you will excuse me, I just had to get this off my chest.

Just one additional thing though. I want to ask you, were you thinking the whole time about writing that? Now I hear you were back and forth there to Tessa's several times on your own. You never mentioned that to me or asked me to go with you. You never indicated that you were getting Material (I believe that is how you would refer to it), and as far as I can recall you tossed off the whole experience in quite a snippy way. And in your whole piece there is not one word about how I took you there or introduced you to Tessa. There is no recognition of that at all, any more than there has been any private recognition or thanks. And I wonder how honest you were to Tessa about your intentions or if you asked her permission to exercise—I am quoting you now—your Scientific Curiosity? Did you explain what you were doing to her? Or did you just come and go and make use of us Prosaic People here to embark on your Career as a Writer?

Well good luck Ollie, I don't expect to hear from you again. (Not that we ever had the honour of hearing from you once.)

Your cousin-in-law, Nancy.

Dear Nancy,

Nancy I must say that I think you are getting your tail in a spin over nothing. Tessa was bound to be discovered and "written up" by somebody, and why should that somebody not be me? The idea of writing the piece took shape in my mind only gradually as I went to talk to her. And I was quite truly acting out of my Scientific Curiosity, which is one thing I would never apologize for in my nature. You seem to think that I should have asked your permission or kept you informed of all my plans and movements, at a time when you were running around in the most monumental flap about your wedding dress and your showers and how many silver platters you were receiving or God knows what.

As for Tessa, you are quite mistaken if you think that I have forgotten about her now that the article has appeared or have not considered what this will do to her life. And actually I have had a note from her which does not indicate that things are in such a turmoil as you have described. At any rate she will not have to put up with her life there for long. I am in touch with some people who read the article and are very interested. There is research of a legitimate nature being done into these matters, some here but mostly in the States. I think that there is more money available to spend on this sort of thing and more genuine interest over the border so I am investigating certain possibilities there—for Tessa as a research subject and for me as a scientific journalist along these lines—in Boston or in Baltimore or perhaps North Carolina.

I am sorry you should think so harshly of me. You don't

mention—except for one veiled (happy?) announcement—how married life is going for you. Not a word about Wilf, but I imagine you took him along to Quebec City with you and I hope you enjoyed yourselves. I hope he is flourishing as ever. Yours, Ollie.

Dear Tessa,

Apparently you have had your phone disconnected, which may have been necessary with all the celebrity you are enjoying. I don't mean that to sound catty. Often things come out these days in a way I do not mean them to. I am expecting a baby—I don't know if you have heard—and it seems to make me very touchy and jumpy.

I imagine you are having a very busy and confusing time, with all the people who are now coming to see you. It must be difficult to get on with your normal routine. If you get a chance it would be very nice to see you. So this is an invitation really to drop in and see me if you ever get to town (I heard in the store that you now get all your groceries delivered). You have never seen the inside of my new—I mean newly decorated and new to me—house. Or even my old house, now that I come to think of it—it was always me running out to see you. And not so often as I would have liked to, either. Life is always so full. Getting and spending we lay waste our powers. Why do we let ourselves be so busy and miss doing things we should have, or would have, liked to do? Remember us beating down the butter with the old wooden paddles? I enjoyed it. That was when I brought Ollie to see you and I hope you do not regret it.

Now Tessa I hope you don't think I am meddling or sticking my nose in where I have no business, but Ollie has mentioned to me in a letter that he is in touch with some people who are doing research or something in the States. I suppose he has been in touch with you about this. I do not know what kind of research he means but I must say that when I read that part of his letter it made my blood run cold. I just feel in my heart it is not a good thing for you to leave here—if that is what you are thinking about—and go where nobody knows you or thinks of you as a friend or normal person. I just felt I had to tell you this.

Another thing I feel I have to tell you though I don't know how to. It is this. Ollie is certainly not a bad person but he has an effect—and now I think of it, not just on women but on men too—and it is not that he does not know about this but that he does not exactly take responsibility for it. To put it frankly, I cannot think of any worse fate than falling in love with him. He seems to think of teaming up with you in some way to write about you or these experiments or whatever goes on and he will be very friendly and natural but you might mistake the way he acts for something more than it is. Please don't be mad at me for saying this. Come to see me. xxx Nancy.

Dear Nancy,

Please do not worry about me. Ollie has kept in touch with me about everything. By the time you get this note we will be married and may already be in the States. I am sorry not to get to see the inside of your new house. Yours truly, Tessa.

A HOLE IN THE HEAD

The hills in central Michigan are covered with oak forests. Nancy's one and only visit there took place in the fall of 1968, after the oak leaves had changed color, but while they still hung on the trees. She was used to hardwood bush lots, not forests, with a great many maples, whose autumn colors were red and gold. The darker colors, the rusts or wines, of the big oak leaves did not lift her spirits, even in the sunlight.

The hill where the private hospital was located was entirely bare of trees, and a distance away from any town or village or even any inhabited farm. It was the sort of building you used to see "made over" into a hospital in some small towns, after being the grand house of an important family who had all died off or couldn't keep it up. Two sets of bay windows on either side of the front door, dormers all the way across on the third story. Old grimy brick, and a lack of any shrubs or hedges or apple orchard, just the shaved grass and a gravel parking lot.

No place for anybody to hide if they ever had a notion of running away.

Such a thought would not have occurred to her—or not so quickly—in the days before Wilf got sick.

She parked her car beside a few others, wondering if these belonged to the staff or visitors. How many visitors would come to such an isolated place?

You had to climb a number of steps to read the sign on the front door, which advised you to go around to the side door. Close up, she saw bars on some windows. Not on the bay windows—which were, however, without curtains—but on some windows above and some below, in what would be a partly aboveground cellar.

The door that she had been advised to go to opened on that low level. She rang the bell, then knocked, then tried the bell again. She thought she could hear it ringing, but she wasn't sure because there was a great clatter inside. She tried the doorknob, and to her surprise—in view of the bars on the windows—it opened. There she was on the threshold of the kitchen, the big busy kitchen of an institution, where a lot of people were washing up and clearing away after lunch.

The kitchen windows were bare. The ceiling was high, amplifying the noise, and the walls and cupboards were all painted white. A number of lights were turned on, though the light of the clear fall day was at its height.

She was noticed at once, of course. But nobody seemed in a hurry to greet her and find out what she was doing there.

She recognized something else. Along with the hard pressure of the light and the noise, there was the same feeling she got now in her own house, and that other people coming into her house must be aware of even more strongly.

The feeling of something being out of kilter, in a way that could not be fixed or altered but only resisted, as well as you could. Some people entering such places give up immediately, they do not know how to resist, they are outraged or frightened, they have to flee.

A man in a white apron came pushing a cart with a garbage can in it. She could not tell whether he had come to greet her or was just crossing her path, but he was smiling, he seemed amiable, so she told him who she was and who she had come to see. He listened, nodded several times, smiled more broadly, began to wag his head and pat his fingers against his mouth—to show her that he could not speak or was forbidden to do so, as in some game, and continued on his way, bumping the cart down a ramp to a lower cellar.

He would be an inmate, not an employee. It must be the sort of place where people were put to work, if they could work. The idea being that it would be good for them, and maybe it was.

Finally came a responsible-looking person, a woman of about Nancy's own age in a dark suit—not wearing the white apron that enfolded most of the rest of them—and Nancy told everything again. That she had received a letter, her name having been given by an inmate—by a resident, as they wanted you to say—as the person to be contacted.

She had been right in thinking that the people in the kitchen were not hired help.

"But they seem to like working here," the Matron said. "They take a pride." Smiling a warning left and right, she led Nancy into her office, which was a room off the kitchen. It became clear as they were talking that she had to deal with all sorts of interruptions, making decisions about kitchen work and settling complaints whenever somebody bundled into a white apron came peering around the door. She must also have to handle the files, the bills or notices that were stuck in a rather unbusinesslike way on hooks around the walls. As well as dealing with visitors like Nancy.

"We went through what old records we had and got out the names that were given as relatives—"

"I am not a relative," said Nancy.

"Or whatever, and we wrote letters like the one you received, just to get some guidelines on the way they might want these cases handled. I must say we haven't had many responses. It was good of you to drive all this way."

Nancy asked what was meant by *these cases*.

The Matron said that people had been here for years who perhaps didn't belong here.

"You must understand that I am new here," she said, "but I will tell you what I know."

According to her the place had been a catchall, literally, for those who were genuinely mentally ill, or senile, or those who would never develop normally, one way or another, or people whose families could not or would not cope with them. There had always been, and still was, a wide range. The serious problems were all in the north wing, under security.

Originally this had been a private hospital, owned and run by a doctor. After he died, the family—the doctor's family—took it over, and it turned out that they had their own ways of doing things. It had been partly turned into a charity hospital and there were some unusual arrangements made to get subsidies for charity patients who were not proper charity cases at all.

Some of those still on the books had actually passed away and some did not have the proper claim or records to be here. Many of those, of course, worked for their keep and this may have been—it was—usually good for their morale, but it was nevertheless all irregular and against the law.

And now, the thing was that there had been a thorough investigation and the whole place was being closed down. The building was antiquated anyway. Its capacity was too small, this was not the way things were done now. The serious cases were going to a big facility in Flint or Lansing—it wasn't quite definite yet—and some could go into sheltered housing, group homes, as the new trend was, and then there were some who could manage if they were placed with relatives.

Tessa was considered to be one of these. It seemed that she had needed some electrical treatments when she came in, but for a long time now she had been on just the mildest medication.

"Shock treatments?" Nancy said.

"Perhaps shock *therapy*," the Matron said, as if that made some special difference. "You say you are not a relative. That means you don't intend to take her."

"I have a husband—" said Nancy. "I have a husband who is—he would be in a place like this, I guess, but I am looking after him at home."

"Oh. Really," the Matron said, with a sigh that was not disbelieving, but not sympathetic either. "And a problem is that apparently she is not even a citizen. She herself does not think she is—so I suppose you are not interested now in seeing her?"

"Yes," said Nancy. "Yes, I am. That's what I came for."

"Oh. Well. She is just around the corner, in the bakery. She's been baking here for years. I think there was a baker hired at first, but when he left they never hired anybody else, they didn't have to, with Tessa."

As she stood up she said, "Now. You may want me to look

in, after a while, and say there is something I'd like to speak to you about. Then you can make your getaway. Tessa is quite smart and she knows the way the wind is blowing and she could be upset to see you leave without her. So I'll give you an opportunity just to slip away."

Tessa wasn't entirely gray. Her curls were held back in a tight net, showing her forehead unwrinkled, shining, even broader and higher and whiter than it used to be. Her figure had broadened, too. She had big breasts that looked as stiff as boulders, sheathed in her white baker's garb, and in spite of this burden, in spite of her position at the moment—bent over a table, rolling out a great flap of dough—her shoulders were square and stately.

She was alone in the bakery, except for a tall, thin, fine-featured girl—no, a woman—whose pretty face was constantly twitching into bizarre grimaces.

"Oh, Nancy. It's you," said Tessa. She spoke quite naturally, though with the gallant catch of breath, the involuntary intimacy, of those who carry a noble load of flesh on their bones. "Stop that, Elinor. Don't be silly. You go get my friend a chair."

Seeing that Nancy meant to embrace her, as people did now, she was flustered. "Oh, I'm all over flour. And for another thing, Elinor might bite you. Elinor doesn't like when people get too friendly with me."

Elinor had returned in a hurry with a chair. Nancy made a point then of looking into her face and speaking nicely.

"Thank you very much, Elinor."

"She doesn't talk," said Tessa. "She's my good helper, though. I couldn't manage without her, could I, Elinor?"

"Well," said Nancy. "I am surprised you knew me. I've withered quite a bit since olden times."

"Yes," said Tessa. "I wondered if you would come."

"I could even have been dead, I suppose. Do you remember Ginny Ross? She's dead."

"Yes."

Piecrust, was what Tessa was making. She cut out a round of dough and slapped it into a tin pie plate, and held it aloft, expertly turning it on one hand and cutting it with a knife held in the other. She did this rapidly several times.

She said, "Wilf's not dead?"

"No, he's not. But he's gone a bit round the bend, Tessa." Too late, Nancy realized that this had not been a tactful thing to say, and she tried to insert a lighter note. "He's taken up some strange ways, poor Wolfie." Years ago she had tried calling Wilf Wolfie, thinking that the name suited his long jaw and thin moustache and bright stern eyes. But he did not like it, he suspected mockery, so she had stopped. Now he didn't mind, and just to say the name made her feel more bright and tender towards him, which was a help under the present circumstances.

"For instance, he's taken a scunner against rugs."

"Rugs?"

"He walks around the room like this," said Nancy, drawing a rectangle in the air. "I had to move the furniture away from the walls. Around and around and around." Unexpectedly and somehow apologetically, she laughed.

"Oh, there's some in here that do that," said Tessa with a nod, an insider's air of confirmation. "They don't want anything to get between them and the wall."

"And he's very dependent. It's *Where's Nancy?* all the time. I'm the only one he trusts these days."

"Is he violent?" Tessa spoke again, as a professional, a connoisseur.

"No. He's suspicious, though. He thinks people are coming in and hiding things on him. He thinks somebody goes around changing the clocks and even the day on the newspaper. Then he'll snap out of it when I mention somebody's medical problem and do a spot-on diagnosis. The mind's a weird piece of business."

There. Another nice lapse of tact.

"He's mixed up, but he's not violent."

"That's good."

Tessa set the pie plate down and began to ladle filling into it from a large, no-brand tin labelled *Blueberry*. The filling looked rather thin and glutinous.

"Here. Elinor," she said. "Here's your scraps."

Elinor had been standing just behind Nancy's chair—Nancy had been careful not to turn around and look. Now Elinor slid around the bake table without glancing up and began to mold together the pieces of dough that the knife had cut away.

"That man is dead, though," Tessa said. "I know that much."

"What man are you talking about?"

"That man. That friend of yours."

"*Ollie*? You mean Ollie's dead?"

"Don't you know that?" Tessa said.

"No. No."

"I thought you would've known. Didn't Wilf know?"

"*Doesn't* Wilf know," said Nancy in an automatic way, defending her husband by placing him amongst the living.

"I thought he would," said Tessa. "Weren't they related?"

Nancy did not answer. Of course she should have thought of Ollie's being dead if Tessa was here.

"I guess he kept it to himself then," Tessa said.

"Wilf was always good at that," said Nancy. "Where did this happen? Were you with him?"

Tessa wagged her head to say No, or that she didn't know.

"Well when? What did they tell you?"

"Nobody told me. They never would tell me anything."

"Oh, Tessa."

"I had a hole in my head. I had it for a long time."

"Is it like you used to know things?" said Nancy. "You remember the way?"

"They gave me gas."

"Who?" said Nancy sternly. "What do you mean they gave you gas?"

"The ones in charge here. They gave me the needles."

"You said gas."

"They gave me the needles and the gas too. It was to cure my head. And to make me not remember. Certain things I do remember, but I have trouble with telling how long ago. There was that hole in my head for a very long time."

"Did Ollie die before you came in here or after? You don't *remember* how he died?"

"Oh, I saw him. He had his head wrapped up in a black coat. Tied with a cord around the neck. Somebody did it to him." Her lips for a moment were clamped together. "Somebody should have gone to the electric chair."

"Maybe that was a bad dream you had. You might have got your dream mixed up with what really happened."

Tessa lifted her chin as if to settle something. "Not that. I haven't got that mixed up."

The shock treatments, Nancy thought. Shock treatments left holes in the memory? There would have to be something in the records. She would go and talk to the Matron again.

She looked at what Elinor was doing with the discarded bits of dough. She had molded them cleverly, sticking heads and ears and tails onto them. Little dough mice.

With a sharp swift motion, Tessa made air slits in the top crusts of the pies. The mice went into the oven with them, on their own tin plate.

Then Tessa held out her hands, and stood waiting while Elinor got a small damp towel to wipe away any sticky dough or dusting of flour.

"Chair," said Tessa in an undertone, and Elinor brought a chair and placed it at the end of the table, near Nancy's, so that Tessa could sit down.

"And maybe you could go and make us a cup of tea," Tessa said. "Don't worry, we'll keep an eye on your treats. We'll watch your mousies.

"Let's forget all we were talking about," she said to Nancy. "Weren't you going to have a baby, the last I heard from you? Was it a boy or a girl?"

"A boy," said Nancy. "That was years and years ago. And after that I had two girls. They're all grown-up now."

"You don't notice in here how time goes by. That may be a blessing or it may not, I don't know. What are they doing then?"

"The boy—"

"What did you call him?"

"Alan. He went in for medicine too."

"He's a doctor. That's good."

"The girls are both married. Well, Alan's married too."

"So what are their names? The girls'?"

"Susan and Patricia. They both took up nursing."

"You chose nice names."

Tea was brought—the kettle must be kept on the boil here all the time—and Tessa poured.

"Not the best china in the world," she said, reserving for herself a slightly chipped cup.

"It's fine," said Nancy. "Tessa. Do you remember what you used to be able to do? You used to be able to—you used to know things. When people lost things, you used to be able to tell them where they were."

"Oh no," Tessa said. "I just pretended."

"You couldn't have."

"It bothers my head to talk about it."

"I'm sorry."

The Matron had appeared in the doorway.

"I don't want to disturb you having your tea," she said to Nancy. "But if you wouldn't mind popping into my room for just a minute when you're finished—"

Tessa hardly waited until the woman was out of earshot.

"That's so you won't have to say good-bye to me," she said. She seemed to be settling into appreciation of a familiar joke. "It's that trick of hers. Everybody knows about it. I knew you hadn't come to take me away. How could you?"

"It's not anything to do with you, Tessa. It's just that I've got Wilf."

"That's right."

"He deserves something. He's been a good husband to me, just as good as he could be. I made a vow to myself that he wouldn't have to go into an institution."

"No. Not into an institution," Tessa said.

"Oh. What a stupid thing to say."

Tessa was smiling, and Nancy saw in that smile the same thing that had puzzled her years ago. Not exactly superiority, but an extraordinary, unwarranted benevolence.

"You were good to come to see me, Nancy. You can see I've kept my health. That's something. You better pop in and see the woman."

"I don't have any intention of popping in to see her," said Nancy. "I'm not going to sneak out. I fully intend to say good-bye to you."

So now there was no way she could ask the Matron anything about what Tessa had told her, and she didn't know if she should ask, anyway—it seemed like sneaking around behind Tessa's back, and it might bring some reprisal. What could bring reprisals, in a place like this, you could never know.

"Well, don't say good-bye till you've had one of Elinor's mice. Elinor's blind mice. She wants you to. She likes you now. And don't worry—I make sure she keeps her hands good and clean."

Nancy ate the mouse, and told Elinor that it was very good. Elinor consented to shake hands with her, and then Tessa did the same.

"If he wasn't dead," said Tessa in quite a robust and reasonable tone, "why wouldn't he have come here and got me? He said he would."

Nancy nodded. "I'll write to you," she said.

And she meant to, truly, but Wilf became such a care as soon as she got home, and the whole visit to Michigan became so disturbing, and yet unreal, in her mind, that she never did.

A SQUARE, A CIRCLE, A STAR

One late summer day in the early seventies, a woman was walking around Vancouver, a city she had never visited before and so far as she knew would never see again. She had walked from her downtown hotel across the Burrard Street Bridge, and after a while found herself on Fourth Avenue. At this time Fourth Avenue was a street given over to small shops selling incense, crystals, huge paper flowers, Salvador Dali and White Rabbit posters, also cheap clothes, either bright and flimsy or earth-colored and as heavy as blankets, made in poor and legendary parts of the world. The music played inside these shops assaulted you—it seemed almost to knock you over—as you went by. So did the sweetish foreign smells, and the indolent presence of boys and girls, or young men and women, who had practically set up house on the sidewalk. The woman had heard and read about this youth culture, as she believed it was called. It had been in evidence for some years now and in fact was supposed to be on the wane. But she had never had to make her way through such a concentration of it or found herself, as it seemed, all on her own in the middle of it.

She was sixty-seven years old, she was so lean that her hips and bosom had practically disappeared, and she walked with a bold gait, head thrust forward and turning from side to side in a challenging, inquisitive way.

There did not seem to be a person within three decades of her age anywhere in sight.

A boy and girl approached her with a solemnity that nevertheless seemed slightly goofy. They had circlets of braided ribbon around their heads. They wanted her to buy a tiny scroll of paper.

She asked if it contained her fortune.

"Perhaps," the girl said.

The boy said, reprovingly, "It contains wisdom."

"Oh, in that case," said Nancy, and put a dollar into an outstretched embroidered cap.

"Now, tell me your names," she said, with a grin that she could not suppress and that was not returned.

"Adam and Eve," the girl said, as she took up the bill and tucked it away in some part of her drapery.

"Adam and Eve and Pinch-me-tight," said Nancy. *"Went down to the river on Saturday night . . ."*

But the pair withdrew, in profound disdain and weariness.

So much for that. She walked on.

Is there any law against my being here?

A hole-in-the-wall cafe had a sign in the window. She had not eaten since breakfast at the hotel. It was now after four o'clock. She stopped to read what they were advertising.

Bless the grass. And behind these scrawled words there was an angry-looking, wrinkled-up, almost teary creature with thin hair blowing back from her cheeks and forehead. Dry-looking pale reddish-brown hair. Always go lighter than your own color, the hairdresser had said. Her own color was dark, dark brown, nearly black.

No, it wasn't. Her own color now was white.

It happens only a few times in your life—at least it's only a few times if you're a woman—that you come upon yourself like this, with no preparation. It was as bad as those dreams in which she might find herself walking down the street in her nightgown, or nonchalantly wearing only the top of her pajamas.

During the past ten or fifteen years she had certainly taken time out to observe her own face in a harsh light so that she could better see what makeup could do, or decide whether the time had definitely come to start coloring her hair. But she had never had a jolt like this, a moment during which she saw not just some old and new trouble spots, or some decline that could not be ignored any longer, but a complete stranger.

Somebody she didn't know and wouldn't want to know.

She smoothed out her expression immediately, of course, and there was an improvement. You could say then that she recognized herself. And she promptly began to cast around for hope, as if there was not a minute to lose. She needed to spray her hair so it wouldn't blow off her face like that. She needed a more definite shade of lipstick. Bright coral, which you could hardly ever find now, instead of this nearly naked, more fashionable, and dreary pinkish brown. Determination to find what she needed at once turned her around—she had seen a drugstore three or four blocks back—and a desire not to have to pass by Adam-and-Eve again made her cross the street.

If this had not happened, the meeting would never have taken place.

Another old person was coming along the sidewalk. A man, not tall, but upright and muscular, bald to the crown of his head, where there was a frill of fine white hair, blowing every which way just as hers did. An open-necked denim shirt, old jacket and pants. Nothing that made him look as if he was trying to resemble the young men on the street—no ponytail or kerchief or jeans. And yet he could never have been mistaken for the sort of man she had been seeing daily for the last couple of weeks.

She knew almost right away. It was Ollie. But she stopped dead, having a considerable reason for believing that this could not be true.

Ollie. Alive. Ollie.

And he said, "Nancy!"

The expression on her face (once she got over a moment of terror, which he didn't seem to notice) must be pretty much the same as the expression on his. Incredulity, hilarity, apology.

What was the apology about? The fact that they had not parted as friends, that they had never been in touch with each other in all these years? Or for the changes that had taken place in each of them, the way they had to present themselves now, no hope for it.

Nancy had more reason to be shocked than he had, surely. But she would not bring that up for a moment. Not until they got their bearings.

"I'm just here overnight," she said. "I mean, last night and tonight. I've been on a cruise to Alaska. With all the other old widows. Wilf is dead, you know. He's been dead for nearly a year. I'm starving. I've been walking and walking. I hardly know how I got here."

And she added, quite foolishly, "I didn't know you lived here." Because she hadn't thought of his living anywhere. But she hadn't been absolutely sure of his being dead, either. As far as she could make out, Wilf hadn't had any news of that kind. Though she could not get much out of Wilf, he had slipped out of reach, even during the short time she had been on that jaunt to see Tessa in Michigan.

Ollie was saying that he didn't live in Vancouver, he too was in town just briefly. He had come for a medical thing, at the hospital, just a routine sort of thing. He lived on Texada Island. Where that was, he said, was too complicated to explain. Enough to say that it took three boats, three ferries, to get there from here.

He led her to a dirty white Volkswagen van, parked on a side street, and they drove to a restaurant. The van smelled of the ocean, she thought, of seaweed and fish and rubber. And it turned out that fish was what he ate now, never meat. The restaurant, which had no more than half a dozen little tables, was Japanese. A Japanese boy with the sweetly downcast face of a young priest was chopping fish at a terrifying speed behind the counter. Ollie called out, "How's it going, Pete?" and the young man called back, "Fan-tas-tic," in a derisive North American voice without losing a bit of his rhythm. Nancy had a flash of discomfort—was it because Ollie had used the young man's name and the young man hadn't used Ollie's? And because she hoped Ollie wouldn't notice her noticing that? Some people—some men—set such store on being friends with people in shops and restaurants.

She couldn't stand the idea of raw fish, so she had noodles. The chopsticks were unfamiliar to her—they didn't seem like the Chinese chopsticks she had used once or twice—but they were all that was provided.

Now that they were settled, she should speak about Tessa. It might be more decent, though, to wait for him to tell her.

So she began to talk about the cruise. She said that she would never go on another one of those to save her life. It wasn't the weather, though some of that was bad, with rain and fog cutting off the view. They got enough view, actually, more than enough to last a lifetime. Mountain after mountain and island after island and rocks and water and trees. Everybody saying, isn't that stupendous? Isn't that stunning?

Stunning, stunning, stunning. Stupendous.

They saw bears. They saw seals, sea lions, a whale. Everybody taking pictures. Sweating and cussing and afraid their fancy new cameras weren't working right. Then off the boat and the ride on the famous railway to the famous gold-mining town and more pictures and actors dressed up like the Gay Nineties and what did most people do there? Lined up to buy fudge.

Singsongs on the train. And on the boat, the boozing. Some people from breakfast time on. Card games, gambling. Dancing every night, with ten old women to one old man.

"All us ribboned and curled and spangled and poufed up like doggies in a show. I'm telling you, the competition was wild."

Ollie laughed at various points during this story, though she caught him once looking not at her but towards the counter, with an absentminded, anxious expression. He had finished his soup and might have been thinking about what was coming next. Perhaps he, like some other men, felt slighted when his food did not come promptly.

Nancy kept losing her grip on the noodles.

"And God Almighty, I kept thinking, just what, whatever, am I ever doing here? Everybody had been telling me I should get away. Wilf was not himself for a few years and I'd looked after him at home. After he died people said I should get out and join things. Join the Seniors' Book Club, join the Seniors' Nature Walks, join the Watercolour Painting. Even the Seniors Volunteer Visitors, who go and intrude on the poor defenseless creatures in the hospital. So I just didn't feel like doing any of that, and then everybody started with Get away, get away. My kids as well. You need a total holiday. So I shillied and shallied and I didn't really know how to get away, and somebody said, well, you could go on a cruise. So I thought, well, I could go on a cruise."

"Interesting," said Ollie. "I don't think losing a wife would ever make it occur to me to go on a cruise."

Nancy hardly missed a beat. "That's smart of you," she said.

She waited for him to say something about Tessa, but his fish had come and he fussed with it. He tried to persuade her to taste a bit.

She wouldn't. In fact, she gave up on the meal entirely, lit a cigarette.

She said she had always been watching and waiting to see something more he had written after that piece that made all the furor. It showed he was a good writer, she said.

He looked bewildered for a moment, as if he could not recall what she was talking about. Then he shook his head, as if he was amazed, and said that was years ago, years ago.

"It wasn't what I really wanted."

"What do you mean by that?" said Nancy. "You're not the way you used to be, are you? You're not the same."

"Of course not."

"I mean, there's something just basically, physically different. You're built differently. Your shoulders. Or am I not remembering right?"

He said that was it, exactly. He had realized he wanted a more physical kind of life. No. What happened, in order, was that he had a return of the old demon (she supposed he meant the TB) and he realized that he was doing all the wrong kinds of things, so he changed. That was years ago now. He apprenticed to a boatbuilder. Then he got in with a man who ran deep-sea fishing. He looked after boats for a multimillionaire. This was in Oregon. He worked his way back up to Canada, and he hung around here—Vancouver—for a while and then picked up a bit of land on Sechelt—waterfront, when it was still going cheap. He started a kayak business. Building, renting, selling, giving lessons. There came a time he began to feel that Sechelt was too crowded, and he let his land go for practically nothing to a friend. He was the only person he knew of who hadn't made money from land on Sechelt.

"But my life's not about money," he said.

He heard about land you could get on Texada Island. And now he didn't often leave there. He did this and that to make a living. Some kayak business still, and some fishing. He hired out as a handyman, a housebuilder, a carpenter.

"I get by," he said.

He described to her the house he had built for himself, in outside appearance a shack, but delightful inside, at least to him. A sleeping loft with a little round window. Everything he needed right where he could put his hand to it, out in the open, nothing in cupboards. A short walk from the house he had a bathtub sunk in the earth, in the middle of a bed of sweet herbs. He would carry hot water to it by the pailful and lounge there under the stars, even in the winter.

He grew vegetables, and shared them with the deer.

All the time he was telling her this, Nancy had an unhappy feeling. It was not disbelief—in spite of the one major discrepancy. It was more a feeling of increasing puzzlement, then of disappointment. He was talking the way some other men talked. (For instance, a man she had spent time with on the cruise ship—where she had not been so consistently standoffish, so unsociable, as she had led Ollie to believe.) Plenty of men never had a word to say about their lives, beyond when and where. But there were others, more up-to-date, who gave these casual-sounding yet practiced speeches in which it was said that life was indeed a bumpy road, but misfortunes had pointed the way to better things, lessons were learned, and without a doubt joy came in the morning.

She did not object to other men talking this way—she could usually think about something else—but when Ollie did it, leaning across the rickety little table and across the wooden platter of alarming pieces of fish, a sadness spread through her.

He was not the same. He was truly not the same.

And what about her? Oh, the trouble there was that she *was* quite the same. Talking about the cruise, she had got all keyed up—she had enjoyed listening to herself, to the description that was pouring out of her. Not that that was really the way she used to talk to Ollie—it was more the way she wished she had talked, and had sometimes talked to him in her mind, after he was gone. (Not until she got over being angry at him, of course.) Something would come up that made her think, I wish I could tell Ollie about that. When she talked the way she wanted to other people, she sometimes went too far. She could see what they were thinking. *Sarcastic,* or *critical,* or even *bitter.* Wilf would not use those words, but he would perhaps be thinking them, she never could tell. Ginny would smile, but not the way she used to smile. In her unmarried middle age she had become secretive, mild, and charitable. (The secret came out shortly before her death when she admitted to having become a Buddhist.)

So Nancy had missed Ollie a lot without ever figuring out just what it was that she missed. Something troublesome burning in him like a low-grade fever, something she couldn't get the better of. The things that had got on her nerves during that short time she had known him turned out to be just the things, in retrospect, that shone.

Now he talked earnestly. He smiled into her eyes. She was

reminded of the handy way he used to have of being charming. But she had believed that was never to be used on her.

She was half-afraid he would say, "I'm not boring you, am I?" or, "Isn't life amazing?"

"I have been incredibly lucky," he said. "Lucky in my life. Oh, I know some people would not say so. They'd say I hadn't stuck with anything, or that I hadn't made any money. They'd say I wasted that time when I was down-and-out. But that's not true.

"I heard the call," he said, raising his eyebrows, half smiling at himself. "Seriously. I did." I heard the call to get out of the box. Out of the got-to-do-something-big box. Out of the ego box. I've been lucky all along. Even lucky that I got struck down with TB. Kept me out of college, where I'd have clogged my head up with a lot of nonsense. And it would have kept me from being drafted if the war had come along sooner."

"You couldn't have been drafted anyway once you were a married man," said Nancy.

(She had been in a cynical enough mood, once, to wonder out loud to Wilf whether that could have been the reason for the marriage.

"Other people's reasons aren't a great concern of mine," Wilf had said. He said there was not going to be a war, anyway. And there hadn't been, for another decade.)

"Well, yes," said Ollie. "But actually that wasn't a thoroughly legal arrangement. I was ahead of my time, Nancy. But it always slips my mind that I wasn't really married. Maybe because Tessa was a very deep and serious sort of woman. If you were with her you were with her. No easygoing sort of thing with Tessa."

"So," said Nancy, as lightly as she could manage. "So. You and Tessa."

"It was the Crash stymied everything," Ollie said.

What he meant by this, he went on to say, was that most of the interest, and consequently the funding, had dried up. The funding for the investigations. There was a change in thinking, with the scientific community turning away from what they must have judged to be frivolity. Some experiments were still going on for a while, but in a half-arsed way, he said, and even the people who had seemed the most interested, the most committed—people who had contacted him, said Ollie, it wasn't as if he had contacted them—those people were the first to be out of reach, to fail to answer your letters or get in touch, until they finally sent you a note by their secretaries to say the whole deal was off. He and Tessa were treated like dirt by these people, like annoyances and opportunists, once the wind had changed.

"Academics," he said. "After all we went through, putting ourselves at their disposal. I have no use for them."

"I'd have thought you were dealing mostly with doctors."

"Doctors. Career builders. Academics."

To move him out of this byway of old injuries and ill temper, Nancy asked about the experiments.

Most of them had involved cards. Not ordinary cards but special ESP cards, with their own symbols. A cross, a circle, a star, wavy lines, a square. They would have one card of each symbol faceup on the table, the rest of the deck shuffled and held facedown. Tessa was supposed to say which symbol in front of her would match the symbol on the top card of the deck. That was the open matching test. The blind matching test was the same, except the five key cards were facedown as well. Other tests increasing in difficulty. Sometimes dice were used, or coins. Sometimes nothing but an image in the mind. Series of mind images, nothing written down. Subject and examiner in the same room, or in separate rooms, or a quarter of a mile apart.

Then the success rate Tessa got was measured against the results you would get from pure chance. Law of probability, which he believed was twenty percent.

Nothing in the room but a chair and a table and a light. Like an interrogation room. Tessa would emerge from there wrung out. The symbols bothered her for hours, wherever she looked. Headaches began.

And the results were inconclusive. All kinds of objections were coming up, not about Tessa but about whether the tests were flawed. It was said that people have preferences. When they flip a coin, for instance, more people will guess heads than tails. They just will. All that. And added to it what he had said previously, about the climate then, the intellectual climate, putting such investigations into the realm of frivolity.

Darkness was falling. The CLOSED sign was put up on the restaurant door. Ollie had trouble reading the bill. It turned out that the reason he had come down to Vancouver, the medical problem, had to do with his eyes. Nancy laughed, and took the bill from him, and paid.

"Of course—aren't I a rich widow?"

Then, because they were not through with their conversation—nowhere near through, as Nancy saw it—they went up the street to a Denny's, to drink coffee.

"Maybe you'd rather someplace fancier?" Ollie said. "Maybe you were thinking of a drink?"

Nancy said quickly that she'd done enough drinking on the boat to last her for a while.

"I've done enough to last me my whole life," said Ollie. "I've been off it for fifteen years. Fifteen years, nine months, to be exact. You always know an old drunk when he counts the months."

During the period of the experiments, the parapsychologists, he and Tessa had made a few friends. They got to know people who made a living from their abilities. Not in the interests of so-called science but by what they called fortune-telling, or mind reading, or telepathy, or psychic entertainment. Some people settled down in a good location, operating out of a house or a storefront, and stayed for years. Those were the ones who went in for giving personal advice, predicting the future, doing astrology, and some sorts of healing. Others put on public performances. That might mean hitching up with Chautauqua-like shows made up of lectures and readings and scenes from Shakespeare and somebody singing opera and slides of travels (Education not Sensation), all the way down the ladder to the cut-rate carnivals that mixed in bits of burlesque and hypnotism and some near-naked woman wrapped up in snakes. Naturally Ollie and Tessa liked to think of themselves as belonging to the first category. Education not sensation was indeed what they had in mind. But there too the timing was not lucky. That higher-class sort of thing was almost done for. You could listen to music and get a certain amount of education on the radio, and people had seen all the travelogues they needed to see at the church hall.

The only way to make any money that they discovered was to go with the travelling shows, to operate in town halls or at fall fairs. They shared the stage with the hypnotists and snake ladies and dirty monologuists and strippers in feathers. That sort of thing, too, was winding down, but the war coming along gave it an odd sort of boost. Its life was artificially prolonged for a while when gas rationing stopped people from getting to the city nightclubs or the big movie houses. And television had not yet arrived to entertain them with magic stunts while they sat on their couches at home. The early fifties, Ed Sullivan, et cetera—that really was the end.

Nevertheless there were good crowds for a time, full houses—Ollie enjoyed himself sometimes, warming up the audience with an earnest but intriguing little lecture. And soon he had become part of the act. They had had to work out something a little more exciting, with more drama or suspense to it, than what Tessa had been doing alone. And there was another factor to be considered. She stood up to it well, as far as her nerves and physical endurance went, but her powers, whatever they were, didn't prove so reliable. She started to flounder. She had to concentrate as she never had done before, and it often didn't work. The headaches persisted.

What most people suspect is true. Such performances are full of tricks. Full of fakery, full of deception. Sometimes that's all it is. But what people—most people—hope for is occasionally also true. They hope that it's not all fake. And it's because performers like Tessa, who are really honorable, know about this hope and understand it—who could understand it better?—that they can begin to use certain tricks and routines, guaranteed to get the right results. Because every night, every night, you have to get those results.

Sometimes the means are crude, obvious as the false partition in the box of the lady who is sawed in half. A hidden mike. More likely a code is used, worked out between the person onstage and the partner on the floor. These codes can be an art in themselves. They are secret, nothing written down.

Nancy asked if his code, his and Tessa's, was an art in itself?

"It had a range," he said, his face brightening. "It had nuance."

Then he said, "Actually we could be pretty hokey, too. I had a black cloak I wore—"

"Ollie. Really. A black cloak?"

"Absolutely. A black cloak. And I'd get a volunteer and take off the cloak and wrap it around him or her, after Tessa had been blindfolded—somebody from the audience did that, made sure it was a proper blindfold—and I'd call out to her, 'Who have I got in the cloak?' Or 'Who is the person in the cloak?' Or I'd say 'coat.' Or 'black cloth.' Or, 'What have I got?' Or 'Who do you see?' 'What color hair?' 'Tall or short?' I could do it with the words, I could do it with tiny inflections of my voice. Going into more and more detail. That was just our opening shot."

"You should write about that."

"I did intend to. I thought of an exposé sort of thing. But then I thought, who would care anyway? People want to be fooled, or they don't want to be fooled. They don't go on evidence. Another thing I thought of was a mystery novel. It's a natural milieu. I thought it would make a lot of money and we could get out. And I thought about a movie script. Did you ever see that Fellini movie—?"

Nancy said no.

"Hogwash, anyway. I don't mean the Fellini movie. I mean the ideas I had. At that time."

"Tell me about Tessa."

"I must have written you. Didn't I write you?"

"No."

"I must have written Wilf."

"I think he would have told me."

"Well. Maybe I didn't. Maybe I was at too low a point then."

"What year was it?"

Ollie could not remember. The Korean War was on. Harry Truman was president. It seemed at first as if Tessa only had the flu. But she did not get better, she grew weaker, and became covered with mysterious bruises. She had leukemia.

They were holed up in a town in the mountains in the heat of summer. They had been hoping to get to California before winter. They were not able even to make it to their next booking. The people they had been travelling with went on without them. Ollie got some work at the radio station in the town. He had developed a good voice doing the show with Tessa. He read the news on the radio, and he did a lot of the ads. He wrote some of them, too. Their regular man was off taking the gold cure, or something, in a hospital for drunks.

He and Tessa moved from the hotel to a furnished apartment. There was no air-conditioning, naturally, but luckily it had a bit of a balcony with a tree hanging over it. He pushed the couch up there so Tessa could get the fresh air. He didn't want to have to take her to the hospital—money came into this too, of course, for they had no insurance of any kind—but he also thought she was more peaceful there, where she could watch the leaves stirring. But eventually he had to take her in, and there in a matter of a couple of weeks, she died.

"Is she buried there?" said Nancy. "Didn't you think that we would send you money?"

"No," he said. "No, to both. I mean, I didn't think of asking. I felt that it was my responsibility. And I had her cremated. I skipped town with the ashes. I managed to get to the Coast. It was practically the last thing she had said to me, that she wanted to be cremated and she wanted to be scattered on the waves of the Pacific Ocean."

So that was what he had done, he said. He remembered the Oregon coast, the strip of beach between the ocean and the highway, the fog and chilliness of the early morning, the smell of the seawater, the melancholy booming of the waves. He had taken off his shoes and socks and rolled up his pant legs and waded in, and the gulls came after him to see if he had anything for them. But it was only Tessa he had.

"Tessa—" said Nancy. Then she couldn't go on.

"I became a drunk after that. I functioned after a fashion, but for a long time I was deadwood at the center. Till I just had to pull out of it."

He did not look up at Nancy. There was a heavy moment, while he fingered the ashtray.

"I suppose you found that life goes on," said Nancy.

He sighed. Reproach and relief.

"Sharp tongue, Nancy."

He drove her back to the hotel where she was staying. There was a lot of clanking of gear in the van, and a shuddering and rattling throughout the vehicle itself.

The hotel was not particularly expensive or luxurious—there was no doorman about, no mound of carnivorous-looking flowers to be glimpsed within—and yet when Ollie said, "I bet there hasn't been any old heap like this drive up here in a while," Nancy had to laugh and agree with him.

"What about your ferry?"

"Missed it. Ages ago."

"Where will you sleep?"

"Friends in Horseshoe Bay. Or I'll be all right in here, if I don't feel like waking them up. I've slept here enough times before."

Her room had two beds in it. Twin beds. She might get a dirty look or two, trailing him in, but surely she could stand that. Since the truth would be a far cry from what anybody might be thinking.

She took a preparatory breath.

"No, Nancy."

All this time she had been waiting for him to say one true word. All this afternoon or maybe a good part of her life. She had been waiting, and now he had said it.

No.

It might have been taken as a refusal of the offer she had not quite made. It could have struck her as arrogant, insufferable.

But in fact what she heard was clear and tender and seemed at the moment as full of understanding as any word that had ever been spoken to her. *No.*

She knew the danger of anything she might say. The danger of her own desire, because she didn't really know what sort of desire it was, what it was for. They had shied away from whatever that was years ago, and they would surely have to do so now that they were old—not terribly old, but old enough to appear unsightly and absurd. And unfortunate enough to have spent their time together lying.

For she had been lying too, in her silence. And for the time being, she would go on lying.

"No," he said again, with humility but without embarrassment. "It wouldn't turn out well."

Of course it wouldn't. And one reason was that the first thing she was going to do when she got home was write to that place in Michigan and find out what had happened to Tessa, and bring her back to where she belonged.

The road is easy if you know enough to travel light.

The piece of paper Adam-and-Eve had sold to her remained in her jacket pocket. When she finally fished it out—back home, after not having worn that jacket again for nearly a year—she was bewildered and irritated by the words that were stamped on it.

The road wasn't easy. The letter to Michigan had come back unopened. Apparently no such hospital existed anymore. But Nancy discovered that there were inquiries you could make, and she set out to make them. There were authorities to be written to, records to be unearthed if possible. She did not give up. She would not admit that the trail had gone cold.

In the case of Ollie, she was maybe going to have to admit it.

She had sent a letter to Texada Island—thinking that address might be enough, there must be so few people there that any of them could be found. But it had come back to her, with one word written on the envelope. *Moved*.

She could not bear to open it up and read what she had said. Too much, she was sure.

FLIES ON THE WINDOWSILL

She is sitting in Wilf's old recliner in the sunroom of her own house. She does not intend to go to sleep. It is a bright afternoon late in the fall—in fact, it is Grey Cup day, and she is supposed to be at a potluck party, watching the game on television. She made an excuse at the last moment. People are getting used to her doing this sort of thing now—some still say they are worried about her. But when she does show up old habits or needs reassert themselves and she sometimes can't help turning into the life of the party. So they stop worrying for a while.

Her children say that they hope she has not taken to Living in the Past.

But what she believes she is doing, what she wants to do if she can get the time to do it, is not so much to live in the past as to open it up and get one good look at it.

She doesn't believe she is sleeping when she finds herself entering another room. The sunroom, the bright room behind her, has shrunk into a dark hall. The hotel key is in the door of the room, as she believes the keys used to be, though this is not something she has ever encountered in her own life.

It is a poor kind of place. A worn-out room for worn-out travellers. A ceiling light, a rod with a couple of wire hangers on it, a curtain of pink and yellow flowered material that can be pulled around to hide the hanging clothes from view. The flowered material may be meant to supply the room with a note of optimism or even gaiety, but for some reason it does the opposite.

Ollie lies down on the bed so suddenly and heavily that the springs give out a miserable whine. It seems that he and Tessa get around by car now, and he does all the driving. Today in the first heat and dust of spring it has made him extraordinarily tired. She cannot drive. She has made a good deal of noise opening the costume case and more noise behind the thin plank partition of the bathroom. He pretends to be asleep when she comes out, but through the slits of his eyelids he sees her looking into the dresser mirror, which is speckled in spots where the backing has flecked away. She is wearing the yellow satin ankle-length skirt, and the black bolero, with the black shawl patterned with roses, the fringe half a yard long. Her costumes are her own idea, and they are neither original nor becoming. Her skin is rouged now, but dull. Her hair is pinned and sprayed, its rough curls flattened into a black helmet. Her eyelids are purple and her eyebrows lifted and blackened. Crow's wings. The eyelids pressed down heavily, like punishment, over her faded eyes. In fact her whole self seems to be weighted down by the clothes and the hair and the makeup.

Some noise that he did not mean to make—of complaint or impatience—has reached her. She comes to the bed and bends down to remove his shoes.

He tells her not to bother.

"I have to go out again in a minute," he says. "I have to go and see them."

Them means the people at the theater, or the organizers of the entertainment, whoever they are.

She says nothing. She stands in front of the mirror looking at herself, and then still bearing the weight of her heavy costume and hair—it is a wig—and of her spirit, she walks around the room as if there are things to be done, but she cannot settle herself to do anything.

Even when she bent to take off Ollie's shoes she has not looked into his face. And if he shut his eyes the moment he landed on the bed—she thinks this—it might have been to avoid looking into her face. They have become a professional couple, they sleep and eat and travel together, close to the rhythms of each other's breathing. Yet never, never—except during the time when they are bound together by their shared responsibility to the audience—can they look into each other's faces, for fear that they will catch sight of something that is too frightful.

There is no proper space against a wall for the dresser with the tarnished mirror—part of it juts across the window, cutting off what light can get in. She looks at it dubiously for a moment, then concentrates her strength to move one corner of it a few inches out into the room. She catches her breath and pulls aside the dirty net curtain. There on the farthest corner of the windowsill, in a spot usually hidden by the curtain and the dresser, is a little pile of dead flies.

Somebody who was in this room recently has passed the time killing these flies, and has then collected all the little bodies and found this place to hide them in. They are neatly piled up into a pyramid that does not quite hold together.

She cries out at the sight. Not with disgust or alarm but with surprise, and you might say with pleasure. *Oh, oh, oh.* Those flies delight her, as if they were the jewels they turn into when you put them under a microscope, all blue and gold and emerald flashes, wings of sparkling gauze. *Oh,* she cries but it cannot be because she sees insect radiance on the windowsill. She has no microscope and they have lost all their luster in death.

It is because she saw them here, she saw the pile of tiny bodies, all jumbled and falling to dust together, hidden in this corner. She saw them in their place before she put a hand on the dresser or shifted the curtain. She knew they were there, in the way that she knows things.

But for a long time, she hasn't. She hasn't known anything and has been relying on rehearsed tricks and schemes. She has almost forgotten, she has doubted, that there ever was any other way.

She has roused Ollie now, broken into his uneasy snatch of rest. What is it, he says, did something sting you? He groans as he stands up.

No, she says. She points at the flies.

I knew they were there.

Ollie understands at once what this means to her, what a relief it must be, though he cannot quite enter into her joy. This is because he too has nearly forgotten some things—he has nearly forgotten that he ever believed in her powers, he is now only anxious for her and for himself, that their counterfeit should work well.

When did you know?

When I looked in the mirror. When I looked at the window. I don't know when.

She is so happy. She never used to be happy or unhappy about what she could do—she took it for granted. Now her eyes are shining as if she has had the dirt rinsed out of them, and her voice sounds as if her throat has been freshened with sweet water.

Yes, yes, he says. She reaches up and puts her arms around his neck and presses her head against his chest so tightly that she makes the papers rustle in his inside pocket.

These are secret papers that he has got from a man he met in one of these towns—a doctor who is known to look after touring people and to oblige them sometimes by performing services that are beyond the usual. He has told the doctor that he is concerned about his wife, who lies on her bed and stares at the ceiling for hours at a time with a look of hungry concentration on her face, and goes for days without saying a word, except what is necessary in front of an audience (this is all true). He has asked himself, then the doctor, if her extraordinary powers may not after all be related to a threatening imbalance in her mind and nature. Seizures have occurred in her past, and he wonders if something like that could be on the way again. She is not an ill-natured person or a person with any bad habits, but she is not a normal person, she is a unique person, and living with a unique person can be a strain, in fact perhaps more of a strain than a normal man can stand. The doctor understands this and has told him of a place that she might be taken to, for a rest.

He is afraid she will ask what the noise is that she can surely hear as she presses against him. He does not want to say *papers* and have her ask, what papers?

But if her powers have really come back to her—this is what he thinks, with a return of his nearly forgotten, fascinated regard for her—if she is as she used to be, isn't it possible that she could know what was in such papers without ever laying her eyes on them?

She does know something, but she is trying not to know.

For if this is what it means to get back what she once had, the deep-seeing use of her eyes and the instant revelations of her tongue, might she not be better off without? And if it's a matter of her deserting those things, and not of them deserting her, couldn't she welcome the change?

They could do something else, she believes, they could have another life.

He says to himself that he will get rid of the papers as soon as he can, he will forget the whole idea, he too is capable of hope and honor.

Yes. Yes. Tessa feels all menace go out of the faint crackle under her cheek.

The sense of being reprieved lights all the air. So clear, so powerful, that Nancy feels the known future wither under its attack, skitter away like dirty old leaves.

But deep in that moment some instability is waiting, that Nancy is determined to ignore. No use. She is aware already of being removed, drawn out of those two people and back into herself. It seems as if some calm and decisive person—could it be Wilf?—has taken on the task of leading her out of that room with its wire hangers and its flowered curtain. Gently, inexorably leading her away from what begins to crumble behind her, to crumble and darken tenderly into something like soot and soft ash.

A Note About the Author

[illegible]

[illegible] Munro grew up in W[illegible] [illegible] versity of Wester[illegible] Ontario [illegible] [illegible] of stories—[illegible] [illegible] Moving to tell You [illegible] [illegible] Good Woman, and [illegible] [illegible] [illegible] Selected Stories.

During her distinguished career [illegible] many awards and prizes, [illegible] [illegible] W. H. Smith Award, given [illegible] lished in the United K[illegible] National Book Critics [illegible] *The New Yorker*, *The Atlantic* [illegible] publications, and her collection[illegible] languages.

Alice Munro and her husband [illegible] ton, Ontario, near Lake Hur[illegible]

A Note About the Author

Alice Munro grew up in Wingham, Ontario, and attended the University of Western Ontario. She has published nine previous collections of stories—*Dance of the Happy Shades, Something I've Been Meaning to Tell You, The Beggar Maid, The Moons of Jupiter, The Progress of Love, Friend of My Youth, Open Secrets, The Love of a Good Woman,* and *Hateship, Friendship, Courtship, Loveship, Marriage*—as well as a novel, *Lives of Girls and Women,* and a *Selected Stories.*

During her distinguished career she has been the recipient of many awards and prizes, including three Governor General's Literary Awards—Canada's highest; the Lannan Literary Award; the W. H. Smith Award, given to *Open Secrets* as the best book published in the United Kingdom in 1995; and the United States' National Book Critics Circle Award. Her stories have appeared in *The New Yorker, The Atlantic Monthly, The Paris Review,* and other publications, and her collections have been translated into thirteen languages.

Alice Munro and her husband divide their time between Clinton, Ontario, near Lake Huron, and Comox, British Columbia.

A Note on the Type

Pierre Simon Fournier *le jeune,* who designed the type used in this book, was both an originator and a collector of types. His services to the art of printing were his design of letters, his creation of ornaments and initials, and his standardization of type sizes. His types are old style in character and sharply cut. In 1764 and 1766 he published his *Manuel typographique,* a treatise on the history of French types and printing, on type-founding in all its details, and on what many consider his most important contribution to typography—the measurement of type by the point system.